the
Inexplicable
Logic
of my
Life

cable

of my

Life

A NOVEL BY

BENJAMIN ALIRE SÁENZ

SIMON & SCHUSTER

First published in Great Britain in 2017 by Simon & Schuster UK Ltd
A CBS COMPANY

First published in the USA in 2017 by Clarion Books, an imprint of
Houghton Mifflin Harcourt Publishing Company

1 3 5 7 9 10 8 6 4 2

Simon & Schuster UK Ltd
1st Floor, 222 Gray's Inn Road
London
WC1X 8HB

www.simonandschuster.co.uk
www.simonandschuster.com.au
www.simonandschuster.co.in

Simon & Schuster Australia, Sydney
Simon & Schuster India, New Delhi

A CIP catalogue record for this book
is available from the British Library.

PB ISBN 978-1-4711-7103-1
eBook ISBN 978-1-4711-7104-8

Printed and bound by CPI Group (UK) Ltd, Croydon, CR0 4YY

MIX
Paper from
responsible sources
FSC® C020471

Simon & Schuster UK Ltd are committed to sourcing paper
that is made from wood grown in sustainable forests and support the Forest
Stewardship Council, the leading international forest certification organisation.
Our books displaying the FSC logo are printed on FSC certified paper.

For my younger sister, Gloria,
whom I loved as a boy. And love even more as a man.
And in memory of my older sister, Linda,
who lived her life with grace in the face of suffering.

Prologue

I HAVE A MEMORY that is almost like a dream: the yellow leaves from Mima's mulberry tree are floating down from the sky like giant snowflakes. The November sun is shining, the breeze is cool, and the afternoon shadows are dancing with a life that is far beyond my boyhood understanding. Mima is singing something in Spanish. There are more songs living inside her than there are leaves on her tree.

She is raking the fallen leaves and gathering them. When she is done with her work, she bends down and buttons my coat. She looks at her pyramid of leaves and looks into my eyes and says, "Jump!" I run and jump onto the leaves, which smell of the damp earth.

All afternoon, I bathe in the waters of those leaves.

When I get tired, Mima takes my hand. As we walk back into the house, I stop, pick up a few leaves, and hand them to her with my five-year-old hands. She takes the fragile leaves and kisses them.

She is happy.

And me? I have never been this happy.

I keep that memory somewhere inside me — where it's safe. I take it out and look at it when I need to. As if it were a photograph.

Part One

Maybe I'd always had the wrong idea as to who I really was.

Life Begins

DARK CLOUDS WERE gathering in the sky, and there was a hint of rain in the morning air. I felt the cool breeze on my face as I walked out the front door. The summer had been long and lazy, crowded with hot and rainless days.

Those summer days were over now.

The first day of school. Senior year. I'd always wondered what it would be like to be a senior. And now I was about to find out. Life was beginning. That was the story according to Sam, my best friend. She knew everything. When you have a best friend who knows everything, it saves you a lot of work. If you have a question about anything, all you have to do is turn to her and ask and she'll just give you all the information you need. Not that life is about information.

Sam, she was smart as hell. And she knew stuff. Lots and lots of stuff. She also *felt* stuff. Oh, man, could Sam feel. Sometimes I thought she was doing all the thinking, all the feeling, and all the living for both of us.

Sam knew who Sam was.

Me? I guess I wasn't always so sure. So what if sometimes Sam was an emotional exhibitionist, going up and down all the time? She could be a storm. But she could be a soft candle lighting up a dark room. So what if she made me a little crazy? All of it — all her emotional stuff, her ever-changing moods and tones of voice — it made her seem so incredibly alive.

I was a different story. I liked keeping it calm. I guess I had this control thing over myself. But sometimes I felt as if I weren't doing any living at all. Maybe I needed Sam because being around her made me feel more alive. Maybe that wasn't logical, but maybe the thing we call logic is overrated.

So on the first day of school, the supposed beginning of our lives, I was talking to myself as I headed toward Sam's house. We walked to school together every day. No cars for us. Shit. Dad liked to remind me that I didn't need a car. "You have legs, don't you?" I loved my dad, but I didn't always appreciate his sense of humor.

I texted Sam as I reached her front door: *I'm here!* She didn't answer.

I stood there waiting. And, you know, I got this weird feeling that things weren't going to be the same. Sam called feelings like that premonitions. She said we shouldn't trust them. She consulted a palm reader when we were in the ninth grade, and she became an instant cynic. Still, that feeling rattled me because I wanted things to stay the same — I liked my life just fine. If things could always be the way they were now. If only. And, you know, I didn't like having this little conversation with myself — and I wouldn't have been having it if Sam had just had a sense of time. I knew what she was up to. Shoes. Sam could never decide on the shoes. And since it was the first day of school, it really mattered. Sam. Sam and her shoes.

4

Finally she came out of the house as I was texting Fito. His dramas were different from Sam's. I'd never had to live in the kind of chaos Fito endured every day of his life, but I thought he was doing pretty well for himself.

"Hi," Sam said as she walked over, oblivious to the fact that I'd been standing there waiting. She was wearing a blue dress. Her backpack matched her dress, and her earrings dangled in the soft breeze. And her shoes? Sandals. Sandals? I waited all this time for a pair of sandals she bought at Target?

"Great day," she said, all smiles and enthusiasm.

"Sandals?" I said. "That's what I was waiting for?"

She wasn't going to let me throw her off her game. "They're perfect." She gave me another smile and kissed me on the cheek.

"What was that for?"

"For luck. Senior year."

"Senior year. And then what?"

"College!"

"Don't bring that word up again. That's all we've talked about all summer."

"Wrong. That's all *I've* talked about. You were a little absent during those discussions."

"Discussions. Is that what they were? I thought they were monologues."

"Get over it. College! Life, baby!" She made a fist and held it high in the air.

"Yeah. Life," I said.

She gave me one of her Sam looks. "First day. Let's kick ass."

We grinned at each other. And then we were on our way. To begin living.

The first day of school was completely forgettable. Usually I liked the first day — everybody wearing new clothes and smiles of optimism, all the good thoughts in our heads, all the good attitudes floating around like gas balloons in a parade, and the pep rally slogans — *Let's make this the greatest year ever!* Our teachers were all about telling us how we had it in us to climb the ladder of success in hopes that we might actually get motivated to learn something. Maybe they were just trying to get us to modify our behavior. Let's face it, a lot of our behavior needed to be modified. Sam said that ninety percent of El Paso High School students needed behavior modification therapy.

This year I just was *not* into this whole first-day experience. Nope. And then of course Ali Gomez sat in front of me in my AP English class for the third year in a row. Yeah, Ali, a leftover from past years who liked to flirt with me in hopes that I'd help her with her homework. As in do it for her. Like that was going to happen. I had no idea how she managed to get into AP classes. She was living proof that our educational system was questionable. Yeah, first day of school. For-get-ta-ble.

Except that Fito didn't show. I worried about that guy.

I'd met Fito's mother only once, and she didn't seem like she was actually living on this planet. His older brothers had all dropped out of school in favor of mood-altering substances, following in their mother's footsteps. When I met his mother, her eyes had been totally bloodshot and glazed over and her hair was all stringy and she smelled bad. Fito had been embarrassed as hell.

6

Poor guy. Fito. Okay, the thing with me is that I was a worrier. I hated that about me.

Sam and I were walking back home after our forgettable first day at school. It looked like it was going to rain, and like most desert rats, I loved the rain. "Air smells good," I told her.

"You're not listening to me," she said. I was used to that I'm-annoyed-with-you tone she sometimes took with me. She'd been going on and on about hummingbirds. She was all about hummingbirds. She even had a hummingbird T-shirt. Sam and her phases. "Their hearts beat up to one thousand, two hundred and sixty beats per minute."

I smiled.

"You're mocking me," she said.

"I wasn't mocking you," I said. "I was just smiling."

"I know all your smiles," she said. "That's your mocking smile, Sally." Sam had started calling me Sally in seventh grade because even though she liked my name, Salvador, she thought it was just too much for a guy like me. "I'll start calling you Salvador when you turn into a man — and, baby, you're a long way off from that." Sam, she definitely didn't go for Sal, which was what everyone else called me — except my dad, who called me Salvie. So she got into the habit of calling me Sally. I hated it. What normal guy wants to be called Sally? (Not that I was going for *normal.*) Look, you couldn't tell Sam not to do something. If you told her not to do it, ninety-seven percent of the time she did it. Nobody could out-stubborn Sam. She just gave me that look that said I was going to have to get over it. So, to Sam, I was Sally.

That's when I began calling her Sammy. Everyone has to find a way to even up the score.

So, anyway, she was giving me the lowdown on the statistics of hummingbirds. She started getting mad at me and accusing me of not taking her seriously. Sam hated to be blown off. WOMAN OF SUBSTANCE LIVES HERE. She had that posted on her locker at school. I think she stayed up at night thinking of mottoes. The *substance* part, well, I got that. Sam wasn't exactly shallow. But I liked to remind her that if I was a long way off from being a man, she was an even longer way off from being a woman. She didn't like my little reminder. I got that shut-up look.

As we were walking, she was carrying on about hummingbirds and then lecturing me about my chronic inability to listen to her. And I was thinking, *Man, when Sam gets going, she really gets going.* I mean, she was really jumping into my shit. Finally I had to — I mean, *I had to* — interrupt her. "Why do you always have to pick a fight with me, Sammy? Look, I'm not making fun. And it's not as if you don't know that I'm not exactly a numbers guy. Me and numbers equals *no bueno.* When you give me stats, my eyes glaze over."

As my dad liked to say, Sam was "undeterred." She started in again, but this time it wasn't me who interrupted her — it was Enrique Infante. He'd come up behind us as Sam and I were walking. And all of a sudden he jumped in front of me and was in my face. He looked right at me, pushed his finger into my chest, and said, "Your dad's a faggot."

Something happened inside me. A huge and uncontrollable wave ran through me and crashed on the shore that was my heart.

I suddenly lost my ability to use words, and, I don't know, I'd never been that angry and I didn't know what was really happening, because anger wasn't normal for me. It was as if I, the Sal I knew, just went away and another Sal entered my body and took over. I remember feeling the pain in my own fist just after it hit Enrique Infante's face. It all happened in an instant, like a flash of lightning, only the lightning wasn't coming from the sky, it was coming from somewhere inside of me. Seeing all that blood gush out of another guy's nose made me feel alive. It did. That's the truth. And that scared me.

I had something in me that scared me.

The next thing I remember was that I was staring down at Enrique as he lay on the ground. I was my calm self again — well, not *calm,* but at least I could talk. And I said, "My dad is a man. He has a name. His name is Vicente. So if you want to call him something, call him by his name. And he's *not* a faggot."

Sam just looked at me. I looked back at her. "Well, this is new," she said. "What happened to the good boy? I never knew you had it in you to punch a guy."

"I didn't either," I said.

Sam smiled at me. It was kind of a strange smile.

I looked down at Enrique. I tried to help him up, but he wasn't having any of it. "Fuck you," he said as he picked himself up off the ground.

Sam and I watched as he walked away.

He turned around and flipped me the bird.

I was a little stunned. I looked at Sam. "Maybe we don't always know what we have inside us."

"True that," Sam said. "I think there are a lot of things that find a hiding place in our bodies."

"Maybe those things should keep themselves hidden," I said.

We slowly made our way home. Sam and I didn't say anything for a long time, and that silence between us was definitely unsettling. Then Sam finally said, "Nice way to begin senior year."

That's when I started shaking.

"Hey, hey," she said. "Didn't I tell you this morning that we should kick some ass?"

"Funny girl," I said.

"Look, Sally, he deserved what he got." She gave me one of her smiles. One of her take-it-easy smiles. "Okay, okay, so you shouldn't go around hitting people. *No bueno*. Maybe there's a bad boy inside you just waiting to come out."

"Nah, not a chance." I told myself that I'd just had this really strange moment. But something told me she was right. Or halfway right, anyhow. Unsettled. That's how I felt. Maybe Sam was right about things hiding inside of us. How many more things were hiding there?

We walked the rest of the way home in silence. When we were close to her house, she said, "Let's go to the Circle K. I'll buy you a Coke." I sometimes drank Coke. Kind of like a comfort drink.

We sat on the curb and drank our sodas.

When I dropped Sam off at her house, she hugged me. "Everything's gonna be just fine, Sally."

"You know they're gonna call my dad."

"Yeah, but Mr. V's cool." Mr. V. That's what Sam called my dad.

"Yeah," I said. "But Mr. V happens to be my dad — and a dad's a dad."

"Everything's gonna be okay, Sally."

"Yeah," I said. Sometimes I was full of halfhearted *yeahs*.

As I was walking home, I pictured the hate on Enrique Infante's face. I could still hear *faggot* ringing in my ears.

My dad. My dad was *not* that word.

He would never be that word. Not ever.

Then there was a loud clap of thunder — and the rain came pouring down.

I couldn't see anything in front of me as the storm surrounded me. I kept walking, my head down.

I just kept walking.

I felt the heaviness of my rain-soaked clothes. And for the first time in my life, I felt alone.

Me. Dad. Trouble.

I KNEW I WAS in deep trouble. Deep, deep. We're talking deep shit. My dad, who was sometimes strict but always thoughtful, *and who never yelled,* came into my room. My dog, Maggie, was lying on the bed next to me. She always knew when I was feeling bad. So there we were, Maggie and me. I guess you could say I was feeling sorry for myself. That was a strange feeling, too, because feeling sorry for myself was definitely not one of my hobbies. That would be one of Sam's.

Dad pulled the chair away from my desk and sat down. He smiled. I knew that smile. He always smiled before he gave me one of his serious talks. He ran his fingers through his thick salt-and-pepper hair. "I just got a phone call from the principal at your school."

I think I averted my eyes.

"Look at me," he said.

I looked into his eyes. We looked at each other for a long instant. I was glad I didn't see anger. And then he said, "Salvador, it's not okay to hurt other people. And it certainly isn't okay to go around punching people in the face."

When he called me *Salvador,* I knew it was serious business. "I know, Dad. But you don't know what he said."

"I don't care what he said. No one deserves to be physically attacked just because he said something you didn't like."

I didn't say anything for a long time. Finally I decided I needed to defend myself. Or at least justify my actions. "He said something really shitty about you, Dad." On another day, I might have cried. But I was still too mad to cry. Dad always said that there was nothing wrong with crying and that if people did more of it, well then, the world would be a better place. Not that he took his own advice. And even though I wasn't crying, I guess you could say I was a little ashamed of myself — yeah, I was — otherwise I wouldn't have been hanging my head. I felt my dad's arms holding me, and then I just leaned against him and whispered, "He called you a faggot."

"Oh, son," he said, "do you think I've never heard that word? I've heard worse. That word doesn't carry any truth, Salvie." He took me by the shoulders and looked at me. "People can be cruel. People hate what they don't understand."

"But, Dad, they don't want to understand."

"Maybe they don't. But we have to find a way to discipline our hearts so that their cruelty doesn't turn us into hurt animals. We're better than that. Haven't you ever heard the word *civilized*?"

Civilized. My father loved that word. That's why he loved art. Because it civilized the world. "Yeah, Dad," I said. "I *do* understand. But what happens when a friggin' barbarian like Enrique Infante is breathing down your neck? I mean"— I started petting Maggie — "I mean, Maggie is more human than people like Enrique Infante."

"I don't disagree with your assessment, Salvie. Maggie's very tame. She's sweet. And some people in this world are lot wilder than she is. Not everyone who walks around on two legs is good and decent. Not everyone who walks on two legs knows how to use their intelligence. Not that you don't know that already. But you just have to learn to walk away from wild people who like to growl. They might bite. They might hurt you. Don't go down that road."

"I had to do something."

"It's not a good idea to jump into the sewer to catch a rat."

"So we just let people get away with things?"

"What exactly was Enrique getting away with? What did he take?"

"He called you *faggot,* Dad. You can't just let people take away your dignity."

"He didn't take away my dignity. He didn't take away yours either, Salvie. You really think a punch to the nose changed a damn thing?"

"No one gets to call you names. Not when I'm around." And then I felt the tears falling down my face. The thing about tears is that they can be as quiet as a cloud floating across a desert sky. The other thing about tears is that they kind of my made my heart hurt. *Ouch.*

"Sweet boy," he whispered. "You're loyal and you're sweet."

My dad always called me sweet boy. Sometimes when he called me that, it really pissed me off. Because (1) I wasn't half as sweet as he thought I was, and (2) what normal boy wants to think of himself as sweet? (Maybe I *was* going for *normal.*)

When Dad left the room, Maggie followed him out the door. I guess Maggie thought I was going to be all right.

14

I lay on the floor for a long time. I thought of hummingbirds. I thought of the Spanish word for them: *colibrís*. I remembered that Sam had told me that the hummingbird was the Aztec god of war. Maybe I had some war in me. No, no, no, no. It was just one of those things. It wasn't like it was ever going to happen again. I wasn't the punching-other-guys-out kind of guy. *I wasn't that guy.*

I don't know how long I lay on the floor that evening. I didn't show up in the kitchen for dinner. I heard my father and Maggie walk into my darkened room. Maggie jumped on my bed, and my father turned on the light. He had a book in his hand. He smiled at me and placed his hand on my cheek — just as he'd done when I was a boy. He read to me that night, my favorite passage from *The Little Prince,* about the fox and the Little Prince and about taming.

I think if someone else had raised me, I might have been a wild and angry boy. Maybe if I'd been raised by the man whose genes I had, maybe I'd be a completely different guy. Yeah, the guy whose genes I had. I hadn't ever really thought about that guy. Not really. Well, maybe a little.

But my father, the man who was in my room and had turned on the light, he'd raised me. He'd tamed me with all the love that lived inside him.

I fell asleep listening to the sound of my father's voice.

I had a dream about my grandfather. He was trying to tell me something, but I couldn't hear him. Maybe it was because he was dead and the living didn't understand the language of the dead. I kept repeating his name. *Popo? Popo?*

Funerals and Faggots and Words

THE DREAM ABOUT my Popo and the word *faggot* got me to thinking. And this was what I was thinking about: Words exist only in theory. And then one ordinary day you run into a word that only exists in theory and meet it face to face. And then that word becomes someone you know.

Funeral.

I met that word when I was thirteen.

That was when my Popo died. I was a pallbearer. Up until then I hadn't even known what a pallbearer was. You see, there are a lot of other words you meet when you run into the word *funeral*. You meet all Funeral's friends: Pallbearer, Casket, Undertaker, Cemetery, Headstone.

It felt so strange to carry my grandfather's casket to his grave.

I was unfamiliar with the rituals and prayers for the dead.

I was unfamiliar with how final death was.

Popo would not be coming back. I would never hear his voice again. I would never see his face again.

The cemetery where he was buried still had an old-world approach to funerals. After the priest had commended my grandfather to paradise, the funeral director stuck a shovel in the mound of dirt and held it out. Everybody knew exactly what to do. A silent and somber line formed, each person waiting for their turn to grab a fistful of dirt and pour it over the casket.

Maybe it was a Mexican thing. I didn't really know.

I remember my Uncle Mickey gently taking the shovel out of the funeral director's hands. "He was my father."

I remember walking up to the shovel and taking a fistful of dirt and looking into my Uncle Mickey's eyes. He nodded. I still see myself throwing the dirt and watching it hit Popo's casket. I see myself burying my face in Aunt Evie's arms. I see myself as I looked up and saw Mima sobbing into my dad's shoulder.

And I remember one other thing about my Popo's funeral. A man standing outside smoking a cigarette was talking to another man, and he said, "The world doesn't give a damn about people like us. We work all our lives and then we die. We don't matter." He was really angry. "Juan was a good man." Juan, that was my Popo. I can still hear that man's anger. I didn't understand what he was trying to say.

I asked my father, "Who are people like us? And why did he say we don't matter?"

My dad said, "Everybody matters."

"He said Popo was a good man."

"Popo was a very good man. A very good and flawed man."

"Did the two of you talk? I mean, like you and I talk?"

"No. He wasn't like that. I was close to him in my own way, Salvador."

I was so curious at thirteen. But I didn't understand much. I took words in and even remembered them, but I don't think I understood anything.

17

"And *people like us*? Did he mean Mexicans, Dad?"

"I think he meant poor people, Salvie."

I wanted to believe him. But even though I didn't understand anything at thirteen, I already knew there were people in the world who hated Mexicans — even Mexicans who weren't poor. I didn't need my father to tell me that. And I also knew by then that there were people in the world who hated my father. Hated him because he was gay. And to those people, well, my father didn't matter.

He didn't matter at all.

But he mattered to me.

Words exist only in theory. And then one ordinary day you run into a word that exists only in theory. And you meet it face to face. And then that word becomes someone you know. That word becomes someone you hate. And you take that word with you wherever you go. And you can't pretend it isn't there.

Funeral.

Faggot.

Dad and Sam and Me

DAD TOOK ME to school the next day. To have a chat with the principal. When we picked Sam up in front of her house, she was all smiles, trying too hard to pretend everything was cool. "Hey, Mr. V," she said as she jumped into the back seat. "Thanks for the ride."

My dad just sort of smiled. "Hey, Sam," he said. "And don't get used to it."

"I know, Mr. V. We have two legs." She rolled her eyes.

I could see that my dad was stifling his laugh.

Then the car got real quiet, and Sam and I started texting each other.

Sam: Stand ur ground

Me: This ur idea of life beginning?

Sam: Worry, worry, worry. And b sides, I'm not the one who punched Enrique

Me: True that. Am in deep truble

Sam: Yup yup yup. Lol

Me: Zip it

Sam: Dn't apologize for anythng. Enrique had it coming. He's a pig oink

Me: Lmao. I dont think any1 else shares our pov ☺

Sam: Well F them!

Me: No cussing in dad's presence

Sam: Lol

Dad interrupted our texting. "Will you guys stop that? Were you raised by wolves, or what?"

Raised by wolves. One of my dad's favorite expressions. Old-school. "No, sir," I said. "Sorry."

Sam just couldn't help herself. She always had to say something — even if it was the wrong thing. She wasn't good at shutting up. "I can show you our texts, if you like —"

I could see a small grin on my father's face as he drove. "Thanks, Sam. I'll pass on that one."

And then we all started laughing.

The laughing didn't mean I was in less trouble.

When my father and I walked into the principal's office, Enrique Infante and his father were sitting there, both of them with their arms crossed, looking sullen. *Sullen* was a Sam word. On certain days she was very good at being sullen.

The principal, Mr. Cisneros, looked right at me when I walked in. "Salvador Silva, give me one good reason why I shouldn't suspend you." It wasn't really a request — it was more of a statement. It was like he'd already decided.

"He called my dad a faggot," I said.

Mr. Cisneros looked over at Enrique and his father. Enrique shrugged. Like he didn't give a damn. He definitely wasn't sorry. Unrepentant — that was the exact word for the look on his face.

The principal's eyes shifted back to me. "Physical violence is unacceptable behavior — and it's against school rules. It's grounds for suspension."

"Hate speech is against school rules too." I wasn't really upset. Well, maybe I was and trying to act like I wasn't. Anyway, the words I spoke came out calmly. For the most part, I was actually a pretty calm guy. Well, I had my moments. Apparently.

"The way I understand what transpired," Mr. Cisneros said, "you weren't on school grounds. We can't be held responsible for what our students say when they're no longer on campus."

My father smiled, kind of a snarky smile. I knew all about his smiles. He looked at Mr. Infante — then directed himself to Mr. Cisneros. "Well, then we have nothing to discuss, do we? If the school can't be held responsible for the things students *say* off school grounds, then the school can't possibly be held responsible for the things they *do* off school grounds either. I'm wondering if anything can be accomplished here." Dad paused. He wasn't finished. "In my opinion, neither of these boys has anything to be proud of. I think they deserve some kind of punishment. But you can't punish one without punishing the other." My dad paused again. "It's a question of fairness. And apparently it's also a question of school policy."

Mr. Infante had this really angry look on his face. "My son just called you what you are."

My father didn't flinch, didn't skip a beat. "I happen to be gay. I don't think that makes me a faggot. I'm also a Mexican-American. I don't think that makes me a taco bender. I don't think that makes me a beaner. I don't think that makes me a spic. And I don't think that makes me an illegal." There wasn't any anger in his voice — or on his face. It was as if he were a lawyer in a courtroom,

21

trying to make his point to the jury. I could tell he was trying to think of what he was going to say next. He looked at Mr. Infante. "Sometimes," he said, "our sons don't fully understand the things they say. But you and I, we're men. We *do* understand, don't we?"

Mr. Cisneros nodded. I didn't know what that nod meant. I'd never been in his office before. I didn't know anything about him — except that Sam said he was an idiot. But Sam thought most adults were idiots, so maybe she wasn't a reliable source of information regarding Mr. Cisneros.

The room was quiet for a long second or two. Finally Mr. Cisneros arrived at a solution: "Keep away from each other." Sam would have said it was a chicken-shit solution. And she would have been right about that too.

Mr. Infante and Enrique just sat there, spreading their sullenness around like it was peanut butter. And then Mr. Infante's voice filled the small office. He pointed his finger at me: "You're really going to let him get away with this?" That was the first time I really understood why people used the expression *stormed away*. That's exactly what Mr. Infante and Enrique did — they stormed away.

It was hard to read what my father was thinking. Sometimes he had an amazing poker face. Too bad he didn't like to gamble. Then he looked at me. I knew he wasn't very happy with me. "I'll see you after school," he said. "I want to have a few words with Mr. Cisneros."

Later, Sam asked me what I thought my dad and Mr. Cisneros had talked about. I told her I didn't know.

"Don't you want to know?"

"I guess I don't."

"Well, I'd want to know. It's not as if that conversation had nothing to do with you. Why don't you want to know?" She crossed her arms. Sam was an arm crosser. "What are you afraid of?"

"I'm not afraid of anything. There are just certain things I don't need to know."

"Need to know? Or want to know?"

"Take your pick, Sammy."

"Sometimes I don't get you."

"There's not much to get," I said. "And besides, you're the one who needs to know — not me."

"I don't need to know," she said.

"Sure," I said.

"Sure," she said.

Later that evening Sam texted me the word for the day — another one of our games: Wftd = bigotry.

Me: Good one. Use word in sentence

Sam: Mr. Cisneros is a party to bigotry

Me: Harsh

Sam: Being kind. Btw, u kno Infante means infant

Me: Yup

Sam: Yup yup yup

Fito

"MAN, THAT ENRIQUE INFANTE. I mean to tell you, Sal, you made an enemy for life."

"You hang out with that guy?"

"Nope. He's always trying to sell me cigarettes. He's always talkin' shit. Bad news."

"It's not as if I plan on having a long-term relationship with him. He's not exactly best-friend material."

That made Fito laugh. "That's for sure. World's full of guys like that. Today, he's sellin' cigarettes; tomorrow he'll graduate to sellin' dope." Then he shot me a smile. "Didn't know you liked to pull out your fists and shit. Guy like you, I mean, you got it made in the shade, and you're pullin' shit like that."

"What d'ya mean by that?"

"Dude, you got this great thing goin', you and your dad. I mean, I know you're adopted and shit, but you know, you got a good thing."

"I know. And it's not as if I've ever really felt adopted."

"That's cool. Me, I mean, most of the time I feel like I was taken in from the streets because someone had thrown me fuckin' away. For reals. I mean, that's how it feels around my house."

"That sucks," I said.

"Well, at my house, everything sucks. I mean, my dad's kinda cool. He wanted to take me with him. That would've been the bomb. But he didn't have a place of his own and shit and he couldn't find a job and he finally gave up on this place and moved to California to live with his brother. Hell, at least he said goodbye and shit, and he was all broken up about not being able to take me with him and shit. At least I knew he cared. He did. And that's somethin'."

"Yeah," I said, "it is something. It's more than something." I felt bad for Fito. And one thing about him, he didn't go around feeling sorry for himself. I wondered how he turned out to be such a good guy. How did that happen? There didn't seem to be any logic behind who we turned out to be. None at all.

WFTD = Origin

I RESPECTED FITO, but Sam didn't like him all that much. She said it was because of his walk. "He doesn't walk. He slinks. And why does he have to add *and shit* to the end of every other sentence? What's that about?" This from the girl who was having a fling with the F word.

I'd read some of the essays Fito had written for school, and he sounded like an intellectual. I mean it. That guy was smart. But he didn't like parading that fact. Maybe Fito talked like that because of the words people tossed around in his house — and because he was always wandering the streets. Not because he was looking for trouble, but because he wanted to get the hell out of his house.

I had a theory that everyone has a relationship with words — whether they know it or not. It's just that everybody's relationship with words is different. Dad told me once that we have to be very careful with words. "They can hurt people," he said. "And they can heal people." If anyone was careful with words, it was my dad.

But I owe my real awareness of words to Sam. It began when she was in the spelling bee. I was her coach. She had thousands of words on these index cards, and I'd read and pronounce the words and she would spell them. We spent hours and hours and hours getting her ready. We lived and breathed it. She was so focused and fierce. Some days she would break down and cry. She wore herself out. And I was worn out right along with her.

She didn't win.

And man oh man, was she pissed. "The moron who won didn't even know the meanings of the words he was spelling," she said.

I tried to comfort her, but she refused to be comforted.

"Don't you know the word *inconsolable*?"

"You can try again next year."

"Hell, no," she said. "Fuck words."

But I knew she'd already fallen in love with words, and she dragged me into that love affair.

That's when we started the word-for-the-day thing. Wftd.

Yeah. Words. Fito and words. Me and words. Sam and words. As I was thinking about that, the doorbell rang. And there was Sam.

"I was just thinking about you," I said.

"Anything nice?"

"About how pissed you were when you lost the spelling bee."

"I'm over it."

"Sure you are."

"I didn't come over to talk about a stupid spelling bee."

"So what's up?"

"My mom and I just got into it."

"Like that's news."

"Look, not everybody has conversations like you and your dad. I mean, you guys are so *not* normal. Fathers and sons do not talk.

They do not talk. I mean, sometimes you talk like you're friends or something."

"Wrong," I said. "My father doesn't pretend to be my friend. Not even close. He's my father. It's just that we happen to like each other. I think that's awesome. Really awesome."

"Fucking awesome."

"Why do you like to cuss?"

"Everybody likes to cuss."

"I don't."

"They don't call you Mr. Excitement for nothing."

"Who's they?"

"Me."

"*Me* is they?"

"Yes."

"See, there, you've managed to interrupt me. You're always doing that."

"Look, you're always interrupting yourself, *vato*."

I liked when she called me *vato*. It was way better than "dude." And it meant she respected me. "What was I talking about?" I said.

"You were waxing eloquent about your dad."

"You're starting to talk like the last book you read."

"So fucking what. At least I know how to read."

"Stop cussing."

"Stop judging and get on with whatever you were going to say about your dad."

"I'm not judging."

"Yes, you are."

"Okay. Okay. My dad? See, my theory is that most people love their parents. Not all, but most. But sometimes some parents aren't very likable, so their kids don't like them. That's only logical. Or sometimes it's the kids who aren't likable. It's damned hard to talk to someone if you don't like them — even if that someone is your father or your mother."

"I totally get that."

Sometimes Sam really did get what I was saying. And sometimes I knew exactly what she was going to say next.

"I don't like Sylvia at all. She is the most unlikable mother on the planet." Sam called her mother by her first name. But only behind her back. Hmm.

"No," I said. "Fito's mother is the most unlikable mother on planet Earth."

"Really? And you know this because?"

"I met her once. She's a meth head."

"So she has a problem. *No bueno*. But —"

I interrupted her. "There's always a *but* when you're losing an argument."

"I was about to say that comparisons are odious."

"Yeah, yeah, odious. A spelling bee word. A word you got from the new book you're reading."

"Shut up. *And I do have a horrible mother.*"

I really felt bad for Sam. Maybe someday something would happen and Sam and Sylvia would have what Dad and I had. Maybe. I hoped so.

Fights. Fists. Shoes.

ON THE THIRD day of school I punched another guy. I mean, it just happened. Sam always said, *Nothing just happens.* I tried to keep her voice out of my head. See, I was walking toward the Circle K before school to buy me a Coke. I was in the mood for one. So this guy in the parking lot gives me this shit-eating grin and calls me a *pinche gringo*.

"Don't call me that again," I said. And then he did it: he called me that again.

So I punched him. No thinking involved, just a reflex. Punched him right in the stomach — and there was that rush of adrenaline running through my veins all the way to my heart.

I watched him as he bent over in pain. Part of me wanted to say I was sorry. But deep down I knew I wasn't sorry.

I stood there. Numb.

Then I felt a hand on my shoulder. It was Fito pulling me away. I kept staring at my fist, as if it belonged to someone else. "What's up with you, Sal? When did you start beating up on people? One day you're this really nice guy, and — well, I never took you for that kind of guy."

"What kind of guy?"

"Peace out, Sal."

I didn't say anything. I felt nothing.

And I was shaking.

And then this thought entered my head. Maybe the kind of guy I was, well, maybe I was like someone I didn't know. You know, the guy I'd never met whose genes I had.

I walked over to pick up Sam. She was at the door waiting for me. "You're late."

"Sorry."

"You're never late."

"I am today."

She gave me one of her suspicious looks. "What's wrong?"

"Nothing."

"I don't believe you."

"Nothing's wrong."

"Which means you don't want to talk about it."

"Nothing's wrong."

She gave me one of her I'm-going-to-let-you-off-the-hook smiles. It meant she was going to change the subject. Not that she wouldn't come back to it at a later date. Sam wasn't the kind of girl to let things go. At best she gave you a reprieve. I was glad she was in a reprieve sort of mood. "Okay," she said. "Okay." Then she pointed down. "How do you like my shoes?"

"Love them."

"Liar."

"They're very pink."

"Snark."

"Why do you have so many shoes?"

"A girl can't have too many pairs of shoes."

"A girl? Or just you?"

"It's a gender thing. Don't you get that?"

"Gender, gender," I said. I don't know, but she must have heard something in my voice.

"Something's going on with you."

"Shoes," I said.

"Shoes, my ass," she said.

Mima

SAM AND I, we're always telling each other stories, stories of what happened to us, stories about other people, stories about my dad and her mom. Maybe that's how we explained things to each other — or to ourselves.

Mima. She was the best storyteller ever. Her stories were about real things — not like the crap stories I heard in the hallways of El Paso High. Some stories, well, they were closer to lies.

But Mima's stories were as real as anything, as real as the leaves on her mulberry tree. I hear her voice all the time, telling me her stories: "When I was a girl, I used to pick cotton. I worked alongside my mother and my brothers and sisters. At the end of the day I was so tired I would just fall into bed. My skin was burned. My hands were scratched. And my back felt as though it was going to break."

She told me about how the world used to be, about the world she grew up in, a world that was almost gone. "The world has changed," she said. There was a lot of sadness in her voice when she told me that.

Once, Mima drove me out to a farm. I must have been about seven. She taught me how to pick tomatoes and jalapeños. She pointed to the onion fields. "Now, that's work." She knew a lot about that word. I don't think I knew anything about work. It wasn't a word I'd met yet.

That day, when we were picking tomatoes, she told me the story about her shoes: "When I was in the sixth grade, I left my shoes on the bank of the ditch so I could go swimming with my friends. And then they were just gone. Someone had stolen them. I cried. Oh, I really cried. It was my only pair of shoes."

"You only had one pair of shoes, Mima?"

"Only one pair. That's all I had. So I went to school barefoot for a week. I had to wait until my mother gathered enough money to buy me a new pair."

"You went to school barefoot? That's cool, Mima."

"No, that wasn't so cool," she said. "It just meant that there were a lot of poor people."

Mima says we are what we remember.

She told me about the day my dad was born. "Your father was very small. He almost fit in a shoebox."

"Is that really true, Mima?"

"Yes. And just after he came into the world, I was holding him in my arms and it started raining outside. We were in the middle of a drought, and it hadn't rained for months and months and months. And that's when I knew that your father was like the rain. He was a miracle."

I love what she remembers.

I thought about telling Sam the story of Mima's shoes. I decided against it. She would say something like *You're only telling me that story to make me feel guilty*. And she would probably be right.

The Story of Me (Me Trying to Explain Things to Me)

Mima says you should never forget where you came from. I get what she's saying — but that's a little complicated when you're adopted. Just because I don't *feel* adopted doesn't mean that I'm not adopted. Most people think they know something important about you if they know where your story began, though.

Fito says it doesn't really matter where you come from. "I know exactly where I come from. So what? See, some people have famous parents. So what? Being born to talented people doesn't make you talented. Charlie Moreno's father is the mayor. But look at Charlie Moreno. He's an asshole. Everybody in my family's an addict. But, see, it's not where I come from that matters — it's where I'm going." I couldn't argue with that one.

I thought that wanting to know where it all began is part of human nature. Yup. Not that I know much about human nature. Sam said I wasn't good at judging other people: "You think everybody wants to be good."

I have pictures of my mother holding me. Lots and lots of pictures. But looking at photographs of your dead mother isn't the same as remembering.

She died when I was three.

That's when I came to live with my dad.

Maybe another guy would be sad that he didn't have a mother. But I didn't feel sad, not really. I loved my dad. And I had uncles and aunts who loved me. I mean, they really loved me. And I had Mima. I don't think anybody loved me as much as Mima loved me. Not even my dad.

It's not as if my life was like Fito's. Fito had the most screwed-up family on planet Earth. And look at Sam. I really wouldn't have wanted Mrs. Diaz to be my mother. No, thanks. *No bueno.*

I had this sociology teacher who was always droning on and on about family dynamics. You know, me and my dad and Maggie constituted a family. I liked our family. But maybe there isn't a logic behind the word *family.* The truth is, it isn't always such a good word.

I wondered why I didn't have any memories of my mother. Maybe not remembering was worse than misremembering. Or maybe it was better. But here I was, asking myself questions about her and about the guy whose genes mixed with hers to make me.

I was starting to ask myself a lot of questions that I never used to ask. I used to be okay with everything, and now I was going around hitting people. I heard Sam's voice in my head: *Nothing just happens.*

Photographs

I HAD A PICTURE of my dad teaching me how to tie a tie, taken the morning before my First Communion. Dad was smiling, and I was smiling. We were both so happy. And I had a picture of Mima holding me in her arms when I was four. She had all this love in her eyes, and I swear I could drown in that love.

The pictures of my mom and me are different. See, the pictures with Mima and Dad, well, I remembered those things. Those pictures made me feel something. But the pictures with my mom? I didn't feel anything. Sam told me that I didn't remember because I didn't want to. She said it would make me feel sad.

Sam liked to look at my photos. But she said it was too weird to see all the happiness in them. "It's just not real."

"Really?"

"Well, it *is* real, but it's kind of creepy."

"Happiness is creepy?"

"Okay, it's nice. But most people don't do nice. I mean, no one in the entire universe is as nice as your Mima. And your dad, I have to admit: he's the bomb. True that. He's actually a super-great guy. But there's only about ten of those kind of guys walking around this town, so if you're thinking that your sweet little family is a mirror for the rest of the world, I've got a news flash for you."

If the word *cynical* hadn't been invented, Sam would have invented it. And she would go around introducing everybody to that word. But she didn't fool me. There was a lot of kindness in her. A lot. But she had her bad moments. I'd known her since kindergarten. She used to cry at the end of the day when I said goodbye. Ever since then, I'd always listened to what Sam thought — even when I should have known better. Sam was emotionally confused and confusing. It had to do with her family dynamics. Yeah, what the hell did I know? She was really mad at me once. I told her she needed to calm down. And she told me I was an "emotional anorexic." I don't think she meant it as a compliment. Sometimes I wondered why I'd picked her to be my best friend.

Mima said that God gave Sam to me.

It was a beautiful thing to say. And she also said that God gave me to her. And to my dad.

I guess God did a lot of giving. But He did a lot of taking, too. Exhibit A: He took my mom. But if He hadn't taken my mom, I wouldn't have Dad. And I wouldn't have Mima.

Dad:
WFTD = College

THE FIRST CHAOTIC week of school was over. And only two fistfights. *Let's make this the greatest year ever!*

I was sitting in my dad's studio, half watching him paint and half looking over the final list of colleges I was applying to. All summer long it was all about getting my college apps together — financial forms, forms for this and forms for that, looking at websites, and sending emails to admissions counselors and programs and degree plans and on and on and on. Sam was way into it.

One day she'd come over and really ripped into her mother. "She's put a hold on my application process, that witch. She said the schools I applied to were way out of my league, and where the hell did I think I was going to get the money to pay for it all? And who the hell did I think I was anyway? I hate her. I really hate her. She told me I was going to UT, and that was final. I. Hate. Her." Not the first time I'd heard that *hate her* thing.

At my house, I was trying to keep the whole process as low-key as possible. I didn't want to move away. I was thinking I could just take a year off and hang out at home. Like that was gonna happen.

So I'd finally come up with my list. And the only thing I had left to do was get my letters of recommendation and write some damn stupid essay on why they should accept me. I had time. I put the list on my father's desk:

1. *University of Texas*
2. *UCLA*
3. *Columbia*
4. *University of Chicago*
5. *NYU*
6. *University of New Mexico*
7. *University of Arizona*
8. *University of Colorado*
9. *University of Washington*
10. *University of Montana*

The future. All on one list. Change. *Shit.* I watched my dad, lost in his work. I liked watching him paint — the way he held the brush, the way his whole body seemed alive, the way he made painting look so easy. I wondered what that felt like. "The final list is on your desk," I said.

"'Bout time," he said.

"You can stop badgering me now."

"I don't badger," he said.

I knew he was smiling. He knew I was smiling too. He just kept working. And then he asked me something he'd never asked before. "Do you ever wonder about your real father, Salvie?" He didn't stop painting, and I couldn't see his face.

As I sat down on his old leather chair, I heard myself say, "*You're* my real father — and yes, I wonder about you all the time."

The light in the room made his messy salt-and-pepper hair

look like it was on fire. He stopped painting for just a moment, and I wondered about the look he was wearing right then. I knew that what I'd just said made him happy. Then he just continued painting in silence. I let him be. Sometimes you have to let people have their own space — even when you are in the same room with them. He taught me that, my dad. He taught me almost everything I know.

I didn't remember a time when my dad wasn't around. And there was a reason for that: He had always been around. He was there when I was born. He was with my mom in the hospital. He was her coach. He witnessed me coming into the world. That's the word he uses. He says, "I was there to witness the whole beautiful thing."

So he was there from the very beginning.

This is the thing. The truth is, I *did* sometimes wonder about my real father, especially lately for some reason. And I felt like a traitor. I'd lied to Dad just then. Suppose it was half a lie. Call it a half-truth. If something was half a lie, it was just a lie. Period.

Mima and Sam

MIMA REALLY LIKED Sam. And Sam really liked Mima.

When we were little, sometimes Mima would spend the weekend and take care of us when Dad was away at one of his out-of-town art shows. She was great with Sam. I had always liked to watch the two of them together.

I was on the phone with Mima. It made her feel good when I called. It made me feel good too. What did we talk about? Anything. Didn't matter. She asked me about Sam.

"She likes shoes," I said.

"She's a girl," Mima said. "Some girls are like that. But she's a good girl."

"Yeah," I said, "but she likes bad boys, Mima."

"Well, your Popo was a bad boy when he was young."

"And you still married him?"

"Yes. He was beautiful. I knew he was a good man even though a lot of other people didn't think so. I knew what I saw in him. He settled down."

My memories of my grandfather didn't include the phrase *settled down.* "I just worry about Sam sometimes," I said.

"If you're so worried, why aren't you her boyfriend?"

"It's not like that, Mima. She's my best friend."

"Isn't your best friend supposed to be a boy?"

"Well, Mima," I said, "I don't think it really matters if your best friend is a boy or a girl. As long as you have a best friend. And anyway, girls are nicer than boys."

Somehow I could tell Mima was smiling.

The Letter

SATURDAY. I WAS all about Saturdays.

My dad walked into the kitchen and poured himself a cup of coffee. He didn't look at the newspaper — which was weird. My dad was a creature of habit. He had his daily rituals. Coffee and the morning newspaper. He didn't read newspapers online. He was old-school. He wore Chuck Taylors, black high-tops. He wore 501s and khakis — pleated with cuffs. And he wore thin ties. Always. Old-school all the way. On Sundays he read the *New York Times* — that was definitely one of his things. But on this day Dad didn't even look at the paper. He was petting Maggie, but he didn't seem to be in the room. He had a very serious look on his face. Serious, not in a bad way.

Finally Dad nodded. I knew he'd been having a conversation with himself and he'd settled some kind of debate. He got up from the table, leaving his coffee behind. Maggie followed him. A few minutes later, Maggie and Dad appeared back in the room. He was holding an envelope in his hand. "Here," he said. "I think it's time I gave you this."

I took the envelope. My name was written on the front in neat and deliberate handwriting. It wasn't Dad's handwriting. Dad scrawled. I stared at my name. "What's this?"

"It's a letter from your mother."

"A letter from my mother?"

"She wrote it to you just before she died. She said she wanted me to give it to you when I felt it was the right time." He had that I-think-I'll-have-a-cigarette look on his face. He smoked sometimes. Not very much. He kept his cigarettes in the freezer so they wouldn't go stale. "I think this is the right time," he said.

I kept staring at my mother's handwriting. I didn't say anything.

My dad took his cigarettes out of the freezer, removed one, and fished his lighter out of the drawer where he kept it. "Let's have a cig," he said. Not that he'd ever let me smoke. It was just an invitation for me to sit on the back steps with him.

Maggie followed us outside. Maggie was like me — she didn't like feeling left out. I watched Dad light his cigarette. "You can read it when you're ready," he said. "It's up to you now, Salvie."

He leaned toward me and nudged me with his shoulder as we sat there.

"This is freaking me out," I said. "I mean, a letter from your dead mother would freak anyone out."

"Well, your mother —" He stopped. "She didn't write it to freak you out, son."

"I know," I said.

"You don't have to read it right away."

"So, if I don't have to read it right away, why give it to me now?"

"Should I have waited till you were in college? Till you were thirty? When is the right time for anything? Who knows? Living is an art, not a science. Besides, I promised your mother I'd give it to you."

"You made a lot of promises to her, didn't you?"

"Yes, I did, Salvie."

"And you've kept your promises, haven't you?"

"Every damn one of them." He took a drag from his cigarette and blew the smoke out through his nose.

"Were they hard to keep? All those promises?"

"Some of them."

"You want to tell me about them?"

"Someday."

That wasn't exactly the answer I was looking for. I looked at my dad. He was grinning. "Well, there *is* one promise that was easy to keep."

"Which one was that?"

"I promised her I'd love you. I promised her I'd keep you safe. That was the easy one."

"Sometimes I'm a lot of trouble."

"No," he said. "You were never trouble. Not ever."

"Well, I did almost break Enrique Infante's nose. And there was that rock I threw and broke Mrs. Castro's window. And then there was that phase when I loved killing lizards." I wasn't going to tell him that I broke Mrs. Castro's window on purpose. She was mean.

Dad laughed. "Yeah, the killing-lizards thing. You were just a boy."

"But I liked killing them. Remember when you caught me and we had a little funeral for the poor dead lizard?"

"Yeah."

"Your way of telling me to knock it off."

Dad laughed again. "You're not perfect, Salvie. But there's so much decency in you that I sometimes wonder where you came from. Take your friend Sam. Now, she's trouble." He laughed, not a loud laugh. It was a joke. He loved Sam. "Look," he continued, "like I said, living is an art, not a science. Take your Mima for example. She's the real artist in the family." He looked up at the sky. "If living is an art, your Mima is Picasso."

I loved the look on his face when he said that. I wondered if Mima knew how much he loved her. I didn't know anything about the love between mothers and sons — and I never would.

My father put his cigarette out. "Here's the thing about the letter. I had to decide when to give it to you. Maybe it's not the right time. Only you can decide that. Read it when you're ready."

"What if I'm never ready?"

He gave me a look, leaned into me, and nudged me again with his shoulder.

We sat there for a long time, the September breeze and the morning sun on our faces. I wanted to stay there forever, just me and Dad and Maggie. A father and a son and a dog. I was thinking that I didn't really want to grow up. But I didn't really have a choice.

My dad had a quote taped to a wall along with some sketches: "I want to live in the calmness of the morning light." I liked that a lot. But I was beginning to understand that time wasn't going to stand still for me. I had photographs to prove that things changed. I'd been seven once. And I wasn't always going to be seventeen. I had no idea what my life was going to be like. I didn't want to think about the letter. Maybe there was something in it that would change things in ways I didn't want them to change.

I don't know why she left me a letter.

My mom was dead.

I didn't even remember loving her. And the letter wasn't going to bring her back to life.

WFTD = Fear

I STARTED TO PUT the letter in my bottom drawer, where I kept my socks. But I figured that wasn't a good place to store it, because I wore socks every day, and every time I opened the drawer, I'd think of the letter. So I paced my room trying to think of the perfect place to keep it. Maggie was lying on my bed watching me. Sometimes I got the feeling that Maggie thought I was nuts. Finally I put the letter in the box where I kept all my pictures. I didn't take that box out very often. That was the perfect place.

I texted Sam: Wftd = fear.

    Sam: Fear?

    Me: Yeah

    Sam: Explain

    Me: It's a scary word. Lol

    Sam: Funny boy. You afraid?

    Me: I didn't say that

    Sam: Spill it

    Me: U ever been afraid of something?

Sam: Course. U?

Me: Yeah

Sam: Talk to me

Me: I was just thinking, that's all

Sam: I'll get it out of u

Sam

TEXT FROM SAM: What up?

    I texted back: Took a quick rinse. No plans. U?

    Sam: Wanna hang out?

    Me: Yup

    Sam: U got eggs?

    Me: Yup

    Sam: Bacon?

    Me: Yup

    Sam: ☺! Wftd = breakfast

    Me: C u in 5

Sam — that girl, she was always hungry. Her mother never kept any food in the house. It wasn't as if they were poor. They weren't rich, but they weren't exactly using a Lone Star card to get their groceries. Sam's mom was more into fast food and takeout. Dad and I almost never did takeout. We did the takeout pizza thing, sometimes Tara Thai. Otherwise we cooked. I liked it.

Dad was talking on the phone as I walked past him toward the front door. "Who are you talking to?" I asked. For some reason I always wanted to know who he was on the phone with. Not that it was any of my business — but I had a (bad) habit of asking him. "Mima," he whispered — then shook his head and kept talking. I think I annoyed my father sometimes. It worked both ways. Sometimes he annoyed me. Like him not buying me a car, even though we had enough money. That really annoyed me. And it didn't matter how many times I brought the subject up — he'd shoot it down like it was a duck in hunting season. "But we can afford it," I'd say. And then he'd say: "No, *I* can afford it. You, on the other hand, can't even afford to pay for your cell phone." He'd give me his snarky smile, and I'd give it right back to him.

Maggie and I sat on the front porch and waited for Sam. She lived a few blocks away, but we never hung out at her place — not ever. "Sylvia likes to listen in on conversations that are none of her business," Sam said. She always claimed she liked hanging out with Maggie. "Sylvia won't let me have a dog." And even though Sam and Maggie had their own love affair going on, I knew Maggie had nothing to do with her wanting to come over. My theory was that Sam and her mother were too much alike. I told her that once. "You're full of shit" — that's all she had to say on the subject. One thing about Sam, she could be direct as hell. And like everybody else in the known universe, she didn't always let herself in on the truth.

I saw her walking up the street. I waved.

"Hi, Sally!" she yelled.

"Hey, Sammy!" I yelled back. Maggie ran out to greet her. Sam was wearing a yellow blouse with printed daisies all over it. She looked like a summer garden. I mean that in a good way. She bent down and let Maggie lick her face. It made me smile watching Sam and Maggie loving on each other. I bounced down the steps, and she gave me a hug. "I'm starving, Sally."

"Let's eat," I said. I knew I was going to be making the breakfast. Sam *was* like her mother. The only part of the kitchen she was familiar with was the kitchen table.

We walked into the kitchen. Maggie scratched at the door, and I let her out. I noticed my father sitting on the back steps smoking another cigarette. That was strange. Dad rarely had a two-cigarette morning. I got that same feeling I had on the first day of school, like something was shifting in my world.

"What's wrong?" Sam asked.

"Nothing," I said, grabbing a pan and taking some bacon out of the fridge. Sam poured herself a cup of coffee. Sam, she was a walking advertisement for Starbucks.

"Your house is always so clean," Sam said. "That's so frickin' weird."

"There's nothing weird about wanting to live in a clean house."

"Well, our house is pretty much a pigsty."

"True that. I wonder why," I said.

"Funny, funny. The thing is, you guys live like girls, and we girls live like guys."

"Cleanliness — I don't think that's a gender thing," I said.

"Maybe not. You know, I think maybe I should move in with you guys."

That really made me smile. "I don't think you'd like my dad's rules."

"Your dad's super cool."

"Yeah, but he has rules. They're mostly unwritten. Keeping the house clean is one of them. Somehow I can't picture you cleaning a toilet."

"I can't either. Sylvia hires a maid to clean the house once a week."

"I hope she pays her a lot of money."

"Don't be snarky." She glanced at her cell phone — then looked at me. "Unwritten rules, huh? Sylvia doesn't have any of those. She's not that subtle. She writes down all her rules in lipstick on my bathroom mirror."

"Serious?"

"Serious."

"In this house most of the rules are unwritten. No drugs. No drinking. Well, I can have a glass of wine with him on special occasions."

"On second thought, if I lived here, you guys would bore the crap out of me."

"Yeah, to begin with, we don't have lipstick. And we don't have collections of shoes."

She shot me a look.

"And we don't like to argue. You, on the other hand —"

"Don't finish that."

"Dad and I *would* bore the crap out of you. What would you do in a house where people didn't argue?"

"Shut up."

I tried to picture her living with us. I shot her a look. She practically *did* live with us. I didn't think it was a good idea to verbalize what I was thinking. *Verbalize* was a Sam word.

"Oh, and by the way, Mr. I Follow All the Rules — I've seen you down a few beers at parties."

"I don't go to that many parties — and have you ever seen me drunk?"

"I'd love to see you drunk. Then I could tell you what to do."

"You already tell me what to do."

"Snark, snark, snark." We both laughed. "I just don't get it, Sally. Your father's an artist. How the hell did he wind up being such a straight-edger? I bet he's never even done drugs."

"I wouldn't know."

"Have *you* ever done drugs?"

"Why do you always ask me questions you already know the answers to?"

"Why don't you just let loose, Sally? Let yourself go. Live. The now."

"Yeah, the now. Look, you let loose enough for both of us."

She gave me another one of her looks. We both knew she was no stranger to experimenting with mood-altering substances. She especially liked 420. Not me. I tried it once at a party and wound up kissing a girl I didn't even like. I took kissing very seriously. When I kissed a girl (not that it happened very often), I wanted it to mean something. I just wasn't that casual about things.

"Get me the eggs from the fridge."

She opened the refrigerator. "Crap! Look at all that food."

I shook my head. "Most people's refrigerators have food in them. I hope you know that."

"God, you are snarky today, white boy."

She knew I hated being called white boy. Even though I *was* technically a white boy, I was raised in a Mexican family. So I didn't qualify as your average white boy. Not in my world. I knew Spanish better than Sam — and she was supposed to be Mexican.

She handed me the carton of eggs. She knew I was ignoring her comment.

"Chill," she said. She opened the refrigerator door again. "Nope, this does not look like my refrigerator at all. I don't even know why we have one. Maybe I should sell it on eBay."

"And what would Sylvia say about that?"

"She probably wouldn't even notice it was missing." She watched as I cracked two eggs and fried them in bacon grease. "Who taught you how to do that?"

"My Mima." I wanted to add, *You know, my Mexican grandmother,* just to underline my point that I was not your ordinary milquetoast white boy.

"Wish I had a Mima," she said. "My mother says she doesn't want anything to do with her family. You know what I think? I think it's the other way around." She scarfed down a piece of bacon. "I love bacon. Did you go out last night?"

"I went to a movie."

"Who with?"

"Fito."

"Why do you hang out with him? He's a dork. He always has his face stuck in a book, and he cusses way too much."

"Are you telling me that you, Samantha Diaz, find cussing offensive? Really?"

"You're mocking me."

"Yup. And you know I'm a dork too."

"Yeah, but you're an interesting dork. Fito is definitely not interesting."

"Wrong. He's interesting as hell. I like the guy. He actually knows how to think. And he knows how to hold his own in an intelligent conversation — which is more than I can say for most of the guys you hang with."

"Not that you'd know."

I rolled my eyes. I may have been a dork, but I wasn't an idiot.

"Like how many of my boyfriends have you ever gotten to know?"

"You never give me a chance. They're here one day and gone the next. And I *do* know the guy you're going out with now. Let's just say he's not college material."

"Eddie's nice."

"Nice. That guy wouldn't go near that word with a ten-foot pole. He spends all his money on body art."

"I like his tats."

"What's with you and all these bad boys?"

"They're handsome."

"In a raised-by-wolves kind of way. I mean, you go for a certain kind of aesthetic." *Aesthetic* was a Sal word. And then I grinned at her. "Besides, I'm handsome — and you don't go out with me."

She grinned back at me. "Yeah, you *are* handsome. Not very modest — but handsome. But you don't have tattoos, and, well, you're not boyfriend material. What you are is best-friend material."

That made me happy. I liked our friendship just the way it was. It worked for me. It worked for both of us. But the guys she

went out with? Bad news — every single one of them. *No bueno.*
"Look, Sammy," I said, "these guys always wind up hurting you.
And you wind up crying and sad and depressed and sullen and
all those things, and I wind up having to talk you down from the
tree."

"Well, since you don't have a life, you have to get your drama
from somewhere."

I rolled my eyes again. "I don't do drama."

"Yes, you do, Sally. If you didn't do drama, you wouldn't be
my best friend."

"True that."

I loved Sammy.

I really loved her. And I wanted to tell her about the guy I'd
punched because he'd called me a *pinche gringo.* I wanted to tell
her that there was an anger in me that I just didn't understand. I'd
always been this sort of patient guy — and now I'd started thinking I was surrounded by idiots. The guy next to me in English class
passed me a note asking for Sam's number. I passed a note back:
"I'm not her pimp, and I ought to kick your ass." So much for being laid-back and calm.

But Sam, she had this image of me that I was a good boy, and
she was in love with that image. She was in love with simple, uncomplicated, levelheaded Sally. And I didn't know how to tell her
that I wasn't all those beautiful things she thought I was. That
things were changing, and I could feel it but couldn't put it into
words.

I felt like a fraud.

But what if I found the words? What then? What would I do
if she didn't love me anymore?

WFTD = Maybe

DAD AND I sat at the kitchen table. He was making spaghetti and meatballs for dinner. I watched him form the meatballs. His hands were big and rough. I guess it's because he was always making frames, stretching them, painting. Painting and painting and painting. I liked his hands.

We were listening to the Rolling Stones. I liked his music, but it was *his* music, not mine. "Dad," I said, "why don't we listen to something else?"

"Something wrong with my music?"

"Move forward," I said.

"Hmm. Not sure I want to."

I smiled.

He smiled. "Every generation thinks they're the coolest canoe that's ever come down the river."

"That's not true."

"Yes, it is. Every generation thinks they're the ones who are going to reinvent the world. News flash: the world has been around for millions of years."

"But it keeps changing. Besides, what's wrong with thinking you can improve the world? Just a little."

"Nothing wrong with that. When I was in college, high-tech meant having an electric typewriter."

I laughed.

"I never imagined how fast things would change."

"Like — for instance?"

"Cell phones, computers, social networking, attitudes —"

"Attitudes?"

"The gay thing, for instance."

Dad hardly ever talked about the gay thing. Only when he had to.

"You know, when I was growing up, it was so hard. Really hard. And now it's better. A lot of young people don't think being gay is a big deal."

"True that," I said. "I mean we have gay marriage and everything." And then I looked right at him and said, "Dad? Are you ever gonna get married?"

He just shrugged.

"Of course you'd have to have a boyfriend."

He threw a meatball at me, and it bounced with a thud on the table. "Do I feel a lecture coming on?"

I saw this quiet and sad look wash over his face. "But you know we're always going to have to rely on the goodwill of those of you who are straight for our survival. And that's the damned truth."

I saw how he hated that. I saw *it isn't fair* written in his eyes. *It isn't fair.* I wanted to tell him that all the awful things that happened in the old world were dead. And the new world, the world we lived in now, the world we were creating, *that* world would be better. But I didn't say it, because I wasn't sure it was true.

I didn't really like change, but I'd just lectured my dad about

60

change. Maybe change could be good. Like the gay marriage thing and equality and all that. But I wasn't sure I liked all the changes. I mean the changes in me. Maybe I was afraid of who I was becoming. Mima said we become who we want to be. But that meant we were in control. I liked control. But maybe control was just an illusion. And maybe I'd always had the wrong idea as to who I really was.

I decided to text Sam and tell her that the word for the day was *maybe*.

Unwritten Rules

DID YOU TELL Sam about the letter from your mother?"

"Nope."

"I thought you told her everything."

"Nobody tells anybody everything."

My father nodded. "I'll keep that in mind."

"You don't tell me everything."

"Of course I don't. I tell you what I think is important. And your letter — I'd say that was pretty important."

"Yeah, I guess so. But Sam would just push me to read it. I don't want her to make my decision for me. She'd probably say something like *Well then, let me read it,* and then we'd get into it. And she wouldn't stop until I'd read it. Sam's pushy — and she has a way of getting me to do things I don't want to do."

"Like what?"

"Never mind, Dad."

"No, no. Now you've stepped into it. You have to give me an example." That was one of the unwritten rules — you couldn't bring up a subject without finishing it. Not that we always followed our own rules.

"Okay," I said. "Sam taught me how to kiss."

"What?"

"You can't get upset."

"I'm not upset."

"That 'What?' sounded like you were upset."

"That 'What?' sounded like I was surprised. I thought you and Sam were just friends."

"We are. Best friends. Look, Dad, we were in seventh grade and—"

"Seventh grade?"

"Do you want to hear this story or not?"

"I'm not sure I do."

"Too late."

He shook his head—but he was grinning. "I'm listening."

"I really liked this girl. Her name was Erika. And sometimes we held hands. And I wanted to kiss her. And I told Sam, and she said she'd teach me. And I told her I didn't think that was a good idea. But she talked me into it. More like badgered. And, well, in the end it wasn't any big deal."

"So she taught you how to kiss."

I laughed. "She was a good teacher."

Dad laughed too. He looked at me again and shook his head, not upset. "You and Sam. You and Sam." And then he smiled. "Did you ever get to kiss her, this Erika girl?"

I smiled. "I don't kiss and tell, Dad."

My father just laughed. I mean, he really laughed.

"You would do anything for Sam, wouldn't you?"

"Just about."

He nodded. "I admire your loyalty. But I worry sometimes."

"You don't have to worry, Dad. I'm cursed with being a straight-edger."

"Straight-edger?"

"I think you know what I mean." I wanted to tell him how confused I was. I was in the middle of something, and I couldn't quite get at what that something was. I started to get mad at myself. Maybe I didn't do drugs or stuff like that, but I sure as hell was learning how to keep secrets.

"Yeah, Salvie, I think I do know." He took out his cigarettes from the freezer. "Want to have a cig?"

"That's your third cigarette today, Dad."

He nodded as he opened the back door. He sat on the back steps and lit his cigarette.

I sat next to him. "What's up, Dad?"

"Your Mima," he said.

"What about her?"

"Her cancer's back."

"I thought it was all gone."

"Cancer's tricky business."

"But she's been cancer-free since I was —"

"Twelve." He took a deep drag on his cigarette. "It's metastasized."

"What does that mean?"

"It means that there were still some cancer cells in her body, and they shifted to another site."

"Where?"

"Her bones."

"Is that bad?"

"Very bad."

"Is she going to be all right?"

He took my hand and squeezed it. "I don't think so, Salvie." He looked like he was going to cry, but he didn't. If he wasn't going to cry, I wasn't going to cry either. He put his cigarette out. "Your Aunt Evie and I are going to spend the rest of the day with your Mima."

"Can I go?"

"You and I will go to Mass with her tomorrow. Then we'll cook for her. Does that work?"

I knew what he was saying. They had things they wanted to talk about, and they didn't want to have me hanging around. I really, really hated to be left out. "That works," I said.

I knew my dad heard the disappointment in my voice. He put his hand on my shoulder. "I don't have a road map for this trip, Salvie. But I won't be leaving you behind, I promise."

My father, he knew how to keep a promise.

Fito

DAD HAD GONE to see Mima. *Cancer.* I pictured my dad and
Mima and my Aunt Evie talking. About cancer. Them talk. Me
not included. Not happy.

I didn't want to think about Mima, about losing her, and I
kept seeing the look on Dad's face when he said *Very bad.*

I sat on the front porch with Maggie and was about to text
Sam. But I didn't know what to text. So I just sat there staring at
my cell phone.

I looked up from my phone and saw Fito coming down the street.
He walked like a coyote looking for food. For reals. I mean, he was
one skinny guy. I always wanted to give him something to eat. He
waved at me. "How's it goin', Sal?"

"Oh, just hanging out."

He walked up my sidewalk, sat next to me on the steps, and
slid his backpack off. "I just got out of work."

"Where you working?"

"At the Circle K up the street."

"Yeah? You like it?"

"Bunch of crazy people walk in there twenty-four seven. Every druggie in the neighborhood is waiting till it's seven in the morning so's they can buy some booze so's they can come down."

The thing about hanging out with a guy like Fito was that he provided me with an education. Between him and Sam, I was all set. "Well, it least it's not boring."

"Yeah, well, I could go for boring. Some guy was trying to get me to hook him up with free cigarettes. Like that was gonna happen. I gotta quit one of my jobs."

"How many jobs do you have?"

"Two. Beats the hell out of staying home. But I gotta keep my grades up."

"I don't know how you manage that."

"See, it's like this, Sal. I don't have a dad like yours. Your dad, he figures your job is to go to school and get good grades and shit. Me, I haven't seen my dad since he said goodbye to me a few years back. I know he's trying to keep it all together. I mean, my mom did him some damage. I get that. Bottom line is that he's not around to support me. My mom's on public assistance, and I guess I'm just lucky she hasn't been arrested. They arrest her, I'm screwed. The last thing I need is a foster home. The good news is that I'll be eighteen in another couple months. Then I'm free and clear."

"Are you gonna move out?"

"No. I've been saving money for college, and I don't want to use that money for rent. I'm only home long enough to sleep, anyway. It's just a bed. I have to stick it out a little longer. Won't kill me."

God, he looked tired. "I was about to fix me a sandwich," I lied. "You want one?"

"Yeah," he said. "Starving."

Starving was the right word. That boy wolfed that sandwich down in a nanosecond. Fito was an interesting guy. He was all street-smart, and the thing was that he had this really clean-cut look. Short hair, dorky glasses, white shirt, khakis, and he liked to wear these thin black ties. Like my dad. You know, he had a look. Me, I didn't have a look.

"So," he said, "how come you and Sam don't hook up?"

"She's my best friend."

"Why can't she be more than a friend? She's hot."

I gave him a look.

"What?"

"She's like my sister. Guys don't want to hear other guys say things about their sister — things like *She's hot.*"

"Sorry."

"No worries."

"And she's really smart, that Sam. Guess you're not her type anyway."

I just shook my head. "Let's not go there." I didn't like talking about Sam behind her back. It was easy enough to change the subject. "You got a girl, Fito?"

"No girls. I had this thing with Angel for a while."

Until then I hadn't known he was gay. I mean, he didn't act gay — whatever that meant. "He's a nice guy."

"Ahh, he's high maintenance. Don't have time for that. Guys suck."

That made me laugh.

"You ever been with a guy, Sal?"

"Nope. Not my thing."

"I just thought that because your dad was gay —"

I laughed again. "Like it works that way."

Fito started laughing at himself. "I'm, like, an asshole."

"No, you're not," I said. "I like you, Fito."

"I like you too, Sal. You're different. I mean, you say things like 'I like you, Fito.' Most guys don't say shit like that. Well, gay guys do, but they're not really sayin' they like you. They're sayin' they're interested in maybe gettin' you in the sack. Know what I'm sayin'?"

I made him another sandwich. He wolfed down the second one same as the first. He kept petting Maggie and saying, "Man, wish I had a dog and lived all normal and shit." And he just got to talking and talking. He talked about work and about his screwed-up family and about school and about how he really liked Angel, but he was too young for any serious stuff anyway, and he didn't want to be spending his money on a guy who was maybe just using him. "The only thing I'm serious about is getting into college."

If my dad had been there, he would have called Fito a sweet guy. And lonely. That's what I really noticed. He was lonely.

Finally he looked at the time on his cell. "I got to hit the downtown library. That's where I study. That be my home away from home."

After he left, I kept thinking that he deserved better.

And I wondered how Fito got to be so decent when there wasn't anybody around teaching him how to be decent. I just

69

didn't understand the human heart. Fito's heart should have been broken. But it wasn't. And even though there were times when he texted me and told me that life sucked, I knew he didn't believe it. It's just that life hurt him sometimes.

I guess life hurt everybody. I didn't understand the logic of this thing we called living. Maybe I wasn't supposed to.

Sam (and Me)

SAM CAME OVER (again). She brought her backpack, and we studied all afternoon. That was one of our things. Sam hadn't been much into studying when we were in grade school. But once we got into middle school, she got to be a really great student. Sam was extremely competitive. She liked to win. I mean, she was all about winning. She was always better at soccer than I was. Getting the good grades was all about winning. A lot of girls didn't much like Sam. Not that Sam helped herself out on that count. "F all those bitches."

I hated that word. "Have some self-respect, Sammy. The B word is the N word for girls. I hate that. What kind of a feminist are you, anyway?"

"Who said I was a feminist?"

"You did — when we were in eighth grade."

"I didn't know shit in eighth grade."

"Look, just don't use that word around me. It pisses me off."

She stopped using that word around me. But sometimes she did say things like *She's such a B.*

I'd shoot her a look.

So I had this theory that Sam competed with me. And it wasn't just about grades. She wanted to prove to herself (and to me) that she was as smart as I was. And she was. Smarter, I'd say. A lot smarter. Sam didn't have to prove a damn thing — not to me, anyway. But Sam was Sam. So we studied together. All the time. And it was because of her that I had A's (well, two B's) in my math and science classes. If it weren't for her, I wouldn't have known a sine from a cosine. Trigonometry, biology, statistics — anything having to do with numbers and science was really hard for a guy like me.

But Sam, she was actually brilliant — frickin' brilliant. And she was pretty, too. Really pretty. Well, more than pretty. She was beautiful. So she had a beautiful face and a beautiful mind. But there was more to the equation of being a person than a face, a body, and a mind. There was that other thing called a psychology. Sam's psychological makeup was, well, complicated. When it came to schoolwork, Sam was all A's. When it came to picking boyfriends, she was all F's.

I read her paper on *Macbeth*. It was good. Really good. She had style, and I thought maybe she should become a writer. I had the feeling that her life was going to provide her with plenty of material.

"So what do you think?" She was smiling. She already knew her paper was good.

"Brilliant."

"Are you mocking me?" She crossed her arms.

"Nope. And uncross your arms."

She threw herself on my dad's reading chair. "You're quiet today."

"Yeah."

"What's wrong?"

"Who, me? There's nothing ever wrong with me. Don't you know that?"

"Now I know there's something really wrong. You've been a little different lately. Like there's something eating at you."

"Yeah, well, maybe I'm figuring a few things out."

"Like what?"

"Like I don't really want to go to college, for one thing."

"That's crazy."

"Can we not talk about college? Please." I combed my hair with my fingers and started biting one of my fingernails.

"You haven't done that since fifth grade."

"What?"

"Bite your nails."

"It's Mima," I said.

"What?"

"Mima. Remember how she had cancer?"

"Yeah, I remember. That was a long time ago, Sally."

"The cancer's back. It's metastasized. You know what that is?"

"Of course I do."

"Of course you do." I tried to smile.

"Is it serious?"

"Yeah, I think so."

"So what's going to happen?"

"I guess we know how this is going to end. Dad's not optimistic."

"Aww, Sally —"

"Shit, Sam. I'm — I just am, hell, I don't know."

"Oh," she said, "I get it. But — But I don't know, ever since school started, you've been a little — I don't know."

73

"I don't know either. But now this thing with Mima. Ouch."

"Ouch," she said.

All of a sudden she was sitting right next to me on the couch. She took my hand. "I know how much you love her," she whispered. I was the one who should have been crying—but it was Sammy who had tears running down her face.

"Don't cry, Sammy."

"I love her too, you know?"

"Yeah, I know." And Sam *did* love her. She had a lot of empathy. Maybe that's why she liked all those bad boys. They were outcasts. It was like she was picking up strays and taking them in. It's like she could see past their rough exteriors and see the parts of them that hurt. Maybe she thought she could take away the hurt. She was wrong, of course. But I found it hard to fault her for her good heart.

"Sally, you know you're going to have to be a man about this, don't you?"

"I don't think I know how to be a man," I said.

"It sucks, I know, but sooner or later—"

"Yeah, sooner or later," I said.

We were quiet for a long time.

"You want to throw the ball around?"

She smiled. "Yeah, I think that sounds like a great idea."

We did that, Sam and I—we'd take out the baseball gloves and play catch. One of the great things about Sam was that she didn't throw like a girl. She had a good arm, and she knew how to handle a ball. My dad taught her that—he taught both of us. You know, for a gay guy, my dad was pretty straight.

We tossed the ball around until twilight. Sam and I didn't

always talk when we played catch. It was like we could be together and be alone all at the same time. After we put the gloves away, I told her about Fito. "Did you know he was gay?"

"No, but I've seen him and Angel together, and I thought it was kind of an odd pair. I mean, Angel's such a pretty boy. And Fito's such a schizophrenic dork. I mean, they don't make a good couple."

"Like you really know. You don't like Fito."

"Look, I like him better now that I know he's gay."

"That makes no sense."

"It makes perfect sense."

"In your world, I guess so. He's just a guy, Sammy. A lost soul. I like him."

"Oh, so you're into picking up strays."

"No, Sam, that would be your specialty." I gave her a look.

"I don't want to have this discussion."

"I know you don't. Then you'd have to explain your obsession with bad boys."

"I don't have to explain anything to anyone."

"Wrong. Sometimes you have to explain things to yourself."

"Look who's talking."

"Touché."

Sam laughed. "Well, now that we've agreed not to talk about what really matters, what shall we talk about next?"

I shrugged.

But then she said, "You know the other day, when you showed up at my door and there was something going on with you and I let you off the hook by changing the subject to my shoes?"

"Yeah. And?"

"What happened?"

Sam. She really knew me. "I punched a guy in the stomach," I said. Like it was nothing.

"What?"

"You heard me."

"Why?"

"He called me a *pinche gringo,* and I just, hell, I punched him."

"What's that about, Sally? You planning on becoming a boxer?"

"I don't want to talk about it."

She was wearing a question on her face, but she didn't say anything.

I walked her home. That was my dad's idea. He said he didn't like the idea of Sam walking by herself at night. "You never know," he said. Sometimes I thought he cared more about Sam than her own mother did.

As we were standing in front of Sam's front door, she looked at me and said, "There's something different about you, Sally."

I shrugged.

"You're a lot more complicated than I thought you were."

I didn't know why I was hanging my head.

She put her hand on my chin and gently raised my head and looked straight into my eyes. "Whatever it is that's going through that pretty little head of yours, well, you can't hide it from me."

I didn't say a word.

She kissed me on the cheek — and then she said, "I'll love you till the day I die, Sally."

I cried all the way home.

What If

SAM AND I had this game. I think it started as a cell phone game when we both got phones in the ninth grade. The game was called "What If." We'd be talking or texting, and one of us would say something like *What if hummingbirds lost their wings?* And the other person would have to think of an answer that began with *Then.* In fact that was one of the first questions I texted Sam: *What if hummingbirds lost their wings?* We had twenty-four hours to come back with an answer, and it took her precisely ten hours and seven minutes to text me back: *Then it would rain for days and the world would know the rage of the grieving sky.* I mean, it took her a while to get back to me — but her answer was brilliant. At least I thought it was.

Once, when we were walking to school, I asked her, "What if we'd never met?"

"Then we wouldn't be best friends."

"Not," I said. *Not* meant that the answer was unacceptable. You only got three *nots* and you were out. Like in baseball.

"You shit." She hated getting *not*ted. Then she smiled. I knew she'd come up with something. "If we'd never met, then there would be only three seasons."

"Hmm," I said. "Am I supposed to guess which season?"

"Yup."

I thought a moment — then I smiled. "Spring. Then there would be no spring."

"Spring," she said.

"Sometimes you're really, really awesome, Sam."

"You too," she said.

It was a good game, but it was serious. Sometimes, *what ifs* could make us sad. And I thought, *What if I hadn't punched Enrique?* Then — then what? Then things would be the way they always were? Not. Not, not, not. Things weren't going to be the way they were. Senior year. College. Change. *And what if Mima's cancer hadn't come back?* Then I would have her forever. *Not.*

Dad and Me and Silence

DAD CALLED ME on my cell. He was still at Mima's. "You going out tonight?"

"Nah."

"Want pizza?"

"Yup."

"Eat in or out?"

"In. Let's watch a movie."

"Be there in an hour. Order the pizza."

As soon as I finished talking to my dad, Sam texted me: Should I wear red or black?

Me: Red. Out w/ Eddie?

Sam: Jealous?

Me: Lol have fun

Sam: I think I'll wear black

Me: Tht's wht I'd wear if I were going out w/ him

Sam: Dn't be a shit

Me: Try & b gd

Sam: Ur no fn

Me: Fn is overrated

Sam: Get a girlfrnd

Me: Been there done tht

Sam: Try try again oh gotta go

Sam, she always had to have a guy. Me, well, the last girl I was with, she was all about me. I sort of felt like she'd been in a race and I was the trophy she'd won. I was way into her — way, way into her. Turns out she was also seeing some guy who went to Cathedral High School. Her nice way of dumping me was by telling me, "You know, Sal, you're just way too smart for me." Melissa — that was her name — she liked her guys dumb and good-looking. Not that I was ugly. It's just that, well, Melissa needed to be the smart one in a relationship. Do we have relationships in high school? Maybe so. Anyway, I'm not into playing dumb. And besides, she hated Sam. And before Melissa, there was Yolanda. She told me it was either her or Sam. "Sam?" I said. "I've known her since I was five. We're just friends." She dropped me like a water balloon. I went splat. I'm not sure what I was looking for in a girl. Some guys just wanted sex. Not that I didn't want sex, but, well, that wasn't happening for me. Not yet. Well, there was always hope.

Sam had this to say about my dating behavior: "You're way too invested in your identity as a good boy."

Shit, I couldn't pull off the bad-boy thing. I did think Jeff Buckley singing "Hallelujah" was badass. Didn't that count for something?

And I wasn't a good boy. Not a real good boy. And what was that whole good-boy, bad-boy thing anyway? What did any of it mean?

My dad was a little low-key when he got back. "Your Aunt Evie and I are taking Mima to the Mayo Clinic."

"Where's that?" I said.

"In Scottsdale."

"Scottsdale?"

"It's a suburb of Phoenix. It's about seven hours from here. If you're driving."

I nodded. "When?"

"Day after tomorrow."

"That's soon," I said.

"Time is something we don't have," he said. He had a can-we-talk-about-this-in-the-morning look on his face. Some days I gave that same look to him. Guess he was entitled.

We ate pizza and watched an old movie — *To Kill a Mockingbird*. Dad loved old movies. He liked Gregory Peck. Definitely old-school. Nobody at El Paso High even knew who Gregory Peck was. Well, except for Sam. She was all about movie trivia. That had been one of her phases — between her humming-bird phase and her famous architects phase, then back to hummingbirds. She was currently in her shoe phase. For a while before that, she'd worn only flip-flops and tennis shoes. I thought the shoe phase was probably here to stay.

It was a quiet night. Before I went to bed, I asked Dad, "Are we still making lunch for Mima tomorrow?"

"Well, we're going over. But your Mima said nobody was going to cook in her kitchen except her."

We both smiled. That's how she loved people — by feeding them.

Before I went to bed, I studied a photograph of Mima and me. We were sitting on her front porch, and we were both laughing at something. All the pictures I had of Mima and me together were happy pictures. I wondered if happiness would go away when she died. But maybe she wouldn't die. Maybe she wouldn't.

I opened my laptop and looked up the Mayo Clinic. It seemed as if those people knew what they were doing. And then I looked up cancer. Serious business. But I had no idea what stage Mima's cancer was in. Stage one: lots of hope. Stage four: not so much. Not that I was about to throw hope out the window. I didn't consider myself a very serious Catholic. I mean, my dad was gay, and the Catholic Church was not big on gay people. Guess you could say I held a grudge even if my father didn't. But Mima and the Catholic Church got along just fine. I took out my rosary and prayed. Mima had given it to me when I made my First Communion. So I prayed. Maybe it would help.

Sam

WHEN MY CELL phone rang, I was still clutching my rosary. My phone kept ringing and ringing, but by the time I found it in my pants pocket, it had stopped. Maggie was growling. She hated cell phones. I looked at the time: 1:17 a.m. The call had been from Sam. Then the phone rang again.

"Sam?"

"Oh, God," she said. "Sally, Sally, Sally —" She was sobbing into her phone.

"Sammy? Where are you? What's wrong?"

Finally she calmed down enough to spit out, "Can you come get me?"

"Where are you?"

She started crying again.

"Where are you, Sam?" I think I was almost yelling. "Where are you? Where are you?"

"I'm just outside the Walgreens."

"Which Walgreens, Sam? Shit! Which one?" I was getting scared. "Are you hurt, Sam? Are you hurt?"

"Just come get me, Sally?" God, she sounded hurt.

"Sam? Sam, are you okay?" She was crying again. "Sam? Hang on, Sam. Don't go anywhere. I'll be right there. Just hang on."

Part Two

We'd been so sure of ourselves, but now we were lost.

Sometimes in the Night

DAD? DAD!" I was glad he was a light sleeper.

"What's wrong?"

"It's Sam."

He reached over and turned on the lamp on his nightstand. "Is she okay?"

"I don't know. She couldn't stop crying. She sounds really scared."

"Where is she?"

"Walgreens."

"I'm driving."

I didn't argue with him.

She was sitting on the sidewalk, her head down. My dad saw her as soon as we drove up. Walgreens wasn't exactly crowded at that hour of the morning. He jumped out of the car, and I was right behind him. "Sam?"

She ran into his arms, sobbing.

Dad put his arms around her. "Shhh. It's okay. I gotcha, Sam. I gotcha."

———

Sam and I sat in the back seat as my dad drove. I squeezed her hand. She'd stopped crying, but she was still shaking. Almost as if she was cold. I pulled her closer, and I could feel her shivering against my shoulder.

"Do we need to take you to the hospital?" I knew my dad had thought carefully about what questions to ask — and what questions not to ask.

"No," she whispered.

"You sure?"

"I'm sure."

"Where's your mother?"

"She's on a date. She turns her phone off."

"You sure you don't need to go to a hospital?"

"Yes. Just take me home."

No one said anything as we drove. When my dad parked in front of Sam's house, he got out of the car. "I need to talk to your mother."

"I don't think she's home."

"Her car's there."

"Yeah, but Daniel picked her up."

"Maybe she's home." My dad was insistent.

It turned out that Sam was right. No one was home.

"I don't think it's a good idea that you stay here alone tonight."

I could tell that Sam was relieved. She got some things together, and we drove back home. Dad made tea. He sat us both down at the kitchen table. "You want to talk about what happened?"

Sam didn't say anything.

"I know I'm not your dad, Samantha. But there are certain

things you can't keep from the adults around you — adults who care about you."

Sam nodded.

"You don't have to tell me — but in the morning, when your mother comes to get you, you're going to have to tell her what happened. Look at you — you're still shaking. How did your blouse get torn?"

She shook her head. "I don't want to tell my mom."

"I don't think that's an option, Sam. I really don't." There was so much kindness in my father's firm voice that I almost wanted to break down and cry. But I was angry, too. Mad as hell. I wanted to get in the car, find Eddie, and beat the holy hell out of him.

Sam looked up at my father. "I'm sorry I'm such a pain in the ass."

My dad smiled at her. "That's part of your charm."

She laughed — then started crying again.

"Let's all try to get some rest."

All the words inside us had gone to sleep — so we didn't talk. Sam fell asleep on my bed right next to Maggie. We had an extra bedroom, but she didn't much feel like being alone. I'd always done the alone thing much better than Sam. I was on the floor in my sleeping bag, unable to sleep. I kept wondering what had happened. It wasn't like her to be so quiet about things.

And then I started thinking about what Dad was going to tell Sylvia. He'd had chats with her before. Lots of them. That's what Dad called them. Chats. Yeah. And then, all of a sudden, a river of rage shot right through me. I hated Eddie. I hated that son of a bitch. And I wanted to hurt him. And then I thought, *I wish I were more like my dad.* My dad wasn't the kind of guy who'd ever taken out his fists to solve a problem. But I wasn't like him. And he was an artist. I had no art in me. And then I thought that I must be more like my biological father — the man who'd slept with my mother one night. And I hated that thought.

God, I wanted to stop all those thoughts that were turning around in my mind like a gerbil running on his little wheel.

Finally I just got up.

3:12 in the morning.

I walked into the kitchen to get a glass of water. My dad was on the back steps, smoking a cigarette.

I sat next to him. "How many cigarettes is that today, Dad?"

"Too many, Salvie. Too, too many."

Sam (and Her Mother)

I MANAGED TO PUSH open my eyes when I woke up. Some days you really have to push. I looked at the clock. It was already past ten o'clock in the morning. My bed was empty — Sam was up. I was carrying this feeling in the pit of my stomach. This much I knew — it wasn't going to be a normal day. But I had a feeling that normal days were disappearing. I managed to stumble into the bathroom and wash my face and brush my teeth. I could hear the water running in the guest bathroom, so I knew Sam was taking a shower. Sam and her showers. She'd take three a day if you gave her half a chance. She had this thing about being clean. I wondered if she felt dirty. Not that she *was* dirty — but some people felt that way about themselves.

Sometimes I felt that way about myself too. Like when I hit people.

I walked toward the kitchen, but stopped myself. My dad and Mrs. Diaz (a.k.a. Sylvia) were having a *chat,* Dad coming as close to lecturing someone as he got. I could've stood there and listened in on the conversation — but that wasn't my style. So I took a breath and walked into the kitchen.

"Morning," I said. I grabbed a cup and poured myself some

coffee. Dad and Mrs. Diaz had stopped talking, and I knew this was one of those uncomfortable silences. I decided to seize the moment. "Sam didn't tell me anything about what happened — just for the record."

"Surely you must have some notion of what must have occurred." Mrs. Diaz had a deep voice. Sam always said she sounded like the old actress Lauren Bacall.

I shook my head. I wanted to tell her that I had my theories — but that's all they were. "No," I said.

"She didn't say anything to you?"

"No, she didn't." We all turned around and looked at Sam.

She crossed her arms. "I'll give you the short version and spare you the details. I was at a party with Eddie. He wanted me to go into one of the bedrooms and have sex with him. I think he wanted everyone to know that he could have me. That's what I think." She looked at her mother. "And yes, I'd been drinking — but I *wasn't* that drunk." Last night she'd been scared and lost — but now she was just angry. "Any questions?"

"You could have been raped, Samantha." I couldn't tell if Mrs. Diaz was angry at Sam or angry at Eddie or just angry at the whole situation.

"Yeah, I could've been."

"I didn't raise you to make stupid choices —"

Sam interrupted her mother. "Mom, you didn't raise me at all. I raised myself." She gave her mom a look. I mean, she gave her *a look*. "I'm going to go dry my hair."

"I'm taking you home right now." By the time Mrs. Diaz's words were up in the air, Samantha was leaving the room. "How dare you walk out on me, young lady!"

91

Sam swung herself around and looked straight at her mother. I thought she was going to yell at her — but she didn't. "Did anybody ever tell you that you talk in clichés?" She took a deep breath and shook her head. "You're never there, Mom. You've *never* been there."

I realized that Sam wasn't angry at all. She was hurt. At that moment I heard all the hurt she'd ever held. And it seemed to me that the whole house had quieted down to listen to her pain.

But I looked at Mrs. Díaz — and just then I understood that her daughter was a book she didn't know how to read — her own daughter. She had an expression on her face that looked almost like hate. "You ungrateful, spoiled child." She got up from where she was sitting at the kitchen table and looked right at my father. "I'm sure you think that I'm to blame." Then she pointed her eyes toward Sam. "Do whatever the hell you want — you always have." She headed for the front door.

My father followed her out.

Sam and I just stood there, not knowing what to do. Finally I said, "I'm sorry, Sam, I'm really, really sorry."

"This is all my fault," she said.

"What's all your fault?" I said.

"Everything."

I wanted to tell her that I hated Eddie and that I hated her mother. Really hated them. But I didn't think I should say anything. I heard my dad and Mrs. Diaz talking on the front porch. I could hear Mrs. Diaz raise her voice, and I could also tell that my dad was trying to calm her down. "Everything is not your fault. It'll all be okay, Sam." I wasn't sure that everything was going to be all right. But I said it anyway. I gave her a crooked smile. "Want some coffee?"

She nodded.

We sat at the kitchen table and had coffee, the muffled conversation between her mother and my father in the distance.

I looked at her and said, "Everything is not your fault, Sam." I wanted her to believe me.

And yeah, that urge to beat Eddie until he couldn't walk was like a monster growing inside me. I was glad I didn't know where he lived.

Sam. Promises.

BEFORE DAD AND I left for our forty-five-minute drive to Las Cruces to see Mima, I texted Sam: You OK?

She texted back: It sucks being me.

Me: Dnt say that

Sam: Sorry bout evrythng

Me: No worries

Sam: U still love me?

Me: Always ☺

Sam: I AM DONE W BAD BOYS!

Me: Hmmm

Sam: I SAID I WAS DONE

Me: Promise?

She didn't text me back. One thing about Samantha, she didn't make promises she couldn't keep. She was like my dad in that way. There was a big difference, though. Sam hardly ever made any promises. That way, her conscience was clear.

Me. And Dad. Talking.

WE TOOK THE back roads to Las Cruces. Sometimes we did that. Much better than driving I-10. I wanted to ask Dad about his conversation with Mrs. Diaz, so I tried an indirect approach. "Dad, do you like Mrs. Diaz?"

"That's an interesting question."

"That's an interesting answer."

My dad grinned. "It's not whether I like her or not that's important." I knew he was thinking. He was trying too hard to focus on the road. "Sylvia and I are friends."

"Really?"

"Yeah, we are. It's not that we really get along—but we learned a long time ago that as long as you and Sam were friends, well, we were stuck with each other. We both respect your friendship."

"But do you think she's a good mother?"

"I think you already know the answer to that question."

"It makes you mad, doesn't it, that she's so absent?"

"Yes, it does. But there's nothing I can do about it. I can't tell Sylvia how to raise her own daughter. It's none of my business."

"That's not true," I said. "You love Sam. Don't you?"

"I've known her since she was five. Of course I love her."

"The only reason you love her is because you've known her since she was five?"

"Of course not. I love Sam for a lot of reasons. But I'm not her father."

"You kinda are, Dad."

He shook his head, but I could see him grinning. But I could also tell he was a little frustrated. "Look, I've always told Sylvia what I think. Always. Sylvia hasn't always appreciated my opinions. But she knows I care for Sam and that I care very much what happens to her. She appreciates that. She more than appreciates it. And she knows that when Sam is at our place, she's safe. And she's grateful for that."

"She has a funny way of showing her gratitude."

"She's hard, Salvie. She's been through a lot."

I nodded. "Okay," I said, "but I don't like her."

"I know you don't. You don't think she really loves Sam — but she does. Everybody doesn't love in the same way, Salvie. And just because she doesn't love Sam the way you or I would like her to doesn't mean she doesn't love her daughter. It's very difficult being a single mom."

"Oh, and it's so easy being a single dad."

"I'm not complaining."

I didn't know what to say after that. And I didn't even get to the part of what their conversation on our front porch had been about. Shit.

Dad and I were quiet for a while. I looked out at the autumn fields. If it weren't for the river, the whole area would have been nothing but desert. But the river brought water to the fields and turned the landscape into a fertile valley. And I thought, *My dad, he is like the river. He brought water to a lot of people — mostly to me, but also to Sam.*

The Story of Mima and Me

SAM ONCE SAID, "We are what we like." My response: "Does that mean you're a pair of shoes?" It sort of shut down the conversation. But I knew what she was getting at. I didn't know why that popped into my head as we were driving up to Mima's house. I texted Sam: We r what we remember.

Sam: Good one

Me: Mima said that

Sam: Knew it was too smart to be urs

"Get that out of your system before we go inside." Dad hated when I texted in other people's presence. It was the whole raised-by-wolves thing.

Me: Laters

Sam: Dad on ur ass lol laters

I showed my cell to my dad, smiled, and put it my pocket. "Happy now?"

"Very."

Mima was sitting on the front porch dressed in a flowered pink dress and surrounded by the flowers in her garden — roses, geraniums, and others I didn't know the names of. In another few weeks the flowers would be gone.

When I reached out to her, she felt so small. I could feel her bones against her thin, aging body. "You didn't call me this week, *malcriado.*" She always called me *malcriado* when I didn't call her. It meant I hadn't been brought up properly — yeah, yeah, wolves. I laughed. "I love you," I whispered. We were pretty much an I-love-you family — especially with Mima.

"Mijito," she said, "are you taller?"

"Probably."

She wrapped her hands around my face and looked into my eyes. Her hands were old, but they were the softest, kindest hands that had ever touched me. She didn't say anything. She just smiled.

Dad watched us. I always wondered what he was thinking when he saw Mima and me together. Good things. I knew he was thinking good things.

I was sitting at the kitchen table. Mima didn't seem sick. Well, she looked a little tired, but there she was, rolling out flour tortillas, and there I sat, across from her, watching her. My uncles and aunts were watching a football game in the living room. Mostly my aunts talked and my uncles were lost in a sea of Dallas Cowboys uniforms. A Cowboys family. My dad and I weren't much for football. Dad read the sports page. My theory was that he kept up with the sports world in order to be able to have a decent conversation with his brothers — that was the way he loved them.

I watched Mima's hands as she kneaded the dough.

She smiled at me. "You like to watch me make tortillas."

I nodded. "Remember that day when I was mad at Conrad Franco?"

"Yes, I remember. You told me you hated him."

"And you said, 'Oh, *mijito,* you don't hate anybody.' And I said, 'Yes, I do.'"

She laughed.

"Do you remember what you told me?"

"I remember," she said. "I told you that there were only two things you needed to learn in life. You needed to learn how to forgive. And you needed to learn how to be happy."

"I *am* happy, Mima." I was lying to her, but not all lies were bad.

"That means you've learned to forgive."

"Maybe not." I didn't say anything about wanting to go around punching guys' lights out.

She grinned as she rolled out a perfectly round tortilla. How did she do that? She put the tortilla on the *comal.*

I was ready with the butter. She always gave me the first tortilla, and I'd slather it with butter and wolf it down.

"Ay, Salvador, did you even taste it?"

We both started laughing. Laughing was part of the way we talked. I could hear my uncles cheering about something, and Mima and I looked at each other. "I hate football," she said.

"Popo loved football."

"And he loved baseball. He didn't have to talk to anybody when he was watching his games." She shook her head. "Your Popo didn't know how to talk to people."

"He liked talking to dogs."

"That's true."

"Do you miss him?"

"Of course I do."

"I miss him too. I miss his cussing."

She smiled and shook her head again. *"Ave María purísima,* your Popo never met a bad word he didn't like. He knew every bad word in two languages. And used almost all of them every day of his life. He fooled me, you know. He never said one bad word around me when we were dating. Oh boy, was I in for a surprise. But he went to Mass every Sunday."

"I don't think God minded — that he liked to cuss."

"Don't get any ideas."

"I like ideas," I said.

"Hmm," she said.

"Hmm," I said. I liked the *hmm* thing. Dad got that from her. And I got it from him. Maybe a part of me was old-school too.

"Como te quería tu Popo."

"Yeah, I know. But he had a funny way of loving people, didn't he?"

"You know, when I met him, I thought he was so beautiful."

"Maybe it was you who was beautiful, Mima."

"You know, you're a lot like your father."

"Not really, Mima."

"Yes, you are."

I wasn't going to argue with her.

And then she said, "You like to talk. Just like Vicente."

"Yeah. He's good that way, Dad. He talks about things that matter."

She nodded. "He should have become a writer."

"Why didn't he?"

"He said there were too many words in the world already."

I nodded. "He's right about that."

"Yes," she said. *"Creo que sí."*

"Dad, he's more like you. He's not like Popo at all."

"That's right. I loved your Popo — but there's enough men like him in the world already." She laughed. "I'm mean. Your Mima's mean."

"No," I said. "You're sweet. *Dulce,* Mima, that's what you are."

She stopped rolling out tortillas and looked at me. I looked back at her — and then I said, "Are you afraid, Mima?"

"No," she said. "I'm not afraid."

I didn't know I was going to start crying. She put down her old rolling pin and sat next to me. "Maybe they'll take the cancer away at the Mayo Clinic."

I couldn't understand how she could be so calm. If I were dying, I would be really sad. And pissed off. And I *was* pissed off. I was pissed off as hell.

She held me in her arms. I wanted to hold on to her and never let go. But I *was* going to have to let go. And that hurt. Why does it hurt when you love someone? What is it with the human heart? What was it with *my* heart? I wondered if there was a way to keep her in this world forever. And it was as though she were reading my mind. "No one is meant to live forever," she whispered. "Only God lives forever. You see these hands? Hands get old. That's the way it's supposed to be, *mijito.* Even the heart gets old."

She let me go and went back to her work. She handed me another warm tortilla. "This will make everything better."

She watched me slather butter onto the fresh tortilla.

"You have big hands," she said. "Your Popo had big hands." She nodded. I knew that nod. It was her nod of approval. "You're turning into a man."

I didn't feel like a man just then. I felt like a five-year-old boy who didn't want to do anything except play in a pile of leaves. A five-year-old boy with a greedy heart who wanted his grandmother to live forever.

My Uncles and Aunts (and Cigarettes)

WATCHING MY UNCLES and aunts was much better than watching the Kardashians. Not that I liked watching the Kardashians. I only watched because Sam wouldn't shut up about them.

I sometimes joined the conversation — but mostly I listened. Mima was taking a nap, and everyone was sitting around the television, watching the Dallas Cowboys game. My Uncle Mickey was about to light a cigarette. Aunt Evie shot him a look. "Take it outside."

"I'm watching the game."

"Ah, a multitasker. Take it outside. Your mother's sick, idiot." Aunt Evie liked that word: *idiot*.

Uncle Mickey headed out the front door, cigarette and beer in hand. I was raised in a family of smokers. For the most part, I didn't much care for cigarette smoke. Not that it kept me from liking my uncles and aunts. Uncle Mickey said that smokers were more interesting than nonsmokers. Aunt Evie told me not to listen to my Uncle Mickey. "He's an idiot." She never sounded mean when she said things like that. I wondered how she managed it. Maybe it was because she was really sweet. Everyone loved her. My

Uncle Tony said that Evie was Mima with a potty mouth. "She got the potty mouth from Popo." I thought that sounded about right. And my Aunt Lulu, well, she was the only one who didn't smoke. And she didn't drink beer, either. She and my dad, they were the wine drinkers. They were also the only ones who went to college. Uncle Mickey said that going to college turned you into a snob. My dad usually just listened to his brothers talk, without adding his own commentary.

I walked out the door and joined Uncle Mickey on the front porch.

"So, *vato,* you gonna graduate or what?"

"Or what," I said.

"You're a wiseass."

"Yup," I said.

I really liked my Uncle Mickey. He had long hair and a goatee and the straightest teeth I'd ever seen. His skin was weathered from working in the sun, and he didn't seem to give a damn about what anyone thought about him. He was tall and had tattoos, and a lot of people were afraid of him. But he was really a sweet guy. When I was a kid, he used to pick me up, and I thought I could see the whole world as I sat on his shoulders. And he was always sneaking bills into my hand — ones, fives, tens, twenties — his way of loving me.

"When are you going to quit smoking those things?" I asked.

"When I fuckin' die." He laughed. My uncles loved using the F word. Dad said they threw that word around like it was a football. That was his way of saying that just because my uncles loved that word didn't mean I had permission to throw it around the house. Nope.

I sat there next to him, not saying much. "You're like your dad," Uncle Mickey said. "You like to sit and think too much."

"Well, I was just thinking that if you quit smoking, you'd live longer. You know, you could stick around and put more bills in my pocket."

He grinned at me. "So, *cabrón,* the only reason you want me to live longer is so I can give you more money?"

"Nope," I said. "I want you to live longer because I effen' love you."

"You can say *fuck* around me."

"I know."

He rubbed his knuckle against my head. He'd always done that. Dad was right: everybody had their own way of loving.

"I'm proud of you," he said. "You're a good kid. You're gonna be somebody."

We're all somebody. That's what I thought.

I walked back into the living room. The game was over. The Cowboys lost, which didn't put anybody in a good mood. Dad was talking to my Uncle Julian on the phone, and he had a serious look on his face. Uncle Julian and my dad — they were really close, even though Uncle Julian was a lot older. Dad shut off his phone, and my uncles and aunts just looked at him like *What did he say?*

"Julian agrees with me."

Uncle Tony looked a little disgusted. "Well, that's a fucking surprise, Vicente."

"Look, Tony, don't start."

My Aunt Evie looked at Uncle Tony and said, "No more beers for you."

Uncle Tony shook his head. He pointed at my father. "Why does he always have to be in charge?"

My dad had this very patient look on his face. "Nobody's in charge, Tony. We're all in charge."

Uncle Tony put a cigarette in his mouth but didn't light it. "What's the Mayo gonna do? Not a damn thing. *Pinche gringo* doctors don't know shit."

Aunt Lulu did the crossing-her-arms thing. "That's not true. And they're not all gringos. There are good doctors, and there are bad doctors. Mom needs to go to the Mayo."

And then my dad made an announcement using his firm voice. "Evie and I are taking her — and that's all there is to it. I've already scheduled her appointment. We have to be there on Wednesday."

Uncle Tony didn't seem very happy. "And then what, Vicente?"

Aunt Evie wasn't hiding her impatience with Uncle Tony. "Like he knows. We don't know. We have to find out what's going on in Mom's body."

Uncle Tony took the unlit cigarette out of his mouth. "And what about your classes? Or don't art professors have to show up for work?"

My dad gave him a snarky smile. "Only when we want to."

Uncle Tony was quiet for a little while — then he said, "Sorry, I didn't mean —"

"I know," my dad said.

Somewhere along the line Uncle Mickey had walked back into the living room. "How long will she be there?"

"I don't know," Dad said. "We'll just have to see."

Uncle Mickey had this strange look on his face. "Well, just don't let her fucking die there."

Everyone was quiet for a long time. Then my dad said, "Mickey, we're not going to let her die there."

Aunt Lulu looked at Uncle Mickey. "We don't know that she's dying."

"You're right," Dad said. "There'll be tests. And then we're bringing her back. We just have to know what's going on."

Uncle Mickey nodded. And then he looked at my dad and whispered, "At least you know how to talk to doctors. You're good for somethin', *puto*."

And then everyone in the room started laughing. My dad and my uncles and aunts — if there's one thing they knew how to do, it was laugh. My dad called that sort of behavior *whistling in the dark*. Well, I guess that when you found yourself in the dark, you might as well whistle. It wasn't always going to be morning, and darkness would come around again. The sun would rise, and then the sun would set. And there you were in the darkness again. If you didn't whistle, the quiet and the dark would swallow you up.

The thing is, I didn't know how to whistle. I guessed I was going to have to learn.

WFTD = Prayer

I WALKED PAST MIMA'S room and noticed that the door was halfway open. I peeked in, the way I'd always done since I was a kid. She was awake and praying her rosary. She motioned me to come in, patting the bed. I sat next to her. She brushed her hand across my arm. "You're strong," she said.

I didn't believe her, but I nodded. "Who are you praying for?" I whispered.

"Your Uncle Mickey."

"He needs prayers," I said.

She smiled and nodded. "We all need prayers."

She shut her eyes and continued praying. I listened to her whispers, and my mind wandered. I was getting worse about the thinking thing. See, if you wanted to pray, you had to focus. Thinking wasn't prayer — I knew that much. I'd never been able to focus and keep all the thoughts away. Maybe prayers were too old-school for me. My dad said that when he was a kid, he wanted to be Saint Francis — and then he found out he didn't have it in him. I didn't know yet what I did and did not have in me, but Saint Francis wasn't in the cards for me, either.

As Mima prayed, I closed my eyes. I told God that I needed

Mima a lot more than He did. *You already have more than your fair share.* I wondered if Mima would approve of my prayer. Probably not. She would have told me I was a *malcriado*. I thought that later I would text Sam: Wftd = prayer. I wondered if it was normal for guys my age to be thinking about prayer. Maybe it was. Maybe it wasn't. What was it with me and that *normal* word?

As I listened to Mima's soft Hail Marys, I thought, *What if prayer disappeared from the world? Would the world still be okay?* Not that the world was so okay. The real world wasn't my father's world. The real world believed in fists and guns and violence and war. And I was beginning to think I was a bigger part of the real world than I cared to admit.

I saw guys like Enrique Infante and that idiot Eddie, guys who had no respect for anybody. It pissed me off, and there were little explosions inside me, and I even wanted to hit God because He was taking my Mima away, which was super stupid because God wasn't someone you could hit, and what kind of guy was I anyway, a guy who wanted to hit God? My father didn't believe in hitting or punching. And I guess I *did*. I mean, that Eddie guy, I had my sights on him. And I knew my father would say that hurting another human being just because he hurt you is no way to live your life. And maybe he was right. But that thought didn't live inside me.

Me (and Prayer)

BEFORE WE LEFT Mima's house, I texted Sam: What if prayer disappeared from the world?

Sam: Hard one. Not my subject

Me: Mine neither

Sam: Time to consult Sylvia lol

Me: Seriously U think world needs prayers?

Sam: Don't know. Makes us feel better I guess

Me: If no one prayed would the world go to hell?

Sam: World has gone to hell

Me: B serious

Sam: Am being serious

Me: Ur no help

Sam: I'll pray for U

Me: Very funny

Sam: Serious Sally

Me: Laters

Sam: Don't be mad

Me: If on phone I be hanging up

As we drove away from Mima's house, my dad looked at me and asked, "What's so funny?"

"Nothing," I said.

"You were texting Sam, weren't you?"

I nodded.

"You and Sam — you're a pair."

I couldn't argue with that. Part of me wanted to sit in the quiet of my own thoughts, and another part wanted to talk to my dad. Then I heard myself asking, "What would happen if prayers disappeared from the world?"

"That's an easy one," he said. "The world would disappear too."

"You mean that?"

"I guess I do."

"You have proof?"

"Don't get smart. No, I don't have proof. I don't need proof."

"Mima prays for us. Does that mean that our world will disappear — when Mima dies?"

"No."

"No?"

"Because she leaves us behind. And she leaves others behind too — others who pray."

"You?"

"I'm one of them. Yes."

"What do you pray for?"

"More kindness in the world. And then I pray for you."

If Dad hadn't been driving, I would have hugged him. And then I thought: *How can this man love me so much?* I felt like such an asshole. How could I even think or wonder about the man whose genes I had? What did genetic makeup mean anyway, compared with the man who raised and loved me? I *was* such an asshole.

And prayer? How could you pray to a God you wanted to hit?

My Dad

DAD WASN'T VERY talkative on the drive home. But sometimes silences are comfortable and sometimes they aren't. Finally I said, "It was different today, at Mima's."

"Yeah," he said. "I guess that's the way it's going to be for a while. I hope —" He didn't finish his sentence.

"You hope what?"

"I hope we can all handle this."

"We all did fine when Popo died."

"I guess we did. But Popo was Popo and Mima is Mima — and it's not the same."

I knew what he meant. "Yeah, I guess."

"Families can be messy. People get angry when they're afraid."

"Especially Uncle Tony."

"Yeah, your Uncle Tony, he's —"

"I get it, Dad. I do."

My dad nodded. "We're all doing the best we can."

"I know," I said, "but me and you, we aren't messy. And we're a family, aren't we?"

"Yes, we are, Salvie. As families go, you and I and Maggie are about as un-messy as it gets. But we're not a self-contained unit. We belong to something bigger than just ourselves, right? You know, when I was young, I tried my damnedest to divorce my family."

"Why?"

"It was too hard, too messy, too complicated. I sort of lived in a self-imposed exile for a good many years. I went away to college, lived my own life, chased my dreams, tried to face some demons. I guess I thought I could do all those things on my own. I thought that because I was gay, my family, well, they'd hate me or they wouldn't understand me or they'd send me away. So I just sent myself away. It was easier for me to pretend that I didn't belong to a family. I tried to pretend I didn't belong to anyone."

"What changed, Dad?"

"I changed. That's what changed. Me. I didn't want to live without my family. I didn't. And then there was you."

"Me?"

"Yeah. Your mom was living here. She needed help. I came back."

"You really loved my mom, didn't you?"

"Best friend I ever had. You brought me back to my family. I want you to know that."

"Me?"

"Yup." He stopped talking. He pulled over to the side of the road. "Here, you take the wheel."

Me? I had brought him back to his family? Wow. I'd have to think about that. It made me happy that he could tell me about things he felt. And that he needed me to drive — that he needed me to do something for him. That made me happy too.

As I drove down I-10, I wondered if my father was going to continue the conversation he started. He sometimes started telling me something about himself and left off right in the middle of it.

"I need a cigarette," he said.

"No smoking in cars," I said.

"I didn't bring them anyway."

"Good."

"Good," he said. "You love your uncles and aunts, don't you?"

"Yeah, I do. I like that they don't pretend to be anything. They're just themselves. I like that."

My dad nodded. "Me too. But the thing is that we don't do normal in this family. We're not a pretty photograph on Facebook. We misbehave and cuss and drink too much beer and say all the wrong things. We don't try to be the portrait of the American family. We're just who we are. And we don't do perfect. But you know something? It was wrong of me not to trust them. Mima has a saying: *Solo te haces menos.* You know what that means?"

"I know Spanish, Dad."

"Yeah, but do you know what that means?"

"I think it means that it's not other people who make you feel like you're alone. You do it to yourself."

"Smart boy. I lived apart from my family because I didn't trust them. I didn't trust that they loved me enough. Shame on me. I'll never get those years back." He looked over at me. "Don't ever underestimate the people who love you."

I nodded.

"I know you sometimes think that people are like books. But our lives don't have neat logical plots, and we don't always say beautiful, intelligent things like the characters in a novel. That's not the way life is. And we're not like letters —"

"You mean like the one Mom left me."

"I wasn't referring to that, but now that you mention it — look, we can't fit what we feel and think — we can't put what we are and stuff it into an envelope and say *This is me.* I don't know what I'm trying to say. I guess I just have some regrets. I'm sorry to report that regrets are part of living."

"But does it have to be that way?"

"Yes, I think it *does* have to be that way. Because we're always going to make mistakes." He took a breath. He was trying to explain something to me — and maybe even to himself. "Let's put it this way: Show me a man without regrets and I'll show you a man without a conscience."

I nodded. "Well, Dad," I said, "at least you have a conscience."

He started laughing.

And then I started laughing.

Whistling in the dark.

WFTD =
Nurture? Nature?

WHEN WE GOT home, my dad headed straight for his studio. Work was better than cigarettes. I knew he would begin a new painting. He'd take out one of his already stretched canvases and start. And then he'd be able to sleep. He'd told me once that art was not something he *did*. "It's something I am."

Since I didn't have art in me or hadn't found anything that resembled what my dad had, I headed for my room.

I texted Sam: U home?

Sam: Where else?

Me: Skool tomorrow

Sam: Yup broke up with Eddie

Me: ☺

Sam: Guys suk. No wonder ur dad doesn't date

Me: Lol

Sam: Seriously

Me: Can't blow all guys off the planet

Sam: Y not? Lol

Me: Can u live without me?

Sam: Conceited shit

Me: Lol. going to sleep

Sam: Sweet dreams

Me: Ditto

I plugged my phone into the charger and set the alarm for 6:30.

I took a deep breath and tried to remember if I'd brushed my teeth. Didn't matter — if I hadn't, it wasn't going to happen. I petted Maggie as she lay next to me on the bed.

Before I nodded off, I thought about what my dad had said — that life wasn't all nice and neat like a book, and life didn't have a plot filled with characters who said intelligent and beautiful things. But he wasn't right about that. See, my dad said intelligent and beautiful things. And he was real. He was the most real thing in the entire world. So why couldn't I be like him?

I got an idea in my head, so I went on the Internet and started fishing around for information. I found a discussion: "Nature vs. Nurture in Psychology. This debate within psychology is concerned with the extent to which particular aspects of behavior are a product of either inherited (i.e., genetic) or acquired (i.e., learned) characteristics."

I read some articles, and it seemed to me that nobody really knew the answer to that question. To *my* question: What mattered most? What was it that made my engine run — the genetic characteristics I got from my biological father or the characteristics I acquired from my father, the man who raised me?

Which of my fathers was going to have the *big* say on the man I would become?

Me (in the Dark)

I WOKE UP AT 3:14 in the morning. I'd had a dream about walking in the rain. In the dream, I was lost. I thought of the first day of school, when the rain had come down on me and I'd felt so alone. I stared at my cell phone. I couldn't catch up with what was happening. Sam and her scare with that bastard Eddie. I did not want to go there. Sam and her mother. I did not want to go there. Me and my mom's letter. I did not want to go there. Mima and cancer. I did not want to go there. Me and the changes I felt churning inside me. I did not want to go there. Me and college and the future and the stupid admissions essay I hadn't even thought about writing. I did not want to go there.

So I started thinking about my family and all the good things I remembered about them: the time my Uncle Mickey whisked me up in his arms when a loose dog was heading straight for my throat; the morning Aunt Evie wound up in a hospital because she fell off a ladder putting up Christmas lights, and the string of cuss words that came out of her mouth as she lay on the ground; the afternoon Popo fell off the roof and just dusted himself off, laughing, Mima shaking her head and making the sign of the cross; the weekend Uncle Mickey spent in jail and missed my birthday party;

the summer morning when I was throwing rocks at a wasps' nest and wound up in the ER, my Aunt Lulu rubbing some kind of ointment on me for three days in a row; the summer I spent at Mima's because my dad was teaching in Barcelona, and the barbecues we had at Mima's, me counting all the beer cans and the money I got from the aluminum recycling place; and the time we built a human pyramid in our backyard on my fifteenth birthday and I got to be the top of the pyramid. It was as if all the scenes of my life were running through my brain like a pack of dogs running through the streets, dogs running and running, unable to stop even though they were tired.

I smiled to myself. A lot of people in the world had really shitty lives, and it wasn't even their fault. Like Fito. Some people were just born into the wrong family or adopted by the wrong family, or they were born with something broken inside them. There wasn't anything broken inside my dad, even though some people thought there *was* because he was gay. But those people were wrong. They didn't know him.

Me. And My Fists.

I WALKED PAST THE guy I punched in the stomach for calling me a *pinche gringo*. And he gave me this look. Part of me wanted to say *I'm sorry* and *I'm really not that guy*. But, well. I *was* that guy. I was wondering if I shouldn't confess that incident to my father, because I mostly told him what was going on with me. But I hadn't really put anything into words yet. Sam always said, "If you can't put it into words, then you just don't know."

I'm making a fist.

This is my fist.

I want to punch a wall and tell God to make Mima well. And after that, punch Him too.

I want to punch Eddie's lights out and make him tell Sam he's sorry.

I kept thinking I just might turn out like the guy whose genes live in me. And I kept hating that thought.

Sam

SAM CALLED ME after school. She had stayed home sick.

"Are you really sick?"

"Yup. Sick of Sylvia."

"What happened?"

"We got into an argument."

"Like that's news."

"Fuck you." Sometimes, when Sam and her mother got into a catfight, Sam went into a funk. The other thing that told me she was in a super-bad space was that she had called me. We didn't talk on the phone much. We mostly texted.

"Wanna talk about it?"

"Of course I wanna fucking talk about it. I called you, didn't I?"

"I think you should come over," I said.

"Okay."

"I'll make you something to eat."

"I'm fucking starving."

"Okay, okay, enough with the F word."

"Am I offending you, Sally?"

"There are other words in your lexicon. Use your imagination."

"Straight-edger."

"Sewer for a mouth."

"White boy."

"Bad-boy lover."

I walked into my dad's studio. He was looking through old photographs. "Hi," I said.

He smiled at me. "Hi."

"Whatcha doin'?"

"I'm looking for a picture of Mima. One in particular."

"How come?'

"I need it for a painting."

I nodded.

"Your Aunt Evie and I and Mima are leaving for Scottsdale tomorrow afternoon." We sort of studied each other for a moment. "I know you want to come —"

I interrupted him. "Dad, I'll hold down the fort."

He smiled — then laughed. "You remember?"

I nodded. "I remember."

It's what he told me to do the first time he left me alone in the house.

He looked at me. "I'm going to be honest with you."

"You've always been honest with me, Dad."

"As far as you know."

I laughed. "As far as I know."

"I'm a little scared. No, let me start this again. I'm a lot scared."

"Mima?"

"Yeah. I have this feeling. You know what I'm trying to get at? You'll have to be patient with me. It's a little like learning how to speak a new language. It's not something you master easily."

Sam texted: Send Maggie outside to greet me.

I opened the front door and watched as Maggie ran toward Sam, her tail wagging. I watched the familiar lick on the face, Sam's smile, and then the hug.

Sam and Maggie leaped up the front porch steps. Sam looked me over. "You know, you really should get a tattoo."

"It's not me."

"You're right. It isn't you. I like you the way you are. More or less."

"More or less?"

"Yeah. I like that you're not like the other boys I like."

"Yeah, I know."

"You sound disappointed, Sally."

"Well —"

"What?"

"Nothing . . . What if you discovered I was someone else? You know, someone who turned out to be not who you thought I was?"

"I know you, Sally."

"Do you?"

"You're not making sense. Come on. Let's go in."

Dad was making his famous tacos. Sam loved my dad's tacos. Me too. Maggie three. Sam and I went into the living room, and I could smell the corn tortillas as my father shaped and fried the taco shells. God, I loved that smell. Sam kept crossing her arms and uncrossing them as she talked. "My mom is such a bitch."

"Take it back," I said.

"Once you say something, you can't ever take it back."

"Yes, you can."

Sam could give looks that could stop you in midsentence. But I could give those kinds of looks too.

"I take it back." She crossed her arms. "She's mean. She can be really mean."

I nodded.

"You know what she told me? She said, 'If you don't watch yourself, little girl, you're going to wind up dancing around a pole, half naked, surrounded by salivating dirty old men. And you think you want to go to Stanford?' She had no right to say something like that."

"I have to admit that I don't like your mother very much right now."

Sam smiled. "Good." She threw herself on the couch. "Can I ask you a question?"

"Sure."

"Have you ever liked my mother?"

"Well, I don't really know her. She doesn't seem that interested in being known. Not by me, anyway."

"Yeah, guess that's about right."

"Do you ever want to be a mother, Sam?"

"I've never thought about it."

"Never?"

"Not really. What about you, Sally? You want to be a dad someday?"

"Yup. I sure do. I want three kids."

"Three?"

"Maybe four. That would be awesome."

"Well, good luck trying to get a girl to marry you."

That made me smile. But then I noticed she had a sad look on her face.

"You know, Sally," she said, "I think I'd be afraid to be a mother. I don't think I'd make a very good one."

"Hey," I said. "I think you'd make a great mother."

"What makes you say that?"

I pointed to my heart and tapped on it. "Because you have a lot of this. That's all it takes."

"You're like your dad, you know that? I mean, I know he's not your real —"

"Yes, he is."

She nodded. "Yeah, he is."

And right then I wished with all my crooked heart that my dad had been the man who'd fathered me.

Then his voice echoed through the room. "Tacos, anyone?"

Maggie ate one taco. That's all she was allowed. Dad ate three. Sam and I had five each.

I walked Sam home. The night was quiet, the weather almost too perfect. "Dad's leaving tomorrow."

"He taking your Mima to the Mayo Clinic?"

"Yeah."

"You don't want to talk about it right now, do you?"

"No, guess not."

127

"Do me a favor: Don't bring up subjects you don't want to talk about."

"Okay, okay. Give me a break. I do and don't want to talk about it."

"I get it. Your Mima's really sweet."

"Yeah, she is."

"Are you scared, Sally?"

"I never really lost anyone I loved. Well, that's not true. I lost my Popo."

"And you lost your mom."

"Yeah, Sam, I did. But I don't remember that. If you don't remember something, it doesn't hurt."

"Wouldn't it be great, Sally, if we could just push the delete button in our brains and forget the times somebody hurt us?"

"Would be nice. But maybe not. I mean, hurt's a part of life, right?"

"Right," Sam said. "Sometimes that really sucks."

"I guess we can't just pick the good things to remember, can we?"

I watched her walk into her house. I stood there a moment. She poked her head out the door, smiled at me. She waved. Real sweet-like. And I waved back.

Me and Dad

THE WIND AND THE RAIN pelting my window woke me up. Then the lightning started. And the thunder, as if the sky were trying to break itself in half.

I grabbed my pants and headed for the front porch, Maggie following me. I needed to watch the show — it was one of my hobbies. I wasn't surprised to find my dad standing there, smoking a cigarette. Watching the lightning and the rain come down. I stood next to him. He put his arm around me. I leaned into him, watching the lightning and hearing the crack of the thunder and the rain coming down in sheets. I don't know how long we stood there. Sometimes there were moments when time didn't exist. Or maybe it did exist, but, well, it just didn't matter.

We didn't say a word. Dad was right. The world *did* have too many words. The sound of the rain was all we needed.

The storm was fierce. But I wasn't afraid. I knew my father's love was fiercer than any storm.

"Will you be okay?" he whispered.

"Yeah."

"No wild parties?"

"Just Sam," I said. "Guess that's wild enough."

He laughed. "I'll call you every day."

"How long will you be gone?"

"I don't know."

I nodded.

"Let's get some sleep. I have to get up early."

"No," I said. "Let's wait for the storm to end."

Between Storms

THE AIR WAS CLEAN, the sky as deep a blue as I had ever seen.

I thought of what my father had told me one summer day. I'd fallen down, and my knee was all scraped up and bleeding. We sat on the back porch, and he cleaned my wound and put a Band-Aid on it. The sky had cleared after a summer storm. I'd been crying, and he tried to get me to smile. "Your eyes are the color of sky. Did you know that?" I don't know why I remembered this. Maybe it was because I knew he was telling me he loved me.

Anyway, my eyes weren't nearly as beautiful as the sky. Not even close.

I sat on the front steps and breathed in the air as Aunt Evie and Mima drove up in front of the house. Mima got out of the car and smiled as if there were nothing wrong with her. She was standing on the sidewalk, wearing a pastel blue dress that reminded me of a summer day. She looked the way she'd always looked: pretty and strong and happy. I bounded off the steps and hugged her. *"Mijito de mi vida,"* she said, "you look so handsome."

"Looks aren't so important."

"That's right." She held my face in her hands as she'd done so many times before. "Everyone is beautiful," she said.

"Not everyone," I said.

"Yes. Everyone."

I smiled at her. I wasn't going to argue with her.

My dad came down the front steps carrying a suitcase. I watched as he and my aunt rearranged everything in the trunk.

Aunt Evie winked at me. "Hey, sweetie." That was her thing. Everyone was *sweetie.*

"Hi," I said.

"Are you gonna be a good boy?"

"I'm always a good boy, Aunt Evie."

"Always?"

"Well, most of the time."

"Well, that's good enough for me."

My dad opened the door for Mima. "Ready?"

She nodded, and something sad passed over her face.

She waved at me.

I waved back.

I hugged my dad.

He looked serious. "Take good care of Maggie."

"I will."

"Tell Sam I'm counting on her to keep you out of trouble."

"I'll tell her."

Aunt Evie gave me a hug and jumped into the back seat. I watched as they drove away. I thought about last night's storm. One had ended, and another one was beginning.

Me. Fito. Friends.

THAT NIGHT, DAD called just to tell me they were checking Mima into the Mayo Clinic. He'd left me an ATM card in case I needed anything. "Don't go crazy with that card." He was joking. I knew that. I was sitting on my dad's leather chair, and Maggie was lying at my feet. When I finished talking to Dad, I looked around the house. I stared at the picture my dad had painted that hung on the wall. It was a large painting that almost took up the whole wall. It was a portrait of a bunch of kids around a piñata. The kids were his brothers and sisters. And it was my Uncle Mickey who was swinging at the piñata. And the kid who was my father was off to the side. I loved that painting. But as I looked at it, I felt alone again. I didn't feel like being alone. I knew I'd start thinking about things. Shit.

As I poured myself a glass of cold milk, this thought entered my head: *If I ran into my biological father, would we recognize each other because we looked alike? Would we know?* He isn't my dad, he isn't my dad, he isn't my dad.

—

I texted Sam: Lonely. Slumber party?

    Sam: Aww. Can't. School night. And Sylvia's on the warpath

    Me: What happened?

    Sam: She b like upset about the Eddie thing and she's holding up my college apps. She's pissed. I'm pissed. Living in hell

    Me: Sorry.

    Sam: Gotta go. Sylvia just walked into room. She's been writing something on my bathroom mirror TTYL

I decided to text Fito: Dad's gone. Alone. Wanna come over?

    Fito: It's getting late

    Me: Where r u?

    Fito: Working at Cr. K. Not supposed to be texting

    Me: That sux. U get off when?

    Fito: 11

    Me: My place when ur off?

    Fito: K. Cool for a bit. Not like I have a curfew

    Me: Cool cool. Can make sandwiches

    Fito: Sweet

Maggie and I went out to sit on the front steps a little after eleven to wait for Fito. I didn't normally stay up late on a school night unless I was doing homework, but I wasn't out there long. Maggie barked, and Fito appeared out of the darkness. "Hey," I said.

"Hey. What up?"

"The stars," I said.

Fito grinned. "Got no time to look up at the stars."

"That sucks."

"Yup."

We went inside and I made Fito a sandwich. "Don't you want one?" he asked.

"Nah. I think I'll just make some popcorn."

"You got popcorn?"

"Yup." I grabbed a bag and put it in the microwave. Fito was chowing down. "Don't you ever eat?"

"Oh yeah, my mom's a regular chef." He sort of laughed. "My mom gets food stamps. She fuckin' sells her Lone Star card for drugs."

"No bueno," I said.

"No bueno is right," he said. "So where's your dad?"

"My Mima's sick. Cancer. They took her to the Mayo in Scottsdale to check things out. So he'll be gone a few days."

"That sucks about your Mima."

"Yeah," I said. "I've been thinking a lot."

"That's not good. When I get to thinking, I wind up in a bad place."

"I guess I do too. But, well, you know that thing about the unexamined life that Mrs. Sosa is always talking about?"

"Yeah, yeah, Mrs. Sosa." And then he put on the voice of our English teacher, and he got this really goofy look on his face. "'The unexamined life is not worth living. Are you listening to me, Fito? Can you tell me which philosopher said this?'" And then he laughed. "That teach always thinks I'm not listening. Shit, I'm always listening."

People never gave Fito enough credit. I hated that. Not even Sam gave him enough credit.

It was good to sit there and talk to Fito. We talked about school and teachers, and we ate popcorn and then ate more popcorn and

135

drank a couple of Cokes. And then Fito, out of nowhere says, "You know, someday I'm gonna go looking for my father."

"Really?" I said.

"Yup. I mean, me and him have a chance. You know, to have something."

I nodded.

"You ever gonna go looking for your bio dad?" That's how he put it, my bio dad.

"What would I say to him?"

Fito shrugged. "Maybe nothing. Maybe it would just answer a question you had in your head."

"Maybe," I said. "I don't know. I try not to think about it."

"Yeah, I get that." Fito was good at reading people. Then he said, "So how did you get the name Salvador?"

"Good question."

"I mean, your mom was a *gringa,* right?"

"Yup."

"And I take it your bio dad wasn't Mexican."

"Don't think so. I don't know. She just liked the name, I guess."

"It's a pretty heavy-duty name."

"Yeah, I guess so." Then I looked at him and asked, "What's your real name, Fito?"

"Adam."

"No frickin' way. Adam?"

"Yup. My mom, when I was born, she'd been clean for a while, and Adam, well, he was the new man and I was supposed to represent the new life. And hell, we know how that turned out. And I don't know, my brothers always called me Fito because I had little fect. So feet equals Fito." He shrugged. "Stupid. I have a stupid family."

"I like Fito," I said.

"I like Fito too," he said.

Dad called every day.

We talked, but he didn't seem like himself. And there wasn't that much to talk about. Or maybe there was too much to talk about. Still, it was good to hear his voice, and I liked that he told me he loved me. I wondered if it was easier for him to say the words *I love you* because he was gay. I asked Sam about that. She said, "Don't be stupid, Sally."

Even a smart guy could be stupid. I was living proof.

The rest of the week that Dad was gone, I got on Facebook — not that I was big Facebooker and not that I posted anything. I was one of those that just like to read everybody else's posts. I guess I just needed some company. My friends mostly posted stupid stuff. But sometimes I didn't mind stupid. I always clicked on LIKE. I guess you could say I was an indiscriminate liker. No harm done. My way of making people feel good. When I logged off, I scooped myself a whole bowl of ice cream. I sat on the back steps and stared out at the stars. I remember teaching Mima the constellations and how she'd been so proud of me because I'd been interested in the heavens. And I remembered what Fito said — *Got no time to look up at the stars.*

As I sat there and looked up at all the stars, I felt really, really small.

Me and Sam

SAM TEXTED ME: Friday! Slumber party!

I texted back: Slumber party!

God, we could be such dorks. But if I ever said that to Sam, she'd be pissed. She wasn't going for dork. No way in hell. Then I got to thinking that most people thought I was the boy who kept Sam from walking on the wrong side of the street. People gave me too much credit.

She came over and asked the eternal question: "What's for dinner?" God, for a girl who ate the way she did, you'd think she'd be fat. But nope, she wasn't.

"We could order pizza."

"Ardovino's!"

"Yup."

"They don't deliver."

"Dad left the car."

She was already on her cell phone, ordering the pizza.

"Don't forget the salad."

We decided to watch an old movie from my dad's collection. "*To Kill a Mockingbird*," Sam said.

"I just watched that with my dad."

"Well, I didn't."

"Well, I *did*."

"Tough cookies, baby. It's not going to kill you to watch it again."

"Really," I said. "Look, they published that sequel thing — and Atticus turns out to be a racist."

"Yeah, yeah, and have you read that book?"

"No, but —"

"But — but nothing, Sally. In this version, Atticus is *not* a racist. So let's focus, Sal."

I don't know why I bothered arguing with Sam. The result was always the same. So rather than prolong a debate that I was destined to lose, I just said, "Next time I get to pick."

"Deal."

In the middle of the movie Sam poked me and said, "I think your dad's a little like Atticus Finch."

"The unracist one."

"Yup, that one."

"You think so, Sammy?"

"Yup. And he's just as handsome as Gregory Peck."

"Yup," I said.

"How come when you sleep over, you always get the bed?"

"'Cause I'm the girl."

"Sometimes you're so full of shit, Sam."

"Yeah, yeah."

"And how come you always get to sleep with Maggie?"

"You should ask Maggie that."

I looked at Maggie: "Traitor." Then I looked at Sam. "I think you should sleep on the floor sometimes."

"Shut up." She turned off the light. "Go to sleep." But we couldn't stop laughing.

Everything was quiet. Then I heard Sam say, "Tell me a secret."

"A secret."

"We all have them."

"You first."

She was real quiet. Then she said, "I'm still a virgin."

I was smiling to myself, happy that she hadn't slept with any of those bad boys. "I am too."

She laughed. "Everyone knows that, you idiot. Tell me a real secret."

I didn't know I was going to tell her. "I have a letter from my mother."

"What? Really? Really?"

"Yeah, my dad gave it to me."

"When?"

"A while ago."

"What did it say?"

"I haven't opened it."

"What? What's wrong with you?" She turned on the light so I could see that look of hers. "You have a letter from your mother, your mother who's dead, and you haven't opened it? What an asshole."

"I'm not an asshole. I'm just not ready to open it."

"Well, when will you be ready? After the earth dies from global warming?"

"Now *you're* being an asshole."

"Okay, talk to me. I knew something was going on with you. I just knew it."

"Yeah, yeah."

"Don't *yeah, yeah* me, you jerk. Talk to me."

"It's just that, well, I'm not ready."

"What is that about?"

"I don't have an answer."

I could tell she was exasperated. "Look, I'll read it to you," she said.

"That is *exactly* what I thought you'd say — which is exactly why I didn't tell you about it."

She didn't say anything for a long time — but I could tell she was pouting. She turned off the light.

"Don't be mad at me, Sam," I whispered.

"Are you scared to read what it says?"

"I guess I am."

"Why, Sally?"

"I don't know."

"You know what I think? I think you're angry with your mom. Because she died. You just never let yourself in on that dirty little secret."

"Oh, so now you're the frickin' Dalai Lama?"

"Yup."

I gave her a snarky smile in the dark.

"Well, when you're ready and you read it, Sally, will you tell me what she said?"

"I promise. And will you promise not to nag me about it?"

"I promise."

"I'm glad we're friends, Sammy."

"Me too, Sally."

She stopped talking, and I could hear her breathing. I wondered why girls didn't snore. Maybe they did, but Sam didn't. I knew I snored sometimes. I was no expert on snoring. I lay on the floor in my sleeping bag and started making a list of things I was no expert on. Cancer. Girls. Gay men. Mothers. Bio fathers. Nature vs. nurture. Anger. Fear. Prayer. I fell asleep in the middle of making my list.

Me and Dad

I WOKE UP EARLY. Sam was fast asleep. She was definitely a sleeper. Me, well, not so much.

I sat and watched the sun come up. My dad called. He said Uncle Julian had taken time off and was going to Scottsdale to be with Mima while she was at the Mayo. "I'm flying home tonight."

"Flying? I thought you drove."

"No. The drive was too long for Mima. And the flight's only an hour."

"Oh."

"I thought I'd told you."

"Guess I didn't remember. Glad you're coming home," I said. "The fort isn't the same without you."

"What? You didn't tear up the place?"

"Nah. Sam came over. We had our usual slumber party."

"You didn't practice any more kissing, did you?"

"Course not. I should never have told you."

"Just checking."

I noticed he didn't say anything about Mima. If the news had been good, he would have said something.

Sylvia

I WAS MAKING OMELETS, and Sam was feeding Maggie bacon. "It's bad for her," I said.

"She doesn't seem to think so."

I gave her a look.

She gave me a look back. Then she started texting.

"Who you texting?"

"It's private."

"Yeah, well, if it's so private, why are you doing it in front of me?" I gave her one of my best smirks.

"If you must know."

"And I must."

"I'm texting Sylvia. We're supposed to go shopping today."

"That's nice. More shoes."

"That was just a phase."

"Bullshit. Hummingbirds were a phase. Well, you relapsed on that phase and it came back. But shoes. That's chronic."

"Chronic?"

"Yup. So what's the new phase?"

"Vinyl."

"Vinyl?"

"Sylvia has old albums and a record player. I took it out the other day and played some of her stuff. It belonged to her uncle. I have to hand it to Sylvia. She can't keep a clean house, but she can keep her old record collection in mint condition. Go fucking figure."

"There's that word again."

"Say it with me." That girl could smile.

"Nope."

"C'mon. It won't kill you."

"I use that word sparingly."

"I bet you're gonna marry a bad girl."

"Nope."

She shook her head. She kept playing with her phone. "Sylvia didn't text me back. She promised. She's trying to make up for the fact that I'm not allowed to go out on any more dates unless she meets the guy first. And she promised, if I behaved myself, we'd discuss my application to Stanford. If I behaved? What does that mean? Who gets to evaluate my behavior? Me or her?"

"I think she gets the honors," I said. "And at least she's being motherly. That's progress."

"Not in my world."

"You want her involved or not?"

"Involved? She's the one who got me addicted to uninvolved. So what's a girl to do?"

"Go with it."

"I'll try it on for size. But if it doesn't work for me, I'll tell her to buzz off."

I put her omelet in front of her. "Just the way you like 'em."

She smiled as she was calling her mother. "You can always work as a short-order cook."

"Oh yeah, my life's ambition."

"Shit!"

"What?"

"Her phone went straight to voice mail. Things never change. The boyfriends always come first."

"Relax. It's not even noon yet."

"She usually gets home by ten."

"Well, maybe this guy's special."

"They're all special."

That's when her phone rang.

It was all so strange, almost as if we'd been walking along in one direction and all of a sudden we were going in another and we were suddenly on an unfamiliar road, finding our way in the dark, and we didn't know where we were going anymore. We'd been so sure of ourselves, but now we were lost. Lost like we'd never been lost before. I heard Sam's voice as she answered the telephone — "Yes, this is Samantha Diaz . . ." — and I watched as Sam kept nodding, and then the tears came flooding down her face and she kept whispering in disbelief, *"But how, when, no no."* And then she looked at me with those pleading, hurt eyes, asking me to tell her that this wasn't real, that it wasn't happening, and she whimpered, *"Sally, Sally, Sally. She's dead, Sally, she's dead."*

I remembered what Dad said when we'd picked Sam up from Walgreens that night. "I gotcha," I whispered. "I gotcha, Sam." And I held her.

Sam and Me and Death

WHAT DID I know about death? Hell, I didn't even know very much about life. Sam sobbed on my shoulder as I called Dad. "Are you almost home?"

"I'm at the airport."

I was trembling, and crying too — though I didn't know why I was crying. Yes, I *did* know. I was scared. I was so scared. And I couldn't stand it. That the hurt in Sam was so bad.

"What's wrong?"

"Sylvia, Dad. She and her boyfriend . . ."

"She and her boyfriend what, Salvie?"

If I said the words, the whole thing would be true. And I didn't want it to be true.

"Salvie?"

Then I blurted out the words. "They were killed in a car accident."

My dad was quiet on the other end of the phone. "Where's Sam?"

"She's here."

"Good," Dad said. "Does her aunt know?"

"I don't know."

"How's Sam?"

"She's crying on my shoulder."

"She's going to need that shoulder. Call her aunt. I'm about to board the plane."

"Dad?"

"What, son?"

"I don't know. I don't know. I don't know what to do, Dad." I was trying to keep myself from falling apart, but I knew Sam needed me, so I just took a swallow, like I was drinking a glass of water and a Tylenol, and made myself stop shaking. "Dad, just come home."

"The flight's only an hour," he said. "Just stay calm."

Sam and I hung on to each other. That's what we did, we hung on to each other. "I'm here, Sam. I'm here. I'm always gonna be here."

"Promise," she whispered.

"Promise."

I thought of Sylvia.

Sylvia would never be coming back. Not ever.

I thought of my mom.

Part Three

Somehow, because she was all over the map, it helped me to not be all over the map. That didn't make sense, but me and Sam, what we had, well, it had a logic all its own.

WFTD = Comfort

WHAT HAPPENED BETWEEN the time I called Dad and the time he arrived, well, I'm not very clear about that. I remember Sam sitting in my dad's reading chair, stunned or numb or — I don't know, I can't explain. Everything was *I don't know, I can't explain*. Everything. I *do* remember that Sam got into the shower. I could hear her sobbing through the walls. I couldn't stand it. I didn't know exactly what was going on in her heart — some kind of riot, I think. Maybe she was fighting with herself, feeling guilty because she and her mother had had such a difficult relationship — a relationship that was almost unkind. Difficult. I guess sometimes love is difficult and complicated. Guess I'd known that. But no, I hadn't known that.

I don't think I'd ever seen pain written on a face. Not that kind of pain. It was something awful. And I had this thing going on in the pit of my stomach, and it wouldn't go away.

I remember asking Sam for her aunt's number. "Her name's Lina," Sam whispered as she handed me her cell. I must have called her — but I don't remember. I *must have* called her, because she showed up at the door and I know Sam didn't call her. I think I knew she existed, but I'd never met her. She looked like Sylvia

— only she was a little older. And she seemed a lot softer than Sylvia. She looked at me and I looked at her. "So you're Sal?" she said.

I nodded.

I invited her in. But not with words. She looked around the room. She smiled at me. "I haven't seen your father for a while."

"He's on his way back from Scottsdale."

She nodded. "Yes. Sylvia told me your grandmother is sick."

I nodded.

Her voice was soft. "I'm sorry. Maybe she'll get better."

"I hope so," I said. "Sam's just getting out of the shower."

"Sylvia said you are a very sweet boy."

I shrugged. I tried to imagine Sylvia saying something like that.

I don't think either one of us knew what to say. We didn't exactly know each other. It was clear that she knew something about me — but not much. I didn't particularly care for being reduced to a sweet boy. My father saying things like that to me was one thing, but a stranger? Anyway, it wasn't true. And why the hell was I thinking this crap while Sam was in the other room with a heart that would never be unwounded again? Maybe her heart would never heal. Maybe the hurt would live in her forever. So why in hell was I thinking such stupid and shallow things?

I had my head bowed. I was silent. I felt like an idiot. I felt her eyes on me. Sam's aunt.

"Are you hungry?" Her voice was kind.

"No. Yes. I don't know." I didn't know anything.

She smiled. "Where's your kitchen?" She looked up, and I knew Sam had walked into the room. I turned around and saw that strange and sad look on Sam's face. I watched her and her Aunt Lina stare at each other for what seemed a long time. Something was being said. Something important. Something that had to be said without words.

And then Sam's aunt was holding her. Silent tears falling down both their faces.

The world had changed. And this new world was quiet and sad.

Somehow we wound up in the kitchen. Sam seemed calmer. Too calm. She wasn't a calm person, and it scared me that she could be that way. I kept studying her. And finally she said, "You're staring. It's creeping me out."

I smiled. The Sam I knew was still there. "Sorry."

Sam's aunt opened the refrigerator. "Your dad keeps a well-stocked kitchen."

"We like to cook," I said.

"Call me Lina," she said. "That's what Samantha calls me."

I nodded. She was like my Aunt Evie. She took charge. Sam and I had managed to hold things together. We'd managed — but it was hard to manage when you didn't know what to do. Lina seemed to know exactly what to do. She had more experience with these things than we did. And right now, experience mattered.

"You like tortillas?"

"Yeah, there's some in the fridge."

"Not those," she said.

Sam smiled. "You'll make us some?"

"Sure, *amor*. I'll make you some of my tortillas."

Sam and I watched her as she made the dough, never measuring, just working out of years and years of memory. Like Mima.

I guess there were some women who just knew how to make tortillas, who liked making them, who fed people with their art. I guess there were people walking around in the world who understood how to comfort people. *Comfort,* that was the word for the day. I liked that word better than *death.*

No one said anything. There was only the sound of Lina rolling out tortillas on the kitchen table.

I was thinking about Mima.

In the middle of all our silence Dad walked into the room. "I'm home," he said. "Hello, Lina."

"Vicente."

"Tortillas," he said.

Lina nodded. "It's what I do. I make tortillas."

Until then, I didn't know that they'd even met. That they knew each other. God, I really didn't know a damn thing.

My dad looked at Sam. "Hi," he said.

Sam fell into his arms and sobbed. "I'm all alone now," she kept repeating.

And Dad kept whispering, "No, you're not, Sam. No, you're not."

And all I did — all I could do? All I could do was watch.

Dad and Lina
(and Secrets)

DAD AND LINA were having coffee and eating tortillas in the kitchen. They were talking about funeral arrangements. They were talking about Sylvia's insurance — whether she had any. And a will? Did she have one of those? Dad seemed to have all the answers. Yes, she had insurance. Yes, she had a will.

Lina was surprised.

Sam was surprised too.

"I have copies," Dad said. I had a funny feeling that somehow my dad had helped Sylvia organize her life. She hadn't been the most organized person in the world — judging from the way she kept her house. Could you think bad things about the dead? Was that allowed?

But then I got to thinking that it was strange to live one's life and still be prepared for death. I didn't get it. I mean, I got it a little bit. I mean, it was a good thing that Sylvia had left a will. Sam would be taken care of.

Lina and Dad started making a list of what needed to be done. I guess that's part of what the living did — they took care of their dead.

Sam and I got bored. Or maybe we just couldn't deal with it. But I was glad about the whole discussion Dad and Lina were having, because it seemed to calm Sam down. They were taking control. Adults could be good that way. Some of them, anyway.

And this thought entered my head: Sylvia was dead, and she wasn't ever coming back. And there was nothing Dad or Lina could do about it; this was something beyond their control.

Sam and I slipped out into the living room, not knowing what to do with ourselves. I kept studying her face.

"Stop doing that," she said. Maggie placed her head on Sam's lap. "Tell him, Maggie, tell him to stop staring at me."

"I'm not staring. I'm just worried about you."

"Well, I'm worried about me too." And there was a moment of real grief in her voice. "I feel strange," she said. "And empty. I feel empty."

"And you sound tired."

"It's all that crying."

"Crying is good."

"But it makes you tired." She kept petting Maggie's head. "She's gone, Sally. She's gone." She wasn't going to cry, not then. I think she just needed to say it.

"Yes," I said.

"I didn't tell her I loved her."

"She knew."

"You think so?"

"Samantha, she knew."

She nodded. "I want to sleep forever."

"Sleep. Yeah, try and get some sleep."

I watched her get up quietly and walk toward the spare bedroom, Maggie following close behind. *Sleep, Sam, and when you wake, I'll be here. I promise. I'll be here.*

I shouldn't have listened in on the conversation. But I'm not really sorry. Dad and Lina were sitting on the back steps. And the door was open. I could hear every word. Both of them smoking cigarettes. Yeah, I could've just walked into the backyard and they would have changed the subject, but — I just stood there, listening.

"Vicente, I'm so damned angry with her."

"It doesn't do much good to be angry with the dead."

"I know that. Don't you think I know that? She was driving. And she was drunk. God, who does that? Who pulls shit like that? She had a daughter."

"Calm down, Lina. Just —"

"Just what?"

"Let's just do this. For Sam. Her mother's dead. It was an accident."

"Her whole life was an accident."

"So how long are you going to stay mad?" There was a pause, and I could picture my dad taking a drag from his cigarette. "You've been mad at her for how long?"

"My whole fucking life."

"So you're going to keep a grudge? She's dead. Really? Let it go."

"Just like that, huh? Just like that? You have no idea what my sister put me through."

"Oh, I have a pretty good idea. I may not know the details, but I have a pretty good idea." There was another pause, and then I heard my dad saying, "Promise me something, Lina. Just promise me one thing."

"Promise you what?"

"Don't tell Sam how her mother died."

"You mean lie to her?"

"What do you suggest? Hurt her a little more? Is that what you want?"

"You know that's not what I want."

"Then all we have to say, Lina, is that it was a car accident. What's so hard about that? And it *was* a car accident."

"It's a lie."

"Promise me."

I know I shouldn't have heard that conversation. I should have walked away from the kitchen, far away from their voices. But I wasn't sorry. I wasn't sorry at all. As I walked toward the front porch, I wondered who was right, Lina or my father. I didn't know my father was capable of lying about things that really mattered. But I thought I understood that Sam mattered more to him than the truth behind an accident report. I was glad I'd heard. It helped me. It was time for me to grow up — even though I had always wanted things to stay the same. I wasn't in charge of the world around me. My dad had spent most of his energies protecting me. Maybe there had been a time for that. Now the time for protecting me was coming to an end. But I wasn't ready to be a man. That was the truth. And Sam wasn't ready to be a woman. And I guessed a little more protecting wasn't necessarily a bad thing. Because Sam and I still needed it.

Lipstick

I WANT TO GO home."

I just looked at her.

"Will you come with?"

"Sure." I knew I was wearing a question mark on my face.

"I need to get some things."

"We'll take the car."

Sam nodded.

Sam stood outside her house for a long time, staring at the door. She handed me her key. I opened the door. I took her hand. "It's okay," I said.

"Nothing's okay."

"I'm here," I said.

She looked around the house as if she'd never seen it. She walked toward her mother's bedroom. The door was open. "She made her bed," she whispered. She looked at me. "She never made her bed."

I kept studying her.

"You're doing it again."

"Sorry."

"I can't go into that room."

"Then don't. You don't have to."

I followed her as she walked into her bedroom. "It's a disaster," she whispered. "I'm a disaster."

"Shhh," I said. "No beating up on yourself. That's my job." That made her smile. She took out a suitcase, started packing a few things, then walked into the bathroom. I heard her sobbing. Then I saw why. Her mother had left a note on the bathroom mirror, written in lipstick: *just because my love isn't perfect doesn't mean i don't love you.*

Sam fell into my arms. My shirt was wet with her tears. And she kept whispering over and over again, "What am I gonna do, Sally, what am I gonna do?"

Sam and Me and Something Called Home

We sat on Sam's bed, looking around the room. I'm not sure what we were looking for. She texted me. We did that sometimes, texted each other even though we were in the same room: I can't live here.

> **Me:** U don't have to
>
> **Sam:** where is home?
>
> **Me:** I'll be ur home

She leaned into me.

"Get me out of here, Sally."

Before we left Sam's house, I used my phone to take pictures of Sylvia's last note to her daughter. I wanted Sam to have a copy. So she'd never forget. As if she ever would.

Dad and Sylvia

"How could this happen?"

We were sitting at the kitchen table, eating soup. It was cold outside, and it seemed to me that winter had come early this year.

I heard my dad answer Sam's question. "People die in accidents all the time, Sam. Do you ever read those warning signs on the freeway? The last one I read said three thousand, nine hundred and twenty-one deaths on Texas freeways this year. Drive safely. Accidents are the cruel part of life. It's part of the equation of this thing we call living. Accidents are normal, if you stop to think about it."

"Well, that's consoling," she said.

I was glad she was being sarcastic. It was a good sign.

"I don't have any explanations, Sam. In the end, life and death are mysteries."

Sam just looked at my dad. "Which explains nothing."

"Which explains everything. We say things to each other like: *It's God's will.*"

"Do you believe that?"

"No, I don't believe that, so I don't say it. I can't say it. But some people do believe it. People say all kinds of things to try to explain what they can't explain. All I know is that your mother and her boyfriend were killed in a car accident. That's all I know."

"So what am I gonna do now?"

"Well, you can live here if you want."

"Can I do that? Don't I have to go live with my Aunt Lina?"

"No."

"No?"

Dad had a serious look on his face. When he was deciding, he had a specific look. "I need to tell you something, Samantha."

He called her *Samantha*. This was serious. I wondered if he was going to tell her the truth about how her mother died.

"When you and Salvie were about six years old, your mother got arrested for driving while intoxicated."

"She did?"

"Yes. I'm not trying to make your mother look bad here, Samantha. I'm not. Just hear me out. It was like this: She called me on the phone in the middle of the night. She told me she was in jail. It was the second of July." He looked over at me. "You were having one of your slumber parties that night. I had your Aunt Evie pick you both up the next morning. You spent the Fourth of July weekend at Mima's house. Both of you. I don't know if you remember."

Sam and I looked at each other. "I don't," I said.

"I do," Sam said. "It was the first time I got to blow up fireworks. But that's the only thing I remember."

My dad nodded. "I got your mother out of jail. In the end, she got to keep her license. They weren't as strict back then as they are now about that sort of thing. But I made your mom make a will. I guess you could say I gave her a lecture."

"What did you tell her?"

"Believe me, you don't really want to hear all the details."

"I do." Sam gave Dad one of her looks. "I *do* want to hear all the details."

Dad shook his head. "I told your mother she could live her life any way she wanted. I told her that her life was none of my business. But I also told her that she had you to think about. She had a few choice words for me. I remember losing my temper with her. I know how to throw words around too. So I guess you could say we threw some words around that day." Dad laughed. "The funny thing is, that's when Sylvia and I became friends. At least we came to a sort of understanding.

"The point of the story is this —" There were tears running down my father's face, and he looked straight into Sam's eyes. "When she handed me a copy of the will she'd had made up, she said to me, 'If anything should ever happen to me, Vicente, I've had you appointed as Samantha's legal guardian.' Your mother loved you very much, Sam." He stopped. "And so do I." He got up from the kitchen table. "I'm going to have a cigarette."

Sam. Dad. Me. Home.

SAM AND I looked at each other. We were both crying, but, you know, just tears. Those silent things again. Then I said to Sam, "You're going to have to learn how to clean."

She laughed and I laughed, and I guess we needed to laugh, because we couldn't stop. Were we learning to whistle in the dark?

When we finally pulled ourselves together, I said, "Let's go sit with Dad." So we sat on the steps as he smoked.

And then my dad said, "Anybody want to play catch?"

So we played catch all afternoon. Sometimes we said something. Mostly we didn't. And everything in the world was calm again. All the tears were gone. At least for now. The tears would come back again — but we had this little piece of quiet that was helping us survive.

We were safe. We were home.

WFTD = Extinct

I SAT AT MY desk, staring at my computer. I wanted to write something, but I didn't know what. I saw Sam's text appear on my cell. She was sitting in the living room deciding whether she wanted to watch television.

Sam: Wftd = extinct

Me: ? Use word in sentence

Sam: My mother's voice is extinct

Me: ☹

I knew why people were afraid of the future. Because the future wasn't going to look like the past. That was really scary. What was Sam's future going to look like now that her mother's voice was extinct? What was my future going to look like when Mima's voice left this world?

I kept hearing Sam's whispers: *What am I gonna do?*

Me and Sam. And a Word Called Faith.

ON THE MORNING of Sylvia's funeral, I lay in bed, thinking about things. I texted Sam: You awake?

Sam: Yup

Me: Did u sleep?

Sam: A bit

Me: Do you believe?

Sam: ?

Me: U know like faith?

Sam: No don't have that. Want to but don't. U?

Me: Don't know

Sam: Ur Dad?

Me: Yeah think so. But not like Mima

Sam: Wish I had what she has

Me: Maybe we can learn how to get it

Sam: My mom = no faith = ☹

Me: U sure?

Sam: She told me

Me: Oh

Sam: U think God cares?

Me: Yes

Sam: Really?

Me: Yeah

Sam: Then why is the world so screwed up?

Me: Because of us, Sam

Sam: We suck

Sylvia. Goodbye.

IT WAS SUNNY and cold that day.

Sylvia's body was cremated. She hadn't wanted a church service. But in the end, for Sam, Dad and Lina decided to have a quiet Mass at St. Patrick's Cathedral. There weren't a lot of people there — a few — some of Sylvia's coworkers, who seemed to be genuinely sad. Lina was there with her husband and her three children, older cousins whom Sam barely knew — but they were very nice and friendly. And Fito was there. I'd texted him about what happened. So he just showed up. He was wearing a tie and a black sports coat. Fito, he had some class, that's for sure.

Sam wore a black dress and her mother's pearls.

For a moment I thought she'd suddenly become a woman.

Me, I felt awkward in the suit I was wearing.

The thing that impressed me the most about Sam was that she didn't fall apart. She sat next to me, and there were times during Mass when she grabbed my arm and I could see the tears running down her cheeks, but she seemed in control of her emotions. Then I thought of the word for the day: *dignity*.

The Sam I knew was never in control of her emotions.

But on that day she was wearing dignity.

So much more beautiful than pearls.

It was only on the short drive to the house that she leaned into me in the back seat of my dad's car and sobbed. Like a hurt animal. And then she was calm again.

"I'm a fucking train wreck," she said.

"You're not," I said. "You're a girl who lost her mom."

She smiled. "Fito was there. That was really sweet."

"Yeah."

"Tell me again why I never liked him."

There was a small reception at our house. I guess that's what people do. Not that I knew. Lina told me I was a handsome young man. "Not quite as handsome as your father," she said. And then she winked. She was a very decent human being. I knew that much. And though I knew she had been angry with her sister, I knew there were reasons behind her anger, because a woman like her, well, she didn't seem to be an angry person. And she really liked my dad. So I asked her. "How do you know Dad? Through Sylvia?"

"No. Actually, I met your dad years ago at an art gallery in San Francisco. I bought one of his paintings." She smiled. "Imagine my surprise when I found out that we had Sylvia in common."

That made me smile. "How close with her were you?" I asked.

"Not very. I didn't like Sylvia very much. But I loved her anyway. She was my sister."

Somehow that made sense to me.

"You know, Sal," she said, "there was a time I threatened to take Samantha away from her."

"Why didn't you?"

"Your dad. We talked. I knew Samantha would be okay."

"Because my dad said so."

"Yes."

"You trusted him that much?"

"Men like your father are very rare. I hope you know that."

"I think I do know," I said. "You don't mind that Sam's going to live with us?"

"Why would I mind? I want to be close to her. I've always wanted to be close to her. But her mother wouldn't allow it. If I took her to live with me, she'd begin to hate me — and she'd probably wind up running away. She'd run straight here. She'd run back to what she knows, to what she loves."

I nodded. "Yeah," I said. I wanted to tell her that I thought she had a beautiful heart. But I realized there would be time for that. Or maybe I was just scared of saying something like that to an adult I barely knew.

Sam held the urn that contained her mother's ashes. "What am I supposed to do?"

"I don't know."

"You're no help."

"Nope."

She finally put the urn in front of the fireplace. We just sort of looked at each other.

———

Sam and Fito and I sat on the front steps. Sam was staring at a piece of cake as if she didn't recognize what it was. I was drinking a cup of coffee. Fito was on his third serving of potato salad. I swear that guy just couldn't get enough to eat.

Then Fito looked at Sam and said, "What about your father?"

"My father? I met him once. He showed up at the door asking Sylvia for some money. A real winner."

"So why'd your mother marry him?"

"That's an easy one. He was good-looking."

"There must have been another reason."

"My mother wasn't that complicated." She laughed. I think she was laughing at herself. "I'm just being mean. My mother wasn't as shallow as I make her out to be. Yeah, my father must have had some good qualities. Maybe he was smart, who knows? He was broke, that was for sure."

"Well, at least you met him. That's something."

But what? I thought. *Why was that something? What?*

"You can always look for him, Sam," Fito said.

"Why would I want to do that?" Sam said. "I'm just not interested."

"Why?" I asked.

"The day he came over. He wasn't interested in me. Not at all. Funny thing was, I wasn't interested in him either. It was just this weird and awkward moment. He didn't care. And for some reason, it didn't hurt."

I wondered about that. I guess Sam and Fito and I had a lot in common. We had this absent-father thing going on. Except that I *did* have a father who took care of me and loved me. And now Sam and I had this dead-mother thing going on — except that was different. Sam had actually known her mother. And just like the dad thing didn't hurt her, I guess the mom thing didn't hurt me. Sam said it did hurt me. But I wasn't feeling that. I wasn't.

And then it was like Fito was reading my mind. "You ever think about your mom?"

"Yeah, but it's weird — since I don't really remember her."

"And you're never gonna look for your bio dad? I mean, you said you think about him sometimes."

Sam decided to enter the conversation. "Sally, you've never told me you thought about your birth father. Not ever."

"I hadn't thought about him much. Until recently."

"How recently? Since the letter?"

"Yeah. Well, maybe a little before."

"Hmm," she said. "There's a lot of things you're not talking about these days, Sally."

Fito was just looking at us. "What letter?"

Sam answered his question. Of course she did. "Sally has a letter from his mother. She wrote it before she died. And he's afraid to open it."

"Open it, dude. I'd open it. What's wrong with you?"

"I didn't say I wasn't going to open it. I just haven't done it yet."

Fito shook his head. "What are you waiting for, dude? Maybe you'll find out some cool stuff about your parents and shit."

"I have a dad!"

"And he's the bomb, dude. But you're sounding all pissed off and shit — and there is definitely something goin' on with you."

"Something's going on with everybody, Fito."

Sam kept looking at me. That I'm-studying-you thing she did. And then she smiled. "At least you've given me something to think about besides the fact that my mother's dead."

Everybody had gone home.

Except Lina.

Lina and Dad were having a glass of wine. Sam and I had gotten out of our funeral getups.

There was a cold drizzle falling, and I wondered if we were going to have a cold winter. Maggie was scratching at the door. I let her in. And then I thought that maybe life was like that — there would always be something scratching at the door. And whatever was scratching would just scratch and scratch until you opened the door.

I sat back down at the kitchen table. What was it about kitchen tables?

Lina looked over at Sam. "I have something for you."

She reached into her purse, pulled out a ring. She placed it in Sam's palm.

Sam stared at it. She kept staring and staring. "It's an engagement ring," she whispered.

"She was wearing it the night of the accident."

"She wasn't wearing it when she left the house."

Lina nodded. She was wearing a sad smile. "I think your mother got engaged the night she died."

"To Daniel?"

Lina nodded.

"So she got what she always wanted."

"Yes, she got what she always wanted."

"And Daniel?"

"His family took his body to be buried in San Diego."

Sam kept staring at the ring. She kept nodding. "Then she must have died happy."

She laid her head on the table and cried.

River

I WAS LYING ON MY BED, thinking about things. I could hear the wind outside. Maggie was on loan to Sam. Not that there was really any lending going on. Maggie seemed to know that Sam was sad. So it was okay. Still, I missed Maggie.

Then I got a text from Sam: The world has changed.

Me: We'll make it through

Sam: I love u and ur dad. U know that, right?

Me: We love u back

Sam: I won't cry anymore

Me: Cry all you like

Sam: I didn't hate her

Me: I know

Sam: Slumber party?

Me: Absolutely

I got out of bed, turned on the lamp, put on my sweatpants. I took my sleeping bag out of the closet. Sam and Maggie came walking through the door. Sam threw herself on my bed. Maggie licked my face before jumping up on the bed.

"Let's listen to a song, Sally," Sam said.

" 'K," I said. "What about 'Stay With Me'?"

"Sam Smith is gay. You *do* know that?"

"You got something against gay people?"

And there we were, laughing again. What was it with this laughing thing? We were not supposed to be in the laughing mood. But there it all was. Me and Sam laughing.

Whistling in the dark?

Whistling in the dark.

"Give me a song, will you, Sammy?"

"What?"

"I need a song. Give me one."

I thought a moment. "I got one," I said. "It's called 'River.'"

"Who sings it?"

"Emili Sande."

"I like her."

"Me too."

"'K," I said. I took out my laptop and found the song on YouTube.

Sam turned off the light.

We lay there in the dark listening to Emili Sande's voice.

And when the song ended, it seemed that the world had gone completely silent.

Then I heard Sam's voice in the dark. "So you'll be my river, Sally?" She was crying again.

"Yeah," I said. "'I would do all the running for you.'" I would have sung her the whole song, but I have a not-so-great singing voice.

"And you'll move the mountains just for me?"

"Yeah," I whispered.

And then I was crying too. Not out-of-control crying, but crying. Soft, like it was coming from a place inside me that was quiet and soft too, and that was better than the hard place inside me when I made a fist, or wanted to make one.

Maybe the river was made of our tears. Mine and Sam's.

Maybe the river was made of everybody's tears. Everybody who had ever lost anybody. All those tears.

Cigarettes

I WOKE EARLY, MY MIND trying to catch up with everything that had happened. Life had always been slow and easy, and all of a sudden I felt like I was living my life in a relay race and there was no one else to hand the baton to. I lay in bed, repeating the names of my uncles and aunts. I'd always done that when I was stressed. And all of a sudden I panicked. *School! Oh, shit, school!* And then I realized it was Saturday. I'd missed a whole week of school. I wondered if my dad had called the school. Of course he had. I got up. Sam was fast asleep, and Maggie was looking at me like it was time for her to go outside and do her morning thing. Maggie. Her life was simple. I used to think mine was too.

Maggie and I made our way to the kitchen.

My dad was pouring himself a cup of coffee. I opened the back door to let Maggie out. She looked up at me, barked, wagged her tail, and ran out into the yard. Dogs are amazing. They know how to be happy.

My dad took out another cup and poured a coffee for me. I grabbed it and took a sip. Dad made really good coffee.

"How'd you sleep?"

"Good. Sam came over to my room and we had a slumber party."

"You stay up talking all night?"

"Nah. I think she just didn't want to be alone. She needed to sleep."

"Sleep is good," he said.

"You?"

"Okay. I slept okay."

He opened the drawer where he kept his cigarettes. He wasn't storing them in the freezer anymore. "It's a little cold," he said. "Wanna grab me a coat?"

I went to the closet in the entryway and put on a coat and grabbed one for my dad.

He handed me his coffee, and I held it as he put on his coat.

"Sometimes I wish we could sleep through all the bad stuff," I said as we sat down. "You know, like the song. Wake me up, you know, when it's over. It would be good to sleep until we woke up wiser."

"I like that song—but it doesn't work that way, does it, Salvie?"

"Yeah, I know. I don't like death."

"I don't think anyone does. But it's something we have to live with." He took a drag from his cigarette and looked at me. "The news isn't good about Mima."

I nodded.

"She's coming home. There's not much we can do but keep her comfortable."

"She's going to die?"

"Yeah, Salvie, I think we're going to lose her."

"I hate God."

"That's an easy thing to say. Let you in on a little secret, Salvie. Hating God is a lot of work."

"He doesn't need her. *I do.*"

He put out his cigarette and wrapped his arm around me. "All your life I've tried to protect you from all the shit in the world, from all the bad things. But I can't protect you from this. I can't protect you and I can't protect Sam. All I have is a shoulder. And that will have to do. When you were a little boy, I used to carry you. I miss those days sometimes. But those days are over. I can walk beside you, Salvie — but I can't carry you. You get what I'm saying?"

"Yeah," I whispered. And then I got up. "I'm gonna take a walk."

"Walking is good, Salvie."

I was trying not to think about things as I walked. But it was hard to keep my mind blank. So I put in my earphones and listened to music. There was this guy I liked, a singer, Brendan James, and he had this song, "Nothing for Granted," and I listened to it over and over and sang with him. So I wouldn't have to think about anything.

But as I was walking back toward the house, the thought occurred to me that I'd like to get drunk. I'd never been drunk. And I thought it might help. If you got drunk, you didn't think about things, did you? I was thinking stupid thoughts and doing stupid math inside my head. I was going a little crazy.

Sam (Moving In)

JUST AS I reached the front porch, the cold rain started falling. Lina's car was parked in front of the house. I figured she'd come to visit Sam.

I could smell bacon when I walked inside. Lina and Sam were drinking coffee and talking. Maggie was sitting patiently, waiting for a crumb to come her way.

It was warm in the kitchen and I felt safe. I kept studying Dad as he served everyone scrambled eggs and bacon. Sam and Lina were talking about heading over to Sam's house to go through Sylvia's belongings. "You'll want to keep some things, Samantha."

Sam seemed calm enough. Not normal, really, but she wasn't falling apart, either. I really wanted to know what was going through her head. No, that wasn't right. I wanted to know what was going through her heart.

I heard my dad's voice as I chewed on my bacon. "You're quiet over there."

"Yeah, don't have that many words living inside me today."

Sam smiled. "That's normal."

"Yeah," I said, "normal."

———

It was a good thing the spare bedroom was big. And it was an even better thing that it had a big closet. Dad and I cleared the closet of the crap we'd put there. Clothes we no longer wore, miscellaneous stuff we never got around to getting rid of. "Leftovers," Dad called them. "There are always leftovers in people's lives." Dad said it was all going to St. Vincent De Paul, the Catholic version of Goodwill. Yup. Mima would approve of that. She was all about the Catholic thing.

It took all evening to move Sam in. "Too many shoes," I said. "And too many blouses and skirts and pants and dresses and —"

"Shut up," she said.

My dad and I went to pick up an antique dresser that had belonged to Sylvia. It had a big mirror attached to the back, and we set the whole thing up in Sam's room. It was the only piece of furniture she wanted. "You can sit around all day and look at yourself," I said.

"Shut up," Sam said.

We kinda joked around all evening. Everything was nice and orderly, as if nothing had happened. Sam was just moving in. No big deal. Life went on. And maybe that was good. Sylvia was dead and Mima was dying, but Sam and Dad and Lina and I, we were alive. And the only thing to do was keep on living. So that's what we were doing. We were living. Or trying to.

I was happy that Sam was going to live with us. Very happy. But Sam? Maybe she was a long way from happy.

Well, hell, I was a long way from happy too.

Behind

THURSDAY. A NORMAL DAY. Back at school. At the end of the day when I met Sam at her locker, some asshole walked by and gave her this really lecherous look. I flipped him the bird and stared him down.

"You're feisty today," Sam said.

"I don't like the way he looked at you."

"So you're paying attention to assholes these days?"

"Sorry, Sam."

"Things didn't use to bother you." But then she must have seen something written on my face. "And you didn't use to beat up on yourself either."

"Maybe I did," I said. "Maybe I just hid it well."

"Aww, Salvie." She leaned over and kissed my shoulder. "Let's go home."

Home. That's where Mima was. She'd come back home to Las Cruces.

Sam and I were settling back into the school-routine thing. We were behind, so we had a lot of homework. We stayed up late every night to catch up, and somehow homework helped us both.

Sam was fiercely determined to keep up her GPA. She was little bit crazy. "No B's," she said, "Just A's."

"I'm good with B's," I said.

"Don't settle," she said.

"I'm not settling," I said. "I just don't want to make myself crazy."

"I'm already fucking crazy." She flipped the page on the book she was studying. "And you're not far behind."

"LOL," I said. It was no use talking to her. I wished she'd go back to buying shoes or something. She was all over the map with those emotions of hers. Studying helped her focus. So I guess it was okay that she was diving into the waters of homework. At least she knew how to swim there. And somehow, because she was all over the map, it helped me *not* be all over the map. That didn't make sense, but me and Sam, what we had, well, it had a logic all its own.

Dad had been working a lot. Said he was behind. Yeah, behind — everyone was behind.

And it had been really cold — which wasn't normal for this time of year. What was up with the weather? *No bueno*.

I watched Sam as she read. Her eyes were as sad as they were fierce. Dad was talking to Mima on his cell. He was wearing a look. I have a word for that look: *concerned*. And I was wondering what kind of look was on *my* face. I didn't have a word for the day.

Other People's Tragedies

SAM WALKED INTO THE KITCHEN as I was having a cup of coffee. "It's Saturday," she said.

"Yup."

"New phase."

"New phase?"

"Pawnshops."

"Pawnshops? You've already gone through that phase."

"Yeah, well, sometimes phases boomerang back."

"Fun. History repeating itself. It's called recidivism."

"A word I taught you."

"A word you live."

"Shut up, Sally. I'm going to ignore your lack of enthusiasm. I won't interpret it as a lack of empathy for a person in my situation."

"Sam, sometimes you really are shamelessly manipulative."

"Let's just get to it, Sally. Dave's Loans on El Paso Street. That's our destination."

"The one with Elvis standing out front?"

"The very one."

"Why back to pawnshops?"

"Because, as I've tried to impress upon you in the past, there's a sad story behind every item that's for sale in pawnshops."

"Impress upon me," I said. "How could I forget? So we're into sad. No, even worse, we're into voyeurism? Looking in on or making up other people's tragedies. Great."

"Sounds good to me."

"You're weird. Fantastically weird."

"I'm fantastically everything." She shot me a fake smile. "Humor me." Then she texted me. I reached for my phone and gave her one of my looks. I read her text: I'm grieving. U can deny me nothing.

I texted her back: U need a therapist.

She read the text and smiled — then put down her cell. "No," she said. "I need other people's tragedies."

Mima

I WAITED FOR SAM to get ready to go to the pawnshop. She always had to get ready. "What? We're going to run into some bad boy you may want to flirt with?" I got the look.

I decided to call Mima. I hated the waiting thing. I heard Mima's voice.

"Hi," I said, as if nothing were wrong.

I could almost see her smile. "I was wondering when you were going to call me." She said things like that when she missed me.

"Sorry, Mima."

"It's okay."

And then we just talked. I told her everything I could remember about what happened to Sylvia and how Sam was living with us now and how she was sad and about how I didn't like death, and she just listened and she told me that she was sorry and that it was okay to be confused and that I should trust in God — and even though I didn't like God lectures, I didn't mind them when they came from Mima. Then I finally got around to asking her how she felt, was she okay, and she said she was tired all the time, and I asked her again if she was afraid.

"No, I'm not afraid."

And then there was a silence on the phone and she said, "I want you to take care of your father." And I wanted to say *Isn't he supposed to take care of me?* but I didn't. Then I got mad at myself: *When are you going to stop being such a boy?* Then I heard Mima say, "Your father is very sad."

"I know."

"Your father has a soft heart."

"I know."

"I've always worried about him."

"Why?"

"Your father knows how to give. But sometimes he needs someone to give him something too."

"Like what?"

"Love."

"But I love him."

"I love him too."

"I don't understand."

"When I'm gone —"

"I don't want to talk about that."

"Salvador, everyone dies. It's a very normal thing."

"It doesn't feel normal. When Mrs. Diaz died in a car accident — that didn't feel normal."

"People die in accidents all the time."

"That's what Dad said."

"Your father's right."

"I don't like that. I want you to live forever."

"Then I would be God. I don't want to be God. That's a sin, to want to be God. *Ay, mi* Salvador, we've talked about this before."

Mima got very quiet. Then she said, "It would be a curse to live forever. Vampires live forever. You want to be a vampire?"

We both started laughing.

And then we just started talking about other stuff. Normal stuff. What I wanted to tell her was that I didn't care about sin or about God. I wanted to tell her that God was just a beautiful idea and I didn't care about beautiful ideas and that He was just a word I hadn't run into yet, hadn't met yet, and so He was still a stranger. I wanted to tell her that she was real, and she was so much more beautiful than an idea. I know she wouldn't like what I had to say, and I didn't want to argue with her, so I didn't say any of those things.

"You have to have faith," she said.

I wished that word were my friend. "I'm trying, Mima."

"Good," she said. "Tomorrow, when you come, tell Samantha I want to talk to her."

"About what?"

"I just want to talk to her."

That meant she wasn't going to tell me. And then I got a little upset. There was that left-out thing that was living inside me. "I'll tell her."

I think she could tell I was upset. "She doesn't have her mother anymore."

"That's sad."

"Just like you."

"I don't really remember her."

"That's okay. You were little. But she was beautiful, your mother. It's hard to lose your mother."

I thought about my letter.

"But I have Dad," I said. "That's enough." I wasn't sure that was the truth — but I wanted it to be.

"Yes, you have your dad. But he's lonely. Did you know that?"

"Did he tell you that?"

"He doesn't have to tell me. I'm his mother. I can see."

When was *I* going to learn to see?

Me and Sam
(and Pawnshops)

WHEN I TURNED off my cell, I noticed Sam in the room. I looked up at her. "Eavesdropping?"

"A little bit. I hate to see you sad," she said.

"I hate to see you sad too," I said.

"We can do this," she said.

"You believe that?"

"Yes," she said.

Faith. Sam had faith. She just didn't let herself in on that secret.

There it was, that dorky Elvis with a microphone, greeting us outside Dave's Loans. Sam took a selfie of her and Elvis. "Come on, give him a kiss."

"Nope."

"C'mon."

"Nope."

"My mother died."

"Don't start."

"Well, she did."

"Mine died too."

She gave me a look. Then I gave her a look. We were definitely two very weird human beings.

So we walked into the pawnshop. It was littered with junk. Sam went straight for the jewelry. "Look at that ring."

"Looks like an engagement ring."

"Yup. That's what it is. Bet she hocked it after she dumped his ass. I bet he was cheating on her."

"Well, maybe she's still married to the guy and they just needed the money. Maybe they lost their jobs. People are sometimes down and out."

"I like my story better."

"Yeah, it's more tragic."

"No, it's probably closer to the truth."

"You don't have a high opinion of human nature, do you?"

"Your problem, Sally, is that you think everybody is like you and your dad and your Mima. I got a news flash for you."

"Your problem, Sammy, is that you think everybody is like the bad boys you like to date."

"For one, I don't date bad boys anymore. And second of all, the world is full of a lot of screwed-up people." She turned around and searched the store with her eyes. "See that? It's a laptop. I bet some druggie stole it and hocked it."

"That's not legal, is it?"

"Okay, let's say some druggie was jonesing—"

"Jonesing?"

"You know, craving his next hit."

"How do you know these things?"

"You really *do* have to get out more." She gave me one of her smirks. "You make me want to smoke."

"Bad idea."

"So this druggie had to pawn his laptop so he could get another hit. Either that or he owed his dealer money."

"You really are going to be a writer."

"Well, there are a lot of sad stories in the world."

"And you're going to give it your best shot at telling all of them."

"Nobody wants to read happy stories."

"I do."

Then her eye fell on a tennis bracelet. "Look at all those diamonds."

"Why do they call them tennis bracelets?"

"Because you can play tennis and not have to take it off."

"Is that true?"

"I have no fucking idea." She laughed.

"Man, the F word has come into your mouth with a vengeance."

"My mother died."

"Stop."

She kept staring at the bracelet. "My mother had a bracelet just like that one."

"Well, they all kind of look alike."

"No, they don't."

"So?"

"I'm thinking that bracelet might have belonged to my mother."

"That's crazy."

"Why is it crazy?"

"It just is."

"Well, her bracelet wasn't in her things."

"Are you sure?"

She gave me a look.

"Maybe she lost it."

"That's definitely a possibility. One time she lost a pair of four-hundred-dollar shoes."

"She spent four hundred dollars on a pair of shoes? That's crazy."

"She was like that."

"How do you lose a pair of shoes?"

"She went dancing with some guy. She took them off. She forgot them. When she went back, surprise surprise, they were gone."

I thought of Mima and her story of the stolen shoes. The shoes thing. Lots of tragedies in lost shoes. I kept shaking my head. "Let's go."

She gazed at the tennis bracelet again. "Maybe she lost it and some guy hocked it."

"Really? Look, let's just get out of here."

On the way back home I kept thinking that the world was not only crazy, it was super crazy. Laptops and tennis bracelets and four-hundred-dollar shoes. Crazy. Nuts. I guess I was thinking out loud, because Sam said, "Four hundred bucks for a pair of shoes isn't so crazy."

"Too much money for shoes, Sammy. Did you know that when Mima was a girl, she only had one pair?"

"But that was the Stone Age."

"You calling my Mima a dinosaur?"

"No, no, that's not what I'm saying. The world was different

194

back then; that's all. Today four hundred dollars for a pair of shoes — that's nothing."

"Well, all I can say is that I could do lots of stuff with four hundred bucks."

"Like what?"

"I don't know. Stuff. I mean, I'm not into buying things."

"Are you trying to tell me you're a cheapskate? I hate cheapskates."

"I'm not a cheapskate. I just don't care about money. And I guess I'm not into spending. And besides, my dad buys me everything I need. Well, some things I have to buy myself. I just don't care. There something wrong with that?"

"Well, I'm way into spending."

"Yeah, the whole world knows that. That's why you never have any money."

"Yeah, not like you, who hoards all his cash."

"I don't hoard it. I save it."

"You have a bank account?"

"Yup."

"How much money do you have?"

"Oh, I dunno, about four or five thousand dollars."

"Holy shit!"

"I told you — I don't like to spend. When I get money from my uncles and aunts and Mima for my birthday and Christmas and stuff like that, I put it in the bank. And my dad gives me money when I need it. I keep some of it and put the rest in the bank. I mean, it adds up. I've been doing that since I was about five. Saving my money."

"God, you're a fucking old man."

"Stop it. Look, if you want it, I'll give it to you."

"I don't want your money, Sally."

"I'm just saying I don't care. I'll give it to you."

"You really would, wouldn't you? You'd give me all that money?"

"Sure I would."

"You are exasperatingly sweet." She leaned over and kissed me on the cheek. "Too bad you're not my type."

"At this point it would be more like incest."

She laughed. "I know. Yuck." She gave me another one of her looks. "You *are* sweet," she said. "But —"

"But what?"

"You don't have to be sweet all the time."

"Good, cuz I'm not."

"But you beat yourself up over it."

"Are you gonna be a therapist or a writer?"

"Whatever I'm gonna be, smart-ass, I'm always gonna be your best friend."

Me and Sam and Maggie

I WAS SLEEPING WITH Maggie again. I heard Sam crying. Her room was right across the hall, and my door was open. So Sam was close. She was close and she was far. I couldn't stand lying there listening to her soft sobs. Dad had told me it would be that way. Up and down and up and down with the emotions thing. I got out of bed. "C'mon, Maggie." She followed me, and I opened the door to Sam's room. "Go on, Maggie." Maggie walked into Sam's room, and I shut the door.

Sam needed Maggie more than I did.

Reading Faces

I WOKE UP REALLY early. It wasn't so cold outside, even though it was late October. The weather had more or less returned to normal. El Paso was like that. I was surprised to find Sam sitting at the kitchen table.

"You look like crap," I said.

"Thanks."

"I have an idea, Sammy."

"What?"

"Why don't we start running every morning? You know, it would be good for us."

"Really?"

"Remember how you were great at soccer?"

"I *was* great."

"And you almost tried out for the track team. Except you said you didn't like the coach. Maybe it would be good for us to get moving. Makes sense."

Sam was thinking. I liked her thinking look. "You know, that sounds okay."

"Just okay?"

"Why the hell not? Let's do it."

That's how it all started, the running thing. Sam ran a little ahead of me. I thought maybe she was crying as she ran, but I thought that was a good thing. I mean, she had a lot to cry about.

When we got back home that Sunday morning from our first run, I smiled at her. We sat on the front steps of the porch and let our hearts slow down. "You know," I said, "you don't really look like crap."

"I know," she said. "It's impossible for me to look like crap."

Suddenly I saw a familiar figure walking up the sidewalk. "Is that you, Salvador?"

I studied his face for a minute. He hadn't changed very much. He had salt-and-pepper hair, and the last time I'd seen him, his hair had been dark, with no sign of aging. But his face hadn't changed. "Marcos?"

"You remember? God, you're practically a man."

"I'm practically lots of things," I said. I don't know why I said that. Sam was rubbing off on me.

He laughed.

"I thought you moved," I said.

"I did. I moved back a few months ago. I live a couple of blocks from here, as a matter of fact."

"Have you seen my dad?"

"No, no, I haven't. Not yet, but, you know, I was taking a walk and thought I'd stop in and see how he was doing."

Sam nudged me.

"This is Sam. Remember her?"

He nodded. "Yeah, I remember." He smiled at her. "Still pretty."

"Of course I am," she said. "And I remember you, too. I don't think I liked you very much."

He really laughed at that one. "No, I don't think you did."

Sam was giving him a look. "You didn't like going to the movies with us. That's what I remember."

"Well, I was never much for movies."

Sam wasn't buying it, I could tell. But, for whatever reason, she decided to be nice. "Well," she said, "we were just kids. We were probably bratty." She gave him a smile. She could charm when she wanted to, I'll say that much for Sam.

That's when my dad stepped out onto the front porch. I saw the look on his face when he looked at Marcos.

I didn't quite understand the look.

I didn't know if it was good or bad.

I'd never seen that look on his face before.

It was one of those awkward moments — you know, one of those times you wish you could just sneak out of the room without anyone noticing. My dad seemed genuinely uncomfortable, and he didn't do that often. He was the kind of guy who just took things in stride. My dad sort of cleared his throat and said, "So how are you, Marcos? It's been a while."

"I'm good," Marcos said.

There was another awkward silence, so I nudged Sam. "Shower time."

"Yup," she said. "I smell bad."

We went into the house and walked straight to my room. I shut the door.

Sam looked at me. "Do you think?"

"Do I think what?"

"Don't play dumb. Do you think that guy was your dad's boy-friend?"

I nodded. "You know, I never thought about it before. I was twelve the last time I saw him. What the hell did I know when I was twelve? I certainly didn't really get the whole gay thing and what that really meant back then. Did you?"

"Hmm, not really. Not really, really."

We both shrugged. "But, Sammy, I think I remember my fa-ther being really upset about something when Marcos left. And one day I asked him why Marcos didn't come over anymore, and he said, 'Well, he just moved away.'

"I remember asking him where he'd moved to, and Dad said somewhere in Florida. That's all he said. I got the feeling that he didn't want to talk about it. And I thought maybe they got mad at each other, you know, like people do. I don't know. Sometimes I don't know shit."

"You got that right." Then Sam paused. "Sally, I got the feel-ing your dad wasn't exactly happy to see him."

"Well, I got a different feeling."

"And —"

"I saw a look on Dad's face. And, well, I don't know. I've never seen it before, and believe me, I'm an expert on reading my father's face."

"Oh, so now you can read faces?"

"Yes. Some people read cards. I read faces."

"You read mine?"

"Absolutely."

"Maybe I'll work on my poker face."

"LMAO. You don't have it in you, Sam. You wear everything you feel on that beautiful face of yours. You have the easiest face to read on the planet."

"That's bullshit."

"Whatever."

Sam smiled. "So your dad was in love with him?"

"Maybe."

"Maybe?"

"It's a plausible scenario."

"Screw plausible scenarios. You should ask him."

"Wrong. What's the matter with you, Sammy? A guy has a right to his own privacy."

"Didn't you get the memo, dude? There is no privacy since Facebook."

"My dad doesn't do Facebook."

"But he has a cell, doesn't he?"

"Yeah, okay, whatever."

"Aren't you curious?"

"Of course I'm curious. But he's my dad. It's none of my business."

"He's your dad, that's right. *And that's why it is your business.*"

Samantha Diaz had a very interesting way of thinking. The thing is, she thought everything about my life was her business. And in her mind, that included my dad's business.

On the Road (to Mima's)

WE WERE ON THE ROAD to Las Cruces to see Mima. Samantha was in the back, texting a few friends. She had categories: school friends, Facebook friends, and real friends. She actually didn't hang out with a lot of her real friends because most of the people in that category were her ex-boyfriends. And she never stayed friends with any of those guys after they broke up. Not that they were the kind of guys you'd want to hang out with. And anyway, Sam was all or nothing. *You don't love me? Get lost.*

Dad was in his head as we drove.

I really *did* want to ask him about Marcos. They'd sat on the back steps and talked for a long while. This time, I hadn't listened in — though I really wanted to. When Marcos left, he told me that it was good to see me. And Sam butted into the conversation to say, "Was it good to see me, too?" her tone dripping in gleeful sarcasm. Marcos smiled good-naturedly. "Sure," he said. "It was great to see you too, Samantha." She rolled her eyes, and she wasn't subtle about it.

I sat in the front seat of the car, wondering why Sam didn't like him. Not that I was all that into him either. The thing was, Sam didn't lie to herself about what she felt. And when she took a disliking to someone, well, it was bad news. That was Sam. Me? Sometimes I didn't know what I thought. Maybe it's because I didn't want to know.

Maybe I was fishing when I said, "What's in your head, Dad?"

"I was just thinking."

"About what?"

"Things."

I hated when he said stuff like that. "Anything I should know about?"

He glanced at me and smiled. "Sometimes we get to keep the things we have in our heads to ourselves."

"You said we shouldn't keep secrets."

"Did I say that?"

"Yup, you did."

"Stupid thing to say."

Guess he shut down the conversation.

Then he said, "What are *you* thinking?"

So I decided to tell him. "Well, I was thinking about how Sam doesn't seem to think very highly of Marcos."

Dad laughed. "He wasn't very good with kids."

"That's an understatement, Mr. V," Sam said. "And I have a long memory."

"Let me translate that for you, Dad," I said. "Sam likes to keep grudges."

"All they have to do is say they're sorry," she said.

"What's he got to be sorry for, Sammy? We were twelve the last time we saw him. He wasn't exactly mean to us."

"He didn't want to play catch with me."

My dad and I started laughing.

"Go ahead, laugh."

Dad didn't quite scratch his head, but he had that scratching-your-head look on his face. "You remember that, Sam?"

"I remember lots of things, Mr. V."

"Well, we all do," Dad said.

"Is it all right if I don't like him, Mr. V.?"

"You can dislike anybody you want, Sam."

"Well," she said, "if you like him, then I'll like him for you."

"Hmm. I'll get back to you on that one."

Sam and I were giving each other knowing looks without actually making eye contact. Just then we took the exit to Mima's house. Dad glanced over at me. "No texting."

"You hear that, Sam?" I said.

WFTD = Tortillas

MIMA WAS SITTING on the front porch talking to my Aunt Evie when we pulled up. She looked a little tired, but she was all dressed up and wearing makeup and the earrings she always wore. I got my usual hug and kiss and lots of *I missed you*s. And when Mima saw Samantha, she just hugged her. *"Que muchacha tan bonita,"* she said. "You've turned into a woman. *Que linda!* Oh, it's been so long since I've seen you." And then she made a joke because Mima loved to joke around. "And do you still like to use bad words?"

Samantha actually blushed.

"She does, Mima," I said.

Mima kissed Sam on the cheek, and I realized how frail and small Mima looked.

We had fun that day. My uncles and aunts and two of my cousins came over. They were way older than me, my cousins, and they were cool—even though they treated me like I was a kid. We watched the Dallas Cowboys, and there was a lot of cussing going on. The team was going down in flames.

At a certain point Mima walked into the living room and

called Sam over with her finger. I watched as they disappeared down the hall, and I wondered why I wasn't included in the conversation — but I was just going to have to deal with it. Anyway, I knew Sam would tell me all about it. Or maybe she wouldn't. Or maybe she'd only tell me some things and not others. Why was I like this? Why did I have this thing about being left out?

I walked outside and sat on Mima's front porch. Uncle Mickey was smoking a cigarette and talking to someone on his cell. He winked at me. He was kind of a winker. I thought that was cool. Fito would have called my Uncle Mickey a cat. To Fito, some guys were cats. Don't know where he got that cat thing.

I stared at Uncle Mickey's tattoos. I thought maybe there were two kinds of people in the world: tattoo people and non-tattoo people. I already knew which category I fit in.

"So," my Uncle Mickey said, "is she your girlfriend now?"

"Nah. It would be too weird."

"Yeah, I guess so. I remember her from when you were little kids. She liked to scream a lot."

"She still does," I said.

We both laughed.

"She's living with us now, you know? Her mom died."

"Yeah, I heard about that. Poor kid. That sucks."

"Yeah, it sucks."

He reached into his pocket and took out his wallet. He handed me a fifty-dollar bill. "Here, give this to her for me."

I nodded. I knew that Uncle Mickey was terrible with words. But he cared, and he showed that care in the only way he knew. I smiled. "You're a good guy," I said.

"For a screwed-up guy, I'm all right."

Uncle Mickey. He was always beating up on himself. I wondered why. But then I thought, *Well, I get that. I so get that.*

I walked into the kitchen, and I couldn't believe what I was seeing — Sam rolling out a tortilla while Mima stood over her. Sam was whining: "Mine aren't round, Mima."

"You have to be patient, Samantha. They don't come out perfect the first time."

I loved the way Mima pronounced her name. The way she said *Samantha* as if it were a Mexican name.

"Mima, Sam's not patient."

"Not true."

"Yes, true."

"You're not patient either, Sally."

Mima smiled and shook her head. "Patience is a gift you have to work for." She looked at me. "Samantha will learn if she wants to."

I offered Sam a crooked smile. "I'm impressed. I didn't know you knew what a rolling pin was."

"Mima, tell him not to be mean to me."

I had to hand it to Sam. She knew how to work it. But I was getting a kick out of her first shot at being domestic. I watched her as she gave the sad flour tortilla she'd just rolled out a look of disgust. "It looks more like a map of South America than it does a tortilla."

"Nope," I said. "It looks more like Africa."

"Australia," she said. "Definitely Australia."

Mima shook her head. "That's okay. It's your first time." She winked at me. "Don't laugh at Samantha."

Actually I thought it was great that Sam was making such an effort. It wasn't like her to please other people. That wasn't her style. She was changing. She really was changing.

I looked at Mima and Sam. "Is it all right if I stay and watch the lesson?"

Sam smirked. "Why not?"

So we sat in the kitchen, Sam trying to learn how to roll out tortillas, Mima telling stories about how things were when she was a girl and how the world had changed, and she seemed a little sad.

Sam and Aunt Evie and I helped her cook. Mima didn't generally like people in her kitchen, but I was thinking she was beginning to let go. When you were dying, you had to let go of the things you loved. And Mima loved her kitchen, so yeah, the letting-go thing was starting to kick in. Me, I wasn't letting go of anything just yet. Not ready. Just not ready.

I grated the cheese for the enchiladas. Mima taught Sam how to make red enchilada sauce, and Aunt Evie fried the corn tortillas. If you don't fry the tortillas, the enchiladas won't be any good. Some restaurants don't quite get that. In our family, frying the corn tortilla was a rule. Nobody was allowed to break it.

You know, it was beautiful to be in that kitchen just then. I guess there are times of quiet beauty in life. My dad had told me that once. At the time I didn't have a clue as to what he was trying to say.

I smiled at my Uncle Mickey staring at his plate of enchiladas. "That's what I'm talkin' about." He loved to say that. Mima always served him first. Don't know why.

As I watched Mima serve everyone that Sunday afternoon, I wondered how many more meals she had left in her.

Sam. Me. The Future.

ON THE DRIVE home, Dad asked me and Sam where we stood on our college applications. Sam said she had all the paperwork but still had to complete some of the forms.

"Lina and I will go over the financial forms ASAP," he said.

"Thanks, Mr. V."

"You've written your admissions essay?"

"I'll get on it," Sam said.

"I know it's been crazy," Dad said. "But this is important. And you, Salvie? How's the essay coming?"

"It's coming," I said.

"Is it, Salvie?"

"Okay, it's not coming." It's not as if my mind was on college. My heart just wasn't in it.

Sam reached into her backpack and took out her list of schools.

"You carry that around?" I asked.

"Yup, Sally. For luck."

She handed it to me. "Read me my list," she said.

"Why?"

"I wanna hear. I wanna hear the sound of the future."

"You cray-cray," I said.

"Humor me. I'm still in mourning."

"You're pulling that card out again?"

"Yup."

I could tell my dad was getting a big kick out of our little exchange.

Sam shoved her list in my face. Literally. I took the list. "You want me to read it like it's a frickin' poem?"

She crossed her arms.

I looked at the list and said, " 'K. Here goes." I put on a formal voice: "Number one on the list: Stanford University. Now, that's a real college. Number two: Brown University. Uhh. Brown. Rhode Island, here I come."

"Skip the commentary, you clown. Just read the list."

"No sense of humor," I said. I got the look. "Okay, okay. Number three: Georgetown. Number four: UC Berkeley. Number five: UC Santa Barbara. Number six: University of Texas. Hey, we have a school in common."

"If you're going there, I'm definitely not."

"Whatever, Sammy. Hmm. Okay, to continue, number seven: Boston College. Number eight: University of Notre Dame. That one's cuz you're such a good Catholic."

"Shut up. Mr. V, tell him to shut up."

My dad was cracking up. "You're doing pretty well on your own, Sam."

"Clocking in at number nine: the University of Miami. And rounding out the top ten is Cornell University, where Sam will text every ten minutes complaining about the winter."

"You mangled my list."

I gave her my best snarky smile. "But seriously, Sam, you'll get into all of them."

"Yeah, well, I'm not sure about the money."

"You have the money, Sam," my dad said.

"Yeah, well, it sucks that I have the money because my mother had a good insurance policy." She was fighting back tears.

"Hey, hey," I said. "It's okay."

"Yeah, Sally, one minute it *is* okay. And then another minute I'm falling apart. You know, Sylvia and I fought all summer about this list."

"Yeah, I know."

I noticed that my dad didn't interject himself into the conversation.

Lists = Future?

I MADE ANOTHER LIST. A list of questions I had in my head. But the list wasn't numbered, and all the questions were wrecking into each other: Was Marcos going to be coming around? If Marcos was once my dad's boyfriend, why did he leave? Why doesn't my dad date? Is that my fault? Why are some people gay? Why do people hate gay people? How much will it hurt when Mima dies? Who invented college? Why didn't I know what I wanted to be? Why couldn't I sing? Why couldn't I draw? Why couldn't I dance? What the hell could I do?

Maybe I could turn my list of questions into my college admissions essay.

I think I'm the stupidest smart boy who ever lived.

Marcos?

SO IT WAS Halloween. Sam's favorite holiday. We'd gone trick-or-treating together since we were five. And the fact that we were seniors wasn't going to stop us from continuing our tradition.

At first Sam fought the idea of Fito's coming along. "Does he have to come?"

And I said, "Yup. I got him to take the night off from working at Circle K. Give him a break. His life sucks."

"Everybody's life sucks."

"Mine doesn't. And yours doesn't either."

"My life does too suck."

"No, it doesn't. Your mom died, that sucks. That hurts. I get that. But your life? Your life doesn't suck, Sammy."

"Whatever."

"Fito lives in a crack house," I said.

"It's not a crack house."

"Looked like one to me."

"How many times did you go in there?"

"Once. That was enough."

She rolled her eyes. "Don't talk like you actually know what a crack house is."

"Okay, okay, but you get what I'm saying. Fito's just trying to make it through the day. Now, that's a life that sucks." And then I gave her one of those smirks that I gave Sam when I knew I had her on the run. "And he went to your mom's funeral. That was sweet. You said so yourself."

"But Halloween's always been our thing."

"I get that, Sam. It's our tradition. But Fito's just — you know."

"I know, I know. Okay. I'm being a shit. He can come."

"And you like him."

"Yeah, I guess I do like him."

So we all went trick-or-treating. Sam went as Lady Gaga. Of course she did. I went as a baseball player. Sammy rolled her eyes. "Booorrrrrriiiiiinnnnngggg." Fito went as a businessman vampire: tie, sports coat, black cape, and fangs. Sam was impressed.

We were a little old for trick-or-treating — but we didn't care. Dorks. Actually it was fun — and we needed to have fun. We just did. Some lady was giving out caramel apples. Sam refused hers. "They probably have razorblades in them."

Fito shrugged and wolfed his down, and then smiled at Sam. "See? No razorblades."

"Do you ever chew your food? It's not gonna run away, you know."

"What are you, Ms. Etiquette? You know, sometimes, Sam, you be like the sweetest girl on the border and shit, and then other times you just got attitude. I mean, at-ti-tude."

"If you were a girl, you'd have my attitude too."

"If I were a girl, I sure as hell wouldn't go out with the kinds of guys you hang with."

I laughed. Sam didn't.

"Oh, so you like nice boys, do you?"

"Yeah, I like nice boys. I like boys who know how to read and don't give me attitude. I get all the attitude I need at home."

Sam looked at him. I knew she was thinking. That girl was always thinking. "You got a boyfriend?"

"Nope."

"Don't I see you and Angel hanging out all the time?"

"Angel's history."

"He's cute."

"Yeah, well, he's high maintenance."

"Examples, please."

Fito just looked at Sam. "I don't do anybody else's homework."

"He wanted you to do his homework?"

"Yup."

"Screw that."

"That's what I said."

"Guys suck."

Fito laughed. "Yeah, they do."

And I said, "I don't suck."

Fito and Sam looked at each other and said, "Yeah, you do."

And we all cracked up. Sometimes when you laugh, it has nothing to do with whistling in the dark.

As we walked the streets, knocking on doors for candy we didn't need, Sam started taking lots of pictures of the little kids. "Adorable," she said.

"See?" I said. "You're going to make a great mother."

"Maybe."

But she was more interested in checking out the boys who

216

were around. Sometimes she'd look over at me and nod. "That one's a bad boy."

"Keep walking," I said.

"Yeah," Fito said, "keep walking."

Sam was Sam. Yup.

Then one bad boy with tats stopped us and said to Sam, "You're hot, bitch."

And I said, "What did you say?"

"You heard me."

And just like that, I took a swing at him. He fell back, but my punch didn't stop him. He put up his fists and started going for me. "Let's have at it, fucker," he said.

But Sam stepped in and said, "Hey! Hey! Stop it! Stop it!"

And the guy looked at Sam, and Sam said, "Please. He didn't mean it."

So the guy calmed down and walked away. But he said, "I better not find you alone, dude."

Sam looked at me and said, "Sally, what's wrong? What the hell's wrong with you?"

And I said, "I don't know. He had no right to call you that." I sat down on the curb. "I'm sorry I'm sorry I'm sorry."

I felt Sam's arm over my shoulder. "Sally, a lot of people think I'm a bitch. Who cares? They're just stupid boys. Who cares?"

I sat there shaking.

"What is it, Sally? What is it?"

I calmed down, and I told Sam and Fito that it was just all these things coming at me and that I was fine. And then we got back into trick-or-treating and we took a bunch of selfies, and we were having fun again. When we headed back home, Dad was sitting on the front porch giving out candy to some trick-or-treaters.

A man sat next to him.

As we walked up the sidewalk, I could see the man's face.

Marcos.

Part Four

Maybe that's what life was. You zigged and you
zagged and zigged and zagged some more.

(Dad) Things
We Never Say (Me)

EVEN THOUGH DAD and I had this great thing going, and even though we talked, and even though we didn't keep a lot of secrets, there were still things we never talked about. Talking wasn't always easy — even for talkers. But I decided I was going to talk to him because I had too many questions hanging around in my head. And I decided I was going to post a No Loitering sign right there in my brain.

Sam had spent the night with her Aunt Lina. I guess they had things to talk about too.

It was a warm Saturday afternoon. Maggie was rolling around in the grass in the backyard.

Dad was sitting on the steps having a cigarette.

I sat next to him and said, "Can I have a drag?"

We both busted out laughing.

"I never want you to smoke. Not ever."

"Not to worry, Dad. I don't like those things."

"I don't either."

"Then why do you smoke?"

"Ahh, they keep me company sometimes. It's a very uncomplicated relationship."

"Yeah, you smoke them and they give you cancer."

"And emphysema."

"And heart disease."

"Are we going to run down the whole list?"

"Nope. Don't really want to talk about cigarettes."

"What's on your mind?" he asked.

"Can I ask you a question?"

"Ask away."

"Why haven't you ever had a boyfriend?"

"I *have* had a boyfriend. I've had several."

"Before me or after me?"

"Both."

"Yeah, but not lately."

"Well, lately I've been busy."

"That's kinda lame, Dad."

"Lame? Me? The place isn't exactly crawling with your girl-friends."

"I'm not in that space right now."

"Maybe I'm not either."

"How come you never talk to me about some stuff?"

"You mean my love life? Well, first of all, you're my son. In my opinion, fathers shouldn't be talking to their sons about their love lives."

"But, Dad, you don't have a love life."

"That sounds like an accusation."

"It *is* an accusation."

"What's this about, Salvie?"

"You know what I think? I think you don't date because of me. I think it's my fault that you don't have a normal life."

"I'm gay, Salvie. I've never had a normal life."

"You know what I mean, Dad. You know exactly what I mean."

"What do you want me to say?" He put his cigarette out. He took my hand in his and squeezed it.

"Dad," I whispered, "was Marcos your boyfriend?"

He nodded. "Yeah, he was."

"What happened?"

My dad was looking up at the sky. Then he said, "He told me he couldn't handle being a stepfather."

"So you chose me."

"Of course I did."

"So it *is* my fault."

My father looked straight at me. And then he kissed my forehead. He let go of my hand and put a cigarette in his mouth but didn't light it. "Don't be an idiot, Salvador. You never were very good at doing math. Look, if Marcos couldn't handle me being a father — well, that was his problem. Not my fault. Nor your fault. It was him. We're a package deal, you and I. And I can't be with anyone who doesn't get what you and I have."

I nodded.

He lit his cigarette.

"Did you love him?"

"Yes."

"Do you still? Love him?"

"Yes."

"Maybe that's why Mima said you were lonely."

"She said that?"

"Yup. You never stopped loving him?"

"I guess not. I guess a guy like me just doesn't know how to stop loving someone."

I could tell he wanted to cry. But he didn't.

"Fito said the problem with being gay was that you had to date guys."

Dad laughed. "Fito's funny. I didn't know he was gay."

"I didn't either. But now I do."

"Is he good with that?"

"Yeah, I think so. It's his family that sucks. It's like he kind of raised himself."

"That's tough."

It was good to talk to my dad. I leaned my head on his shoulder. "Dad," I whispered, "you should let other people take care of you sometimes."

"I guess I don't know how to do that."

"Well, you can learn, can't you?"

"Yeah, well, maybe I can. Maybe you can help me."

And I wanted to learn too, to learn how to take care of my dad when he needed taking care of. But I didn't know how.

Me. Secrets.

OKAY, SO I didn't tell my dad that I'd started going around taking swings at guys who pissed me off. And I didn't tell my dad that I had this fantasy about beating the crap out of Eddie. And I didn't tell my dad that I kept wondering what it would be like to get drunk. And that I didn't even know where that thought came from. And I didn't tell my dad that there was this strange anger living inside me. And I didn't tell my dad that I was sort of mad that he'd given me my mother's letter and that maybe he should have waited. And I didn't tell my dad that I was mad at my mother for having left me a letter in the first place. And I didn't tell my dad that I felt guilty about the fact that I'd hated Sylvia and that I didn't know what to do about that because she was dead.

And I didn't tell my dad that maybe I wasn't so sure about Marcos hanging around, because even though I thought my dad should have a boyfriend *in theory,* I just didn't know about that Marcos guy. And when I asked him if he still loved him and he said yes, I wasn't sure that I liked the answer.

And I didn't tell my dad that I was having thoughts about my bio father. I was wondering if I looked like him, if I acted like him, and that I was starting to have thoughts that maybe I should at least meet him.

Sam had met *her* father.

Fito had met *his* father.

And then there was me.

How could I tell my dad all these things I hadn't told him?

225

Marcos? Hmm.

I TEXTED SAM: Asked Dad about Marcos.

    Sam: Wow! Spill it

    Me: When u get back

    Sam: B home soon. Lina and I cleaned up house. C u in ten

    Me: Wftd = sacrifice

    Sam: As in human sacrifice?

    Me: Wrong!

    Sam: Use in sentence

    Me: My father knows the meaning of the word sacrifice

    Sam: Yup

So when Sam got home, I told her about the conversation I'd had with my father. She listened, asked questions. She loved asking questions. And of course she had a few things to say about the whole situation. "That shit Marcos broke your father's heart. I knew there was a reason I hated him."

"He didn't do anything to you, Sam. It's not your place to hate him."

"That's bullshit."

"No, it isn't. Dad doesn't hate him. And if Dad doesn't hate him, I won't hate him." God, I could be such a hypocrite.

Sam looked at me. "You know, you and your dad, not normal. Sometimes not normal is *no bueno*. Why do you guys always walk around being so nice? I mean, it just isn't *normal*." She kept shaking her head. "And it's not fair. Marcos gets away with being a shit."

"What do we know about Marcos, Sammy?"

"We know he's a worm who came crawling back to the surface after the rain."

Sam, she was always good for a laugh.

"Don't laugh. It was *not* a joke."

"Maybe he realized he was wrong."

"Sally, do you always have to interpret reality with the naiveté of a ten-year-old? Really?"

"Sammy, I don't know a damn thing about reality. And I'm not a ten-year-old."

"So is Marcos gonna be hanging around, stinking up the place?"

I don't know why, but I laughed again.

Sam kept yelling at me, which made me laugh even harder.

But really, I felt the same way she did. Only she was honest about it.

Cake

IT WAS A Saturday evening, and I was hanging out in my room, thinking about that college thing again and that I didn't really want to go. I mean, I *did* want to go, but only after taking a year off. You know, to find myself. Well, that was lame. But it was true. Was there such a thing as being a little lost? I mean, if you were lost — well, then you were lost. I didn't know shit. I was going through the motions. Maybe a lot of people just went through the motions. Maybe that worked for some people. But I knew that the going-through-the-motions thing wasn't going to work for me. *No bueno.*

Sam was in her room working on her admissions essay. I didn't have to wonder what she was going to say, because I knew she'd make me read it. And she'd want to read mine. And I didn't have one to read. What was I supposed to say: *Take me. You won't be sorry. I'm the greatest thing since the invention of the cell phone?* We were supposed to talk about ourselves. Yeah. *Hello, they call me Mr. Excitement. But I am pretty good in a fight.*

Sam texted me: Have a good idea for my essay. U?

Me: No ideas. Not good at selling myself

Sam: I'll help you

Me: I'm worthless

Sam: Ur not. Don't ever say that

Me: I thought u were mad at me

Sam: Nope. We should bake a cake

Me: What?

Sam: U know, a cake?

Me: U know how?

Sam: No. But u do

Me: Where is the we?

Sam: Teach me. We can take it to Mima tomorrow

Me: Good idea

Sam: And we can take her flowers

Me: The evil Sam went away?

Sam: No worries. She'll come back

Me. Saturday Night. Sam.

WE WERE IN THE KITCHEN, and I was teaching Sam how to make a chocolate cake from scratch.

"Why not just bake from one of those Betty Crocker boxes?" she said.

"I'm impressed. You know about Betty Crocker."

"Go ahead. Mock me."

We gave each other looks. Yup, we were all about giving each other looks. "See, Sammy, we have all the ingredients. It's not that hard."

She was watching me put in the dry ingredients as she read them aloud from the recipe book.

"You want to know what each ingredient does?" I asked.

"You're really asking me that question?"

"How are you ever going to learn to cook if you don't know what each ingredient does for the recipe?"

"The physics of chocolate cake? Not interested."

"Now who's mocking whom?"

She watched me as I broke two eggs and beat them. "Guess it doesn't look that hard. Still, Betty Crocker's easier."

"We're not going for easy. We're going for taste."

"Whatever."

"It was your idea," I said. "You said you wanted to learn."

"I lied."

"Yup."

When the cake was in the oven, Sam watched as I made the frosting. "You're not like most guys."

"Thank you. I think."

"What makes you so sure it was a compliment?"

"I don't want to be like most guys. So it *was* a compliment."

Maggie sat there and watched us as we played verbal volleyball. I always wondered what that dog was thinking. Probably nothing complicated.

Dad walked in from the backyard, where he'd been working on a painting. "What's with the cake?"

"We're making it for Mima."

"That's sweet."

Sam smiled. "Well, we're very sweet young people." She couldn't leave out that little teaspoon of sarcasm — part of her recipe for living.

Dad grinned. "I'm going to clean up. I'm going out tonight."

Sam couldn't help herself. "Going out with anyone we know?"

"Just a movie with an old friend."

It's not as if we were surprised when the doorbell rang and it was Marcos. I had never noticed how handsome he was. Still, he wasn't as handsome as my dad. And he was shorter. I wondered if most kids noticed their parents and how they looked. Maybe they did. Maybe they didn't. I hadn't exactly taken a poll.

Dad seemed a little embarrassed by the whole situation.

Sammy didn't help him out one damn bit. "Text if you're going to be out late."

Marcos just shrugged and grinned at her.

Dad couldn't get out the door fast enough.

"I don't care if he is cute. If he hurts your dad, I'll kill him."

"Are we going to start that again?"

"How come you don't care?"

"I *do* care. I learned something about my dad today. Something very beautiful. You know that game What If? Well, Sam, what if my dad hadn't adopted me?"

"I don't know, Sally. I don't have an answer to that one."

"Not," I said. "Not, not, not."

"Enough with the *not*s already. *Basta*."

"I don't know what would have happened to me if Dad hadn't adopted me — but I *do* know I wouldn't have this life. And it's the only life I know. I wouldn't have Mima, who is the greatest grandmother in the fucking world —"

"Did you just use the F word?"

"Sarcasm looks really good on you, you know that?"

"Couldn't help myself."

"I know. I know. But, Sammy, if it weren't for my dad, I wouldn't know you. You wouldn't be my best friend. You wouldn't be living here. You know, I asked my dad once if he believed in God. You know what he said?"

"Tell me."

"He said, 'Every time I look into your blue eyes. Every time I hear you laugh. Every day, when I hear your voice, I thank God for you. Yeah, Salvador, I believe in God.'"

Sam leaned over and kissed me on the cheek. "You're the luckiest boy in the world."

I nodded. "You bet your ass." Yeah, I *was* the luckiest boy in the world. But I was still a boy. Shit.

Sam and I were sitting at the kitchen table admiring the chocolate cake we'd baked.

"Who knew?" Sam said. "Chocolate cream cheese frosting." She was really happy. "Who knew that teaching a girl how to bake a cake could make her happy?"

"Did the girl learn?"

"I took notes." She tapped her temple. "Up here. And it's really beautiful."

"It's all about the aesthetics."

"You love that word."

"My dad's an artist."

Right then, for whatever reason, I got this not-so-great idea to have a glass of wine. So we sat at the kitchen table and opened up a bottle of red. I poured us each a glass. We toasted our cake.

I swear I don't know what got into us. Pretty soon we were having a second glass.

"You think your dad will get mad?"

"Hmm," I said. "It's not as if he's going to kill us."

We both shrugged and kept drinking. The thing is, I didn't want to stop. I wanted to know what it felt like to be drunk. You want me to explain this with logic? Well, where was the logic to loving? Where was the logic to dying in accidents? Where was the logic to cancer? Where was the logic to living? I was starting to believe that the human heart had an inexplicable logic. But I was also starting to get drunk, so I wasn't trusting anything I was thinking.

As I opened up a second bottle, Sam and I looked at each other with a kind of what-the-hell thing on our faces. "Did you know I used to think that every person was like a book?" I said.

Sam laughed. "Boy, you *are* a talker when you drink."

"I can shut up."

I poured us another glass of wine.

"No! Don't! Just talk. You *do* know that I do most of the talking in this little mutual admiration society of ours."

"Yeah, I guess so."

"You *do* know what that means, don't you?"

"It means you like to talk more than I do."

"You're an idiot. It means you know me better than I know you."

"You know me."

Sam looked at me. I wasn't going to argue with her. Not because I wouldn't win the argument, but because I knew she was right.

"I'll try and do better."

She smiled. "So everyone's like a book, huh?"

"Yeah, I used to think that. But it's crap. People aren't like books — they're not like books at all. Books make sense. People don't. You know, like life. All these things happen, and they're not connected. I mean, they are and they're not, and it's not as if my life or your life — it's not as if our lives have this plot, you know? It's not like that. I mean, like some people say, we're born, we live,

234

and then we die. Yeah, well, so fucking what? That doesn't say anything, does it?"

Sam was looking at me.

"You're studying me, Sammy. It's a little creepy."

"You're funny," she said. "This is just how I imagined you'd be when you were drunk."

"That predictable, huh?" I downed my wine.

"Well, you're predictable in some ways. But lately not as predictable as you used to be. I don't understand that fist thing you have going, Sally. I don't know where it comes from. You're not crazy or wild. But sometimes you *are* crazy and wild. That's the greatest thing about you, Sally. You're you. It's like sometimes you're the same old Sally, and then you get into these pensive moods and you don't want to talk, and then all of a sudden you're mad at the world. I get that. I'm mad at the world a lot. But you weren't like that. And now, I don't know."

"I don't know either, Sam. I'm just confused. And everything seems complicated. Mima's sick. And I have this reminder of my mom in a letter that I don't want to read, and it haunts me and it confuses me because I want everything to be the way it was, and it can't be that way anymore, and your mom is dead and that's so strange, and I don't know how you deal with it, and it's weird that we both have dead mothers, only you remember yours and I don't remember mine, and I don't know what the hell I'm trying to say."

"So we're both mad at the world. That's okay."

"Is it, Sam?"

"That's the way it is right now."

"I don't like it."

"It's okay, Sally."

"I don't feel okay. I feel like punching out the world."

"I do too. Only you're being very literal about that, and maybe that's not so okay."

"Where does it come from?"

"You're gonna have to figure that out."

"How?"

"You'll find a way."

"Will I?"

"Yes."

"You're so sure."

"I know you. You'll find a way."

"And you still love me, even though I'm not that good boy you thought I was? The good boy you wanted me to be?"

"I never wanted you to be anything, Sally. I've always just wanted you to be you."

"But I don't know who me is."

"Yes, you do. Deep down you do. Reach out and find him, Sally."

"It hurts."

"So what?"

"I'm not brave like you, Sammy."

"Maybe you're braver than you think."

"Maybe." I looked at the bottle of wine. "I'm drunk. And I'm saying stupid things." Then I smiled at Sam. "We might as well polish it off." I don't know, I guess I felt like talking — so that's what I did. I just kept on talking. "Sammy, remember when Marcos came over that day? I told you I saw a look on my father's face. I didn't understand that look because I'd never seen it. Sam, it was love. You know, a different kind of love. I mean, I can see love on my dad's face when he looks at me. But this was different. I think that's exactly what I saw. Dad loves him."

"Does that scare you?"

"A little bit. That's a lie. It scares me a lot. I mean, I've never really had to share him."

"That's not true. You've always shared him with me. And you've shared him with Mima and with all your uncles and aunts."

"Yeah, I guess so. I just want my dad to be happy. I do. And if Marcos makes him happy, I'm cool with that. No, no, maybe I'm not so cool with it. I'm not."

"You jealous?"

"I don't know. Maybe I am. And then, I mean, the guy hurt my dad. And if he ever hurt him again, I don't know what I'd do. I don't know, Sam."

"I get that. I couldn't stand any of my mother's boyfriends."

"Not any of them?"

"Nope."

"Why?"

"Because I knew they were all going to hurt her. And they did. And Marcos better not hurt your dad, because I'm going to go after him. And I got those fists of yours on my side."

"So we're a team."

"Yeah, we are."

"Me and you against the world?"

"Not exactly. We have your dad. And really, he's my dad too."

"Yeah."

"So?"

"So?"

Then we got to laughing and we just kept drinking wine and

talking and then the room started spinning and there was this salty thing going on in my mouth and the next thing I knew, I had my head in the toilet, spilling my guts out, and Sam was standing over me and handing me a warm washcloth. "You'll be okay," she said. "You're not an alcohol virgin anymore."

I felt terrible, and the room was still spinning and all I could do was moan.

And then I was throwing up again.

Dad. At the Breakfast Table. Me and Sam.

I'M WONDERING WHICH one of you two geniuses thought this was a good idea."

Sam raised her hand, as if she were in a classroom. "My idea, Mr. V."

"Wrong," I said. "I thought, you know, it would be nice to have a glass of wine."

"A glass would have been fine with me. But I'm looking at two dead soldiers on this kitchen table."

"I guess we just got carried away."

"Care to offer an explanation?"

"Well, we stayed home. We didn't drink and drive."

"You don't get extra credit for that. And that doesn't qualify as an explanation."

"You're talking like a dad."

"I'm taking that as a compliment." My father wasn't taking his eyes off me. "I'm waiting."

"I don't have an explanation, Dad. We just, you know, we got a little crazy. Not everything has an explanation. Not everything I do makes sense. It was just one of those things."

"Just one of those things, huh?"

"What do you want me say, Dad? I feel like crap. Isn't that punishment enough?"

"Who said anything about punishment? All I'm asking for is a simple explanation."

"And I'm telling you I don't have one."

Dad looked at Sam, who was hanging her head as low as I was hanging mine. "Sam?"

"I guess I don't have an explanation either. Mr. V — I — well, no, I don't have an explanation."

"I'm going to ask you two a question, and I want you to answer honestly."

Sam and I nodded. We just kept nodding very slowly. God, I thought my head was going to bust open.

"Does this have anything to do with Marcos?"

"How do you mean, Dad?"

"Are you two upset because I went out with Marcos last night? Because if that's the case, if that upsets you, I don't have to see him. We can talk about —"

"Wrong, Dad! Wrong!" I wasn't sure why I was yelling. "Downing two bottles of wine last night was one of those stupid high school things that stupid high school kids do sometimes. That's all! Don't make it more than it is —" And then I said something I had no idea I was going to say. "And if I *was* upset about you and Marcos, you know what? You should be saying, *Then grow up, Salvie!* Stop living your life around me, Dad. Just stop it!"

So there I was, feeling really bad. I was covering my face with my hands. "I'm sorry. I didn't mean that."

My dad had his hand on my shoulder. "Yes, you did," he whispered.

"Dad, I'm going through some stuff."

"What stuff?"

"Stuff, Dad. I can't talk about it right now. But stuff. Things are happening. And I can't control it."

"Who says we're always in control?"

"I used to be in control of me."

"Control can be a lie, son."

"No one ever told me that." And I started to cry.

My dad held me. "Let go, my Salvie. Just let go."

"I did let go. I got drunk."

"Try it without two bottles of wine."

Hangover

Yᴜᴘ, ᴛʜᴀᴛ Sᴜɴᴅᴀʏ morning I ran into the word *hangover*. I didn't exactly want to be *Hangover*'s friend. Sam told me to drink lots and lots of water. Which I did. I took a shower. All I wanted to do was sleep. I felt like crap. I mean, emotionally speaking, I felt really, really bad. Sam said it was called "the walk of shame."

"Yeah," I said. "It's the perfect name for what I feel."

"Well, I feel the same way. I really am ashamed of myself. I mean, your dad's, like, this great guy, and he's all about being good to me, and here I get drunk on his wine. Shit, Sally! I mean, on top of everything else, we stole his wine."

"We're idiots."

"Yeah, we are."

"And then, what I told him. I mean, I shouldn't have said what I said. I told him to stop living his life around me. But the thing is, maybe I've been living my life around *him*. It's like I've always wanted to please him and be a good boy and all that — and I, hell, I mean, I don't want to disappoint him."

"Maybe the truth is that you've been living your lives around each other. And maybe you have to do something about that. Both of you."

"It's what we've done forever."

"He has to live his life. You have to live yours. Me and Sylvia. We had that down."

"Oh, God, what am I gonna do? Can we just pretend none of this happened?"

"That's walk-of-shame talk, Sally. No pretending. Pretending equals *no bueno*."

" 'K. No pretending. Shit. So how many times have you been drunk, Sammy?"

"I don't know. Enough times, I guess. I don't know why I do it. I don't know why I experiment with mood-altering crap. I always wind up hating myself for it."

"Walk-of-shame talk," I said.

And then we both sort of laughed. Halfhearted laughter. Walk-of-shame laughter. Guess we weren't up to whistling in the dark.

There were clouds floating in the autumn air. It wasn't really warm, and it wasn't really cold. But the breeze was *almost* cold. Dad was sitting on the steps. He had a cigarette in his lips, but it wasn't lit.

I had our baseball gloves. "Wanna play catch?"

"Sure," he said.

So we started tossing the ball around.

"I'm sorry I yelled at you," I said.

He smiled. "It's okay, Salvie. But let's make a deal?"

"Okay?"

"I think I need to give you some space, you know? Things are rough for you right now, and you're not used to rough. I think I spoiled you a bit too much."

"Sure. That's why I'm driving my BMW sports car around town."

"That's not what I meant. I just protected you — maybe a little too much. You know what I'm trying to say?"

"Yeah, I think so. You never wanted anything bad to happen to me. Maybe because I lost my mom?"

"I didn't want you to lose anything else. A little overprotective, I guess."

"Just a little." I couldn't help but smile. "I get that, Dad."

"But we're okay, Salvie. Me and you."

"We're okay?"

"Yeah, we're okay." And then he smiled. "But I'm afraid you owe me for a couple of bottles of red wine."

I wanted to tell him that we'd figure out the Marcos thing. We'd figure it out. *I'd figure it out.*

Mima. Cake.

MIMA WAS A REAL TALKER. Loved to talk. But that Sunday, when Sam and I handed her the cake, her face lit up and she hugged us — but she didn't talk much. She held my hand and she held Sam's hand and she held Dad's hand. But she didn't say much. Her eyes searched the quiet room, and I didn't know what she was looking for.

She loved the flowers we gave her, and she asked me to put them on the kitchen table. Dad and Aunt Evie made a late lunch.

Mima didn't eat much — but when it came to the cake, she ate two pieces. "Who made this cake?"

"Sam and I, we made it."

Then she started talking a bit — but I knew it was taking some effort. "My mother used to bake bread every Saturday on a wood-stove. And she knew how to make root beer. Did you know that? She used to make all my dresses. I have her sewing machine. I feel like seeing her again." Her voice sounded strange and far away, as if she'd left the room. But then she took her fork, asked for a little more cake, dug in, and offered me a bite.

She smiled.

I smiled back.

She fed me a bite of cake.

And I remembered those days when I was a small boy.

As we drove home in the dark, it started to rain.

"It will be her last Thanksgiving." Dad's voice was sad. But it was also matter-of-fact. "Everyone will be here," he said.

I didn't feel anything.

I didn't want to feel anything.

I knew Sam was in her own corner of the world. Thinking about her mother.

When we got home, Dad went into his studio. "Think I'll work awhile."

The streets were wet, but it had stopped raining, and it was cool, but it wasn't cold. Sam and I decided to go for a run. I wondered if running in the dark was the same as whistling in the dark.

I don't know if Sam was crying. She did that a lot. She cried when she ran. It was the grief thing. The my-mother-died thing.

I don't know if she cried that night as we ran. But I did.

Poetry. Poetry?

THE HANGOVER WAS nothing more than a memory, and the sadness over Mima's visit seemed to have abated. *Abated.* Another word Sam taught me. Sam and I were walking to school, and I felt oddly normal, meaning I didn't have any feelings running through me. Maybe the weekend had tired me out. I was feeling okay. Like everything was okay — even though it wasn't. And I told Sam what Dad said about the wine.

"Too bad we're not old enough to buy Mr. V some nice wine."

"Yeah, too bad."

"Hey," she said, "maybe we can get Marcos to take us wine shopping."

"So you warming up to him — or what?"

"I'm just pragmatic. That guy should be good for something."

I smiled. "Pragmatic. Remember you spelled that word in the spelling bee?"

"Why do you always have to remind me of that day?"

"Still mad?"

"I still give that creep evil looks when I run into him at school."

"You know how to hold a grudge, don't you?"

"It's not always such a bad thing, you know. Keeps a lot of shit-heads out of my life."

She gave me a look because I was laughing.

"You're laughing at me? Really?"

"What if?"

"What if?"

"Where did our What If game come from?" I don't know. Maybe I just felt like playing. "It seems like we haven't played in a long time."

"Yeah, it does seem that way, doesn't it?"

"What if," I said.

"What if," Sam said.

"What if I were a poet and you were a poet too?"

"If I were a poet, I would write a poem to —" She smiled. "Okay, I need some time with this one."

I opened the front door to the school building.

"By the end of the day I'll have mine ready," she said.

"Me too," I said.

"And don't write it during math. You need to pay attention."

"Bye," I said.

"Bye," she said.

"Great day," I said.

"Great day," she said.

And then I saw Enrique Infante walking in the other direction. "Faggot," he said.

I gave him a cheesy smile. "You want I should bash your face in again?"

"Come at me, white boy."

I almost turned around and went for him. But I kept walking.

We were on school grounds. I actually let a thought come between me and my fist reflex.

During lunch, this is what I wrote in my notebook:

> *If I were a poet*
> *I would write a poem*
> *that would make people's tongues*
> *fall out every time they said*
> *the word* faggot.

I read what I'd written and was pretty proud of myself. But I knew Sam's was going to be really good, and I wanted to remain competitive, so I thought a minute and then wrote:

> *If I were a poet*
> *I would write a poem*
> *so beautiful and moving*
> *that it would cure*
> *cancer, and cancer*
> *would never enter*
> *another human being*
> *ever again.*
> *Not ever.*

And then I was into it, so I started to write another one:

> *If I were a poet*
> *I would write a poem*

that would make my dad's heart
smile. And he would never
feel any sadness, and every day
he would wake
to the beauty of the day.

After school, we met at Sam's locker. "You look smug," she said.

"I don't do smug."

"Oh yeah, you're all about smug right now. You think you wrote a really outta-this-world cool poem, don't you?"

"Yup."

"Yeah, well, we'll see." Then we cracked up laughing and decided to wait till we got home to read each other's poems. I guess they were poems. What the hell did I know about poems? The only poem I really liked was this poem called "Autobiographia Literaria" by some guy named Frank O'Hara. I had it on my bulletin board at home. Sam liked to read it to me.

Sam kicked me as I walked. "Did you have a great day?"

"Yeah. We had a substitute in my English class. He didn't give a rat's tail about teaching, so Fito and I just texted each other."

"What were you texting?"

"Fito's situation at home seems to be getting worse."

"Well, that's *no bueno*."

"*No bueno* is right. And then this morning my good friend Enrique Infante walked passed me in the hallway and called me a faggot."

"He's a sleaze bucket."

"Yup. I told him that maybe I'd bash his face in again."

"*No bueno.*"

"*No bueno* is right. But it really pisses me off that he also called me a white boy."

"Uh-oh." Sam started laughing.

"You're supposed to be on my side."

"But you *are* a white guy."

"Really? We're going to get into this discussion again? Really?"

She messed up my hair and smiled. "Just relax. No worries, Enrique will get his. Yup, that's what I think." I wondered if she was up to something. She had that look.

When we got home, I gave Sam my poems. She gave me hers. This is what she wrote:

> *If I were a poet*
> *I would write a poem*
> *that would make the oceans*
> *clean again.*
> *I would write a poem*
> *so pure that it would rain for days*
> *and when the skies were clear again,*
> *a million stars would fill the summer night.*
> *I would write a poem to make the people see*
> *guns are guns and unworthy of our love.*
> *I would write a poem to make*
> *all the bullets disappear.*

I looked at her. "Wow. Mine are kind of stupid compared to yours."

She smiled at me. "Stupid boy. You're incapable of stupidity."

She got up from the couch and took her poem and mine. "I'm going to put them on the refrigerator. So your dad can read them."

"Good girl," I said. "He would like that."

"Yup."

So Sam took off some of the postcards that were on the refrigerator and replaced them with our poems. "We got to get some new magnets." Sam was starting to get all domestic on me. Who knew?

Sam and I were studying in the living room. I looked up and saw my dad standing there. "So how are my budding poets?"

I kinda smiled at him. "Sam's the better poet."

My father had this incredible look on his face. "Sometimes I love you both so much that I can hardly bear it." Then he turned around and walked toward the kitchen. "What do you want for dinner?"

"Tacos," I said.

"Tacos it is."

I looked at Sam and saw tears running down her face. "What?" I said.

"Your dad. He says things that make me cry."

"Beautiful things," I said.

"Yeah, beautiful. How come more guys aren't like your dad?"

"I have no frickin' idea." And then I thought, *Because most guys are like my bio father.* I had no idea where that thought came from. I didn't know a damn thing about my bio father.

Dad. Marcos.

I'D BECOME a chronic eavesdropper. That's what I thought as I stood at the back door and watched my dad and Marcos having an argument in front of Dad's studio.

My dad had this look on his face that said *I am half angry and half hurt*. And then I heard him saying: "Marcos, you can't just walk back into my life as if nothing happened. You can't just disappear one day and reappear a few years later and expect me to —" And then he stopped in midsentence.

"I said I was sorry, Vicente."

"Cheapest word in the dictionary."

"I was scared."

"I was scared too, Marcos. But I didn't walk away. You didn't see me running, did you?"

"Everybody deserves a second chance. Even me. We, Vicente, you and I, we deserve a second chance."

I watched my dad. He didn't say anything.

Marcos said, "I know how much I hurt you."

"Yes, you *did* hurt me."

"Vicente, not a day went by when I didn't think of you."

"It took you long enough."

I saw the tears on Marcos's face.

Right then I witnessed the world they lived in go completely silent. The world was flooding with their tears.

Marcos slowly walked away and left through the side gate.

I stepped away from the doorway and made my way back to my room.

Dad (Marcos) Me

As I sat in my room, part of me wanted to grab Marcos and punch his lights out. As if that would solve anything. Yeah, a big part of me wanted to hate him. For hurting my dad. But how could I hate him? I knew what I'd seen. Marcos, he loved my dad.

I'd seen the look on Dad's face too. He loved Marcos back.

And I understood that the love they had wasn't easy. And maybe they wouldn't make it, you know, but they were trying, and I knew that. A part of me didn't want that to happen, because, well, hell, it complicated everything, and everything was complicating everything and, you know, I used to think Sam was the most illogical person in the universe, and now I thought I was.

Me. Me? Who?

OKAY, TIME TO GET DOWN to writing my admissions letter. I made a list of things I should include that some bored person in the admissions office would read.

1. ~~My father is gay.~~
2. ~~I am adopted.~~
3. ~~I used to know who I was, but now I don't.~~
4. ~~I'm nothing special.~~
5. ~~My best friend, Samantha, is brilliant — but I am not.~~
6. ~~I got a letter from a dead mother, and man, how many boys applying to your school have that?~~
7. ~~I am a natural-born boxer.~~
8. ~~My grandmother has taught me more than any teacher I've ever had in a classroom.~~

This is not working.
This is not working.

WFTD = Fists. Again?

So AFTER SCHOOL, we were walking home. That familiar walk that had always been so calm and uneventful, walks that had been filled mostly with Sam's words and her curiosity about the world. And now, on many of our walks back home from school, Fito joined us, and it was good. Yeah, we were calmly walking back home from school — Sam and me and Fito. Sam and Fito were talking about *The Grapes of Wrath*. It was Fito's favorite book, a book I hadn't read. Fito said I had to put it on my list. And I thought, *Great, another list.*

And then as we walked, we saw this group of guys that were taunting Angel, calling him faggot and queer and *maricón*. They were talking all kinds of shit, and they had him surrounded, and it looked like they were about to beat the holy crap out of him. I must have run toward them, though I don't remember running. All I remember is that I had this guy by the collar and was shoving him against a chainlink fence. I was right in his face, and I was telling him, "I'm gonna kick your ass from here to Canada."

And then I felt Sam's hand on my shoulder. She kept saying, "Let him go. Let him go."

I slowly let go, and he and his friends took off.

I was numbly staring into Sam's eyes.

I looked over, and Fito said, "I'm gonna walk Angel home."

I nodded.

Sam and I didn't say a word as we started back home.

There were different kinds of silences between us. Sometimes the silences meant that we knew each other so well that we didn't need words. Sometimes the silences meant that we were mad at each other.

And sometimes the silences meant that we didn't know each other at all.

Sam. Grief. Sylvia. Mima.

I WAS IN BED, but I wasn't tired, and I wasn't sleepy. I kept turning the light off and on. I started reading *The Grapes of Wrath,* but put it down. It was too daunting and overwhelming. I turned off the light. I turned it on again. Sam texted me: U know there are five stages of grief.

Me: ?

Sam: Yup. Five stages

Me: Where do u get these things?

Sam: Counselor at school

Me: U went?

Sam: Last week. Been thinking

Me: Good for U

She walked into my room. She was wearing an extra-large El Paso Chihuahuas T-shirt that had an outline of the ears of a Chihuahua dog and said FEAR THE EARS. Stupid. She loved that T-shirt. I was lying in bed. "Five stages, huh?"

"That's what the experts say."

"So what?"

"You're in the anger phase."

"What?"

"Mima's dying and you're in the anger phase."

"Well, you should know. You're the expert on phases."

She uncrossed her arms. She sat on my bed. "Yup, you're definitely in the anger phase. Phase one equals denial, as in *This is not happening.*"

I gave her my best fuck-off look, but I knew she wasn't going to stop.

"Are you listening, Sally Silva?"

"I have a choice here? I mean, you're totally colonizing my space."

"Colonizing. Good one." She didn't skip a beat. "Phase two equals anger, as in *I am so pissed off at God or at whomever because I am not happy that this is happening.* That would be you right now."

"No, I'm not."

"Did you know that you were cussing as we were running?"

"Was I?"

"And lately you're quick on the draw — with your fists, I mean." She gave me a snarky look.

I started to say something, but didn't.

"Yup. Phase three equals bargaining, equals, in my case, *If I am good for the rest of my life and never say the F word again, will you please bring my mother back,* or, in your case, *If I never have a bad thought about anybody ever again in my life, will you cure Mima of cancer?*" She smiled at me. "I know what I'm talking about."

I smiled back at her. There was a lot of snark in my smile.

"Phase four equals depression. Yeah, well, depression. Anger turned inward. Yup. And finally, phase five equals acceptance. See, a fucking happy ending. The thing is, the phases, they come and go and appear in different orders."

"For how long?"

"How the hell should I know? The only phase I've completed is the denial one. I aced that test. The other stages, they're all still clinging to me like bad boys who can't take no for an answer. And stage five, well, that's just a dream right now."

Then she started crying. "I know it's hard, Sally. But you're in your head a lot these days, and I miss you. You know the denial phase? That phase has a partner. Isolation, baby."

"Isolation?"

"Yeah, as in *I don't feel like talking anymore*."

"Well, I *don't* feel like talking."

"I'm trying to figure out if you're in the isolating phase or the depression phase, because you can do two phases at once. But I never knew you to multitask."

And then we both cracked up laughing, but we weren't really laughing, we were crying.

And then I held her as she cried. "I miss Sylvia," she whispered. "I really miss her."

Running. On Empty. Fito.

SAM WOKE ME UP early to go running.

"Let's skip a day," I said.

"Get your ass out of bed. Move it."

"I want to do the isolation thing."

"Up."

"It's Saturday. Let me sleep."

"You can never go back to sleep after you wake up — and you know it."

"I hate you."

"You'll get over it."

Some days getting up seemed like a bigger commitment than I was ready for. Get up and show up. That's what you had to do in life. Well, according to my dad. On the other hand, Uncle Mickey liked to say that everybody deserved a day off from the truth. So there I was, talking to myself as I put on my running shoes.

I told Sam we should change it up, so we decided to run to the Santa Fe Bridge.

It was actually great running through the mostly empty streets of downtown El Paso. I liked that you could see and smell the border in the air and on the streets and in the talk of the few people we passed who spoke the special kind of language that wasn't really Spanish and wasn't really English. My dad said he moved back because he knew he belonged here. Here. I wondered if I would ever know that kind of certainty.

Sam shouted at me as we ran, "Great idea, Sally. I love this route."

When we got to the bridge, we took a rest. And Sam said, "We should run across the bridge and then just cross back."

"No quarters," I said. "*And* no passport."

"Crap. I hate that passport thing." And she got that Sam look in her eyes. "Let's get passports."

I smiled. "Yeah. We should have passports." And we took off running back home. We got into this race. I was a faster runner — but Sam held her own. If I slowed down just a little, she was right on my heels. And she was laughing and I was laughing too, and it was hard to run and laugh and breathe.

By the time we got to the library, we'd tired ourselves out, and we slowed to a jog. There were always homeless guys sleeping on the benches and stuff. We passed one of them, and I stopped and turned around.

"What?" Sam said.

"Isn't that Fito?"

We walked up to the sleeping homeless guy who was not a sleeping homeless guy. It *was* Fito.

I shook him by the shoulder. "Hey," I said, "Fito."

He leaped up with his fists out.

I jumped back. "Hey, it's okay. It's just me."

Fito got this really sad look on his face and slumped down and hung his head. "Sorry," he said.

"What are you doing here, Fito?"

"What the shit does it look like I'm doing here, Sam? I'm sleeping."

We both eyed the backpack. "What's going on?"

Fito just looked at us. "I'm handling it."

Sam took a seat next to him on the bench. "Right."

"Look, my mom threw me out of the house." And then he explained the whole thing, how his mom was high when he got home late and how she started in on him and how she'd found his checkbook in one of his drawers and demanded that he give her all his money as rent. "'*You wanna live here, you little shit? Start paying!*' She had this demonic look on her face, and then she just starts hitting me and saying all sorts of shit and calling me a faggot, and I won't get into the descriptive parts that went along with *faggot,* and so I just packed my things and got the hell out. And as I'm walking out the door, she's in my face and telling me never to come back again and all kinds of shit like that, and well, here I am."

"How come you didn't come to my house?" I asked.

"Really, Sal? I was gonna do that? No, man, I got my pride." He kept talking and saying that he'd find a way to get by, and that nothing was gonna stop him from going to college, and it made me feel like an idiot because college was this gift I had, like a present under a Christmas tree, and I didn't want to open it.

Sam and I sat there listening to him. As he was talking, Sam and I were thinking. Thinking and listening. And when he was done, he shrugged and said, "Well, there it all is. That's how my life rolls."

So I said, "What are you gonna do, Fito?"

"Well, I've been saving my money to go to college. And I've

been working two jobs, so I guess I'm gonna use that money to find me a place to live. The thing about it is that I won't be eighteen until December and shit, which is, like, less than three weeks away. And who the hell is gonna rent to a minor? What? Like I'm gonna be on the streets for three weeks? And I'm not even gonna go near a social worker. Not goin' there. And hell, you think a guy like me is into adult supervision? I mean, I've lived without that all my fuckin' life. Shit, I don't have a clue as to what I'm gonna do. Does it look like I have a plan? This bench, that's my plan. I'm like one of those dogs that jump the fence. They go, like, *Ahh, freedom,* and then they look around all confused and shit because they don't have a plan."

Samantha Diaz had a look on her face. I knew that look.

She leaned into Fito and gave him a shove with her shoulder. "I have an idea," she said. "You and that dog may not have a plan, Fito. But I do . . ."

God, I loved her smile. She hadn't smiled like that in a while.

Sam. Awesome.

OKAY, WE CAN'T tell your dad."

"I don't like keeping secrets from him." Not that I wasn't keeping secrets.

"Well, we're not doing anything wrong."

"That's true. We're just not telling him what we're up to."

"We're not really up to anything. We're just helping our friend. Like that's a bad thing. I mean, adults always want us to be good people and do nice things for others and all that, right?"

"Yeah — well, yeah."

We were walking back toward the library after we'd eaten breakfast, and Sam and I had packed a lunch for Fito. Sam had made him promise to wait for us. He'd shrugged and said, "Like I got somewhere to go."

I looked at Sam as we walked. "You sure this is okay?"

"You are the most risk-averse person I have ever fucking met. *No bueno.*"

"*No bueno,* what?"

"You're a worrier. You're seventeen years old and you're a worrier."

"So what? It means I care."

"I care too. And look at me. Do I look worried?"

The discussion was so not fruitful. I shook my head.

"Look," she said, "just don't tell your dad. That's all you have to do. Just *do not* tell. That's not exactly trigonometry." She rolled her eyes.

I rolled mine.

"Look," she said. "Fito's our friend, right? So we can help him on our own. We don't always need permission to do the right thing. Or do we?"

Fito was sitting on his bench, reading a book in front of the library —kind of a normal sight. But it wasn't really normal, not if you knew the story. Maybe everything looked normal on the outside. On the inside, well, there was always some kind of hurricane spinning around.

So there was Fito, sitting on a bench and reading a book, looking all normal. He waved as he saw us walking toward him. Yeah, normal. "I went into the library and checked out a book. I also brushed my teeth and washed up in the bathroom." He didn't seem as upset as before. I guess he'd had lots of experience in dealing with bad things happening to him.

"You're sure it's okay that I stay in your old house?" he asked Sam after she told him her plan.

"Absolutely. No one lives there. We're going to put it up for sale. But my Aunt Lina said it needs some work. The house is just sitting there. All alone. Like you."

That made Fito smile. He didn't do a lot of smiling. Nope,

not a smiler. Not that he'd ever had much to smile about.

I handed Fito a lunch bag with a couple of sandwiches in it. "Hungry?"

He took the bag. "I'm always hungry." And he wolfed it down. That guy did not eat. That's not what he did. He wolfed.

There we were, me and Sam and Fito sitting in Sam's living room. Not that she lived there anymore. There were a lot of boxes around, most things all packed up, waiting to be moved. "You know," Sam said, "we almost moved everything out. We were going to put a lot of this stuff in storage, and then Lina said, 'What for? We can leave it here.'" She looked at Fito. "So now you have a place to stay. And we still have electricity and we still have water. Very cool. The heater doesn't work. It went haywire on us, and Mom didn't get around to fixing it. Poor Mom." Sam got this look on her face. "But we have lots of blankets. You won't freeze to death. And sorry, no TV and no Internet."

Fito just kind of shrugged. "Don't do TV. And you think I had Internet at my house?" He looked around and kept nodding. And then, I thought he was sort of going to start crying. He looked away, then put his head down — but he kept himself together. "Why are you guys bein' so nice to me?"

"Because we're such fucking nice people." That Sam. Her and that word. But she was the best. Maybe when she was old, she'd be all heart, like Mima. And everybody would love her. Well, maybe not. There was something wild in Sam. But that didn't mean she didn't have a heart. She had a heart, all right. A really good one.

We hung out with Fito most of the morning, listening to

vinyl records. Mostly Beatles stuff. Fito was really into *Abbey Road*. I wondered if we were pretending that everything was fine when it wasn't. I mean, getting thrown out of your own house was pretty drastic. And Sam and I had stuff going on in our heads and in our hearts. Just as I was watching Sam and Fito singing along with one of the songs, I remembered a dream I'd had the night before about Mima — how I couldn't find her — and I thought about the letter my mom left me and wondered what I was so afraid of. Risk averse. That's what Sam said I was. It was a nice way of saying I was afraid of trying new things. Maybe what it really meant was that I was a coward. Maybe I lost my temper with guys who acted like assholes because I wasn't brave enough to talk to them.

I felt a pillow hit my head. "What are you thinking over there?"

I smiled at Sam. "Ah, just stuff."

"I know," she said. "Let's order pizza, and Fito can tell us about his shitty childhood and I can tell you about what stage of grief I'm in today."

"Yup, yup," I said.

Fito looked at her — like *What?*

I texted Dad: Sam and I are hanging out with Fito. It wasn't a lie, but why did I have this thing in me that didn't feel all that good when I kept secrets? What was up with me anyway? I needed to stop analyzing myself. I didn't have the credentials to be my own therapist.

I swear, that Fito could eat. How'd he stay so skinny? He was like Sam. Good thing we ordered a large pizza. "Let's play a game." Sam was always making up games. And she always changed the rules and always said she could do that because, surprise, she was the one who'd invented the game.

"What game?" I said.

"What was the worst moment in your life? The only rule is that you have to be honest."

"Okay, but only if the next game is 'What was the best moment in your life?'"

"Okay, that's fair. If you have to have your optimism fix for the day, I'm good with that."

I could see Fito getting a kick out of the way Sam and I got along.

She looked at Fito. "You first."

"Why me? I'm the new guy in this group."

"Yup. Initiation."

"Well, actually, the worst moment in my life is my whole life."

"Wrong."

I laughed. "Sam's gonna be tough on you. She's like that. I can even tell you why she said *wrong*."

"All right, smart-ass, why did I say *wrong*?"

"Because it's not specific. There's no detail. If you don't get to relish in Fito's tragedy — if you can't do that — it's no fun."

"I don't do relish," Sam said.

"Yeah, you do."

"Oh, you think you know me so well."

"Point out where I was wrong."

She gave me one of her I-think-I-might-hate-you-at-this-very-moment smiles and turned her attention back to Fito. "We're waiting."

"My worst moment. I have a lot to pick from. Let's see, it would have to be when I was about five. Maybe I was six. So this guy came to our house. And he and my mom, they were doing something. Smoking something out of a pipe, and my mom and him, they start taking off their clothes and shit, and they're making out and shit, and I don't really know what the hell is going on and so I ask them. And the guy goes after me. I mean, he goes after me. I thought he was going to kill me. I remember running out of the house to get away. I spent the night hiding in the backyard. In the morning, I didn't go inside until I saw that his car was gone. I had dreams about that for a long time." He looked at Sam. "How'd I do?"

Sam leaned over and kissed him on the cheek. "I'm sorry," she whispered. "This is a stupid game."

But Fito smiled at her. "Not so fast. Your turn."

We all started laughing. And who cared if it was just whistling in the dark? "Okay," Sam said. "Mom left me alone once for a whole weekend. I was seven —"

I interrupted her. "Why didn't you come over? Or call or —"

"You and your dad were somewhere out of town. Some art show or something. And I was scared. Mom told me not to open the door for anyone and just leave it locked. She said she'd be back on Sunday morning. Anyway, I was sleeping that Saturday night, and I woke up. I heard a crash, and I knew someone had broken the window to the back bedroom where my mother slept. I didn't know what to do, so I ran out the front door."

She looked sad.

Fito wore this really kind expression. "And then what happened?"

"I ran to the Circle K up the street, the place where you're working now, and there was a police car parked there. And I saw two policemen in the store and they were paying for coffee. So I just went in and told them someone was breaking into my house. One of the policemen was super nice. 'Did you forget your shoes?' Anyway, I showed them where I lived, and we went inside, and someone had taken the television and some other stuff.

"And the policemen asked me where my mother was. I told them she was away on a family emergency, that my babysitter was here when I went to sleep, but when I heard the noise, she was gone."

"Why did you lie?"

"I didn't want my mother to get in trouble. I don't know what happened, but my Aunt Lina got involved, and she told my mother she was going to take me away from her. I remember that. It was scary. Really, really scary, and my mom never left me alone again. Well — not until I was, like, thirteen. But I spent a lot of weekends at your house, Sally."

"Why do you always call him Sally?"

I rolled my eyes and shook my head. "I think it's a control thing," I said.

That pissed Sam off. "A control thing? Really?"

"Yeah. If you get to name me, you get to tell me what to do."

"You shit. Maybe it's a sign of affection."

Wow. I had actually never thought of that. "My bad," I said.

"Yeah," Sam said, "your bad."

Fito, he was still thinking about Sam's story. He looked at her and said, "That sucks, that she left you alone."

"Yeah, well, my mother was a complicated woman. I used to hate her. Now I miss hating her." She shrugged. "That came out wrong."

"That came out perfectly," I said.

"Yeah, yeah. Your turn, Sally."

"Okay. I don't have horror stories like you guys. See, when you guys are all grown up, you're going to have all these stories about how you survived your childhood. Me, I won't have any of those stories."

And then, both Sam and Fito looked at me and it was as if they'd rehearsed, because they both blurted out at the same time, "Bullshit."

"Bullshit? Really?"

"You heard us," Sam said.

"Whatever," I said. "Let me see. I think the worst moment of my life was that night when you called from in front of Walgreens, Sammy. I was so scared. I thought someone had really, really hurt you. That was the worst moment of my life."

Sam leaned over and kissed me on the forehead. "You are the sweetest boy I have ever known. And — don't take this the wrong way, but maybe it's not such a bad thing that you're going through a crisis. You know, maybe it's a good thing."

"I'm going through a crisis?"

"You're an idiot. But *you are* the sweetest boy in the world."

"Yeah. Too bad you're straight." Fito was wearing this really great smile. I wondered how he could smile like that. His life was complicated, with a capital *C*. I guess all our lives were complicated. Even mine. Sam's mother was dead. Fito didn't have a place of his own. Mima was dying, and everything was changing. I felt as if I needed to do something to fix everything that was wrong with all the people I loved. But I couldn't fix anything. Not a damn thing.

Dad

WHEN SAM AND I got home, Dad was sitting at the kitchen table going through some recipes. "Thanksgiving," he said. "It's coming up on us. I think I'll bake the pies this year."

"Cool," I said. "We'll help you."

"Everyone will be in by Wednesday."

"You excited, Dad?"

"Yeah, I am. It'll be great to see Julian." My Uncle Julian was the oldest. My dad was the youngest, and there was that big age spread. Yet they were so close. Dad was wearing one of those nostalgia smiles. He looked at me and smirked. "Of course, they'll all spoil you."

"Well, it's not my fault I was the baby. Everybody was all grown up when I came along."

My dad laughed. "You were such a great kid, always laughing. When you were about four, you had a habit of exploring everyone's face with your small fingers. You used to run your hands across my face, and if I hadn't shaved, you'd run to the bathroom, get my razor, and hand it to me. For some reason, you hated an unshaved face."

I watched him as he went through his recipes. "What kind of pies are you gonna make, Dad?"

"Pumpkin. One apple pie for Julian. He doesn't like pumpkin. And maybe a couple of pecan pies. Your Aunt Evie loves pecan pies."

"And Mima?"

"Mima's like me. Traditional pumpkin pie."

"Me too," I said.

"Me too," Sam said. "Did you know I've never had a home-made Thanksgiving dinner?"

I looked at her. "What?"

"Don't look at me like that. I'm not an alien from Mars."

"What did you do on Thanksgiving?"

"My mom and I went to the Sun Bowl Parade — which always lasted forever — and we'd watch all the people, and then we'd go out to eat and to a movie. That was our Thanksgiving."

"That's awful," I said.

"I liked the parade and the movie. And you know, I didn't really care."

My dad shook his head. "Well, you're in for a treat."

"The best part of Thanksgiving is on Friday," I said.

Sam was wearing a question mark on her face.

"On Friday we make tamales," I said. "It's a tradition."

Samantha raised her arms, as if she were watching a soccer match and someone had scored a goal. "I'm totally going on Facebook with the tamale thing. For those haters out there who think I know absolutely nothing about being a Mexican."

Dad just grinned.

Me. Sam. Us Doing This.

I WAS LYING in bed. Alone. Maggie was into this taking-turns-sleeping-with-us thing. Sometimes she slept with me. Sometimes she slept with Sam. That dog was all about equality.

I got this idea in my head to make a book for Mima. Well, not a book exactly, but photos with captions on them. I guess I wanted to give her something before she died. Yeah, she was going to die. I hated that word.

I remembered a story my dad told me about Mima, how she'd come upon some thieves on their farm. The thieves were stealing all the sacks of dried red chile she'd worked so hard to harvest. Sacks of chile she'd sell to help support her family. And there they were, these two guys putting the sacks in their truck. She threatened to cut them down like the weeds they were, and she managed to keep them at bay with a hoe until Popo arrived. I loved that story. I tried to picture her as a strong woman, holding a hoe like a baseball player at bat. Protecting what she'd worked for. Protecting her children, who were lined up behind her. I remembered one of our teachers, talking to another teacher in the hallway, saying, "Today's kids don't know shit about what we've been through." Maybe she was right. But maybe she was wrong.

I saw I had a text from Sam: U think Fito's all right?

Me: It's like heaven for him. He lived in hell

Sam: Guess ur right

Me: U were great today

Sam: Y? B-cuz I let him stay in a house that's empty?

Me: U didn't have to do that

Sam: World doesn't need another homeless guy

Me: R we changing Sam?

Sam: Yup called growing up. I was behind. I'm trying to catch up to my hero

Me: ?

Sam: YOU, you idiot

Me: Awwwwww

Sam: No extra credit for being decent human beings. Isn't that what ur dad says?

Me: Yup. I think we should tell him about Fito

Sam: Thought about that. We'll tell him later. This is us. WE R DOING THIS. US. ME N U

Me: U rock

Sam: I m proud of us

Me: Me too

Sam: But we'll tell ur dad

A Father Thing

I CALLED SAM on her cell when I woke up. That was her alarm. Time to run. I changed into my running clothes and sat on my bed for a little while. Sometimes when you get up, you aren't really awake. But you aren't really asleep, either.

I made my way to the kitchen to drink a glass of water. That was the routine now. Drink water, go running, then drink coffee. Coffee tasted better after a run. Well, another glass of water, then the coffee.

Dad wasn't reading the paper. He was sketching something on his pad and drinking his coffee. I sat down. Then Sam walked into the kitchen. "Dad," I said, "we have something to tell you."

My dad got this look on his face.

"Relax, it's nothing bad," I said.

Sam sat down. "Mr. V, we've kidnapped Fito."

"What?"

"Well, we didn't really kidnap him." Then she launched into the whole story, every detail, about how we ran to the bridge and about how we found Fito sleeping on the bench in front of the library. I mean, she certainly didn't leave anything out. Well, she left out the worst-moment-in-our-lives thing.

My dad sat there looking at us as if he were watching a tennis match, his eyes moving from me to Sam to me to Sam. "Part of me says this isn't a very good idea —"

"Dad, he's going to be eighteen in December. That's, like, tomorrow."

"That doesn't mean he should be on his own."

"So what's the solution?"

"No use in calling social services. By the time they process him, he'll age out. They may not even bother." My dad sat there thinking. "So you didn't tell me yesterday because?"

Sam raised her hand. "We weren't sure. I mean, my motto is usually it's better to ask for forgiveness than ask for permission."

My dad put his hands over his face and busted out laughing. *"Ay, Samantha, que muchacha."*

"You know, Dad," I said, "we have to learn how to make decisions on our own. Without you watching over us. Remember that overprotective thing?"

Dad nodded. "God, you're sweet kids, you know that? You're helping a friend the best way you know how. That's a beautiful thing. But —"

I looked at my dad. "But?"

"There have to be rules. He can't have any girls over."

"He's gay, Dad, remember?"

"Oh yeah, I forgot." He grinned. "Well then, no boys. In fact, he can't have company. Just you two. He doesn't party and all that stuff, does he?"

"Dad, he works two jobs and studies. He wants to get into college."

Dad nodded. "He apparently has more ambition than you."

I had the *What?* thing on my face.

"No year off for you. You're going to college next year. And that's that."

My dad never said *That's that.* "Okay," I said.

"Okay," he said. "Go for your run. I'm going to pay Fito a visit."

"What for?"

"It's a father thing. That okay with you?"

My Dad, the Cat

Sam and I ran through the streets of Sunset Heights. Yeah, we were zigzagging through our neighborhood. Maybe that's what life was. You zigged and you zagged, and then you got up every morning and zigged and zagged some more.

Thanksgiving week. A big holiday for Mima.

I was making a list in my head of the things I was grateful for. I had talked to Mima on the phone the night before. She said she'd already made her list.

"Did I make the top ten?" I asked.

She laughed. I liked making her laugh. "Of course you did," she said. I wanted to tell her that she was first on my list. Well, maybe she was second. Dad was first. And Sam was third. Maybe it wasn't a good idea to rank the people in your life. That's not how the heart worked. The heart didn't make lists.

Sam and I sat on the front steps. We did that a lot after our morning runs. If we had time. Today we had time. On Sundays we always had time.

"Great run today," she said.

"Yeah," I said. "You're a great runner."

"You were slow today. That's because you were in your head."

"Yeah, I guess so."

"I'm happy today," she said. "You know something? I don't think I've been a very happy person most of my life."

I leaned in and nudged her. "Most of your life? You say that like you're an old lady. You're only seventeen."

"It's true, though. I think I liked being miserable."

"Yeah, you did."

"Are you making fun of me?"

"Yeah, I am."

I looked up and saw Dad coming up the sidewalk. "How was your visit with Fito?"

"He's a very fine young man."

"His life kind of sucks," I said.

"I get that. He's a survivor, though. Some people can survive just about anything." He started to go inside. "I'm going out back to have a cig. Why don't you guys hit the shower? We can take Fito grocery shopping."

Sam was wearing this giant smile. "Are you gonna adopt him too?"

My dad grinned. "Some people collect stamps. Me? I collect seventeen-year-old kids."

I asked Fito about his conversation with Dad.

"Your dad's cool. I never met a dad like yours. I like that cat."

"So what did you talk about?"

"He just wanted to make sure I was okay. He asked me about

my mom and shit. So I just basically laid it all out, told him how things rolled in our dysfunctional little household. And after I finished telling him all my shit, you know what your dad said?"

"What?"

"He said, 'Fito, I hope you know you deserve better than that. You do know that, don't you?' That's what he said. How cool is that?"

That sounded exactly like something my dad would say.

"Oh yeah, and he gave me some rules for living in the house."

"Rules?"

"Yeah. Like no one else allowed in the house. Just me. Well, you and Sam, you're cool. But no one else. Believe me, I'm down with that. Don't want strays eyeing things in Sam's house. It's called respect. I'm down."

"Any other rules?"

"Yeah. I have to quit one of my jobs. I'm down with that, too. I'm tired. I'm really tired. He said I should just work my weekend job and stick with the school thing. Graduate, go to college, and try to have some fun. That's what he said. Have some fun. Like I know what that is."

"Is that word even in your vocabulary?"

"Nope."

"Sam will teach you how to spell it."

"And one more rule he gave me. Your dad's all about rules."

That made me laugh.

"It's not like I'm bitching about your dad. Look, nobody ever cared enough about me to give me a rule. Your dad said I needed to stop spending so much time alone. I don't know how he knew that. He said I'm isolated. Isolated? Is that a verb?"

"Yeah, it is," I said.

"Your dad, man oh man, he shoulda been a counselor. Anyway, I got an invite to eat at your house anytime I want. A standing invitation."

His smile was breaking my heart.

Hanging Out

SO SAM TEXTED Fito and told him to come over and have some soup. I texted him too: Got homework?

Fito: Yup math and shit

Me: Bring it with

Fito: Damn straight

And then, guess who knocked on the door? Marcos. "Came over for some soup?" I asked.

"Yeah, I guess that was the idea."

Dad was in the kitchen slicing some bread.

Sam was sitting on the couch, texting.

She waved at Marcos. I was hoping she'd be nice.

I was surprised when Marcos sat in my dad's chair. "Can I talk to you two for a sec?"

Sam, boy, she perked right up. She even set her phone down on the coffee table.

"Talk," she said. "We're listening."

He looked a little uncomfortable. "I'm getting this vibe that you don't —" He stopped, trying to find the words, so I thought I'd help the poor guy out.

"We're okay, Marcos." I knew I didn't mean it — but I wanted to mean it.

Sam nodded. "Yeah, we're good." She didn't sound all that convincing.

Marcos smiled. "I'm an idiot — you know that, don't you?"

Sam smiled back at him. "Yeah, I get that vibe from you." But it didn't come out mean or snarky, the way she said that. Well, a little snarky, but a little sweet too. She was trying.

Marcos looked at me and nodded. "Five years ago I left your dad. It was the biggest mistake of my life. I wanted you to know that. I wanted you to know that I hurt him once. You have no idea how much I regret that hurt. For the last five years, not a day has gone by when I didn't think of Vicente. Not one day."

Sam and I were just looking at each other. Marcos smiled at us. "You two are a pair, aren't you?"

"Yeah, we are," I said.

My father walked into the living room. Sometimes when Mima saw me, her face would glow. Sometimes. Because she loved me so much. That's how my dad looked now.

Sam and I sat there looking at each other. Marcos and Dad walked toward the kitchen. And then Sam said, "Sometimes adults can be very cool."

Marcos and Dad looked at her, and she flashed them a smile. "I said *sometimes*."

Sam was washing the dishes. She'd come a long way with stuff like that. The first time she cleaned the bathroom, I swear the people in Juarez could hear her bitching. But now it was a normal thing with her.

Marcos was an engineer, so he was helping Fito with his math. I heard him explaining the concepts. I should've probably been paying attention, but I was so *not* about math. Nope.

Dad was sitting in his chair writing something on a yellow legal pad. Sam came into the living room. I watched her as she walked over to him and kissed him on the cheek. He smiled at her. "What was that for?"

"Just because," she said.

And I heard myself saying, "Oh, now we're into *just because* kisses."

"Yeah. And you're so not getting one."

I thought about how we all sat down tonight to eat my dad's soup — Dad and Marcos and Fito and Sam and me. We'd played a game, the one we didn't finish at Sam's house, the what's-the-best-moment-in-my-life game.

Dad said the best moment in his life was the day I was born. "An emergency C-section. Your mother couldn't hold you. I was the lucky guy. God, did you belt out a cry. Yeah, that was the most beautiful moment in my life."

Marcos said the best moment in his life was the day he met my father. I thought that was a brave thing to say, but I also think it was the truth. Yeah, being brave and telling the truth went together. Whatever happened between them in the past, well, it was in the past. I know I was trying to find all the faults in the guy, but I wasn't getting very far.

And Sam? The best moment in her life? "Well," she said, "the day I came to live here. That was the best moment in my life. Even though I came to live here because my mom died, I feel safe. This feels like home."

And Fito said, "Hell, you know, this is the best moment in my life. This moment. Right now."

I thought Sam was going to cry — but she didn't.

And me? I said the best moment in my life was the day it rained yellow leaves, and I told them all about that afternoon with Mima. I had never told anyone about that. No one. "I don't think Mima even remembers. But I do."

Dad smiled. "Maybe I'll paint that." Yeah, I could see that painting in my head.

For the longest time our house had belonged to me and Dad. It was just the two of us. And life was good — simple and uncomplicated. Or maybe that's the way I saw it. If I stopped to think about it, the whole thing hadn't been that uncomplicated — not for Dad. I remembered him telling me that love was infinite. *Infinity,* that isn't like the *pi* thing in math. Or maybe it is. Love has no end — it just goes on and on.

It was a nice evening. A beautiful evening, really. Yeah, Mima was still dying and Sam's mom was still dead and Fito was living in exile from his family, and I still wasn't dealing with the stupid essay I needed to write to get into college, and I was still staying away from reading my mother's letter, as if it had a snake in it or something. Still, it was a nice evening. Even if I was trying to figure out if Marcos was for real or if he was just playing it all up so he could get my dad back.

Me. Fito. Sam.

ON THE WEDNESDAY before Thanksgiving, Dad said, "Did you invite Fito over for Thanksgiving dinner at Mima's?"

"No," I said.

"No?" He looked at me as if I'd committed a crime. He shook his head. "What are you waiting for?"

I felt bad. I mean, yeah, I felt bad. Shit. Another little slip.

So Sam and I picked Fito up. We always said that. *We'll pick you up.* We weren't really picking him up. I mean, we walked to school. But Sam's house was on the way, and I had always stopped by and we'd go to school.

Fito was waiting for us outside, and Sam and I waved. "Hey."

Fito waved. "Hey." And then Fito said he had had a bad dream.

"Bad dreams suck," Sam said.

"Yeah. I have lots of them."

We walked along, and I asked Fito, "So what are you doing for Thanksgiving?"

"Well, this guy Ernie, he wants me to work for him at the K. So I'm probably gonna work."

"Tell him no," I said. "Tell him you have plans."

"But I don't."

"You do now. You're spending it with us."

"Nah," he says. "No can do. *No bueno.*"

"*No bueno?* What's wrong with you?"

"You know, you and Sam, you show up and you're kind of like these fuckin' angels and you're all, like, sweet and stuff and nice and shit, and I'm this guy who's all messed up. I mean, what have I got? I gotta get my stuff together. I mean, why do you guys keep hanging out with me? I got nothin' to offer."

Sam got a fierce look on her face. "Oh, you think we just feel sorry for you. Is that it? You're full of shit, you know that, Fito? Maybe when Sally looks at you, he thinks you're worth something. Maybe when I look at you, maybe I think you're worth something too. Just because you don't like yourself doesn't mean other people don't like you. And if you ever say you don't have anything to offer in my presence — if you ever say that again — then I'm going to kick your ass from here to Michoacán."

"Michoacán?" I said. And then we got all goofy and laughing. And then Fito sort of hung his head and he was blinking his eyes, like he was trying to blink away all the tears that he'd held inside all his life. "I'm just, you know, I'm just not used to people being so nice to me."

Sam leaned over and kissed him on the cheek. "Well, get used to it, Fito."

And then we walked. Three friends walking to school. Fito was smiling, and Sam was smiling. And I was smiling. And I looked at her and whispered, "I like who you're becoming."

291

Sam. Eddie. Me.

I THOUGHT IT WAS going to be a perfect day, that Wednesday before Thanksgiving.

But it didn't turn out that way. Not perfect. *No bueno.* To begin with, no one wanted to be in school. You could feel it in the hallways. It felt like we were fire ants going crazy on a busy anthill. Or something like that. Sam would have laughed at me if she had been listening in on my thoughts. I was okay with words, but let's just say I wasn't going to grow up to be a writer.

What was I going to be? Maybe a boxer. Ha. Ha.

I decided I was going to wait out the day.

During lunch I went outside to get some air. I needed to breathe. Malaise. That's what I was feeling. Malaise.

But just as I stepped outside, I saw Sam lost in a conversation with Eddie.

Really? She was talking to Eddie? It made me crazy to see them talking to each other as if nothing had happened.

They didn't even notice when I walked up to them.

"Sam," I said, "what in the hell are you doing?"

"I'm talking to Eddie," she said softly. "And why are you yelling at me?"

"Because you're talking to a guy who tried to hurt you."

"Sally —"

I didn't let her finish. "Sam, just walk away right now. Just walk back inside."

That's when Eddie decided to step into the conversation, "Look, Sal, we were just —"

"Say another word and I'll beat the holy crap out of you, you son of a bitch."

That's when I felt Sam's slap.

She slapped me so hard I fell back.

And then we just looked at each other.

"Who are you?" she whispered. "Who are you, Sally? Who are you?"

The rest of the day I could feel my cheek still burning.

Part Five

Highways are nice and paved, and they have signs telling you which way to go. Life isn't like that at all.

Sam. Learning to Talk. Me.

I WAITED FOR SAM at her locker after school. I was scared, and I didn't know what was happening between us. Things had never been this way, and I had this awful feeling in my gut. I saw her walking toward me, but she pretended not to see me. She completely ignored me as she opened her locker, pulled out a couple of books, and then slammed it shut.

"I'm not talking to you," she said.

I had to say something. Anything. "I'm the one that got slapped in the face."

"Maybe you needed it."

"You were talking to Eddie. He hurt you. What the hell's wrong with you?"

"He was apologizing, you stupid shit. I was handling my own shit just fine, Sally."

"Oh," I said. God, there was this thing inside me, this thing that said I really was a stupid shit. I felt like an asshole. I mean, I wanted to hide somewhere, but there was no hiding. "Oh," I said again.

"'Oh.' That's what you have to say? That's articulate."

"I'm sorry, Sam. I really am." God, I sounded stupid.

"I don't get you lately. You used to be really sweet."

"Maybe I wasn't."

"Yes, you *were*. But now you're so inconsistent."

"Well, you're like that sometimes."

"But you're not me, Sally. And you *did* deserve that slap." And then she smiled. "I see what you mean about hitting people. Sometimes it feels good."

"I thought you weren't talking to me."

"Well, we're going to have to figure some things out, aren't we, Sally?"

I nodded. I don't know. I didn't feel like using any words. I didn't. But she was talking to me and maybe there was this little crack in what we had. We weren't broken, though. And that was good. That we weren't broken. I wanted to hug her, but I had the feeling that Sam wasn't quite ready for a hug.

Thanksgiving

WHEN FITO HANDED Mima the flowers he'd brought her, Mima's face really lit up. "Beautiful," she whispered. Sometimes Mima looked like a little girl. Even now. Innocent. And Fito, his face was all red, and he just wanted to find someplace to hide. I mean, that guy was super shy.

Aunt Evie took the flowers and put them in a vase. She looked at Fito and said, "So sweet, Fito."

"Sweet? Not," Fito whispered.

Mima put her hand on Fito's cheek. "You're too skinny. You need to eat."

"I eat."

"Well, you have to eat more."

"Mima," I said, "he eats all the time."

Mima nodded. "When he gets old, he'll be fat. Just like Popo. Popo was skinny too. But then he married me." Her laugh was as fragile as the leaves she had raked when I was five.

Everyone was busy doing something in Mima's kitchen. All the voices seemed to mix together, the voices of my uncles and aunts and some of my older cousins who had made it back home for a few days, Sam's voice, Fito's voice. And Mima's voice. Her fading voice was the one I heard the loudest.

I asked my dad for the keys to the car. I needed cough drops and knew some were stashed in there. I wasn't feeling so hot, and I was afraid I was catching a cold, which was bad news because when I caught a cold, I *caught a cold*. Bad news. *No bueno*. My throat was beginning to swell. I knew what that meant, and I was thinking, *Shit shit shit!* As I walked to the car, I heard my Uncle Tony and my Aunt Evie talking as they sat on the front porch. I *had* become a chronic eavesdropper. "It's the old girl's last Thanksgiving, Evie."

"Don't talk like that, Tony."

"What do you want me to say?"

"We're going to miss that woman. She's something special."

"Yeah, Evie. We're all gonna miss her. We really have to make ourselves strong."

"I know, Tony."

"We can do this, Evie."

"Well, we don't have a choice, do we?" Aunt Evie was quiet for a little while, and then she said, "You know what I think? I think Mickey's gonna take it the hardest."

"Maybe so," Uncle Tony said. "But I think Vicente's gonna take it the hardest. Only he won't show it."

And then I heard Aunt Evie say, "Actually, I think Salvador's gonna take it the hardest. He and Mom have something special. I still remember the day Vicente brought him over for the first time. Mom fell in love with that boy the minute she took him in her arms. It's beautiful to watch them together. I think the kid's gonna be devastated."

Then I heard Uncle Tony say, "Maybe so, Evie. Maybe so."

I told myself not to think too much about that conversation and just enjoy the beauty of the family I was so lucky to have. If it was going to be Mima's last Thanksgiving, I was going to make the best of it.

I walked past the front porch from the side of the house where I'd been listening. I waved at my uncle and aunt as I went to the car and found the cough drops on the driver's side. Dad kept them for what was becoming a smoker's cough. *No bueno*. I popped one in my mouth, then walked toward the front porch. I smiled at Aunt Evie and hugged her.

Uncle Tony slapped me on the back. "You're a good kid."

I made a joke. "Not that you'd know."

"Don't be a smart-ass."

We were making pies. Well, I wasn't doing any making. It was really just my dad. And Uncle Julian. They're, like, this team. They look alike. I sat next to Mima as Dad rolled out the dough.

Mima nodded. "I showed him," she said.

She was calm.

Then Mima said to me, "We should make the corn bread." Yeah, the corn bread. Mima's stuffing was to die for. So I got the ingredients and made room for myself on the kitchen table. I took out a big mixing bowl. We always tripled the recipe. Making the corn bread with Mima was my thing. Our little tradition.

I watched her hands as they worked the batter over with a wooden spoon. I wanted to kiss them.

"Did we add the sugar?" Mima asked.

I nodded.

She winked at me.

Then my dad's cell phone rang. He looked at his caller ID and answered. As he listened to the voice on the other end, he was wearing this really great smile and I knew it was Marcos. Mima was right. She said Dad was sad. No, he hadn't been sad. He'd just been a little lonely — she'd said that, too. He noticed that I was watching him, and I just smiled at him. Like I knew something. And he just smiled back — like he knew that I knew something.

I wondered if Mima knew about Marcos. I wondered what she thought about all that. Maybe it just didn't matter to her. She loved my dad. And all the other complicated stuff, well, maybe it just didn't matter to Mima.

Sam. Talk. Fito. Talk. Me. Talk.

SOMEWHERE BETWEEN MAKING the corn bread and talking to my Uncle Julian, I started feeling a little worse. My muscles ached, and I kept trying to ignore what was going on in my body.

Then Uncle Mickey walked into the kitchen smelling like smoke — not cigarette smoke, but smoke like he'd been camping. "Time to put the turkeys in," he said. I knew what that meant, but Sam and Fito didn't. So I dragged them to my uncle's house, two blocks away. Uncle Mickey dug a big hole in his backyard every year, put all kinds of seasoning on two turkeys, wrapped them in foil, and then wrapped them in gunnysacks that he'd soaked in water for two hours. Then he dropped them into the hole, which was full of red-hot wood — homemade charcoal.

I took Sam and Fito to Uncle Mickey's, and they watched the whole ritual of wrapping the turkeys, dropping them into the hole, and covering it.

Fito was like, *Wow!* And Sam was like, *Wow!* And Uncle Mickey handed Fito and me and Sam each a beer. I noticed that Sam passed on the beer, which made me smile. I thought of the two bottles of wine we'd downed, and I sort of just shook my head.

My Uncle Mickey talked about the whole cooking-in-the-ground thing. And Fito kept saying, "Man, I am totally a city kind of Mexican."

Fito liked the beer thing, but I wasn't into mine and I was beginning to feel not so great. Still, Thanksgiving had to go on.

Fito and Uncle Mickey were talking, well, hell, they were talking turkey. Seriously. "In the morning I'll take those babies out, and it's gonna be the best turkey you'll ever taste."

"You're going to sleep with the boys?" My Aunt Evie had this look on her face.

"Sure I am. Sally and I have had slumber parties since forever."

"Still calling him Sally, huh?"

"Yup. I'm gonna call him that till he grows up."

Aunt Evie laughed. "And there's no monkey business?"

"Monkey business?" That made Sam laugh. "With Sally? With Fito? Monkeys is right. Nope. Not into monkeys."

Aunt Evie shook her head and smiled as she handed us some extra pillows.

Sam got the bed. Of course she did. She was wearing her stupid Chihuahuas T-shirt. Maggie jumped up on the bed with her. Of course she did. If Maggie had the choice between the bed and the floor, Maggie always took the bed.

Fito and I were on the floor.

Sam was looking for some music on her laptop.

Fito was reading a text.

I was lying there thinking about things. And feeling not so

great. I was feeling like I wanted to cry. Maybe it was because I was feeling bad, and it made me feel like a vulnerable little boy, and I didn't like that.

Then Fito said, "Wish that Angel would stop texting me."

"He's cute," Sam said.

"Yeah, well, he acts like a girl."

Sam shot him a look. "What's wrong with that?"

Fito had this I-really-stepped-in-it look on his face. "He wants me to buy him stuff. He be like, *What are you gonna buy me?* What is that? It's like I have to buy him stuff to prove that I like him."

"That sucks," I said.

Sam rolled her eyes. "Well, I used to do that too."

"What's that about?"

Sam was all Ms. Expert. "He's just insecure. No matter what you buy him, he's not going to believe you really like him. Get rid of him."

"Yeah. I told him I didn't have time for that crap. He said, 'Oh, now you be all about your straight friends.'"

"That would be Sam and me?"

"Yup," he said. "I don't know. I don't know shit about love. And even though I'm gay, I don't know shit about being gay."

I laughed. "Well, I'm no expert on love either."

"That's for sure," Sam said.

"Oh," I said, "and how did all those bad boys work out for you?"

"At least I put myself out there. What about you, Sally?"

"I had a few girlfriends."

"Not one date this year."

"I've been busy."

"Whatever," Sam said.

"Well, all the girls think I'm secretly in love with you."

"Yeah, well girls can be such —"

"Don't say the B word, Sammy. Just don't say it."

"Consider it said."

"Dating sucks," Fito said. "Sam, remember that guy Pablo you were hanging with last year?"

"Yeah? Nice tats."

"Yeah, well, he's gay."

"He's gay? For reals? You sure?"

"Yup. We got drunk one night. Man, that guy can kiss."

"Wow," I said.

"Wow," Sam said. "So what happened?" She always wanted to know the sordid details. Sometimes I wanted to tell her to just use her imagination.

"Not much," Fito said. "I mean, he goes, like, 'Let's have a couple of beers.' I could tell he'd already had a few. He parked the car downtown, and we go walking around after we'd drunk our beers, and I thought the guy was gonna rip my clothes off and shit. We were, like, in some alley, and then he got this text and he said he had to take off. He gave me his number, and so the next day I call him on his cell, and he's, like, pretending nothing happened. 'I was just drunk and shit.' That's what he says. Yeah, right, I say. And he goes whatever. And then I just say, 'Laters, dude.' So that's what went down."

Sam said, "He's a selfish asshole, anyway. Thank God this high school crap is almost over. When you're older, Fito, do you ever want to get married?"

"I don't know. I got a lot of things to think about. I just want

305

to get myself into college and shit. Make something of myself. Screwing around with some guy? Don't know about that."

"I get that," Sam said. "But you know, after you graduate and have a job and all that. Would you like to get married?"

He looked over at me. "Yeah, I guess, maybe. I'm kinda used to the alone thing. But why not? I think I'd like to marry someone like your Mr. V. Or someone like Marcos. You know, someone decent. Someone who resembles a human being. I think a lot of gay guys are like *I be a girl,* or they're the opposite and they're like *I be an animal* and shit like that. Why can't they be like *I'm just a guy*?"

I don't know why, but that made me and Sam laugh.

And Fito kept saying, "It's not that funny."

And Sam said, "Maybe we're laughing because the truth is funny."

"Yeah, hilarious. Yup, yup." Then Fito turned to me and asked, "What about you, Sal?"

Sam answered for me. "He wants to have four kids."

"That's cool. Not me. I don't want little Fitos crawling around in the world. Bad idea. And anyway, I'm gay. Maybe that's a good thing. I got a nasty gene pool."

"Beating up on yourself. That your hobby?" Sam could lecture you by just asking a question.

"My hobby is trying to get by. I went to a counselor once. He told me I lived my life in survival mode. I smiled at him. But I was thinking, *No shit.*"

"Well, you know, maybe someday you'll want to adopt a kid who's in survival mode."

"Don't think so. It would be like living my shitty childhood all over again. But you, Sal, I kinda see you doin' something like that. I'm not like you or your dad. Your dad, when he came over to talk to me at Sam's place, I'm like, *Who is this dude?* I'm like, *There are fathers like this in the universe?* Really? Your dad, he's like this fuckin' saint. I bet guys are trippin' all over theirselves to get at your dad."

That made me laugh. "I don't think my dad's into that scene."

"Well, that Marcos guy, I like that cat. Looks like they have something going there."

And out of nowhere, I started to cry. I don't know, maybe I was getting a fever. Hell, I don't know, I just started to cry.

I heard Sam say, "Aww, Sally, you're crying."

I felt sick and hollow, as if there was nothing inside me, and I heard myself saying, "My Mima. My Mima's gonna die."

And then I felt Sam's arms around me, and she was whispering, "Shhh. I gotcha. I gotcha, Sally."

Church

It was a gift. For Mima. Everybody went to Thanksgiving Mass. And everybody got dressed up. We all knew Mima didn't go for the dressed-down thing at Mass — the I'm-dressed-like-I'm-going-to-a-football-game look. Dad and I and Fito wore ties. Mima loved that. She was so, so happy. We took pictures so we could put them on the computer for her to look at.

I felt awful.

I had cotton head. I kept blowing my nose, and everything around me sounded dull and fell on my ears with a kind of thud.

My muscles ached. Everything ached. But I kept smiling.

Fito was a little freaked out. "I don't really do the church thing," he said.

Sam said, "It won't kill you."

"See, you guys really are, like, these angels." That's what he said.

Sam, she just looked at him, and said, "Knock it off with that angel stuff. I'm not an angel. I don't even want to be one. That's not what I'm going for."

I didn't make it through Mass. Right around Communion time I was projectile vomiting in the men's room.

Not Fair. Not Fair?

REALLY? WHO GETS the flu at Thanksgiving? God, I was sick.

I missed everything.

And the worst part was that I cried like a ten-year-old boy. But the best part was that Mima sat next to me on my bed.

"Aren't you afraid I'll get you sick?"

Mima smiled. "I'm already sick."

Then I started crying, and I felt really far away from myself. I had a fever, and I kept telling Mima I was sorry I got sick. She took my hand and held it, and she put a cold washcloth on my forehead. "For the fever," she said.

"Why are you taking care of me, Mima? You're sick."

"Because I want to," she whispered.

"I like holding your hand," I whispered back. It's weird, the honest things you say when you're sick. "I want you to stay with me forever."

"I'll always be with you," she whispered.

"I don't want you to be sick."

"Don't worry," she whispered. "I won't be sad. I don't want you to be sad either."

"Okay," I said. "I won't be." I didn't mean it, but I thought it would make her happy. I fell asleep with Mima holding my hand.

I had bad dreams, but at least I slept. I slept and slept and slept.

I remember Sam and Fito standing over me. And I remember saying, "I'm not a puppy."

I got up from bed on Saturday. It was around noon. And I was really hungry. I mean, I was like Fito-hungry.

The tamales were all made. I missed the tamale-making thing and the everybody-telling-stories thing. I missed all the cussing and all the laughing.

I was sad.

I wasn't allowed to eat tamales. Turkey soup. Yup. I sat in the kitchen and felt sorry for myself eating turkey soup.

I took a shower and changed and felt a little better. You know, I kind of felt like a T-shirt that had been spinning in the dryer for way too long. I was sitting in front of the Christmas tree with Sam and Fito.

"Crap," I said. "I missed everything. I always help Mima put the lights on her tree the day after Thanksgiving. Always. Since I was, like, four. It's not fair."

Sam looked at me. "Enough with the drama. That's my job. You're supposed to be all chilled."

"*Not fair* does not qualify as drama."

Fito kinda stared me down. "You don't know shit about *not fair*."

I wasn't about to argue with him on the fairness thing. "How are this year's tamales?"

310

"Man," Fito said. "Your peeps are all about tamales. That's what I'm talkin' about. They know how to do it right."

Sam laughed. "Like you'd know."

"Well, I know how to eat 'em."

"Right." Sam was shaking her head. "He ate, like, about twelve. And Mima couldn't stop laughing. She asked Fito, 'Don't they feed you?' And Fito started blushing."

"See?" I said. "I missed it all."

"Ahh, watching Fito wolf down twelve tamales? I'd say you didn't miss all that much."

Fito got real quiet. "You got a nice family, Sal. Super nice, you know. Sweet. And Sam here, she got way into making those tamales. You should have seen her. She was like a real Mexican."

"I am a real Mexican."

Fito shook his head. "Don't think so. All three of us put together don't make one real Mexican."

I guess he was right.

Then Sam said, "And all three of us put together don't make one real American."

Fito cracked up laughing. "Well, *gringo* over here had a good chance at being a real American. Only he wound up in the wrong family."

"Yeah," I said. "Looks like I lucked out."

"You bet your ass. And they all had lots of good things to say about you, *vato*. Like you walked on water and shit."

That made me smile. That really made me smile. Sitting there talking to Sam and Fito. Well, I stopped feeling sorry for myself.

Walked on water. Right. More like, learn to swim, baby. Learn to swim.

Mima. Tired.

On Sunday morning I was really in the mood to eat tamales. Dad said it was a bad idea. "I'm hungry," I said. "Enough with the turkey soup. *No bueno.*"

He shook his head. "*No bueno, no bueno.* Where do you get that? Have some leftover turkey and mashed potatoes."

No tamales for me. *Crap.*

Sam sat across from me at Mima's kitchen table — two warm tamales on her plate. I just looked at her and said, "Sam, sometimes you're not a very nice person."

"I'm not the one who's sick."

"Perverse. You're perverse."

"I like it when you exhibit your erudite vocabulary."

"I'm going to walk to the other room."

"You're pouting."

"Yup."

Mima was too tired to go to Mass. Nobody had to tell me that was a bad sign.

Mima

On Sunday afternoon Mima was sitting at the table, looking around her kitchen. I sat down across from her. "It was a beautiful Thanksgiving," she said.

I nodded. I wanted to say something, but I didn't know what. Then I just blurted out, "I've been getting into a lot of fights lately."

She nodded. "I understand," she said.

"I don't."

"Sometimes that happens to boys."

"I don't mean to. I mean, I don't know. Something is mad inside me."

She nodded again. "You're a good boy."

"I'm not, Mima."

She smiled at me. "Listen to your Mima," she whispered. "When you start to become a man, things start happening inside you. Maybe you think you need to be perfect. If you think of that word, don't listen to it."

She got up from the table and put her arms around me.

"I'm sad."

"You won't always be sad," she said. She kissed me on the forehead. Then she let me go.

Leftovers. Lectures.

AT LEAST WE'RE taking home a stash of tamales and leftovers," I said. I was sitting in the back seat with Fito. Sam was riding shotgun. "Hey, I didn't get any pie!"

That made Sam, Dad, and Fito laugh. I have no idea why they found that funny. Hilarious. Yeah.

"I'll make you a pumpkin pie this week," Dad said.

"I'm not going to share."

"You're a funny guy sometimes, you know that, Salvador?"

"Yup."

"You guys want a real tree this year?"

"No. I like the fake one," I said.

"I like real," Sam said.

"Okay," I said. "Then you get to water it every day, put ice cubes in the tree stand every evening, and sweep up the needles every morning."

"Ahh," she said. "So the Grinch in you comes out."

"I'm just saying, Sam."

"And have you finished your essays?" Dad wasn't laying off on the college apps. He'd been leaving Post-it notes on our doors for two weeks.

"I'm turning it in on Tuesday. Then it's all done." Sam was proud of herself.

"I have a sort of draft," I said.

"No bueno," Dad said. "Finish it off. December first."

"That's only a few days away."

"Yup."

"I hate that essay thing," I said.

"December first."

"I like you a lot better when you don't lecture, Dad. I mean, not that you do a lot of that. But right now you're all schoolteacher about this."

I could tell Dad had this snarky look on his face. "December first," he repeated.

Sam texted me: I'll help u

I texted back: My essay. I'll do it

Sam: ☹

I looked over at Fito. Maggie had her head on Fito's lap, and he was asleep.

I texted Sam: Take a picture. U have better view

She turned around, smiled, and took a couple of pics. She texted them to me: Sweet

Me: Sweet, sweet, sweet

Then Dad said, "Why do you two text when you're sitting a foot away from each other?"

"We're discussing my essay," I said.

"Sure you are. Don't fib to your father."

By Me

DAD SAID I should take a day to get my strength back. He didn't want any relapses. By now Sam and Fito were on their way to school, and I felt a little left out. Before Sam left, I was lying in bed, and she texted me: Wftd = lethargy.

Me: Yup. Emotional lethargy

Sam: Idiot. There isn't any other kind

Me: Leave me alone

Sam: WRITE UR ESSAY

Maggie was lying right beside me. I kissed her, and she started licking my face. Then she yawned and nudged herself against me.

I fell back asleep.

I woke up around noon, still groggy, walked into the kitchen, and grabbed some orange juice. Dad was teaching all afternoon, and he'd left a note: "Salvie, be patient with yourself." I thought, *Does that mean I should take a long, hot shower?* Hmm. That's what I did.

Then I sat in front of my laptop at the kitchen table. Kitchens reminded me of my Mima. *Okay, I'm going to write my essay.* That's what I told myself.

I was trying to focus, but my mind was wandering. I felt like a piece of paper in the wind being blown this way and that way and wanting only to land on the ground, but the wind had other ideas.

I thought of Mima. When we were leaving her house, even though she looked more frail and weak than she'd ever looked before, she came outside to see us off. She'd always done that. Aunt Evie had to help her. I hugged her, and she looked at me and smiled. "Just remember," she said.

I wasn't sure what she wanted me to remember.

Then she pointed at my father, who was putting something in the car. "Him," she said. Then she nodded.

Mima. No despair. She was dying, and there was not one sign of despair in her dancing eyes.

There I was, the piece of paper being blown in the air, trying to hit the damned ground.

I have to do this.

Fito had said he was glad he didn't have to write an essay. "All I have to do is make good grades here at UTEP and then transfer to UT. No essays for me. And anyway, what the hell would I say? My father was a good guy who had to leave because my mom is a drug addict who likes to yell and my brothers took after her. I guess I could tell them that I spent about a year waiting for my old man to come back and get me, but then I said, Yeah, like that's gonna happen. That about sums up my life." That Fito. Dad said he was a walking miracle. See, it was so much easier for me to be thinking about everything besides my essay.

Sam had given me the opening lines to *her* essay, which she was putting the final touches on: "My mother used to leave me messages written in lipstick. She'd write them on my bathroom mirror, and when I was a girl, I would study each letter of every word." I mean, she was already accepted.

I looked at what I had so far. "I don't really know that I want to go to Columbia University. I don't really believe that I'd measure up to your other applicants. That's the truth." *No bueno*.

The problem was that I didn't have special gifts or anything like that. And apart from the fact that I seemed to be going through a phase that was confusing the hell out of me — which was at least interesting — I didn't think I had a particularly compelling reason why any expensive university should accept me. Yeah, my dad had gone to Columbia — but he is gifted. Maybe if he'd been my bio father, I'd be gifted too. But I wasn't. I was applying to Columbia because? Because I was sentimental. Maybe my fists weren't, but I was. Columbia. Yeah. For Dad.

I took a deep breath. If Mima was dying and she wasn't despairing, and if Sam could write her essay even though she was still reeling from her mother's death, what the fuck was my problem? Maybe I was ambivalent about college. *Ambivalent*. A Sam word. Yeah, I was ambivalent. Maybe I was going through a phase. And maybe phases were important. Maybe phases told us something important about ourselves.

I texted Sam: Wftd = ambivalent.

I turned off my phone.

I wrote the first sentence of my essay. I looked at it. And then I started writing some more. I wrote and wrote and wrote.

When I glanced up at the clock, it was 2:30. My essay was finished. I read it aloud. I made a few changes. I wasn't so sure it would get me into college, but I thought, *Mima would like it*. So what if she wasn't on the admissions committee?

Friday

WELL, WE DIDN'T quite get to the Christmas tree during the week.

We got busy with school. At least I'd finished my essay — though I hadn't gotten around to telling anyone I was done. But there was still that other letter waiting to be read. Is that what my dad meant when he said *Be patient with yourself*? Sometimes you put things off. And you get addicted to putting things off. That's stupid, I know. And then the thing you put off seems overwhelming.

Sam texted me: Wftd = stasis.

Me: Stasis?

Sam: As in not moving. As in you have a letter from your mom

As in finish your essay. As in NO MOVEMNT

Me: Thanks for lecture

Sam: Ur welcome

I was going to tell her that my essay was done — but she'd just want to read it, and I didn't want anyone to read it. Nope.

After Fito quit his second job, he came over most nights and we all sat and studied together. He said it was weird not to work all the time. He went to visit his mom. "She was high as a kite," he said. "She looked at me with her dead eyes and said, 'You got any money?' So I just walked out the door."

"Why'd you go back?" I asked.

"She's my mother."

Sam put in her two cents. "She's toxic. You do know that, don't you?"

"Yeah," Fito said. "Doesn't change the fact that she's my mother."

"I know," Sam whispered. "I know, Fito."

We left the conversation at that. I mean, there was nothing any of us could do. Dad said there came a time when we had to be in charge of our own lives. I guess that time came a little early for Fito. Dad also said that sometimes things happen that are bigger than we are, because life is bigger than we are. Like Mima dying. Like Sylvia getting killed in a car accident. Like Fito's mom. Like my mom, who died when I was three.

Our kitchen table at night was like a study hall. We asked each other questions sometimes and helped each other out, and Fito said, "I died and went to fuckin' heaven." That's a quote. Fito, he liked the F word. But he also liked to read. Sam said he had a heart as big as the sky. And it was true.

Fito said he learned how to escape from the hell around him by reading all the time. He said he liked *The Grapes of Wrath* because "it's about poor people. That's way cool."

I thought Fito and Mima would've really liked each other. I was sad that they'd never have the chance to be friends.

Fito came over, and since it was a Friday and we hadn't

gotten around to putting up any Christmas stuff, we dragged the Christmas tree out from the garage and put it together. Dad and Marcos did the lights thing, and Sam kept going through all the boxes marked *Christmas*. "You guys have a lot of Christmas stuff."

"We're all about Christmas," I said.

She really liked the wreath we always hung on the front door. "I remember this."

It was nice, the whole thing, everyone decorating the tree. Dad had gotten around to making the pumpkin pie he promised, and it was in the oven.

The house smelled like pie.

But really, the best part, the best part was that Dad was steaming up the tamales. I was finally going to get a taste. I looked at Fito. "I'm giving you a limit on the tamales."

He laughed. "I kinda have this thing with food. I'm always hungry. What do you think that means?"

Sam rolled her eyes. "It probably means you need sex. You're just compensating. You should start running with us. It's called sublimation."

My dad looked at her, trying to suppress his grin. "What?"

"Yeah, it's a gay thing. Gay guys just have to have sex."

Dad looked at Sam and shook his head. "Where exactly did you come by this information?"

I had to insert myself into the conversation. "She just makes it all up."

"I do not."

"Yes, you do, Sam. You surf the Internet and read about a topic and learn a few things — and the rest, you just make up. And then you believe the things you make up."

"That's not true."

"Yes, it is. That's why you're going to be a great writer some-day."

She gave me a look and shifted her gaze to Fito. "Do you or do you not want to get laid?"

Marcos started laughing. "He's seventeen years old. We all know the answer to that one. I don't think it has anything to do with being gay."

"You got that right," I said, and I knew I was blushing, and I sort of wanted to crawl under the couch.

And my dad, who is really a smart guy, said, "Why don't we talk about something else?"

Sam rolled her eyes, "Yeah," she said. "Let's talk about Santa Claus."

Marcos

FITO GOT A TEXT around ten, and all of a sudden he said he was headed for home — which meant Sam's house. But I thought that maybe he was going to hook up with some guy. I don't know, maybe I'd been chumming around with Sam for too long. Maybe I was projecting. That's another Sam word. Ever since her mother died, she'd been turning into a therapist. Hmm.

Sam and I ate two pieces of pumpkin pie each as we listened to this group called Well Strung. They were kind of dorky musicians who played classical music and put it together with pop. Sam said they were way gay, and I said I didn't like that expression, and she countered with, "Well, sometimes that's a compliment."

"I'm not so sure about that."

And she said I didn't know crap about these things.

Dad and Marcos were talking in the living room, and I could hear them laughing. I wondered what it would be like to love someone like my dad loved Marcos. Not that he talked about it. But I could see it. And, really, I was a little jealous. I was. I mean, Marcos gave Dad something that I couldn't give him. And Dad was spending more time with him, and I missed having him all to myself, and I knew that it was really frickin' selfish, and the other thing was that I didn't really know Marcos all that well, and even though we got along, I wasn't making any moves toward getting real close to him. I was a little jealous and I was a little suspicious. And I generally wasn't a suspicious kind of guy. I wasn't making progress when it came to Marcos. Nope. Stasis.

Sam texted me: Wftd = love.

She was sitting across from me at the kitchen table. I gave her a sarcastic look.

I didn't know a damn thing about love. I think all I'd ever had were crushes. Not that crushes didn't have their own emotional thing going on. I really liked the kissing thing. I sometimes day-dreamed that I had a girlfriend. And I pictured her looking at me. I wondered what it would be like to feel a girl's hands on my body. I wondered what it would be like to run my fingers over a girl's lips.

I kept chomping on my pumpkin pie, and Sam asked what I was thinking.

"Nothing important," I said.

"I finished my essay. College apps all done! Yay, Sam! And you should be thinking about *your* essay."

"What if I told you I'd finished it?"

"You finished it? And you didn't let me look at it?"

"I'll let you see it."

"When?"

"When I'm ready."

"Oh, just like when you're ready to read your mom's letter."

"Don't go there."

"Sally."

"Sammy." I grinned at her. "So I guess we're off to college."

"Let's not get all enthusiastic about it."

"Ambivalent," I said.

She smiled. Sometimes it was as if she could read minds. "Don't worry. When you get to college, you'll have girls all over you."

"Sure."

"And you won't have me around to get in the way."

"You're not in the way."

"Maybe a little. You're way too loyal. None of the girls you've ever gone out with — not that they number in the hundreds —"

I shot her the snarkiest smile I could come up with.

"None of them liked me."

"Girls are weird that way," I said. "They're all like — *I'm the only person in the universe.* I don't like that."

"That's because, unlike most boys, you're actually kind of mature. But only in that way. In other ways, well, you're a work in progress."

"Is that a compliment?"

"You bet your ass, white boy."

"Nice girl. See how you are? You give me a compliment. And then you take it away in one fell swoop."

"Yup. No need to give you a big head." Then she turned toward the living room and gave me the eye. "What do you think?"

I shrugged. "Marcos — he's nice, huh?"

"Yeah, he kinda is. He's quiet, but not too shy. And he's actually a good listener. I heard him talking to Fito, who was saying something about school, and it came out like the usual Fito. You know that negative self-talk he's addicted to. And Marcos listened and then said, 'You know, maybe it's not you. Maybe it's that

326

teacher. There are a lot of great teachers out there. But there are also a lot of not-so-great teachers. It's just something you should think about.'"

I looked at Sam. "So are you gonna stop giving him a hard time?"

"I don't think so."

"What?"

"We have this thing. I give him attitude, and he gives me a smile. It's how we get along."

"I get you, and I don't get you."

"Nah. You get me. You totally get me." Then she got real serious. I knew that look. "You see me, Sally. I. Mean. You. See. Me. My mom, well, you know, she loved me. I know that. But she didn't always see me. That's sad. That's really sad. She didn't see me because she didn't see herself. But you? You see me. I remember when we were about six. Maybe seven. I fell on the pavement, and you picked me up. And we walked here, to the house that has become my house. You washed my bleeding knee, which to me was totally traumatic." We both laughed. "You washed it with a warm washcloth and put a Band-Aid on it, and then you kissed it. Do you remember that?"

"No. I don't remember that."

"You were so serious. I'll always remember that look on your face. You saw me. You've always seen me. And I think that's all that anyone wants. That's why Fito loves coming over here. He's been invisible all his life. And all of a sudden he's visible. Seeing someone. Really seeing someone. That's love."

"You know what else love is?" I said. "A friend who slaps you when you need to be slapped."

She smiled at me and I smiled at her. "You want to know a secret?" I asked.

"Yes."

"I'm a little jealous of Marcos."

"Good."

"Good?"

"Yeah."

"And I'm a little suspicious of him."

God, she smiled. "Good to know not all my lessons have been lost on you."

Me. Dreams.

IN MY DREAM I am surrounded by a bunch of guys. And I say, "One at a time. I'll take you on one at a time." So one at a time, I take them all down. I beat the holy crap out of the first guy. He's bleeding, and I watch him lying on the ground. And I just say, "Next." So one by one, I beat the holy crap out of all of them. And they're all lying there on the ground, and I just stand there and stare at them.

And then a man shows up. I look like him, and I know he's my father. And we go for it. I throw the first punch, but it doesn't faze him. And then he starts punching me. He punches me and punches me until I'm on the ground. Then he starts kicking me and kicking me. But I don't feel a thing.

And then I wake.

If I was a bad boy in my dreams, what did that mean? And what did it mean when a father I didn't know showed up in my dream and beat the crap out of me? I'm not going to tell Sam about this dream, because she'll start analyzing me. I don't feel like being analyzed.

I tried to think of something beautiful so I could fall asleep again.

I thought about the day when it was raining yellow leaves. Of course I did.

And then I went back to sleep.

Sam. Dad. Me. Dad!

SAM AND I had just come in from our morning run. Dad was reading the paper. Sam and I had been discussing our plan. I decided to get some input from Dad. Why not? "Dad," I said, "Fito's birthday is Friday. He turns the big eighteen."

"I'm listening."

"So what are you doing on Friday?"

"Well, Marcos and I were thinking about going to a movie."

I almost wanted to ask why they didn't think of inviting Sam and me to go along — but I knew the answer to that one.

"Well," I heard Sam say, "we were thinking of having something for Fito. You know, like cake and tacos."

"Sounds like a winning combination. We can do that."

"I'll even bake the cake," I said.

"And I'll even make the tacos," Sam said.

My dad looked at both of us and said, "Wow." But he knew us. He knew there was something else coming. I could tell by the way he put the newspaper down.

"And?" he said.

"And," I said, "Fito's phone died. Which really sucks. I mean, his phone sucked anyway."

"Yeah," Sam said. "It really sucked. It was one of those cheapos from Walmart."

My dad did a wince thing. "It's what he could afford, Sam."

"I know, I know, Mr. V. I can be such a brat. But we were thinking we wanted to get him a smartphone for his birthday. You know, Lina has me on her family plan, and you have Sally on your plan, so we thought maybe we'd put Fito on one of our plans, and the phone would be, like, super cheap. Sally has some money, and you know — what do you think?"

"Well, if you can't save the world, at least you've decided you're going to save Fito."

Sam crossed her arms. "Don't say it like that —" And then she stopped. "He's not like a project. He's our friend. We love Fito."

"Yeah, we do," I said.

Dad smiled. "I get that. So you need a partner in crime?"

"Something like that," I said.

"Why not? Tomorrow after school, we'll all go get Fito a phone."

"Great," I said.

"Okay, then," my dad said.

"Okay, then," I said.

Sam was smiling. We were happy. And then she got this look on her face — as if she had something else to say. And when Sam had something to say, she was going to say it. She looked right at my dad. "Mr. V? I don't know what to call you now. Mr. V doesn't seem to fit anymore."

"You can call me Vicente. That *is* my name, after all."

"That seems sort of disrespectful."

"This coming from the girl who used to refer to her mother as Sylvia?"

"Yeah, but I only called her that behind her back."

Dad grinned.

"What to call me?" he said. "How to solve this problem. You have something in mind?"

"Actually, I do," she said, sounding very serious.

Dad just waited for her to finish what she'd started to say.

"Well," she said, looking really shy, "I'm going to be eighteen in August. And then I'll be an adult."

"Legally, anyway," my dad said.

"Yeah," Sam said, "legally. I was thinking maybe, well, you know, you're really the only dad I've ever known. You know, it's kind of been like that, hasn't it?"

My dad grinned some more as he nodded.

"Have I been a big pain in the ass?"

"Nope," he said. "I don't know what we would have done without you."

Sam had this I-think-I'm-going-to-cry look on her face. "You mean that?"

"I don't say things I don't mean, Sam."

"I'm glad," she said, "because I have this idea in my head that you might want to adopt me. You know, make things official before I turn, you know, legal."

I saw my dad's face light up. "Are you sure?" he asked.

"I'm sure," she said.

Dad thought a moment. "We can go through a legal adoption, if that's what you want. Let me just say that you've been my daughter for long time now, Sam. Adoption or no adoption. And you don't need a piece of paper to call me Dad."

Tears were running down her face. And then she waved at him. "Hi, Dad," she said.

And Dad waved back. "Hi, Sam."

Sister

I WAS IN MY room thinking about things. Life has a logic all its own. People talk about the highway of life, but I think that's crap. Highways are nice and paved, and they have signs telling you which way to go. Life isn't like that at all. There are days when great things happen and everything is beautiful and perfect, and then, just like that, everything can go straight to hell. It's like getting drunk. At first it feels kinda nice and all relaxed. And all of a sudden the room is spinning and you are throwing up, and, well, maybe life is a little like that.

I was thinking of making a list of all the great things that were happening and all the shitty things that were happening, the things that were making me crazy. But what good was that? Part of me was really happy. It was like Dad said — adoption or no adoption, Sam had always been my sister. And Dad had always been her dad.

To know something you'd always known. To really know it. Wow.

Yeah, Mima was still dying and I still hadn't come up with the courage to open my mother's letter and I still felt unsettled about a lot of things. I heard Uncle Tony's voice in my head: *I think that kid's gonna be devastated.*

I texted Sam: What doing?

Sam: Reading. Thinking

Me: Thinking?

Sam: I want to change my last name

Me: ?

Sam: Want to change my last name to Avila

Me: Avila?

Then I saw her standing in my doorway.

I look at her. "Avila?"

"Yeah, Avila. It was my mother's name before she got married. And I got to thinking that I really never knew my father."

"It's not too late."

"I think it is. Anyway, that's not the point."

"What's the point?"

"See, Sally, she's dead now. And I want to take her name. That's what I want. I asked her once why she didn't take her name back after she divorced my father. She said, 'I married him. I took his name. I'm good with that.' I think my mom always defined herself in terms of the men around her. She kept the name Diaz because she told herself that at least she'd been married once. That's what I think." She gave me one of her I'm-proud-of-myself looks. "Yup, I'm going to officially change my name. In honor of my mother."

She walked up to me and kissed me on the top of the head as I sat at my desk. I was holding my mother's letter.

"God, you're smart, Sammy. And me? Stasis."

She stared at the letter. "You'll figure it out, Sally."

"Will I?"

"I believe in you, Sally." She got real quiet. "I still cry, you know? I still ask myself what if? What if Sylvia hadn't died?"

"Maybe we shouldn't play that game anymore."

"We can't help ourselves. Sylvia and I — we fought to the bitter end."

"Maybe that's how you loved each other."

"It *is* how we loved each other. That's really sad, Sally. And it can't be undone."

"We can't live in regret, Sam."

"Maybe we both live in regret. You've asked yourself a hundred times what if your mother had never died, haven't you?"

I didn't say anything.

"You hate to talk about this."

"Yeah, I do." I put the letter on my desk, ran my hand across it, and asked myself, *What would happen if I met my bio father face to face? What if, Sam? What if?*

Mothers

THE WIND WAS COLD. And it looked as if it might snow.

I loved the snow.

I loved the feel of the cold wind on my face.

Dad didn't much care for cold weather. He said my romance with snow existed only because I didn't live in a place like Minnesota.

I don't know exactly why I was standing in front of my house looking at the lights. I could see the Christmas tree twinkling in the living room. When I was a boy, Mima would hold my hand and take me outside, and we'd look at the lights. Mima always had lights all around her house, and we always sang a Christmas carol. She really liked "O Come, All Ye Faithful," but she sang it in Latin because that's how she'd learned it.

Dad said Latin was a dead language. I wondered about that. Why did some languages die? Sam had a theory that languages didn't actually die. She said we killed them. "Do you know how many languages we've killed off in the history of the world? You kill a language off, and you kill off an entire people." Sam, that Sam.

I decided then and there that Sam and I would print out the words in Latin and sing it to Mima this Christmas. That's exactly what we'd do. I was almost finished with the photo book I was making. I was going to give it to her for Christmas. We could look at it together. That would be the best part.

I took my cell phone out of my pocket and called her. My Aunt Evie answered the phone. "It's good to hear your voice," she said.

"Yeah," I said. "It's just a regular voice from a regular guy."

"Regular." She laughed. "Smart-ass. You want to talk to your Mima?"

"Yeah."

When Mima got on the phone, she sounded tired but she sounded happy, and she told me that Uncle Julian was coming for Christmas even though he'd come for Thanksgiving, and she was really happy about that. I was happy too, and happy that she was talking so much, because that was her normal self. Then she asked me what I was doing.

"I'm standing in front of my house and looking at the lights and thinking of you. That's what I'm doing."

I wanted to say so many things to her. I wanted to ask her about my mother, because she'd known her, and ever since Sam's mom died, I'd begun thinking more about my own mother. It wasn't just the letter; it was this whole thing about mothers that Sam and Fito and I had going on, and maybe that's what we had in common, this thing with mothers who were impossible to talk to. I wanted to talk to Mima about this, but I could hear the tired in her voice. She seemed almost as far away as my dead mother, and there was nothing I could do to bring her closer. Nothing at all.

I texted Sam: Come outside with me.

Sam: It's cold out there

Me: Please

So a few minutes later Sam was standing right beside me and we looked at the lights together. "What's so important?" she said.

"I've been thinking."

"Yeah, you've been doing a lot of that lately."

"Were you mad at your mother?"

"We just had this conversation, didn't we?"

"No. That's not what I mean. Were you mad at her because she died?"

Sam was quiet. Then she took my hand and held it. "Yes," she whispered. "I was fucking furious with her for dying."

"Are you still?"

"It's going away. But yeah, I'm still mad."

"You know something? I think I don't remember loving my mother because I got mad at her. For dying. I got mad at her. I think so."

"You were three, Sally."

"Yeah, I was three."

She squeezed my hand. It started to snow, big flakes that fell silently to the ground.

I wondered if that's what death sounded like. Like a snowflake falling on the ground.

340

Fito. Eighteen. Marcos. Adult?

YOU GOT ME a present? Really. I mean, like a real present?" Fito said.

"What?" I was just looking at Fito. "It's your birthday, *vato*. That's, like, what people do."

"Not in my house," he said, wearing a shy, crooked smile. "The last time I got a present, I was, like, about five." He just kept staring at the box.

"It's from all of us."

Sam pushed it across the kitchen table. "You can open it, you know."

Fito kept looking at his present. "Nice wrapping."

"Thank you," I said. "That would be my handiwork. Sam doesn't wrap. She just buys those gift bags. Me, I like to unwrap stuff."

"How do you even know what I like? I mean, how did you — I mean —" Fito was stumbling all over the place, tripping over his own words.

"You'll like it," Sam said. "I promise."

He just kept nodding and staring at the wrapped box.

Sam did the cross-her-arms thing. "If you don't open it, I'm gonna pop you one. I mean it."

So finally he reached for the box. He opened it really slowly, and then he stared at it. He didn't say anything. He just stared. He looked up at Sam and me. "You got me an iPhone? An iPhone? Wow! Wow! Man, oh man." Then he got real quiet. "Look, guys . . . Man, I can't take this. Man, this is just way too nice. I can't take this. I mean, I can't."

Sam gave him one of those looks. "Yeah, you can."

"See, I can't because, you know, it's like —"

"Just take it," I said. "You need a phone."

I looked up and noticed that my father had been watching us.

"Yeah, but I was gonna get one at Walmart for sixty bucks. You know, like the one that died." Then Fito kept shaking his head. "Look, I'm really sorry. I just can't take this. It's not right."

My dad took a seat at the table. He took the iPhone out of its fancy white box. He held it in his hand. "These things are really light these days," he said. "You like baseball, Fito?"

"Yeah, I love baseball."

"You know, Fito, some people believe from the start that things belong to them. My father used to say, 'Some people are born on third base, and they go through life thinking they hit a triple.'"

Fito laughed. "I like that."

My dad nodded. "Yeah. Fito, you're not one of those people. A guy like you was born in the locker room, no one ever pointed you in the direction of the baseball diamond, and somehow you managed to get yourself into the dugout. And something in you just doesn't believe he belongs in the game. But you do, you *do* belong in the game. One of these days you're going to be up at bat. And you're going to hit it out of the ballpark. Anyway, that's what I think. I'm gonna go outside and have a cigarette."

The three of us sat there. Fito pushed the phone away, and it sat in the middle of the table. "Your dad is really cool, you know. Super cool. He's nice. But —"

Sam stopped him dead in his tracks. "Oh, you think he thinks these things about you because he's a nice guy. Maybe you're a nice guy too. Maybe you deserve more than the shit you've been given most of your life."

"Yeah," I said, "don't you get that, Fito?"

He was biting his lip, and then he sort of pulled at his hair.

"Fito," I said. "This is a present we got you for your fucking birthday. And if you don't take it, I'm gonna kick your ass. I mean it. I'm gonna lay you out flat."

Fito nodded. He slowly reached for the phone, took it in his hand, and stared at it. "I never know what to do when people are nice to me."

"All you gotta do, Fito, is say thank you."

"Thank you," he whispered.

"You're welcome," I whispered back.

The three of us didn't say anything. We just sat there and smiled. And then Fito said, "Your dad, man. I really like that cat."

Sam smiled and shook her head. "Why is everyone a cat?"

"Not everyone's a cat. Just cool people, you know?"

I kinda liked that cat thing Fito had goin' on.

Sam was teaching Fito how to operate his iPhone — and I was sitting next to Dad on the back steps. It was dark out and not too cold. The Christmas lights around the back door were blinking off and on. I was beginning to like the smell of my dad's cigarettes, which was a really bad thing. Then I heard him say, "So how come you're sitting out here with your old man?"

"Do you believe in heaven, Dad?"

"That's a helluvan answer to my question."

"Do you?"

"I'm not sure. I believe there's a God. I believe there is something greater, a force that transcends this thing we call living. I don't know if that answers your question."

"If there's no heaven, I don't really care. Maybe people are heaven, Dad. Some people, anyway. You and Sam and Fito. Maybe you're all heaven. Maybe everyone's heaven, and we just don't know it."

My dad was wearing this great smile. "You know something? I think you're a little bit like Fito."

"How's that?"

"Well, I know you've been going through a lot lately. And it seems that our lives have gotten a little complicated, and I know you well enough to know that that particular word doesn't sit well with you. Me going back and forth to see Mima and talking to doctors, and Sam's mom —"

"And you dating Marcos."

"And me dating Marcos," he repeated. "And it seems you're more in your head than I've ever seen before. I don't know what's going on in there. Not really. But —" He stopped. "But," he repeated, "I do know you. And I'm guessing that you underestimate yourself. That's why you had such a hard time writing your essay."

"I didn't tell you I'd finished it."

"I know."

"How did you know?"

"I just did. One of those things."

"Wow," I said.

"Wow," he said. "Salvie, I have a theory that you can't sell yourself on an application form because you don't believe there's much to sell. You tell yourself that you're just this ordinary guy. Is that true?"

"Yeah," I said. "That's part of it, I think."

"What's the other part?"

"Can I get back to you on that?"

My dad nodded. "Can I just say one thing, Salvador?"

"Sure."

"There's nothing ordinary about you. Nothing ordinary at all."

Sam actually made the taco shells. I taught her how. The first few were total losses, but she got the hang of it. Well, she burned her hand when some hot oil splattered. The F word went flying through the kitchen and landed in the living room, where it hit my dad right in the heart. He walked into the kitchen and looked at Sam, shaking his head. "You okay?"

It wasn't that bad. "She's fine," I said. "Just a little burn. She hasn't had her drama fix for the day."

Marcos dropped in. He looked a little tired. You know, I had never thought of Marcos as a person. Not really. I thought of him only in relation to my dad. And that awkward conversation he had with me and Sam, that sort of impressed me a little. Yeah, it impressed me, but it hadn't impressed me enough. I still saw him as my dad's boyfriend. I guess that's what he was. Or at least they were working toward that, I think. And Dad was shy about the whole thing, which was kind of sweet in a way. Sweet. He's the guy who introduced me to that word. Part of me wanted to like Marcos. He was decent. And him and Fito, they really got along. But part of me wanted to push him away.

I found myself sitting in the living room, where Marcos was having a glass of wine. Dad and Fito and Sam were still eating cake in the kitchen and fooling with Fito's iPhone, so I looked at Marcos and said, "I don't know anything about you. I mean, I know you like my father. But that's about it."

"You mind? That I like your father?"

"Nope. Don't mind." I thought about telling him that if he ever hurt my father again, I'd go after him. I mean, well, I just smiled. Then I found myself opening my mouth and saying, "You hurt him."

"Yes, I did."

I shook my head. "Guess it happens," I said.

We sat there in that awkward silence. And I guess he decided to talk — or at least try. You know, talk like normal people.

"Your mother introduced me to your father. Did you know that?"

"No, I didn't." That surprised me. I wondered why Dad hadn't told me. Not that Marcos came up much in our conversations.

"I was with someone at the time. But I really liked your father. He was real, the kind of guy who never pretended to be anything other than who and what he was. And then I saw his work and I thought, *Wow*. Wow. The funny thing is, I had just moved in with this other guy, and I was so new to this thing called the gay scene.

I wasn't really comfortable in my own skin. And I was so *not* a grownup. Not at all like your dad."

"So when did you start, you know, seeing him?"

"I think you were about ten. I ran into him at an art opening in L.A. I was on vacation and saw this thing in the *LA Weekly* about all the art openings in town. And there was your father's name at some gallery. So I went."

"Did you at least buy a painting?"

"I *did* buy a painting, as a matter of fact. And we started seeing each other. And then something happened."

I looked at him with a question mark on my face.

"I ran. I was so scared of what I felt for your father that I ran. I ran as fast as I could. As far away as I could." He shook his head. "It took me a long time to become a man." It seemed he was still kind of upset with himself. Or maybe he was sad that it had taken so many years to become who he was today. I wondered how long it would take me to become whoever I was supposed to become. How many years? Before the start of the school year, I'd thought I was a totally calm kid who knew himself. But I wasn't so sure anymore.

"You know what I told your dad?"

"What?"

"I told him I couldn't handle kids. That was a lie. But I knew that for your father, that was a deal-breaker."

The guy was being honest. I liked that. And he'd been scared. I got that. Because right now I was scared too. And maybe being scared was part of the whole growing-up thing, the whole living-life thing. "And did you tell my dad the truth? I mean now?"

"Yeah, I did. Why do you think he gave me another chance?"

"Well," I said, "everybody deserves a second chance."

You know, I guess love is a really scary thing. I hadn't ever thought of that. I mean, I didn't think that any of the crushes I'd ever had on girls qualified as love. I think I was the kind of guy who, well, if I fell in love, it was going to hurt. I just had a hunch.

Sam and I walked Fito home. I wanted to ask them both if they'd ever been in love, and I wondered what was stopping me. So I did it. I asked.

"I'm always in love," Sam confessed. "Well, I always think I'm in love, but now that I think about it, I don't think I've ever been in love. Not really. Just these little, I don't know what to call them, these attractions to good-looking bad boys. Nothing serious. They just seemed serious at the time. I'm kind of intense that way."

"I hadn't noticed," I said.

"Shut up. You asked, right?"

"Right," I said.

Fito was shaking his head. "You gotta stay away from those *vatos*, Sam. *No bueno*."

"*No bueno* is right," I said.

"Me?" Fito said. "There was this guy I met last year. He went to Cathedral. Can you believe that shit?"

"Ah," Sam said. "So you have a thing for good boys, do you?"

"Yeah, I guess so. I sort of fell in love with him. Turns out he wasn't such a good Catholic boy. I won't get into it. I'll tell you something: it hurt like hell. I went out and got all fucked up. First and last time I'll ever do drugs. That's bad shit. *No bueno*."

Sam and I both nodded.

"How come we need to love?"

"Maybe we don't," Fito said.

"Like hell," Sam said. "We need it. Like the air we breathe."

I nodded. "Yeah."

"That's the question, isn't it, Sally?"

"Do you think the heart needs love to keep on beating? You know what I mean?"

"Well," Sam said, "isn't that what a heart's for?"

"But not everybody loves. Not everybody." Fito had a real serious look on his face. "And that's the fucking truth."

Sam and I just looked at Fito.

"You okay?" Sam whispered.

"I'm not always okay. I don't want to talk about love. Sometimes life is shit."

(More) Shit Happens

WHEN SAM AND I went for our Saturday morning run, I tried to keep up with her. Lately she'd been stepping it up. We ran to the Santa Fe Bridge, and on our way back home, we stopped in front of the library. After my breathing returned to normal, I glanced over and saw Sam looking up at the sky.

"Hey," I said.

"Hey," she said.

"You thinking?"

"Yeah," she said. "I got a text from this guy at school."

"Yeah?"

"Yeah. He likes me."

"You like him?"

"Sort of. He's my type."

I smiled. "Yeah? Gonna go out with him?"

"Nope."

"Nope?"

"I turned him down flat."

"Really?"

"Yup." She gave me one her fantastic smiles. "I don't always know who I want to be. You think I do. But I don't. But, Sally, I know who I *don't* want to be. A lot of guys got this thing into their head that I was easy."

"They were wrong," I said.

"Yeah, they were wrong."

We just looked at each other. And then I said. "And a lot of people got the idea that I was this calm guy who always had his shit together. They were wrong."

"Hey," she said, "go easy. The jury's still out."

That made me smile. "Let's go home," I said.

"Yeah," she said. "You know we gotta talk to Fito. He's got something going on in that head of his."

"Well, it's not just in his head."

"Yeah," she said. "He doesn't deserve that screwed-up family."

Life wasn't always about deserve. That much I knew.

I was starting to get why Dad has this thing with uncertainty. He told me more than once that you don't need certainty to be happy. And I was starting to get it. You never know what's going happen. You really don't. One day, you're going along with your life and everything is normal. You go to school, you do your homework, you play catch with your dad, and the days go like that, and then bam! Bam! Mima's cancer comes back. Sam's mom gets killed in an accident. Fito gets thrown out of his house. I used to wonder at the emotional ups-and-downs that Sam went through all the time. I mean, *all the time.* But suddenly that's how I felt. I woke up and felt good, at lunch I'd be all pissed off about something stupid, and then I'd be kind of okay. I flipped back and forth between being the old me and the me I didn't know or understand. And just when I'd think that things were more or less balancing themselves out, well, shit happened. It's the perfect way to put it. Shit happens.

I'd just gotten out of the shower after our run, and Sam had gone out with her Aunt Lina. That was nice, that she had her aunt. And it was really sweet, what they had. I walked into the kitchen, and my dad was reading the paper. He put the newspaper down and said, "What's Fito's last name?"

"Fresquez."

"Would you text him and ask him what his mother's name is?"

"What?"

"Just do that for me, will you?" He had a serious look on his face. I didn't like it when he wore that look. So I texted Fito: What's ur mom's name?

Fito texted back: Elena

I looked at Dad. "Her name's Elena."

"How old is she?"

So I texted Fito: How old is ur mom?

Fito texted back: 44

I looked at Dad. "She's forty-four."

And then Fito texted back: ?

"Do you know where Fito used to live?"

"Yeah, on California Street. Close to school."

Now Dad looked really sick. "Fito's mother is dead," he said. He handed me the newspaper. "Forty-Four-Year-Old Woman Found Dead." That was the headline. I started reading. The neighbors found her. "An apparent drug overdose."

I looked at my dad. "So what are we gonna do?"

"It's not as if he's not going to find out. You better tell Fito to get over here."

"I have some bad news for you, Fito." Dad's voice was soft. Kind. Really kind. "There's no good way of breaking this news, Fito."

Fito shrugged. "I'm kinda used to bad news, you know, Mr. V."

"Yeah, Fito, I get that." Dad looked down at the newspaper. "It's about your mom. I read it in this morning's newspaper."

Fito stared at the newspaper. He took it and started reading. When he finished, he put it down. Dad was popping his knuckles and studying Fito. Then Fito started hitting himself. I mean, he was punching the hell out of his chest, and he started crying, like, really loud, and he was saying stuff that I just couldn't make out. And he wouldn't stop hitting himself, and he got up from his chair and he ripped the newspaper up, and he started hitting himself again, and his crying was breaking my heart and I was really glad that Sam wasn't home to see it, really glad she was out with her Aunt Lina, because this would've really killed her, to see Fito that way. And then I just couldn't stand it anymore, and I took Fito's fists and I was stronger than he was, and I held his arms and kept him from hitting himself. And then I just pulled him in to me, and I held him and he cried and he cried and he cried. And I couldn't do anything about all the hurt, but I could hold him. And then Fito whispered in a voice that sounded tired and old, "Why am I crying? She didn't even love me."

Then I heard myself whisper back, "Maybe all that matters is that *you* loved *her.*"

"My life is shit," he said. "That's all it's ever been."

"No, it isn't. I promise you, Fito, it isn't."

Friends

FRIENDS. I GUESS I met that word when I met Sam. But sometimes you get to reintroduce yourself to certain words you already know. That's how it was with Fito. He gave me that word again. It was exactly like Sam had said, about how we had to see people because sometimes the world made us invisible. So we had to make each other visible. Words were like that too. Sometimes we didn't see words.

Friend. Fito was my friend. And I loved him.

And it killed me to see him so broken.

It killed Sam, too.

And it killed my dad.

It's hard to fix a heart when it's been so damaged. But that was our job. *That was our job.*

Dad went out and bought an extra baseball glove. We had only three. Actually, he bought two extra gloves. One for Marcos. Not that he said it was for Marcos. So we played catch. Sam and I tossed the ball to each other. And Dad and Fito tossed the ball to each other. Marcos came over and watched. Then Dad took a break, and Marcos and I tossed the ball to each other, and Sam and Fito tossed the ball to each other.

We weren't really talking. Sometimes there isn't much to say.

Dad was smoking a cigarette on the back steps.

It was a week before Christmas. The day was cold, but not too cold, and the sun was warm on our faces. Then I noticed Lina sitting next to my dad, and they were talking.

Fito said, "You know, my mom, she's not suffering anymore."

Marcos nodded as he tossed the ball. "No, she's not. She's resting."

"Good," Fito said. "She needed to rest." Then he said, "I shouldn't have left her. I should've gone back. It was my job to take care of her."

Marcos looked sad when he heard Fito say that. "You're wrong about that, Fito. It wasn't your job to take care of your mother. It was *her* job to take care of you."

"Yeah, but —"

"Man, you are really into beating up on yourself, aren't you? We gotta get you a new hobby."

Fito smiled. It was a sad smile. But it was still a smile.

Sam said, "Fito, are you hungry?"

"Yeah. Actually. Yeah. I'm starving."

So we all went inside, and Lina started making tortillas, and Sam was giving Fito her spiel about the five stages. And she and Fito were Googling about the five stages in the living room. But me, I was at the kitchen table waiting for the first tortilla so I could slather it with butter. Dad and Marcos were talking. Marcos said he knew of a good counselor and it was probably a good idea for Fito to start seeing one.

"I'll pay," he said.

Dad looked at him. "You sure?"

He made a joke. "You know what they say about gay men, we have expendable incomes."

That made Lina laugh. "Send some my way. I want to buy another of Vicente's paintings, and he's getting awfully pricey." She looked at Marcos. "That's very generous of you."

"That kid needs a break. I know he just turned eighteen. He's not a boy anymore. But that doesn't mean he's a man. And besides, I've been there."

Lina and I were both studying him.

"My dad died hugging a bottle. He sure as hell never hugged me." Marcos took my father's hand. "I'll talk to Fito about seeing a counselor."

I wondered if Fito would go for that.

I reached for the butter and the first tortilla. It was so good, the tortilla. I thought of Mima, and I guess I thought I'd never taste one of her tortillas again. And I thought about what Marcos had said about Fito. *He's not a boy anymore. But that doesn't mean he's a man.* And what about me? What made you a man? What exactly made you a man?

Faggot. That Word Again.

Fito's mom didn't have any kind of religious service. I thought that was a little sad. I wondered if God showed up whether or not your funeral was religious. Mima would probably know the answer to that question. But I didn't.

Fito's mom had a brother who paid for a sort of service at the funeral home. A few people showed up, including Fito's brothers, who acted as if they were high. Sam said they were way scary. Yeah, they were a little rough around the edges. For sure. The casket was at the front of the small chapel at the funeral home, and Fito just kept staring at it. My dad was sitting next to him when one of his brothers came up to Fito and said, "So now you got a sugar daddy or what?" He looked at my dad. "A bit old to be picking up little boys, don't you think?"

It happened pretty fast. Like a bomb going off. Next thing I knew, Fito had his brother on the floor and was punching his lights out. And then his two other brothers jumped in, and hell, I don't know, it was happening so fast — but next thing I knew, I'd joined the fight, and I was pulling one of Fito's brothers off him and I was punching him in the stomach — then in the face, and when I was about to go for one of Fito's other brothers, I felt some guys pulling me off and holding me back and then I saw Dad had Fito, and Fito's face was bleeding. And then Sam was looking at me and she said softly, "Your lip is bleeding."

I realized that the funeral directors were holding my arms, afraid that I wasn't quite finished. I started relaxing and breathing, and they let go of me.

Sam grabbed my arm, whispering, "Let's get out of here."

Everything seemed so quiet.

I saw Dad walking in front of us, and I saw Fito leaning into him, holding his rib — or his arm.

Everything around me had sped up — and now everything was moving in slow motion.

As we walked out the door, I heard a voice yelling, "Fucking faggots!" The words echoed in my ears.

Nobody said a word as we drove off.

Not a word.

Fito sat next to me in the back with his hands covering his face. His fists were a little bloody. He was rocking himself back and forth as tears ran down his face. And I could tell he was in pain.

It was a cold night. Clear sky. I don't know why I noticed that. Maybe a part of me wished that everything could be as clear and simple as the night sky.

Dad pulled into a parking lot, got out of the car, and lit a cigarette. His hands were shaking. He puffed on his cigarette until he was calmer. Then he got back into the car.

———

I knew my dad was thinking. He was very disciplined that way. He pulled in to the emergency room of the hospital. He looked over at Sam. "You wanna park this thing for me?" He opened the door to the back and gently helped Fito out of the car. He looked at me. "You hurt?"

"No," I said. "Just a bloody lip."

"You sure?"

"Yeah, Dad. I'm good." He gave me a look. It was strange. I couldn't tell what was in his head.

I watched Dad and Fito as they walked into the ER, Fito leaning on my dad. I felt the car move as Sam made her way into the parking lot.

I sat in the back, immobile, paralyzed, my heart and head empty. I felt like a bird whose wings were broken but who was still struggling to fly.

I don't know how long we were in the ER waiting room. They let Dad go in with Fito, and Sam and I sat there waiting. She went into the women's room and came out with some wet paper towels and wiped the blood off my lip. "Your mouth is swollen," she said.

"That'll teach me," I said.

"You were just trying to help a friend."

I shook my head. "It's not like that."

"Tell me."

"It's not as if there was any thinking involved. I mean, it was all reflex. It's not as if I said to myself, *I gotta help Fito*. I just jumped in. It just happened."

"Maybe your reflexes are telling you something."

"Like what?"

"Like you'd do anything to protect the people you love." She nudged me. "But you know, you gotta find a better way to help them."

"You're sounding like Dad."

"Am I? I'll take it as a compliment."

"Shit," I said. "I'm screwing everything up."

"Stop it," Sam said. "Stop doing that. Maybe you're beating up on yourself a little too much lately too. *No bueno.* That's not who you are."

"How do you know?"

"I know," she said firmly. "I know."

I nodded.

"I wish I had a cigarette," she said.

"You don't smoke."

"I used to — sometimes."

"Solve any of your problems?"

Our laughter was soft and wounded.

I looked up and saw Marcos standing there. "So how's the home team?"

"We took a beating."

"So I hear."

"Yeah," Sam said. "But you should see the other guys."

That made Marcos smile. Sam stood up and hugged him. Then she leaned into him. "Why is the world so mean, Marcos?"

"I don't know," he whispered. "I just don't know."

I looked up at Sam and Marcos. It seemed to me that Sam had learned how to deal. She hadn't known how to deal with anything for such a long time, and she'd always leaned on me. And even though she gave Marcos a hard time, she'd already learned to be his friend.

I said to myself, *No more, Salvador. No more.* Though I wasn't sure what *no more* meant. But it felt like I was taking a step. A step away from stasis.

Figure it out, Salvador. Figure it out.

Aftermath

THE GOOD NEWS: Fito's ribs weren't broken. But his left hand, well, that was broken. He missed school for a few days — but he seemed okay. He kept staring at his arm in a sling, and I wondered what he was thinking.

On the outside, he was back to his old self. Only, I knew there was a wound living inside him, and that wound wasn't going away anytime soon. There had always been something a little sad about Fito, and that made sense to me. He'd had a really sad life. But he'd always been so tough. And really determined. It wasn't just that he had a broken arm now. Something else was broken too.

Fito moved into my room and slept on my bed. I slept on the floor in a sleeping bag. Fito had bad dreams one night; he was yelling and I had to wake him. "Hey," I said, "it's just a dream."

"Yeah, I get them," he said.

"Want some hot chocolate?"

"That sounds good," he said.

So we walked into the kitchen and Maggie followed us. She'd sort of adopted Fito. That dog, I swear she was the most empathetic dog in the world. "You wanna talk?" I said.

"I guess. Only I don't know what to say. I mean, it's like, it's just too sad, Sal. It's just too fucking sad."

"Sam says you have to grieve."

"I lost my mom a long time ago. So this grief thing, hell, I don't get it."

"You loved her."

"Yeah, I did."

"That's a beautiful thing, Fito."

"Is it?"

"Absolutely."

"How do you know?"

"Because Mima's dying, and that's something I have to deal with. She was the only real mother I've ever known. Only it was better because she was my grandmother. I love her, Fito. And she'll be gone."

Fito nodded. "Why the fuck does it have to hurt so much?"

"I don't know. It just does. You're asking the wrong guy."

The first day Fito went back to school, Sam stayed home with a bad cold. Fito and I didn't say much as we walked. Finally I said, "Fito, it's gonna be okay. *You're* gonna be okay."

He shrugged. "Maybe some people aren't meant to have, you know, a great life. I guess that's that way it rolls."

"Don't you *ever* talk that talk around me. You hear that, Fito? YOU. ARE. GOING. TO. HAVE. A. GREAT. LIFE."

"Never had no friends like you," he said. "Never had that." And then he started bawling like a baby, fell to his knees and bowed his head, and just bawled. I picked him up gently, not wanting to hurt his broken hand. He leaned on my shoulder and after a while stopped crying.

"Hey," I whispered, "people are gonna think I'm gay."

He laughed. I'm glad he laughed.

Me. Dad.

DAD WAS SITTING across from me at the kitchen table reading the morning paper. He put it down and looked over at me. I knew what was coming. "About the incident in the funeral home —"

"Incident," I said. "Yeah. Not my finest moment."

"You're good in a fight."

I nodded.

"Do you need a lecture?"

I shook my head. "I'm no expert on what I need, Dad."

"You know how I feel about solving things with your fists."

"Yeah," I said. "I don't think I jumped in because I was doing problem solving —" I looked at my father's dark, soft eyes. "I don't know, Dad. I have this reflex thing going on."

"I think I understand what happened at the funeral home. You reacted to a situation that you had no control over. I'm not going to make excuses for the way Fito's brothers behaved. I'm sorry he grew up in that family. None of us have any control over that. Look, I'm not going to beat you up about this. And I sure as hell hope you don't beat yourself up over it, either. The real question is: Where do we move from here?"

I nodded. "You mean, where do *I* move from here?"

"Exactly. Can I ask you another question?" He didn't wait for me to answer. "How many fights have you gotten into this year?"

"A couple, three or so."

He nodded. "'A couple, three or so.' There's something going on inside you, son. And you need to figure it out. It's not something I can do for you. I can ground you. I can punish you. I can give you a lecture. I don't think that's going to solve what's going on with you."

"I'm trying," I said.

"Good."

"It's hard," I said.

"Whoever said growing up was easy? But using your fists doesn't make you a man. You already know that. I guess I just had to say it."

"I know, Dad!" God, I was almost yelling. And I was shaking. "But I get so angry. I get really angry."

"Anger isn't a feeling," Dad said.

"That's crazy," I said.

"Okay, maybe I can get this right. Anger *is* an emotion. But there's always something behind anger. Something stronger. You know what that is?"

"Is that a trick question?"

"It comes from fear, son. That's where it comes from. All you have to do is figure out what you're afraid of."

Oh, I thought. *Is that all?*

Dad and I went out into the cold morning and played catch. We didn't talk for a long time. Then he said to me as I caught his throw, "When are you going to let me read your essay?"

"It's not that great. Good thing not all the schools I'm applying to require one."

We kept tossing the ball back and forth. "Still, I'd like to read it."

"Okay," I said. "I'll get around to it." I threw him a fastball.

Dad caught my fastball and threw back a fastball of his own. "'I'll get around to it'? Really?"

The cold wind was picking up. The weather was always changing. One minute almost warm and sunny, the next minute a cold wind numbing my face.

Fito. Sam. Me.

WE WERE ALL sitting at the dining room table doing our homework. Fito was reading his history text. He liked history. I had no idea why. Sam was looking up something on the Internet for her English essay on Langston Hughes. Langston Hughes was her new thing. Me, I was staring at a trig problem. Trig. What the hell was I thinking when I took that class?

Sam glanced at Fito and shut her laptop. "Talk, Fito."

He stared at her. Then went back to the history book.

"Don't play dumb."

"I'm just needin' some Fito space."

"You've been living in Fito space all your life."

"It's got me through so far."

"You wanna live in exile all your life?"

"Exile?"

"Give me another word, and I'll go with it."

"What do you want me to say? That I'm sad and shit?"

"That's a start."

"Well, I *am* sad."

"I feel you," she said. "I get sad too." Then she pointed at me. "Even he gets sad. His Mima's dying. She's a beautiful lady. We all have something to be sad about. We're not pigs, you know. We're not supposed to live in our own shit."

That made me and Fito laugh.

"Good," she said. "Laughter is good. And we do a lot of it. And that's brilliant. When we laugh together, that's truly brilliant."

"Whistling in the dark," I said.

Fito shook his head. "I don't know what I'm gonna do."

"What was the plan before your mother died?"

"Get good grades. Finish high school. Go to college."

"And your mother was gonna pay for all this?"

"Hell, no."

"Then what's changed?"

"She's dead," Fito said.

"Well, join the club. We all have dead mothers. How about that?"

"This isn't a joke, Sam," I said.

"You think I don't know that?"

"It sucks," I said.

"Yeah, it sucks."

"Yeah," Fito said. "I guess I was hoping that someday my mom would, well, just be a mom."

Sam was relentless and fierce. "That ship sailed a long time ago, Fito. That was never gonna happen."

"But I hoped. I had hope. Now it's gone."

"No," Sam said. "It's not."

Then Sam got that I-know-all-kinds-of-shit look. "Look, Fito, your mother was an addict. She had a disease. Addiction is a disease. You *do* know that, don't you?"

She saw me giving her a look. She sort of glared at me. "Look it up, dude. Don't you know anything? In the age of information, we choose to live in ignorance." Then she looked at Fito. "I don't know if your mother was a good person or not. I *do* know that she lived stuck in disease and she died of that disease. Don't judge her. And don't judge yourself. Maybe she couldn't love you, Fito. But maybe in her own way she did. She was sick. Just remember that."

"So now you're a drug counselor, are you?" I said.

She crossed her arms. "You are *no* help. *No help at all.* There are websites, you know."

"And you know all of them," I said.

Fito broke up our little conversation. "I didn't hate my mother," he said. "I thought I hated her, but I didn't. I wanted to help her — but I didn't know how. I just didn't."

Fito + Words = ?

SAM WAS LOOKING for a particular pair of shoes. "I must have left them back at home," she said. "Home," she said. "I guess it's not home anymore."

We took Maggie with us to Sam's old house so she could visit Fito. But Fito wasn't there. I texted him: Where r u?

Fito texted back: Working at the K

Me: We're at Sam's picking up shoes

Fito: Cool, cool, laters, customers

Sam went through her closet, but there was nothing there. She looked in the closet of the spare bedroom — and there they were. "Love these shoes," she said.

"How many pairs of shoes can you love?"

"It's like Dad says, 'Love is infinite.'"

"I don't think he had shoes in mind."

When we walked back into the living room, Sam stopped. "What are those?"

On a small bookshelf Fito had set up next to the couch was a set of leather books.

Sam walked over and picked one up. She opened it. "Wow," she said. "It's a journal. Fito keeps a journal." She shut it, then picked up another one. "Yup, they're all journals. Beautiful ones, too." I thought she was going to start to read the one she was holding.

"Put it down, Sam," I said.

"He never told us he kept a journal."

"Is it something we need to know?" Sam had that look on her face. "Don't answer that question," I said.

"There's a whole life inside these journals."

I knew Fito was in for it.

Sam didn't have it in her to leave things alone.

Homework. Mothers.

I WAS WHINING at the dining room table as I did my homework. "Why do they make us take math?"

Sam said, "Just shut up and work."

"Don't feel like working," I said.

"I'm the one who used to say things like that."

"Maybe we've traded emotional spaces."

"How's it feel to be out of control?"

"Shut up," I said.

I got up and went to the refrigerator. I don't know what I was looking for. There were some store-bought flour tortillas, and I thought of Mima. And I don't know why, but I thought of my mom.

As if Sam were on the same wavelength, she said, "It's time to do something with Mom's ashes."

"What are you planning?" I asked.

"Oh, I've been giving it some thought. And I think I know."

"You want to fill us in?"

"Yeah," Fito said.

"We'll do it soon," she said.

"That's all?"

"Yeah," she said.

Then she looked at me with that question mark on her face. "Where's your mom buried?"

"I don't know."

"You don't know?"

"I never really asked."

"I think you should ask."

"Yeah, maybe."

Sam turned her gaze toward Fito. "Where'd they bury your mom, Fito?"

"They cremated her."

"How'd you find out?"

"I called my uncle. He said he was sorry about the whole thing at my mom's funeral."

"You close to him?"

"Nah."

"You want to be?"

"Nope."

"Why not?"

"He's a dealer. That's where he gets his money. He thinks he's all fuckin' superior because he doesn't do drugs and shit. He lives off addicts. He's scum. Let's not talk about it." Then he looked at me. "Let's make coffee."

I nodded.

Fito kept talking. "Anyway, they spread her ashes in the middle of the desert."

"Did she like the desert?"

"I don't know. I guess she did."

"Why didn't they call you?" I could tell Sam was pissed.

"I don't matter to them."

"Screw them," I said.

"Yeah." And then there were those tears on his face again. "Sorry," he said. "I don't mean to be a downer and shit."

"You're not," I said. "You know what? Let's get the car keys and get us double chocolate mochas with whipped cream."

Fito shot me a crooked smile. "I could go for some of that."

"Me too," Sam said.

I wondered if drinking double chocolate mochas at nine thirty at night was related to that whistling-in-the-dark thing. Maybe so.

Snow. Cold. Fito. Mima.

I TEXTED SAM WHEN I woke up: It's snowing.

No answer.

So I called her. "It's snowing."

"No way."

"Look out the window."

We were both up and dressed in a nanosecond.

Dad was drinking coffee, and Marcos was sitting across from him. I shot my dad a look. He looked back at me and said, "No, he didn't spend the night."

"So what if he had?"

Sam walked into the kitchen and shot Dad and Marcos a smile.

"He didn't spend the night," I said.

"So what if he had?"

Marcos rolled his eyes. "Couple of clowns."

Then I said to Marcos, "Thanks for helping Fito."

Marcos had a puzzled expression on his face.

"I mean, for helping to get him to see a therapist."

"It's no big deal," he said.

"It kind of is," I said.

Marcos nodded. "That kid deserves a break."

"Yup," I said. "He's a good guy."

"Yup," Sam said. "We love him."

Dad had a great smile on his face. I looked out the kitchen window. "It's really snowing."

"You can go play in it. There's no school today."

One thing I loved about El Paso was that if a couple of snow-flakes fell on the ground, school was canceled. Sweet. Sam was already texting Fito. I poured myself a cup of coffee and thought about Marcos sitting there. I really wanted to know why he was here so early in the morning, but I would have looked like a real idiot if I started asking too many questions. It wasn't any of my business. But it sort of was. And, well, I wasn't used to this boy-friend thing Dad had going on — even though I had wanted him to have someone. I guess me wanting Dad to have a boyfriend really was just theoretical.

It was coming down hard when Sam and I stepped outside. Fito was on his way. Sam started dancing around in the snow in the front yard, and I took some pics of her on my phone, then started dancing around too. I thought of Mima's yellow leaves. And then I felt a snowball smack me on the side of the head.

I looked up and saw Fito laughing his fool head off. That was, until Sam got him right in the face with a snowball of her own. We started having a huge snowball fight in the middle of the street, and we were running around, ducking behind parked cars, team-ing up with each other, then betraying each other, and a few of the other neighborhood kids came out and joined the fun, and then it seemed like there were kids coming from everywhere, from every house, from every nearby street — and even Dad and Marcos were having a snowball fight in the front yard, and I thought, *How great is this?*

And it was all so fantastic.

We were playing! We were playing!

One minute there was a fight in a funeral home and ugly words were flying through the air like bullets — and a few days later there was a snowball fight and the sound of Sammy squealing with laugher and Fito kneeling on the ground because he couldn't stand up straight because he was laughing so hard.

God, it really was beautiful. Really, really beautiful.

Rat

I WAS HOPING for less drama in my life. And hoping it would be calm. Yeah, I was going for calm. But no. Something else had to happen. Sure it did. So on the last day of school before the Christmas break, it happened. On my way to lunch, I got a text from Sam: Get to Fito's locker now!

I trotted down to Fito's locker, and Sam was at her drama best, waving a note in front of Enrique Infante's face. "You spell *faggot* with two *g*'s, you ignoramus."

I got right in the middle of it. "Hey, hey, what the —"

"This asshole was pasting this" — she showed me the piece of paper with the word *FAGOT* it on it — "on Fito's locker." Just then Ms. Salcido, my English teacher, joined our little group. Sam was too busy cussing out Enrique Infante to notice, yelling, "Give me one good reason why I shouldn't kick your bigoted little ass."

"Try it, bitch."

And that was it. Sam slapped him so hard he fell back, stunned. I knew he was gonna go for her, so I stepped between them, and I was about to pop him one right between the eyes when Ms. Salcido was all over us like chocolate icing on a cake.

"In the principal's office right now!" Mr. Montes and Ms. Powers had shown up as reinforcements. Enrique Infante wasn't helping himself by repeating, "I can't believe that bitch slapped me," and it took everything I had not to hit the little shit. As we marched to the principal's office, Sam was holding tight to the evidence and was explaining to Ms. Powers that Enrique had it coming. Fito and I, well, we were keeping our mouths shut.

When we all filed into Mr. Cisneros's office, he shook his head. He looked at me and Enrique and said, "I thought you two were supposed to keep away from each other."

I don't know what got into me, but I was feeling feisty. I mean verbally feisty, not, you know, fist feisty. "Well, it didn't quite work out according to plan," I said. "A couple of weeks ago I passed this clown in the hall and he calls me a faggot. Apparently he's fallen in love with that word."

Sam jumped right in. "And when Fito and I were walking toward his locker, this joker" — she pointed at Enrique — "was taping this note to Fito's locker." She placed the evidence on Mr. Cisneros's desk. "And on top of everything else, he can't even spell."

I could see Ms. Powers trying like hell to keep from smiling.

Mr. Cisneros smiled a snarky smile at Sam. "Well, we've been here before, haven't we?"

Then Enrique Infante chimed in, "And she slapped me. I mean, she slapped me, like, hard."

"You deserved it," I said. "And you were about to go at her. You were about to hit a girl. And you would've if I hadn't stepped in. You're lucky I didn't mop the floor with you, buddy. You have some class, don't you?"

Mr. Cisneros looked at the teachers. "Which one of you was first on the crime scene?"

Ms. Salcido spoke up. "I heard an argument, stepped out into the hall just as Mr. Infante let out the B word in reference to Ms. Diaz."

Mr. Cisneros looked at me. "Are you going to have your dad in here again?" That's when I knew that Dad must have really gone off on him — in a good way, a very Vicente Silva kind of way. "That depends on how this goes," I said.

Mr. Cisneros looked straight at Enrique. "You've been in this office, what? Four times this year? Apologize to Mr." — he looked at Fito — "what was your name again?"

"Fito."

"Apologize to Fito here for using that word. I suppose you were trying to humiliate him in front of the entire student body."

Enrique Infante, he was doing that sullen thing again.

Mr. Cisneros was starting to get annoyed. "I said, a-pol-o-gize."

"I'm sorry," Enrique said.

"I'm not sure Mr. Fito over here heard that."

"I'm sorry, Fito." Enrique Infante was not happy. Not happy. I thought I could see his ears burning. Not that he was oozing sorrow. Nope.

"Now apologize to Ms. Diaz for referring to her in that manner."

"I'm sorry, Samantha."

"I didn't quite hear that," she said. I tell you, that Sam, she had some stuff in her.

"I said I was sorry."

Then Mr. Cisneros looked straight into Sam's eyes. "Now you apologize for slapping him."

"Enrique Infante, I'm sorry I slapped you." She almost, *almost* hid the sarcasm. But not quite.

Then Mr. Cisneros did something that nearly made me want to forgive him for being such a pompous asshole. He ripped up the misspelled piece of paper with the word *fagot* on it.

We met at my locker after the last bell. "God," I said, "what a day."

Sam was grinning. That girl could do some serious grinning. "I had kind of a great day."

"Yeah, you got to slap Enrique Infante."

"I've been dying to do that since last year. He's a rat. Still, you know that thing about jumping in the sewer to catch a rat?"

"Yeah?"

"I'm a work in progress, Sally."

"Yup. But you know, Sam, things could have turned out really bad. That guy could have seriously hurt you. Good thing I was right around the corner. Lucky you."

"I know, Sally. And what would you have done — if he had hurt me?"

"Sam, I don't even want to think about that."

"I know what I would have done," Fito said. "I would have killed that *pinche rata*."

"Killing someone. *No bueno*. When's your next session with your therapist?"

Fito smiled. "Good one, Sally." Now two people were calling me Sally.

The truth was, I would have really hurt Enrique Infante. If he'd laid just one finger on Sam, I would have really hurt him. But what if I *had* hurt him? What if I had? I heard my dad's voice in my head: *Figure it out, son.*

Mima. Me.

I PHONED MIMA every day. She always called me *hijito de me vida.* Little son of my life. It didn't have the same ring to it in English. Sometimes things just don't translate. Maybe that's why there were so many misunderstandings in the world. On the other hand, if everybody spoke only one language, the world would be a pretty sad place. Not that I spoke French or Italian or Hebrew.

But Spanish was holy because it was Mima's language. And my dad's language — even though you couldn't tell. He didn't speak English with an accent like Mima. But when he spoke Spanish, it came out perfectly. That language belonged to him the way it would never belong to me or to Sam. Well, at least I didn't speak Spanish like a gringo. Yeah, I had issues about that. The only thing that mattered was that my uncles and aunts always treated me as if I were theirs. As if I belonged to them. No one in my family ever made me feel adopted. Whatever that feeling was.

I called Mima. I heard her fading voice say, "Hello."

"Hi, Mima."

"Hi, *hijito de mi vida.*"

I recorded a part of the phone call, and Mima didn't know it. So her voice would never be extinct.

Part Six

In the distance, I can see a storm coming in, the dark clouds and the lightning on the horizon moving toward me. I wait and I wait and I wait for the storm. And then it comes, and the rains wash away the nightmares and the memories. And I'm not afraid.

Sam. Fierce. Yup.

CHRISTMAS BREAK. And I felt I needed one. We went out to a movie, Fito and Sam and I. We ate lots of popcorn and afterward dropped by some guy's house. Fito scored us beer. One each. Well, it *was* Christmas break. We went to Sam's place and made sandwiches and hung out.

As we were eating our sandwiches and having our beers, Sam said, "I really hate that Enrique Infante. Where do rats like that come from?"

I shrugged. "Families."

Fito nodded. "Fucked-up families."

"Right." Sam said. "Exactly." And then she looked at me and said, "You and me and Dad and Maggie, we are the normalest family on the planet."

"Well," I said, "I don't know if we're normal."

"Guess not," Sam said. "And you know what really pisses me off? People's attitudes. Enrique Infante going around calling people faggots. And then Charlotte Bustamante comes up to me last week and goes, 'Isn't it kind of creepy to live, like, with this gay guy? I mean, I'm sorry about your mom and everything, but isn't it kind of —' I stopped her dead in her tracks. I went off on her like You. Would. Not. Believe."

I pictured the whole scene.

Sam, she was all about telling the story. "I looked right at her and said, 'I know you get this a lot, but it bears repeating. You're an imbecile. And that thing about being sorry about my mom. Don't go around telling people you're sorry when you don't mean it. The next time I hear you do that, I'm. Going. To. Slap. You. Silly.'"

I gave her one of my grins. "Really? You'd slap her silly?"

"Well, no. But can't I just enjoy the fleeting thought?"

"No bueno," I said.

"No bueno," she said.

But I think we were both laughing to ourselves.

Fito. Sam. Me. Texting.

FITO CAME OVER while I was making breakfast. "How come I'm not in on the word-for-the-day thing?"

I shrugged. "I never thought about it. You're not in on the running thing either."

"Screw that," he said. "I'm too skinny for running. And besides, I've been running all my life."

"That makes no sense," Sam said.

"I got my own logic goin' on here," Fito said.

"You sure as hell do," I said. "Want some breakfast?"

"You have to ask?"

I fried him up a couple of eggs as Sam made him some toast. He stared at the plate in front of him. "No bacon?"

"Take it up with Sam. She ate it all."

I sat down with a cup of coffee. "Word for the day," I said. "'K, Fito. Your call."

He took out his iPhone and texted me and Sam: Wftd = mothers.

Sam and I read his text. Sam texted back: Mothers. Yeah.

Me: Yeah

Fito: My mother's name was Elena. Actually Maria Elena

Sam: Sweet

Me: Yeah, sweet

Sam: Sylvia. Sylvia Anne

Me: Sylvia Anne? Nice

Sam: Sally? Urs?

Me: Alexandra. They called her Sandy

Sam: Never knew that! Wow

Fito: Wow. Alexandra. I like

Sam: They had names

Me: Yeah, they had names

We put down our phones. It was as if we'd learned something but didn't quite know how to put it into words. "Let's play catch," I said.

"Without Dad?" Sam said.

"Yeah, without Dad."

Ashes

I WAS IN BED, actually thinking about opening my mom's letter. I got a text from Sam: Tomorrow. Sylvia's ashes.

> **Me:** ?
>
> **Sam:** Talked to Aunt Lina. Talked to Dad. Done deal
>
> **Me:** I'm the last to know? Really?
>
> **Sam:** Relax. Mad?
>
> **Me:** Not really. Tell Fito?
>
> **Sam:** Going to text him now
>
> **Me:** What feeling?
>
> **Sam:** Feeling? Hmm. It's time, Sally
>
> **Me:** Good girl
>
> **Sam:** ☺ Night, Sally
>
> **Me:** Night, Sammy
>
> **Sam:** Want me to send Maggie over?
>
> **Me:** Urs for the night
>
> **Sam:** Sweet

I must've really been out, because I felt someone pulling on my shoulder, and I kept hearing a voice telling me to wake up. "Wake up! C'mon. Wake up, Sally." I thought it was a dream — but there was Sam standing in front of me, holding the urn that contained her mother's ashes. "It's time," she said.

"Time?"

"To spread Mom's ashes."

"Oh, yeah. That's right."

"You need coffee."

"Yeah, I need coffee."

"C'mon, Fito's already on his way over. So is my Aunt Lina. So is Marcos."

"You asked Marcos to come?"

"Yup."

"Look at you," I said.

"I'm warming up to him."

"Yeah, you are," I said.

"You, Sally?"

"I'll get there."

"You'll get there; you'll get there."

"Be quiet."

"You're still half asleep."

"Yup."

"You're still lying there."

"Yup."

"Get up, shithead."

"'K," I said, but I didn't move.

"I'm not leaving this room till you get your ass up, Sally."

"'K. I'm getting up." I sat up and put my feet on the ground. "Turn around so I can put my pants on."

"It's not as if I haven't seen you in your underwear."

"I'm shy."

391

"Silly boy." She turned her back to me. "Shy my ass."

I put my pants on and tapped her on her shoulder. "You can look now."

We stared at each other.

"So this is the day," I said.

"Yeah," she said. "This is the day."

We drove to McKelligan Canyon — Sam and Fito and Marcos and Dad and Lina and me. We parked the two cars, paid the fee, and started up the trail toward the top of the mountain. Sam was carrying her mother's urn in her backpack. We didn't speak. Sam wanted us all to be silent. Sam was good at giving instructions. No talking. No talking was a big deal for her. I mean, Sam and silence just didn't go together.

When we reached the top of the mountain, the wind was cold, but I didn't mind. It was strange and beautiful, and I felt so alive. We looked across the gorgeous vista, and it wasn't hard for me to believe in God at that moment. Who else could've made this? We could see the river and the valley and the houses on the west side of town. The houses looked small and far away, and the streets looked like rivers. You couldn't tell if a house was big and belonged to a rich person or if it was little and belonged to a poor person. All of it was all so large and vast and miraculous. I felt so small, and I didn't mind that at all. I *was* small.

Sam took off her backpack, looked at my dad, and then looked at Lina and nodded. Then Sam looked at me. She was shaking and biting her lip, and I knew she was being as strong as hell and that it was costing her something, but she was willing to pay the price because she needed to do this. "I'm ready now, Sally."

I wiped the tears that were running down her face.

She handed me the backpack. "Will you take the urn out for me, Sally?"

"Yeah," I whispered.

I unzipped her backpack, gently took out the urn. I placed it in her shaking hands.

She held the urn tightly. "She liked this place." Her voice was trembling. "She used to bring all her boyfriends here." She laughed. And then her trembling stopped. "I only know that because I read through her journals. She kept journals. She didn't seem the type. But that was one of her things." She was quiet for what seemed a long time. "Oh, I forgot." She gave me the urn, took out some paper, and handed a sheet to each of us. It was a picture of the mirror where Sylvia had written *just because my love isn't perfect doesn't mean i don't love you.* "That's how I'll always remember her."

Then she took the urn from my hands, raised the lid. She slowly tipped the urn until the ashes poured out. The wind lifted Sylvia's ashes and blew them over the desert.

Sam took my hand and looked at it. Then she whispered, "What would I do without this hand?"

O, Christmas Tree, O, Christmas Tree

SAM PUT ON some Christmas music, and she was singing along to "O, Christmas Tree, O, Christmas Tree." Sam could do a lot of things, but she didn't know how to sing. But she was in a good space, so I didn't mind.

I was lying on the couch, trying to read about the Civil War. Fito was lying on the floor, right in front of the Christmas tree. He was crazy over the Christmas tree. *Loco.* Sam was on her laptop, looking at the Stanford website, dreaming her dream.

"I like Christmas," I said.

"Me, not so much," Sam said. "You and Dad always went to Mima's. And I was always stuck with Sylvia, who was usually not in a good mood. For whatever reason, she was usually without a boyfriend around Christmas, so we watched a lot of movies. But we did buy a lot of shoes. I was always happy when Christmas was over."

Fito was listening to Sam. He was still staring at the lights on the tree. "That doesn't sound so bad to me. I remember one Christmas, my mom actually got a tree. And me and my brothers decorated it, and I was, like, this happy little kid. And I went around the house whistling. I used to love to whistle. Then one night my mom was in a bad mood, or she was high, or she was, I don't know, but she was yelling and acting all crazy, which was normal, and then she went off on me and said she couldn't stand that whistling shit. 'And just for that,' she said, 'I'm getting rid of the tree.' She tossed it out. Yeah, Christmas was shit at my house. But you know, I still liked Christmas. I liked walking around and seeing all the lights, and I liked to see the mangers with Mary and Joseph and the baby Jesus. I liked all that. And there was this song I heard, and I used to sing it to myself as I walked up and down the streets looking at the lights." And Fito started singing this song I really liked, a kind of sad song, "I Wonder as I Wander." And the way he sang it — like he'd written it.

And after he stopped singing, he smiled. "Yeah," he said. "I like Christmas." Sam and I were real quiet, and then Sam said, "Wow, Fito, you have a beautiful voice. You can really sing."

"Yeah," I said. "How come you never told us you could sing?"

He shrugged. "I guess no one ever asked."

Sam shut her laptop. "Fito," she said, "did you know I didn't used to like you? Shame on me. Shame on me."

Dirt. Paper Bags. Candles.

I'VE NEVER MADE luminarias before."

"Me neither."

I gave Fito and Sam a look. "I'm kicking you out of my Mexicans-only club. Have you guys ever done anything Mexican?"

"I've gone to Chico's Tacos."

"Me too."

"Which one?"

"The one on Alameda."

"Me too."

"Well, maybe I'll let you in."

"Shut up, gringo."

I gave them another look. Both of them. "*Pochos*. You're both such *pochos*. Totally half-baked Mexicans."

They just laughed.

I'd taught Fito and Sam to fold the tops of the paper lunch bags. You had to be careful because if you were in too big a hurry, the bags would rip. *No bueno*. So they started getting the hang of folding. I grabbed a shovel and poured about six inches of sand into each bag. As I was doing that, I started thinking of the shovel at my grandfather's burial, and I hated that thought living in my brain, so I just shut it down by thinking of a song. I guess that was another way of whistling in the dark.

We were in my Uncle Mickey's backyard. He had plenty of dirt, since his dog, Buddy, had dug up half the lawn.

There we were, the three of us, making luminarias.

"Who the hell thought of this luminaria stuff anyway?"

"The Spaniards in northern New Mexico. They used to put little fires on paths to light the way to midnight Mass on Christmas. I think that's how it goes. They were the original streetlights. Then the fires became paper bags, just like paper lanterns. Sort of. Only they sit on the ground."

Sam gifted me with one of her looks. If she hadn't been folding paper bags, she would have crossed those arms of hers. "Thank you, Professor Silva, for the little history lesson."

"You don't believe me? Wikipedia it."

She stopped folding, took out her cell phone, and started her thing. She read it, then looked at me. "So yeah, big deal. You know a few things."

I have to say I was feeling a little cocky. I dropped the shovel and started dancing around, waving my hands in the air like a super dork. And then I started singing a tune I made up in my head: "'Call me gringo, now. Call me gringo, now.'"

And Fito, he's laughing his ass off. "*Vato,* you just proved that you're, like, white, white, white. You can't dance worth a shit."

"Ah," I said, "get to work."

We were having fun. I wondered why one of our hobbies was giving each other a hard time — part of the friendship thing. The heart, yeah, sometimes I didn't get it. But if we were making each other laugh and smile, maybe it was part of the way human beings loved each other.

When we finished folding and filling all the paper bags, Fito looked at our handiwork. "You and your peeps, you're up to your ass in traditions, you know that?"

"You want that I should apologize?"

"Is that your way of saying *fuck you*?"

"You're quick, Fito. You're very quick."

We placed a hundred and fifty luminarias all around Mima's house and put a votive candle in the center of each bag. "Ah," Fito said, "the sand. I get it. That way the bags don't catch on fire."

"Like I said, Fito, you're quick."

"You say that one more time, and I'm gonna do to you what I did to my brother at the funeral home."

"I'm not sure that therapist is working out for you."

Sam started laughing, and she said maybe Fito and I should take our show on the road. "Anywhere," she said, "as long as it's far away from me."

Dad and Uncle Mickey and Uncle Julian lit the luminarias as the sun was setting. It was a clear night, and there was only a slight breeze. Perfect weather for luminaria lighting. Mima was no longer walking, and my Aunt Evie and my Aunt Lulu helped her into her wheelchair and bundled her up, and they kept asking her if she was sure she wanted to go outside. "What if you get sick?"

Mima gave them a look. I mean, she could still give looks. "I have cancer," she said. "I *am* sick."

She winked at me. I wheeled her outside and we stopped at the end of the driveway so she could see the luminarias. The lanterns made everything seem so soft, as if a few candles in paper bags could tame the night. Sam and I and Fito started singing her song in Latin. We'd practiced it a bunch of times, but it was Fito who carried us along: *"Adeste fideles laeti triumphantes, venite, venite ..."* When we finished, Mima had tears streaming down her face. I knew they were the good kind of tears.

She took my hand, holding tight — as if she never wanted to let go.

Now I knew why people said things like *I'll take that to the grave.* I had always assumed it was a bad thing. Just then I realized that it could sometimes be a good thing. And not just a good thing, but a great thing.

The luminarias lighting up the winter night.

Candles in paper bags.

Mima's tears.

Christmas.

Midnight Mass

MIMA HAD GONE to midnight Mass every year of her life. Not this year. Not ever again. Dad told us to get dressed, so we did.

Mima sat in a chair in the living room. She was awake. She was thinking. She held Aunt Evie's hand.

We stood in front of her.

Sam and I waved.

Dad kissed her. "We're going to Mass."

Mima's face lit up. Like a luminaria.

Christmas

CHRISTMAS MORNING, and I was sitting next to Mima in the living room. My Aunt Evie and my dad had to help her into her chair, the one she liked to sit on. Dark clouds were moving in. It wasn't cold enough for snow.

Rain.

Rain was bad for paper bags.

Rain was bad for luminarias.

Mima and I were looking at my book of photographs. The one I made for her. She looked at them and smiled, and I knew she was remembering.

She didn't talk much anymore.

A word here.

A word there.

Sometimes a full sentence.

She pointed to a picture of me and her and Popo. I must have been about ten. We were all dressed up. "Dad's birthday," I said. She laughed at my caption: *Mima is prettier than Popo.*

She was staring at a picture of me and Sam when we were seven. No front teeth. We were standing in the front yard. It was summer and the leaves of her mulberry tree were behind us. The caption read: *She was always my sister.*

"Beautiful," she said.

I turned the page, and she smiled. It was a picture of the day when we built the human pyramid in my backyard, and I was at the top. The caption read: *One day, all these Mexicans built a pyramid to the Sun.*

"You were my pyramid," she whispered. "All of you."

Dream

I WOKE UP in the middle of the night. I dreamed I was opening my mom's letter. And my mom was sitting next to me. She took the letter and said, *Here, Salvador, let me read it to you.*

What if I started remembering a mother I had no real memories of?

I couldn't fall back asleep.

I looked around the room and remembered that we were still at Mima's. I was sleeping on the couch. I wanted to walk into her room and tell her about my dream.

But she was asleep.

I didn't want to wake her.

Home

THREE DAYS AFTER Christmas, my dad was sitting on the front porch with Mima, who was having a good day. Dad looked at the mulberry tree. "I remember when Dad planted that tree."

"I remember too," Mima said. "It's a beautiful tree. I've sat in the shade of this tree for many years."

Mima was like the tree. In this desert where I'd grown up, Mima had shaded me from the sun.

She was a tree. How would I live without that tree?

Sam took the wheel and drove us home. "I want a car," she said.

"You have to pay for cars," my dad said. "Are you ready to make payments on a car?"

"I'm ready," she said.

I believed she was.

Fito turned off his phone. He was always fooling with it. "It's almost New Year's," he said. "That means we get to start over."

"You believe that?" I asked.

"Maybe. Maybe I just wanna believe it."

"I wanna believe it too."

"Then believe it," my dad said. "What's stopping you?"

"I believe it," Sam said.

"Let's do something great this New Year's Eve."

"I'm for that," my dad said.

"Me too," I said.

New Year's Eve

I WAS HANGING OUT with Maggie and Dad after our morning run. Dad was looking at the cigarette he was holding. "I hate these things."

"But you love them too."

He laughed. "Yeah."

"You said it was an uncomplicated relationship. That wasn't true, was it?"

"Guess not." He lit his cigarette. "What's the plan for New Year's?"

"Me, Sam, and Fito were thinking of going across the border to New Mexico and getting some fireworks and shooting them off in the desert."

"Oh yeah? You got a car?"

"Don't be a wiseass, Dad."

"That's a sore subject with you, isn't it?"

"I'm the last boy in America who doesn't have a car."

"Not true."

"You know what I mean."

"Wow, I guess I've sent you straight to the therapist's couch."

"What? Are you taking lessons from Sam?"

"You have money in the bank. You can buy a clunker if you want."

"You never said that."

"I never said you couldn't have a car. All I said was that I wasn't going to buy one for you."

"Oh shit! You mean I could have bought a car?"

"Yeah." My dad was laughing. "Not my fault you didn't think of it." He rubbed my hair. "Joke's on you."

I didn't have a choice. I had no one to blame but me. So I sat there laughing at myself.

Then I looked at my dad. "How come you didn't want to buy me a car?"

"I gave you everything you needed. But not everything you wanted. I didn't want you to grow up to be an entitled brat. A lot of kids, their parents get them everything and the kids do a new kind of math: *I want* equals *I get*. As you like to say, *no bueno*." He put out his cigarette. "Anyway, we have reservations at Café Central tonight. Marcos is treating us to a New Year's dinner."

"He must be in the bucks."

"He does all right. Everything he has, he came by honestly. I respect that."

"Does this mean we have to dress up?"

"Yeah. What, you married to your jeans?"

"You're funny today, Dad."

"I got up feisty, I guess."

"Well, can Fito go?"

"He's included. The reservation is for five."

That made me smile. "Marcos likes Fito, doesn't he?"

"Yeah. Marcos had a tough childhood. I guess he sees himself in that kid." He played with his pack of cigarettes. "Besides, we all like Fito. He's a wonderful guy. Pisses me off that his family never gave a damn."

I nudged him with my shoulder. "Dad, I think I like you a little feisty."

He nudged me back. "It's been a weird year. Beautiful. Hard. Sad. Get your fireworks. We can shoot them off after dinner."

So I told Sam that we're having dinner at Café Central. And she was dancing around the living room. "New dress! New dress!"

"Like you have all this cash lying around."

"No, but you do."

"Really," I said. "Really?"

"What are brothers for?"

Dad lent me the car, and we were off to buy a dress. For Sam. Even Fito came along, but only because we were going to buy fireworks.

Sam tried on about twenty dresses. She looked great in all of them. And Fito, after Sam looked at herself in a mirror and shook her head again, Fito, he finally lost it. "Sam, you make me feel all happy and shit that I'm gay. Straight guys have to put up with this shit. Gay guys not so much."

I was grinning, and Sam was crossing her arms and giving us a look that said, *Guys suck: gay or straight, guys suck.* And then Fito walked to this rack, picked out a long red gown, handed it to Sam, and said, "This." And he smiled.

Sam took the dress, looked at the size, and walked into the

dressing room. She came out, inspected herself in the mirror, turned this way, that way, then turned around and smiled at Fito. "You *are* gay!"

We couldn't stop laughing. Just couldn't stop.

Sam bought the dress. Well, I bought the dress.

But do you think she was finished there? Nope. She picked out a shirt for me. And a shirt for Fito. Oh yeah, and ties. Sam, she was all about new clothes. "Dress like men," she told us.

We drove on the 10 right past the state line. New Mexico! Fireworks!

When we walked into the restaurant, I thought Fito's eyes were going to pop out. He looked at me and whispered, "Holy shit! People, like — they live like this?"

Sam kissed him on the cheek. "I love you to pieces, Fito."

Sam was the most beautiful woman in the room. No one else even came close.

At dinner, Sam was all about taking pics. The Facebook thing. Made me crazy. Marcos ordered a bottle of champagne. He and Dad were at ease in places like this. They were used to going out to nice places and traveling and all that. Me, I wasn't quite used to it.

We toasted Mima. My dad raised his glass. "I know it's hard," he said softly, "but we have to remember we'll always have her with us." I think he was talking to me more than to anyone else. So we raised our glasses to Mima. And then I said, "And to the mulberry tree Popo planted." My dad smiled at me. So we toasted that beautiful tree. We talked about everything that happened to us in the past year. Then Sam turned to Marcos and asked, "What's the best thing that's happened to you this year?"

He smiled. "That's easy." He pointed at my dad. Then he pointed at Fito. Then he pointed at me. And then he pointed at Sam.

Sam said, "You're just trying to charm me into liking you, aren't you?"

Marcos nodded. "That's exactly what I'm doing."

Sam smiled. "Well, it's working."

Of course she had to invent some kind of game. Of course she did. "Okay," she said over dessert, "New Year's resolutions."

I said, "I don't do resolutions."

She didn't skip a beat. "That's part of your problem."

And I didn't skip a beat either. "Okay. I resolve not to kill you this year, even when you use my razor to shave your legs."

"You're such a girl about that."

Fito cracked up. And so did Marcos. Dad, not so much. He was used to us.

"Seriously: New Year's resolutions."

Fito went first. "I'm going to try and stop beating up on myself. Yeah, that idea came from the therapist. But, you know, I like it." Everyone clapped.

Sam nudged him: "Just don't go overboard."

Dad said, "I'm going to quit smoking." More applause.

And of course, Sam had to add her commentary. "I'm glad you're quitting smoking, Dad. Nobody likes to kiss smokers." She sort of shot Marcos a little grin.

Marcos looked around. "I'll go next. I'm going to start running again." And he looked at Sam. "What, no editorial?"

Sam didn't hesitate. "And you were doing so well, Marcos. You know, we're still watching you."

Marcos grinned. I noticed there was something very shy about him. I thought that was a good thing. At least he wasn't an arrogant asshole.

Then it was Sam's turn. "I've decided not to date any more boys until I get to college."

And my dad blurted out, "Whooaaa."

Fito was smiling his ass off. "We'll see," he said.

"Yeah, we will," Sam said.

Then it was my turn. "I resolve never to use my fists again."

Sam said, "Not even to protect my honor?"

"Your honor doesn't need protecting," I said.

"Hmm," she said.

"And," I said. "*And* I'm going to let anybody who wants to, read my admissions essay. But I don't want to hear any editorials." That put a smile on my dad's face.

Sam was all over reading my essay. "When? *When?*"

There we were in the New Mexico desert. Fito and Marcos were setting up some fireworks, ready to bring in the new year. Dad popped a bottle of champagne and poured a glass for everyone. Well, a plastic cup for everyone. So the fireworks were all ready to be fired, and we were all standing around, all dressed up with our coats on, and I was glad it wasn't that cold.

And then Marcos looked at his cell and we start to count.

Together. *Ten, nine, eight, seven, six, five, four, three, two, one:*
HAPPY NEW YEAR!

That was the first time I'd ever seen my dad kiss another man.

I don't think I was quite prepared for that. And it wasn't, like, this sexy thing or anything. More like a peck. But still. They had a thing. And it *was* New Year's, after all.

Sam was smiling. No, she was beaming. She kissed me on the cheek. "Happy New Year, Sally. Let's make it count."

Then Fito kissed me on the cheek too. "That cool?"

"That's cool," I said.

Happy. New. Year.

Happy New Year?

WE WENT TO see Mima on New Year's Day.

She was in bed. She'd always made *menudo* on New Year's Day. Not this year. She was hardly eating anything anymore. I knew she was getting ready to say goodbye. Word for the day: *goodbye*. A common word. A sad and common word.

But the good news: she was talking again. "Pray with me," she said. So we gathered in her room and prayed the rosary. It was like this gift. I didn't know if it was Mima who was giving us a gift or us giving *her* a gift. Maybe both. When we finished, she said, "I want to talk to you."

So she talked to us. All of us. One at a time. She pointed at my Uncle Mickey. We all left the room so she could talk to him. It reminded me of going to confession. You know, everybody waiting their turn.

When she was done talking to my dad, he walked into the living room and said, "Son, you and Sam and Fito."

And Fito goes, "Me?"

My dad nodded.

—

I sat down on Mima's bed and held her hand. She squeezed my hand softly. There was so little strength left in that hand. Then she placed that same hand on my cheek and said, *"Hijito de mi vida."*

Sam and Fito were standing close.

And my Mima said, "Samantha, you have to take care of my Salvador. He's your brother, and you have to take care of him." She made a fist. "You're strong."

"I promise," Sam said.

"And, Salvador, you have to take care of Samantha."

"I promise," I said.

Then she looked at Fito. "Vicente talked to me about you." She motioned for him to come closer and she took his hand. "Life can be hard. I know how hard it can be." And then she said, *"Déjate querer."*

Let yourself be loved.

She made the sign of the cross on our foreheads.

I kissed her.

That was how she said goodbye to the world. To the people she loved. She was going to leave this earth the same way her mother had.

With all the grace of the old world. The old, dying world.

Night

No one said a word on the drive home. Dad was trying to be strong for us, for me and Sam.

And I was trying to be strong for him. I'd never thought about that. I knew now, and maybe a part of me had *always* known it, that my dad knew how to keep his pain to himself. He'd learned — maybe because he was born gay — he'd learned how to suffer things in silence. I didn't want that silence for him.

The night seemed so dark.

But I think I'd learned how to whistle in the dark. Maybe that was something.

Thursday. Two O'clock in the Morning.

WE WENT TO MIMA'S every day after that. Back and forth from El Paso to Las Cruces. Marcos came with us. He always drove.

Mima had stopped talking.

Sometimes it seemed that she had already left her body. But sometimes I thought she still recognized me.

On Thursday, at two in the morning, Dad woke me and Sam. "Let's go," he said.

I stumbled into my clothes.

As soon as we walked into Mima's house, Aunt Evie fell into my father's arms. "She's gone."

Gone

THERE ARE A LOT of things I don't remember. I think part of me went away somewhere after Mima died. But this is what I do remember. Someone came and pronounced my Mima dead. My dad and my Aunt Evie made calls and more calls.

Some men from the funeral home came to take Mima away.

Dad and I watched as they placed Mima's body on a stretcher.

As they were wheeling her out, my dad made a motion for them to stop. He kissed her forehead and crossed himself. Then he nodded at the somber funeral men, and they placed her in the hearse.

Dad and Aunt Evie and Sam and I watched them drive away.

My dad turned and walked back inside. I think he was lost in those moments.

Sam took my hand and whispered, "This is killing me. I'm trying so hard."

I nodded. I couldn't talk.

I walked into the house. I found my dad sitting on Mima's bed. My father was sobbing.

My father.

I sat next to him. And then I took him in my arms. My father.

Grief

I WAS SITTING in Dad's car. Mima's house was full of people. Our family. Old friends. Everyone brought food. There was food everywhere. My Uncle Mickey said, "Mexicans love to eat. We eat when we're happy, and we eat when we're sad."

Marcos and Fito were staying at a hotel.

Dad was being very strong. He wrote her obituary for the newspaper. He wrote her eulogy. He was all about taking care of business. He greeted people; he talked to people; he comforted people. I guess my dad wasn't the kind of guy who sat around and felt sorry for himself.

Me, I was just numb and lost.

I tried to think of the stages that Sam talked about. But I couldn't remember what they were.

I didn't want to be around anyone. I didn't want anyone to see my pain. I didn't want to see it either.

I went driving. I found myself driving toward that farm Mima had taken me to once. I'd been trying to find it without knowing it.

And then I reached the farm. It was winter and nothing was growing.

I got out of the car and stared out into the barren fields.

Barren. That's how it felt. That's how *I* felt.

I found myself on my knees. I was wordless and lost, and I had never known anything that felt like this, this, this hurt in the heart, this emptiness, and I wished right then I didn't have a heart, but I knew I had one and I couldn't wish it away. I couldn't wish away the hurt or the tears. I don't know how long I knelt there on the winter soil. But I felt myself taking a breath and let myself feel the cold air on my face.

Cemetery

I FOUND MYSELF HELPING to carry Mima's casket at the cemetery. I was between my dad and Uncle Mickey.

I still see the casket being lowered.

I still see myself pouring a fist of dirt over her casket.

I still see my Uncle Mickey sending some men away after everybody else had left.

I still see my dad and my uncles taking shovels and burying their mother. I still see my dad handing me the shovel and nodding. I still see myself shoveling dirt. Shoveling dirt, shoveling dirt.

I still see myself falling into Sam's and Fito's arms, crying like a little boy. But the strange thing was, I didn't feel like a boy anymore. It had been such a strange time since that first day of school. So many things had happened, and I wasn't in charge of any of them. I didn't control anything, couldn't control anything. I'd always thought that adults had control. But being an adult had nothing to do with control.

I wasn't an adult. I wasn't a man. But I wasn't a boy anymore.

Me. Alone. Not.

AFTER THE FUNERAL, there was a reception. Lots of people. People, people, people. If I heard one more very nice person say, *This is your son, Vicente? God, he's handsome,* I was going to fucking scream.

I was sitting in Dad's car again. Alone. Everybody was inside, and I thought maybe I'd pick up smoking. Then I heard a sound and looked up and saw Sam and Fito knocking on the window. "Get out of the car. We have you surrounded."

I got out of the car. "Very funny."

"Word for the day," Sam said. "Isolating."

"Guess so," I said. "Let's sneak some beers."

"I'm not so sure that's such a great idea."

"Yeah, there's nothing worse than a reformed partier." I shot her a look. "Humor me."

We walked over to Uncle Mickey's house. There were people there, too. We didn't really have to sneak anything. My Uncle Mickey was more than happy to unload a few beers. I drank mine down. Then I drank another.

"Slow down, Cowboy."

I shot Sam another look. And then I downed a third beer. And then a few minutes later, I was feeling those beers. I was like, *Whooaaa.* "I don't think that was such a great idea."

"No bueno," Fito said. "Beer isn't what you need, *vato.*"

I nodded.

"What you need is us," Sam said. "So don't fucking run away."

I offered her a crooked smile. "I won't run anymore," I said.

"Let's put some food in you," Fito said.

"Yeah, good idea."

We walked back to Mima's. I was feeling a little lightheaded. "Chugging three beers on an empty stomach. *No bueno,*" Fito said.

I was kind of leaning on him. "*No bueno* is right, *vato.*"

"Just keep leaning into me, dude. That's all you need to do."

Dad was at the stove warming something up in Mima's kitchen. Marcos and Lina were at the sink, washing pots and pans. Lina? I guess I hadn't noticed. I waved at my dad. "Hi."

"Where have you been hiding?"

I guess I was a little drunk. Yeah, I was a lightweight. I walked up to my dad and put my head on his shoulder.

"Have you been drinking?"

"Yup." I really held on to my dad just then. "No Mima in Mima's kitchen."

"Are you okay?"

"Yeah, Dad," I whispered. "I had a moment."

"Don't drink, son. Don't do that."

I nodded. "Okay," I said.

My dad took me by the shoulders and looked at me. "Do you

want to see something really fantastic?" Then he cocked his head like, *Follow me.* So I followed him, and he motioned for Sam and Fito to follow too.

So there we were in Mima's bedroom. My dad pointed to Mima's bed. "Sit."

Sam and Fito and I just looked at each other.

He handed me an envelope. "Open it," he said. "Be careful. It's fragile."

I held the envelope in my hand and opened it with all the care that was in me. And there in the envelope were some dry leaves. Yellow leaves. And there was a note. I stared at Mima's handwriting: *These are the leaves that my Salvador gave me one Saturday afternoon when he was five.*

I knew then that that day had been just as beautiful for her as it had been for me. She'd remembered.

My dad was smiling.

I handed the note to Sam. She and Fito read it. And then they were smiling too.

Dad. Grief. Marcos.

ONE MORE THING I remember about that time. The day after we got home, Marcos came over in the late afternoon. I answered the door. "Hi," I said. "Dad's in his studio." I walked with him to the back door.

He went through the door, and just as he stepped into the backyard, my dad came out of his studio. I turned to go back into the house, but I don't know why, I stopped, turned around, and looked out. My dad stood there talking to Marcos, and then he was crying. Marcos took him in his arms and held him.

I thought of what Mima had said.

Déjate querer.

Yeah, Dad, let yourself be loved.

But there was something else. In that moment I saw that I wasn't paying attention to my dad's pain. I was only paying attention to mine.

I was ashamed of myself.

Dad. Me.

I COULDN'T SLEEP. Maggie was in Sam's room. I wished Maggie were here, lying next to me. I couldn't stop thinking about my dad's face while Marcos held him. Wasn't it *my* job to take care of him like that?

I got up out of bed and walked toward my father's room. I knocked on the door and slowly opened it. I could see his lamp was still on. "Dad? Can I come in?"

"Sure."

I sat on his bed. "Dad?"

"Yeah?"

"I just wanted to make sure you were okay."

"It's hard," he said. "Grief is a terrible and beautiful thing."

"I don't think it's so beautiful."

"The hurt means you loved someone. That you *really loved someone.*"

"Dad." I reached for his hand. "I'm here, Dad. I mean, *I'm really here.*"

My dad took my hand. "This is a good hand," he said. "A very good hand."

Going for Normal

I THOUGHT THAT MAYBE life would never be normal again. Not ever. And this time I was *definitely* going for normal. Too many things had happened, and I was tired. Sam sat across from me and said, "You're doing it again."

"Doing what again?"

"Isolating."

"No, I'm not. I'm sitting across from you."

"You're in your head."

"Yup."

"So spit it out."

"I was making a list of all the things that have happened."

"Keeping score?"

"Well, maybe. It doesn't feel that way. It just feels like remembering."

"Remembering is overrated."

"And I've decided I'm going for normal."

"Too late for that, Sally."

Things *did* get back to normal, but I felt that something had changed in me, and I didn't know how to put it into words. I framed my leaves and the note from Mima between two pieces of glass and hung them in the living room. It didn't seem right to keep them all to myself.

I was now in the habit of taking out my mom's letter and putting it on my desk in the morning. Then putting it back at night.

Me and Fito and Sam got into going to the movies. We argued about which movies to see. Sam and Fito, they got into it some days. I'd always let Sam have her way. But Fito, man, he wasn't about to let have Sam have her way all the time. I guess he was tired of being on the short end of the stick. I loved watching them.

Lina had everything fixed that was wrong with Sam's house. She and Fito had a mutual admiration society going on. Which was sweet. The Realtor hung up a FOR SALE sign. Sam posed me and Fito leaning on the sign, and she posted it on her wall. Of course she did. Her and her Facebook.

Yeah, life was normal. School, movies, homework, studying. School, movies, homework, studying. Yeah, and I still ran into Enrique Infante, who still called me *faggot*. I stopped him one day and asked, "Is that *faggot* with one *g* or two?"

He didn't like my joke, but I thought it was pretty funny. Sam and Fito thought it was hilarious.

I woke up one Saturday morning. A cold front had come in. No snow, but it was really cold. I walked into the kitchen, and Sam and Dad were talking.

I poured myself a cup of coffee. "Am I interrupting?"

"No," Sam said. "Dad and I were talking about the adoption thing."

"And?"

427

"Well," Sam said, "ever since I brought the subject up, I started calling him Dad. And it felt right. And it kinda, it kinda was enough. Just to be able to call —" She looked at my dad. "Just to be free to call you *Dad*. I don't need the adoption thing. I think I just wanted to know that I belonged. Which is stupid. Because I've always belonged. But I still want to change my last name to my mother's."

I really liked the smile on my dad's face.

Sam. Me. Fito.

TWO WEEKS AFTER Mima died, Sam and I walked over to the Circle K. Fito was getting off at eleven, and it was a Friday and we didn't have any plans. We got to the store just as Fito was clocking out. We grabbed some Cokes and some popcorn and headed to Sam's house.

We put on an old vinyl album. Dusty Springfield. Sam loved Dusty Springfield. We were hanging out and talking, and Sam kept eyeing Fito's journals. I knew she was going to start digging any minute. "So, Fito, how long have you been keeping a journal?"

"How'd you know I kept one?"

"All those volumes sitting on that little shelf."

"She likes to get into everyone's business," I said.

She pointed at me. "Your business" — and then she pointed at Fito — "your business equals my business."

"And I thought *I* was bad at math," I said.

"You *are* bad at math, Sally." I got the look. Yup, Sam was undeterred. "Did it help, Fito, keeping a journal?"

"Yeah. It was almost like having a life. I guess I started when I was in seventh grade. Helped me keep my head on straight. Gave me someone to talk to — even if that someone was just me. You know, I used to go to the library and read. And one day I went to the museum and I was walking around and shit and looking at the art, and before I left, I went into the museum store and they had this really cool leather-bound journal with all these blank pages. So a couple days later I walked into that store and bought it. That's how it started. And the books I read made me think of things, and I wrote stuff down."

Sam grabbed one of the journals and handed it to him. "Read us something."

"No way. That's private shit."

"Give me a fucking break, Fito."

Fito took the journal away from her.

"You're not gonna win this one, Fito," I said. "Trust me. If not tonight, some other night. She'll hound you and hound you till she wears you down."

Sam had her arms crossed. "That's how you talk about me behind my back?"

"You happen to be in the room," I said.

Sam gently took Fito's journal from him. "*I'll* read something," she said.

Fito was quiet. Then he said, "Are you always like this?"

"Bossy, you mean? Yup. Some people would call it leadership skills."

Fito said, "Okay, read something. Go ahead. But if you laugh, I'll fuckin' kill you."

"Fair enough," Sam said. She opened the page and started reading:

"Sometimes, I see myself standing on a beach, my bare feet buried in the wet sand. And there's no one on the beach, just

me, but I don't feel alone. What I feel is alive. And it seems like the whole world belongs to me. The cool breeze whistles through my hair, and something tells me I have heard that song all my life. I'm watching the waves hit the sand, the ebb and flow of the waves crashing against the distant cliffs. The ocean is ever moving — and yet there is a stillness that I envy.

"In the distance, I can see a storm coming in, the dark clouds and the lightning on the horizon moving toward me. I wait and I wait and I wait for the storm. And then it comes, and the rains wash away the nightmares and the memories. And I'm not afraid."

Sam put the journal down. "This is awesome, Fito."

"Yeah, it is," I said. "You can sing, and you can write, and you have beautiful thoughts."

"Nah," he said. "I think I'd just read *The Old Man and the Sea* or something. Anyway, it's bullshit. It's not like I've ever seen the ocean. I don't know what the hell I'm talkin' about."

"Why do you dumb yourself down, Fito? Why do you do that?" Sam was being fierce again.

"You're brilliant as hell," I said.

"You think I'd survive on the streets talking like a fucking book? How long do you think I'd last? I dumb myself down, Sam, to fucking survive. That's how I roll. I carry cigarettes around even though I don't smoke. I hand them out. Make friends. And people won't mess with me. I carry change around, and if someone needs some money, I hand them some change. I carry around M&M's. If I'm sitting around, I pop some. Some guy's always coming up to me and saying, 'Got any more of those?' And I give him some.

I don't like trouble, and I've learned to get along, and it's not any good to pretend you're smart. Not out there.

"And you know, Sam, it's not as if I'm the only one who does that dumbing-down shit. What the hell do you think you're doing when you go out with all those guys? Not a damn one of them is your equal. You know that, don't you, Sam?"

"Yeah, I know that."

Then Fito looked at me. "You do it too. You're better than a fist, Sally. Yeah, you are. You have this letter from your mom, and all of a sudden you can't read. Yeah, we all dumb ourselves down."

I didn't know what to say. And neither did Sam. So we all sat there and listened to Dusty Springfield singing, and then Sam sent me a text: What if you hadn't gotten the brilliant idea of the running thing?

I thought a moment. Then we wouldn't have found Fito sleeping on a bench!

Sam: ☺

Me: And the vato can sing & he can write

Sam: But can he dance? Lol

"You're shittin' me. You're texting. *What in the hell* are you guys texting about?"

"You, Fito," I said. "We're texting about you."

432

Mom

I THOUGHT OF SAM. How she'd been so brave and worked through all those stages. The look on her face when she let her mother's ashes blow into the desert. Tough and brave as hell. I thought about what she'd told me and my dad: *I just wanted to know that I really belonged. Which is stupid. Because I've always belonged.* I thought about how I'd always hated to be left out. That had come from somewhere inside me. I'd never, ever been left out.

For a second the thought passed through my mind that I should text Sam and tell her I needed her, tell her to come to my room. So she could be with me. But I knew this moment belonged only to me. To me and my mom. Only to us.

I couldn't explain everything to myself. I didn't need to know *everything*.

I'd always thought my hands would be shaking when the day came that I decided to read my mom's letter. But they weren't. Nothing inside me was shaking.

I smoothed out the folds of the letter. My mother had beautiful handwriting.

Dear Salvador,

Writing this letter is one of the hardest things I've ever done. I don't know how much longer I have to live, but I know it won't be long now before I die. It's not easy for me to let go, because dying means I have to let go of you. I'm having a pain-free day today, and my mind is clear. So I'm writing this letter and hope I say all the things I need to say to you — though I know that's not possible.

Vicente has you for the day. He adores you. And you? You sometimes cry when he leaves. You adore him back. I love watching the both of you when you're together. It's been that way with you two since the day you were born. After you were born, I was miserable. I didn't want to have anything to do with you. You see, I suffered from a serious bout of post-partum depression. And it was Vicente who cared for you. He was there twenty-four/seven. And he took care of me, too. He took care of both of us.

Then I got better. And then, for a couple of years, I was the happiest woman in the world. I was working in a law office, and I was making decent money. Vicente had landed a job at the university, and he was becoming a successful artist. He paid for your daycare. Not that you went to daycare every day. On days he didn't teach, Vicente kept you. You had a playpen in his studio. You were such a good baby. Good-natured and happy and affectionate. I was so, so happy.

But you have to know what came before to understand why I was so happy in those days before I got sick. I guess I'll start at the beginning. I met Vicente when I was a sophomore at Columbia. I was at a party, and I saw him and I thought, Who is that beautiful man? To say that I wasn't a shy girl is something of an understatement. To be honest, I was more than a little wild. I saw Vicente, and I thought, That man is so going to be mine. I went up to him and said, "My name's Alexandra. You can call me Sandy." No one had to tell me I was beautiful. I was born knowing it. I was born parading my beauty around everywhere I went — not that that's anything to be proud of. There was nothing humble about my beginnings. I came from a family that had wealth and prestige. The word I'd use is entitled. I grew up taking anything I wanted — including boys or men. Life was a party. And there I was in front of Vicente, smiling at him.

We wound up talking most of the night. I thought things were going well. I really liked him. He was different from any man I'd ever met. But then he looked at me and said, "I have to tell you something." And I said, "What?" And he said, "I'm gay." I think I was really disappointed, and it showed. "Sorry," he said, and then he started to walk away. And I thought to myself, So long, buddy. I don't know why, but I went after him. I grabbed his arm and said, "Well, we can be friends." That was the best decision I ever made. And we did become friends. In fact, Vicente very quickly became the best friend I ever had. The best friend I ever had in this world.

I was always getting into trouble. Man trouble, mostly. I'm sorry to have to tell you that I was a lot of drama. I was an incredibly self-destructive young woman. I loved to party, loved to drink, and I loved drugs. Vicente was always pulling me out of messes. I have no idea what I would have done without him. But I was there for him, too. He fell in love with a guy who broke his heart. Vicente doesn't love casually. He's just not built that way. He didn't leave his room for days. I had to drag him down to a restaurant and put some food in him. Then I got him good and drunk and gave him a good talking-to. Vicente had a lot to learn about men, and I decided to be his tutor. I knew plenty about men.

My life was always something of a train wreck. My parents were wealthy, and they were in love with everything that came along with it. My dad enjoyed buying politicians, and in Chicago there was always a politician more than willing to be bought. My mother raised me to be a certain kind of woman, and I wasn't interested in becoming the kind of woman she wanted me to be.

After college, Vicente went on to follow his dream of becoming an artist. I'm not sure I had a dream. Eventually, I got into trouble. I became hooked on alcohol and cocaine. I called Vicente one night. I was living in New York. He came down from Boston, where he was living, and looked after me. He got me into rehab, and I stayed clean for a few years. But I really didn't have any reason to stay sober. I didn't feel I had any purpose in life. And then I met the man who was to become your father. I fell in love with him, and we were happy for a little while. I moved in with him. One day, we got into an argument. I hadn't been feeling well, and I said something he didn't like. He slapped me with the back of his hand and sent me flying. He looked down at me as I lay on the floor. *"Don't ever talk to me like that again."* Then he calmly walked out of our apartment.

I packed my bags. I didn't know where I was going, but I wasn't broke. I went to a hotel. I felt like crap. I thought I was getting sick, so the next day I made an appointment with my doctor. Then I discovered I was pregnant. You. You were living inside me. And I was so happy. I was so, so happy. It was like my life suddenly had meaning. My life had a purpose. There was a life growing inside me.

I don't know why, but I decided to move to El Paso. But I did know why. It was a town Vicente always talked about. He'd get this look on his face, and he'd say, *"I love that border town."* So I moved here. It was far from my family and far from the life I had lived. I was going to start over. I'd lost track of Vicente, but I had his mother's phone number —just in case I ever needed to reach him. That was the first time I spoke to the woman I would come to know as Mima. I told her I was a friend of Vicente's and that I was trying to reach him. She was so kind when she spoke to me. She gave me his number.

I called Vicente and we reconnected. He laughed when I told him I'd moved to El Paso. He said he didn't take me for that kind of girl. About five months into my pregnancy, there were complications, and I went to the hospital because I went into labor. You weren't born then, but the doctor said he was afraid I was going to have to stay in bed for most of the time until you were born. I called Vicente. Mima came

437

to take care of me until Vicente managed to get all his stuff together and move. I fell in love with Mima. She took good care of me. When Vicente arrived from Boston, I felt I could breathe again.

Vicente didn't want me to name you Salvador. He said it was too big and too heavy a name for a little guy to carry. "And besides," he said, "you're not Mexican." I laughed and told him not to be such a snob. But you were my salvation, Salvador. You were.

As I said, the last two years of my life have been so beautiful. And all because of you. I'm dying now. And I am so very sad. But I'm happy, too, because you'll have Vicente as a father. I'm sure you love him. And I know he loves you. I don't know how old you are as you read this letter, but I'm sure Vicente gave it to you at just the right time. He was born with beautiful instincts. I think he got those instincts from his mother.

I didn't want you to grow up with my family. I didn't want you to grow up with your father's family either. I don't believe they're good people — not really. They're too in love with money — and too in love with the things money can buy. I just didn't want you to be raised the way I was raised. Your natural father always wanted a son. But in my opinion, he didn't deserve you. Vicente and I are going to the courthouse tomorrow while I can still walk. We're going to get married. And we've already drawn up the papers for him to adopt you. That was the only way I could be certain that Vicente would be allowed to raise you, to be your father. I'm sure you understand what I'm trying to say.

I had the power to decide who would raise you. (It's strange to talk in the past tense, but by the time you read this, I will have been dead for some time.) But, Salvador, I don't have the right to deprive you of the knowledge of who your natural father was. That is not mine to decide. Inside this envelope is another envelope. It has a name, your father's name. It also has the names of his relatives. It's up to you now to decide if you want to meet him.

I know as you read this that you have already turned into a very fine young man. How could you not be? Vicente Silva raised you.

I love you more than I can bear. You saved my life — if only for a little while. Not everybody lives a long life. But not everybody gets to give life to a boy as beautiful as you.

All my love,
Mom

I remembered what Mima told me. "Your mother was a beautiful person."

I hadn't known so many things, and I'd been so afraid. Maybe I was afraid that she hadn't loved me. Stupid. Here was this letter from a mother who loved me more than she'd loved anything else in the world and who died too soon. I understood what she'd done for me. I understood that she had fallen in love with Mima because she'd never known a Mima in the world she came from. I understood why she married my dad. To give me a family, a family that knew how to love.

I pictured my biological father slapping my mother to the

439

ground. Maybe I had a little bit of him in me. A little bit. But not much. I didn't have to be afraid of becoming like my father. I wasn't that man. And never would be. I think my mom ran away from a selfish and violent man. She saved herself. And saved me, too. I knew myself enough now to know that I'd taken out my fists because of my sense of loyalty to the people I loved. Yeah, I'd struck out at Enrique and other boys, but Dad was right — my anger *had* come from hurt. I wasn't proud of any of those moments. Hurting other people because you've been hurt? *No bueno.*

Every time I'd pulled out my fists, I thought I now understood the reflex. Or at least I was beginning to understand. I couldn't bear to see anyone hurting the people I loved. Because I loved them so much that it hurt me, too. And I couldn't stand anyone calling me a white boy because I belonged to a family, and when people called me that, all I heard was that I did not belong to that family. And I *did* belong to them, and I wasn't going to let anybody tell me otherwise. And one more thing: I didn't want to admit that I had anger living somewhere inside me. But that anger didn't make me a "bad boy." All it did was make me human. There was nothing wrong with getting angry. It was what you did with that anger that mattered.

All this time I'd been so scared that I was going to turn out to be like a biological father I'd never met. I'd underestimated myself. In the end, wasn't it up to me to choose? Didn't we all grow up to be the kind of men we wanted to become?

I was trying to explain to myself why I was so happy. I hadn't ever felt this happy. I finally understood something about life and its inexplicable logic. I'd wanted to be certain of everything, and life was never going to give me any certitude. I thought of Fito, who always lived in hope when life had offered him no hope. Certitude was a luxury he had never been able to afford. All he'd ever had was a heart incapable of despair.

I thought of Mima and Sam's mom and Fito's mom and my mom. They were dead. They were like the falling yellow leaves of Mima's tree. Life had its seasons, and the season of letting go would always come, but there was something very beautiful in that, in the letting go. Leaves were always graceful as they floated away from the tree.

There would always be cancer, and people would always die under its awful and unforgivable weight. There would always be accidents because people were careless and weren't paying attention when they should've been paying attention. There would always be people who suffered and died from addictions that were powerful and mysterious and uncontrollable.

People died every day.

And people lived their lives every day. There were always survivors in the aftermath of all that death.

I was one of those survivors.

And so was Sam.

And so was Fito.

And so was Dad.

I'd watched them in all their beautiful courage. I'd watched them as they struggled through their hurts and their wounds.

And there was one thing I could be certain of: I was loved.

I pictured Mima pointing at my dad. I knew exactly what she had been trying to tell me. She wanted to be sure that I understood that I had been raised by a kind and tender man, that there was no cruelty in the world that could rob him of his dignity. His heart could not, would not, allow it.

God, I was happy.

I texted Sam: Are you awake?

Sam: Just about to fall asleep

Me: Wftd = nurture

Same: What?

Me: As in nature vs. nurture

Sam: You okay cray boy?

Me: Go to sleep. I'll tell you in the morning

Sam: Sweet dreams

I went outside and sat on the back steps. And all of a sudden it mattered so much to me where I went to school. I wanted it to be Columbia. That's where my father had met my mother. That's when they'd fallen in love with each other. It wasn't the usual love story. But it *was* a love story. A love story like mine and Sam's.

I held the letter in my hand. Dad said that Mima would always be with us. And my mom, she'd be with me too. That's the way it was when you loved someone. You took them everywhere you went — whether they were alive or not. I read the letter over and over and over. I didn't sleep all night. I wasn't tired. I wasn't tired at all.

I was happy sitting there on the steps, my mother's letter in one hand and my essay in the other. I remembered the first day of school as I walked home in the rain and how I had never felt so alone, the weight of the rain blinding me.

I wasn't alone. Mom. Dad. Mima. Sam. Fito. My uncles and aunts. My cousins. No, I wasn't alone. I never had been. I never would be. *Alone* was not a word that applied to me as I sat there. Waiting for the sun to rise.

Salvador

I HEARD MY FATHER grinding the coffee beans in the kitchen.

I walked inside. He looked up at me. "You're up early."

"I wanted to watch the sunrise."

Then he studied me. "You look like you've been crying."

I held up the letters. "My essay," I said. "And Mom's letter."

"Oh," he said.

Just then Sam walked in, ready for her morning run.

She looked at me — then at Dad.

I dangled my letters.

Sam's eyes got really big. "Are you okay?"

"Yeah," I said. "I've never been better."

Dad said, "I need a cigarette."

And Sam said, "I'm going to text Fito."

I am watching my father sitting on the back steps. He is smoking a cigarette and reading my mom's letter. Sam and Fito are sitting next to him and reading it with him. I am throwing the ball up in the air and catching it in my glove. I am playing catch with myself as they read.

They have just finished reading the letter.

They are looking at me, Dad and Sam and Fito. I drop the glove and the ball on the ground. I walk toward my father.

I take the sealed envelope from him — the one that holds the information about my biological father.

I ask him for his cigarette lighter.

He hands it to me.

I look at Sam and Fito and say, "Word for the day."

Sam understands and says, "Nurture."

I take the unopened envelope. I am watching myself as I take the lighter and place it over the edge of the paper.

I am watching the envelope burn. I am watching the ashes floating up to the heavens.

I am hearing myself as I tell my father, "I know who my father is. I have always known."

And now I am laughing. And my dad is laughing. And Fito is smiling that incredible smile of his. We are watching Sam dance around the yard as Maggie follows her and jumps up and barks. Sam is shouting out to me and the morning sky, "Your name is Salvador! Your name is Salvador! Your name is Salvador!"

Epilogue

I GOT TO THINKING about the essay I wrote to get into Columbia. I think it might have been different if I'd read my mom's letter first — but it's no use living in regret. My dad told me once, "If you make a mistake, don't live in it." He also said that we do things — important things — only when we're ready to do them. I think he's right. But sometimes life forces our hand. Sometimes we have to make decisions whether we're ready to make them or not. I suppose I will have to learn to bend to the inexplicable logic of my life.

So this is the letter I sent to Columbia University (which fit none of the guidelines):

Dear Admissions Committee,

My name is Salvador Silva. My name represents the story of my life. My name matters more to me than I can ever explain. If things had turned out differently, I would have had a different first name and a different last name. And I would have had a different life.

My mother died when I was three. Her name was Alexandra

Johnston. She met the man who was to adopt me, Vicente Silva, while they were undergraduates at this very university. My father came from a poor Mexican American family, went on to study art at Yale, and has become a rather well-known artist. I think it's important to mention that my father is gay, not that it matters to me (though it seems to be something that bothers other people, mostly people who know nothing about the kind of man my father is).

I believe that the friendship between my dad and my mother was something incredibly rare. Their love created a family. A real family. When I was three, my mother died of cancer, and the man I know as my father adopted me. He was my mother's birth coach, and he was in the room when I was born. You could say quite accurately that he was my father from the very beginning.

For some reason my mother decided to name me Salvador. And I'm very happy to have the name she gave me. My last name, I got from my father. I grew up feeling and thinking that I was as Mexican as my family. And even though, technically, they're not Mexicans — as they have been in this country for several generations — my uncles and aunts and my grandmother have always thought of themselves as Mexican. That's how I think of myself, too.

The most influential person in my life, other than my dad, is my grandmother. I call her Mima. By the time you read this letter, she will probably be dead. She is suffering from the last stages of cancer.

It's difficult to put into words what my Mima means to me, so I'm going to end this essay with a memory I have of her, a memory I have carried all my life and will carry until the day I die.

I want to be worthy of being called her grandson. If I can live up to that, then I think I just might make a very fine addition to your university:

I have a memory that is almost like a dream: the yellow leaves from Mima's mulberry tree are floating down from the sky like giant snowflakes. The November sun is shining, the breeze is cool, and the afternoon shadows are dancing with a life that is far beyond my boyhood understanding. Mima is singing something in Spanish. There are more songs living inside her than there are leaves on her tree . . .

Dad said it was a great letter. "It's really beautiful, son."

Sam said it would get their attention. And she loved my memory of the yellow leaves. She said it was like a poem.

I don't really believe it's the kind of letter that's going to get me into Columbia. Would be nice. I know I have the grades to get me into a few of the schools I've applied to. No matter where I go, I'm going to have to take me along for the ride. But the good news is, I'll be taking everyone I love with me too.

Someday I want to go to the beach with Fito and Sam. Sam and I, we can watch Fito walk on the sands of the beach for the first time. And see the expression on his face when he looks out into the horizon, where the water meets the sky.

Tonight Dad is taking Sam and Fito out for pizza and a movie. Sam and Fito have been arguing about which movie for the past half hour.

And me? I'm going out to dinner with Marcos. It was my idea. He gets to pick the restaurant — and I get to pay.

It's time I get to know the man who loves my father. It's time.

Acknowledgments

WRITING IS A journey. This writer, me, Ben, walks around in the world and one day gets an idea. I live with that idea, and then it starts turning into a story, and the story grows and grows in my head until I have to get it out so I won't go completely mad.

Writing novels is always difficult, challenging, and beautiful. When I got the idea to write about a young man who had been adopted by a gay man, the wheels in my head started turning. Fiction is fiction — but no novel comes from nowhere. I admit there are bits and pieces of my own autobiography scattered throughout this book. Because my own mother had recently died when I began it, I knew the arc of the story would be about the narrator's grandmother dying. In a sense, writing this novel helped to heal my wounds. But writing has always helped me to survive my own pain. This is why I say that writing has saved my life: It's the truth.

It took me a couple of years to finish the novel. And when it finally arrived on the desk of my editor, Anne Hoppe, there was still much work to be done. Countless conversations and emails and revisions. Then more conversations, then more emails, and then more rewriting. Anne always asked the right questions, challenging me to wring the most out of the material. Sometimes I felt she knew my novel better than I did. Her commitment to my work not only challenged but amazed me.

Writers love to thank their agents — and I am no exception. Patty Moosbrugger, who has been my agent for more than a decade, is a true friend. She not only believes in my work—she believes in me. Me. Ben. What more can a writer ask? I do not know where I would have ended up if she had not been traveling by my side. It was she who placed this book in the compassionate and capable hands of Anne Hoppe. It seems impossible to thank her enough.

And then there's this thing called family. This thing called friends. No writer creates a book all by himself. Without the support of the people who love me and have often helped save me from myself, I would be absolutely nowhere. This book is very much a creation of the village around me, the village that raised me and supported me and loved me, the village that gave me words and language and my voice. And so I shout out my gratitude to my village. This is the book that we all wrote together. Let's go write another — shall we?

About the Author

BENJAMIN ALIRE SÁENZ is an acclaimed poet and fiction writer for children and adults. His first book of poetry, *Calendar of Dust,* won the American Book Award, and his most recent volume of short stories, *Everything Begins and Ends at the Kentucky Club,* won the PEN/Faulkner Award for Fiction. His teen novel *Aristotle and Dante Discover the Secrets of the Universe* won a Michael L. Printz Honor, the Pura Belpré Award, the Lambda Literary Award, and the Stonewall Book Award. A visual artist as well as a writer, Mr. Sáenz lives in El Paso, Texas.